JOHN COULD FEEL HIS OWN HEART RACING WILDLY, thumping against his chest where he held Claire's head crushed against him.

She would have gone over the edge if he hadn't caught her. His mind conjured up an image of her broken body lying at the bottom of the cliff, and his hand tightened in her silky hair. His heart continued pumping too much blood too quickly through his veins.

"Uh, John?" Claire asked, after a moment.

"Yes?" He felt adrenaline changing to something else as she stirred against him, her soft breath caressing the skin at the open neck of his shirt.

"I can't breathe."

He loosened his grip, but not by much. She looked up at him. Her gray eyes held a touch of remaining fright, and something else; something that was probably mirrored in his own eyes, John guessed. Attraction. Pure, physical animal attraction to a member of the opposite sex.

True North

Beverly Brandt

St. Martin's Paperbacks

TRUE NORTH

ISBN: 0-312-97985-1

Printed in the United States of America

St. Martin's Paperbacks edition / January 2002

St. Martin's Paperbacks are published by St. Martin's Press, 175 Fifth Avenue, New York, NY 10010.

10 9 8 7 6 5 4 3 2 1

To Wes,
*for always believing that I could do it,
despite much evidence to the contrary*

Acknowledgments

FIRST, I HAVE TO THANK THE WONDERFUL PEOPLE AT ST. Martin's Press who made my dream a reality when they called and offered to publish this book. I believe my first words were, "You're kidding, right?" I'm happy to report they weren't kidding, and even happier that I've had the chance to work with two fabulous editors during the publication of this book. To my previous editor, Ellen Smith, thank you for your insightful comments on how to make the story I sent you even better. To my new editor, Kim Cardascia, thank you for taking me on with such enthusiasm and respect. To all the other people at St. Martin's who have worked behind the scenes, I thank you, too, for your efforts. You can't imagine how excited I am to see the fruits of our labor.

Next, to my agent Deidre Knight, my thanks for patiently answering all the questions I've thrown your way during the past year, and for representing me with such professionalism and grace.

I'd also like to thank my first and most enthusiastic fan, Marci Gamon. Your encouragement at the beginning of this journey helped me more than you'll ever know.

Finally, this section would not be complete without thanking my best writing buddies and critique partners: Laron Glover, Lori Grube, Libby Muelhaupt, and Marthe Arends. Your support, your thoughtful feedback, and, most importantly, your great senses of humor enrich my stories and my life. Thank you!

Chapter 1

GLANCING AT HER WATCH, CLAIRE BROWN DID THE SAME calculation she'd done a hundred times over the past week.

The flight from Seattle to Aspen was scheduled to leave at 7:30 A.M. She'd already called the airline once to make sure the departure time hadn't changed. Counting backward, she gave herself enough time to arrive at the airport an hour early to meet her fiancé and added an extra half hour for bad traffic. She was down to only twenty minutes to finish her makeup, dry her hair, get dressed, and finish the last of her packing.

Claire took a deep breath, picking up the pace of her morning routine. Her first hope of "maybe the cab will be late" turned almost immediately to "please, don't let the cab be late" as a new worry creased her brow. She had better call the cab company again.

With her blond hair mostly dry, she pushed a tortoiseshell headband behind her ears and zipped up the neatly packed bag of toiletries. Although she was accustomed to packing for two- or three-day business trips, not week-long vacations, she made sure that everything fit neatly into one large suitcase and an overnight bag. She refused to be one of those women who felt she had to bring every change of clothing she owned on vacation just in case she got a sudden invitation to meet the queen of England or something equally implausible. She knew plenty of women like that, women who went on two-day business trips with enough junk for a month. Usually, those were the ones who expected her to help them lug their crap through crowded airports or heave their incredibly heavy bags up into the overhead luggage bins.

Claire shook her head, then placed her makeup bag into

the carry-on next to her cell-phone charger, her emergency change of underwear, the book she might want to read during the three-hour flight to Colorado, and four months' worth of back issues of *Money* magazine she hoped to catch up on during her time off. Nobody could accuse her of not being able to fend for herself, she thought proudly. Tightening the belt of her robe, she picked up the telephone and dialed the number of the cab company.

"Star Taxi," came the curt reply after the fifth ring.

"Good morning. This is Claire Brown. I have a cab scheduled to take me to Sea-Tac at five-thirty this morning. I want to make sure he's going to be on time."

There was a long pause on the other end of the line and Claire thought they'd been disconnected. She was about to hang up and redial when she heard a long-suffering sigh.

"Listen, lady, you've called three times in the last twelve hours. The cab's gonna be on time. Please stop calling."

Claire studied her perfectly manicured nails. She hated to be a pest, but she'd always found it worked best to keep on top of people. Otherwise, they ignored you, or forgot about you, or . . . well, they didn't do what you wanted them to do when you wanted them to do it. "I'm sorry, I just wanted to make sure he'll be here on time."

The dispatcher's terse swearing preceded the click of the phone. Claire listened to the dial tone for a second before hanging up her own receiver.

"How rude," she muttered, then turned her attention to the pile of neatly folded clothes sitting on a chair in her bedroom.

She began snipping R.E.I. tags off her new clothes in preparation for loading the last of her gear into her suitcase. Unlike her fiancé, Bryan, Claire was not an avid outdoorsman, so their nine-day sojourn into the wilds of Colorado had meant a brand-new Gore-Tex wardrobe for her. Claire looked over at the colorful brochure sticking out of her carry-on case and had to admit that staying at the luxurious, twenty-room Hunter's Lodge could hardly be considered roughing it.

She smiled, then tucked a snowy white T-shirt into a pair of stiff khakis and slipped a dark brown sweater over her shoulders. A nice pair of leather flats and, ta-da, she thought, eyeing herself critically in the full-length mirror, you are ready for anything, just like that catalog said. The outfit was perfect for an early September day, warm enough to keep out any chilly breezes, but she could always take off the sweater if she got too hot.

After hanging her robe on the back of the bathroom door, Claire hefted the carry-on over her shoulder and glanced at her watch again. Five minutes till the cab—

The knock on her front door interrupted her thoughts. She took a deep, calming breath. The cab was early.

A second knock had her scurrying down the stairs, her suitcase banging against her shins. Glancing through the peephole, she saw a short, elderly man wearing jeans and a light blue jacket with the Star Taxi logo embroidered over the right breast.

"Morning," the man said cheerfully as she opened the door.

"Good morning. Here are my bags." Claire handed him her overnight bag and suitcase, then turned to pick up her purse and the heavy computer bag she'd left in the foyer when she'd arrived home the night before.

Making sure all the lights in the townhouse were off, Claire gave the room one last once-over and saw the light on her answering machine blinking furiously. She cursed silently as the strap of her laptop bag dug into her shoulder. Someone must have called while she'd been in the shower. Or, they could have called last night, she supposed. She was at the office even later than usual, trying to get everything in order so she could leave for her vacation. She'd arrived home after midnight and didn't remember even glancing in the direction of the phone.

A short, yet insistent, burst from the horn of the taxi made the decision for her. She'd have to ignore it. It was probably her friend Meg, calling to wish her bon voyage. Or maybe it was her mother. Had something happened to

Father? Claire hesitated on the threshold. Maybe she should—

The driver tapped his horn again and a light went on in the townhouse next to hers. Claire turned away from the insistent blinking of the message machine. Rather than dawdle and risk the cab driver waking up the entire neighborhood, she shut the door, locking away the sight of the red blink with a click of the dead bolt.

"Brown residence. Sumner Brown speaking."

Claire unconsciously straightened up in the back seat of the cab and cleared her throat. "Hello, Father. It's Claire," she began, then cursed herself for an idiot. Of course it was Claire. Who else would be calling Sumner Brown "Father"? She shook her head, rested her cell phone on her shoulder, and took a deep breath, blaming her nerves on the extra cup of coffee she'd hastily swallowed this morning. "There was a message on my machine this morning but I didn't have time to listen to it before I had to leave. Did Mother call?"

"I don't know why she would have. Everything's fine here."

Claire tried to contain her disappointment at the cool tone in her father's voice. Obviously, he couldn't conceive of either her mother or himself calling their only child just to chat. She supposed she should be grateful that nothing was wrong and attempted to cover her disappointment with her usual Miss Chipper Good Daughter routine.

"Things are great here, too. I landed the Prime Seafood account last week, which puts me in the Million-Dollar Club again this year. My boss said I might be up for another promotion before the year's out." She'd been working on reeling in the Prime Seafood account for over two years and was proud of her coup. The claims-adjusting contract was worth more than two hundred thousand dollars to her office alone, and the promotion would make her the youngest senior account coordinator in the company.

"Hmm. Well, I'll tell your mother you called," Sumner

Brown said before hanging up, leaving Claire staring at the blank display of her cell phone.

The urge to scream was almost overwhelming. It was just like the first time she'd ridden a bike without training wheels. Frankly, it was just like it was with every accomplishment in her life. She'd proudly exclaim, "Look, Daddy. Look what I can do!" only to have her father barely acknowledge her existence. Frustrated, she stuffed the phone into her purse and stared out at the bumper-to-bumper traffic on the dingy gray highway. Red brake lights flashed on and off, on and off, as they crept like multicolored snails on the rain-slick pavement.

How was it that her father could make her feel like an inadequate little girl in the space of a two-minute conversation? And why did she let him? When was she ever going to learn that the parental well was not the place she should dip into for approval? There were other, better places for that—namely, work, where she was consistently rewarded for her efforts. Work never let her down, and for that she was grateful. At least there was something in her life she could count on.

Claire put a hand on the laptop bag sitting next to her on the seat, then looked at her watch and felt her frustration grow. Her thirty-minute cushion had been eaten into by the eight-car pileup they'd passed on the freeway. To make matters worse, she was beginning to suspect the cab company had sent her the only driver in the state who strictly obeyed the speed limit. They were on the last leg of their journey, having just taken the exit to the airport where the speed limit plunged to twenty miles an hour. Other cars sped past them, doing at least forty now that traffic had finally thinned out a bit.

"Could you speed it up a little?" Claire asked the back of the cab driver's head.

He met her eyes in the rear-view mirror and answered earnestly, "I'm sorry, ma'am. I'm already exceeding the limit by three miles per hour."

Claire forced herself to take a calming breath. The urge

to leap over the seat and shove her foot down on the accelerator was almost overwhelming. "You must learn to accept that which you cannot change," she closed her eyes and chanted silently to herself. That's what Nathan, her Guerrilla Yoga instructor would say. Of course, then he'd kick the crap out of something. She'd bet there wasn't much Nathan couldn't change when he set his mind to it, but supposed that was the difference between the Zen of a former Navy SEAL and that of an insurance claims adjuster like herself.

"Here we are." The cab finally crawled to a stop alongside the airport curb.

The airport was already bustling with travelers, even though it was Saturday and just past 7 A.M. The two lanes of traffic reserved for dropping off passengers and luggage moved in a chaotic rhythm as the cars jockeyed for position at the terminal. Claire chastised herself for not allowing enough travel time as she handed some bills to the driver and struggled to balance her luggage.

She pulled her bags into the terminal and got in line behind the single other passenger waiting to check in at the first class counter, wishing she'd been able to cram a week's worth of clothing, hiking boots, backpack, and other associated outdoor gear into something that would fit into an overhead bin. Instead, she'd allowed herself a larger bag, thinking that she'd have plenty of time to get it checked before the flight.

Glancing at the long line of coach passengers waiting to check in, she congratulated herself for having splurged on first class tickets for Bryan and herself and hoped his morning was turning out better than hers. They had agreed to meet at the gate since he was coming from his house south of the airport and she from her townhouse in Kirkland, a suburb east of Seattle. They hadn't talked at all during the past week and Claire assumed the plan hadn't changed since she didn't see him waiting for her here at the check-in counter. She'd been so busy at work trying to make sure everything would continue to run smoothly the week she'd be gone, she hadn't had time to give him a call. He must have been equally busy, since he hadn't called her, either. But the last time they'd talked, he'd sounded excited about the trip, a gift she'd given him two months ago on his thirty-fourth birthday.

Shifting her laptop bag to her other shoulder, Claire wished she shared more interests with Bryan. He loved all kinds of physical activities, especially those that involved rain, dirt, and not taking showers for days on end. Claire preferred her exercise to be of the one-hour, air-conditioned, top-of-the-line-equipment variety. Their differing interests were what had prompted her to send away for a brochure after she'd run across an article about Hunter's Lodge in Colorado. She and Bryan had spent so much time apart these last few months, she hoped this vacation would help them to reconnect emotionally. And what better place to get connected than a romantic lodge in the Colorado wilderness? Hooked by beautiful pictures of nice, clean people wandering around the forest with glasses of wine or plates of sumptuous-looking food in their hands, Claire had spared no expense on her birthday present to Bryan. They were booked into the most expensive suite at the lodge, which featured a whirlpool bath and an authentic river-rock fireplace right there in the room.

"Next, please," the ticket agent called, having finished with the passenger ahead of Claire.

Struggling with her bags, Claire hefted the heaviest one onto the ticket agent's scale before reaching into her purse for her driver's license and frequent flyer card.

"Good morning. I have an electronic ticket on flight 604 to Aspen."

The agent took her identification and began typing rapidly on her computer. Claire started to relax. She was going to make it. She'd just have to rush through security and maybe do a little sprint down the concourse, but she'd be meeting Bryan in less than five minutes and everything would be fine. Claire interrupted her mental pep talk as she noticed a puzzled frown come over the ticket agent's brow.

The woman's nails clackety-clicked over the computer keys at an even faster pace.

"Is something wrong?"

"Mmm . . ." The ticket agent's eyes remained glued to the screen and Claire's blood pressure inched upward. "I'm sorry, Miss Brown, but it appears as if your reservation on flight 604 was canceled a week ago."

"But, but . . ." Claire sputtered, then started over. "I didn't cancel my reservation. Could you please check again?"

The agent eyed her up and down, as if considering whether she was worth the trouble.

"Please," Claire pleaded. "My fiancé and I are going on our first vacation together. He's probably waiting for me at the gate right now, wondering what's happened. Could you check again?"

The clackety-clicking began again, then stopped with an air of finality. "I'm sorry, Miss Brown, but your reservation was canceled by Associated Travel Services last Monday. Is that the travel agent who booked the ticket?"

"Yes," Claire answered, confused. She hadn't asked ATS to cancel her reservation.

"Perhaps you should call them. Can I help the next—"

"No, wait, please," Claire interrupted desperately. "Can I buy another ticket? I can work this all out with the travel agent on Monday."

"Certainly, Miss Brown, but all the first class seats are sold. If you'd like to get in the economy line, I'm sure they can help you. Now, can I help—"

Claire had ten minutes before the plane left without her. She did not consider herself an aggressive person by nature, and, later, she would be slightly embarrassed by the forcefulness brought on by desperation.

"No," she said frantically, raising her arms out at her sides like a traffic cop. The woman in line behind her stopped in her tracks.

Glancing at the agent's name tag, Claire stood her ground. "Please, Amy. You don't understand. I don't know why or how my reservation got canceled, but my flight is leaving in ten minutes and I need to be on it. I'd be happy to go wait my turn in economy if there was a snowball's chance in hell that I could get through that line in time, but we both know that's not going to happen. So, I'm begging you, take my credit card and get me a seat on that flight." Claire took a deep breath, slipped the plastic card across the counter, and pleaded, "Please? Any seat will do."

Her usually soft gray eyes met Amy's light blue gaze over the computer terminal.

It was a Mexican standoff over a set of American Tourister luggage.

As the computer keys started clicking again, Claire released the breath she hadn't realized she'd been holding.

"All right, Miss Brown. The flight is leaving out of gate C16. Here's your ID and your boarding pass. I can't guarantee your luggage will make it."

Claire's face lit up as she smiled. "Thank you, Amy." She turned to the woman in line behind her, who looked just as harried as Claire imagined she herself did. "Thank you, too. I hope you have a good trip."

"You'd better run," the ticket agent interrupted Claire's rush of gratitude. "I'll call the gate and tell them you're on your way, but they have a schedule to keep."

Claire arrived at the gate, sweating, her shoulder aching from the weight of her computer bag and overnight case. She was sure she'd have matching purple bruises on both thighs from where each bag had taken a turn smacking against her as she ran. Bryan wasn't waiting for her and she assumed he had already boarded since the agent at the gate was about to close the door.

"Wait, wait!" Claire yelled, holding out her boarding pass.

"You almost missed it." The agent ripped the ticket, handing Claire her section before waving her on. "Enjoy the flight."

"Thank you," Claire answered automatically before sprinting down the jetway.

As she stepped onto the Boeing 737, she spotted the familiar face of her fiancé and felt an instant sense of relief. They had both made it. Everything would be fine. Obviously, his ticket hadn't been canceled along with hers because Bryan was comfortably ensconced up in first class, sipping what appeared to be a screwdriver and chatting with an attractive woman seated next to the window.

"Bryan, you'll never guess what happened . . ." Claire began, noting the look of surprise on her fiancé's face as he looked up at the sound of her voice. He must have thought she was going to miss the flight. She was a little disappointed that he hadn't waited for her, but she vowed to forgive him since everything had turned out all right.

"What are you doing here?" Bryan asked.

Feeling happy with the world now that she'd made the flight, Claire bent down to hug him, awkwardly balancing her luggage behind her back to avoid smacking the seated passengers. "I almost missed the flight, but don't worry. Everything's going to be fine now."

"Ma'am, you need to be seated right away. The captain's ready to push back from the gate." A tall dark-haired flight attendant began shooing her back to coach.

"I'll have to fill you in later. I'm just glad it's all worked out." Releasing Bryan from her embrace, Claire smiled and allowed herself to be shooed.

"I'm happy just to have made the flight," she repeated to herself as she gazed around the plane. Every seat was taken, as usual. She glanced down at the stub in her hand. Twenty-nine E. A center seat. Oh, well, at least she'd made the flight.

Row 29 was the last row on the plane, conveniently located just in front of the lavatories. The flight attendant working the coach section opened the door of the bathroom to make sure it was empty, then locked the door for takeoff. Claire wrinkled her nose in distaste as the uniquely unpleasant scent of airline toilet wafted out.

Claire glanced at the window seat of the row where a tired-looking woman sat. A little boy who Claire guessed to be about three years old sat in the aisle seat. He looked up at Claire, his thumb in his mouth. She wondered if maybe the little guy was in the wrong seat. After all, wouldn't the child sit next to his mother?

"Is this your son, ma'am?" Claire asked, her overnight bag digging a permanent groove into her shoulder.

The woman in the window seat looked up with a friendly smile. A strand of lank brown hair fell into her eyes and she pushed it back behind her ear. Claire noticed the woman's hands looked younger than the lines on her face would suggest. "Yes, that's my little Billy," she answered, obviously proud of her progeny.

"Shouldn't he sit next to you?" Claire asked, hoping she would be able to get out of being squashed like a human sardine in the middle seat.

"Oh, no," the woman answered. "Little Billy's not potty-trained yet so he needs to sit as close to the bathroom as he can. He has accidents, you know."

"Then, don't you want to sit next to him?" Even in the window seat she'd get an extra inch or two and some semblance of privacy.

Her hopes were dashed as the woman responded, "No, but thank you anyway. You see, I'm terrified of flying and my doctor gave me some sleeping pills to take before the flight. He suggested I make sure to get a window seat so I wouldn't be disturbed by the commotion of people walking up and down the aisles."

Claire sighed, her happiness at making the flight somewhat diminished.

"Ma'am, could you please take your seat?" a blond flight attendant encouraged impatiently.

"Are there any aisle or window seats available?" She tried one last-ditch effort to find a comfortable spot to rest for the next three hours.

"No, this flight is completely full. Perhaps if you'd been an hour early as airline guidelines suggest we could have accommodated you, but, as it is, we just don't have any options. Now, I need you to take your seat immediately. The captain is ready to push back from the gate."

Claire didn't care for the woman's lecture, much less her unsympathetic tone, but reminded herself she was glad she'd made the flight. "I don't suppose there's any room in the overhead bins for this?" Claire asked, pointing to her overnight bag.

"No, I'm sorry. You'll have to store it under the seat in front of you. I'm sure this little guy won't mind if you use his space, too." The flight attendant smiled at little Billy, who continued to stare fixedly at Claire.

"Thanks anyway, I guess," Claire mumbled.

She leaned over Billy to drop her computer bag on her seat, then pushed her overnight bag under the seat in front of the boy.

The logistics of trying to squeeze oneself and one's belongings into a space no bigger than a breadbox while also attempting to not maul, crush or otherwise abuse one's fellow travelers was difficult in the best of circumstances. In the end, Claire managed to get by with only stepping on little Billy's mother's toes once and smacking the toddler's thumb out of his mouth with her purse twice. She apologized profusely after finally managing to contort herself into the seat and considered the feat as no less than a miracle, given the circumstances.

At last, the plane pushed back from the gate. Claire hoped she'd delayed the flight long enough for her luggage to make its way aboard but, what the heck, wouldn't it be every man's fantasy if his fiancée was stranded without any clothes for a week? She grinned to herself at the thought.

The captain announced that they were number one for takeoff, and a male flight attendant came through on his final check of the cabin. Claire fastened her seat belt and closed her eyes, intending to practice one of her yoga techniques to get her elevated blood pressure under control.

"Excuse me, ma'am. Your son's seat belt must be fastened for takeoff."

Claire vaguely heard the flight attendant as she started a relaxation exercise from her Guerrilla Yoga class at the gym. "Breathe in . . . Go to the happy place . . . Breathe out . . ."

"Ma'am," the man's voice insisted.

Claire opened her left eye to see the attendant staring at her with disgust. A loud snore had her glancing right. The plane wasn't even off the ground and little Billy's mother was already sound asleep. The flight attendant obviously thought the boy was *her* son.

"But he's not my . . ." The flight attendant continued staring at her as if wondering what rock Claire had just crawled out from under. Claire sighed. For some reason her week-long adventure was starting off all wrong, and there didn't seem to be anything she could do about it.

"Here, little Billy, the plane can't go bye-bye until you're all buckled up," she cooed in her best kid-pleasing voice, leaning over the silent child to reach for the buckle end of the seat belt.

Little Billy let out a bloodcurdling scream, a direct hit into her left eardrum.

His mother's snoring didn't even change its tempo.

Claire dropped the buckle. People around her stared as little Billy kept up his hollering. She decided to meet the problem head-on.

"Look, little fella, this isn't going to hurt. It's just like the seat belt you wear in your car."

Little Billy cried harder, a feat Claire hadn't thought possible. The flight attendant continued eyeing her with disdain. She tried jostling the boy's mother, but the snoring continued.

"If you stop crying and wear the seat belt, I'll give you a dollar," Claire offered in desperation.

Wiping his runny nose on his sleeve, the boy miraculously stopped crying and held out his hand to accept her bribe. Realizing that she'd been hoodwinked, Claire shook her head. "Uh-uh. Seat belt first."

As the buckle snapped shut, Claire rummaged through

her purse for the payoff. It was going to be a long flight, she thought, as the plane took off down the runway.

"Com-poo-ter, com-poo-ter, com-poo-ter." Little Billy jumped up and down in his seat, excitedly chanting and pointing at the laptop she had balanced on her knees. Claire tried to ignore him and concentrate on the screen in front of her. The Fasten Seat Belt sign was still lit, and people all around her were giving her the stink-eye for letting Billy run amok. The problem was, she didn't know how to stop him. She was the only child of parents who were only children. She didn't have cousins, had never been pressed into baby-sitting service, and had no idea how to get the tyke to behave in the calm, courteous, children-should-be-seen-and-not-heard manner that her parents had always expected of, and received from, her.

Bribery had worked for the first hour of the flight, but she had run out of small bills by now, having already handed over almost twenty bucks to make Billy stay in his chair, stop running up and down the aisle, stop kicking her suitcase, stop yanking on the seat in front of him, stop pressing the button for the flight attendant, and stop flushing things down the toilets.

To make matters worse, about an hour ago, little Billy's slumbering mother had shifted in her seat, reducing Claire's already-cramped seating space by another six inches. Then the guy in front of her leaned his seat all the way back— as if the extra two inches could possibly make him any more comfortable—causing Claire to have to slump in her seat and pull her laptop onto her stomach in order to continue working. To top it all off, the turbulence had been awful and the captain hadn't turned off the seat belt sign once. So, not only was she crammed into a space that was shrinking by the minute, she also hadn't been able to go up and speak to Bryan.

Claire closed her eyes and gladly turned her thoughts to her fiancé. Bryan had seemed surprised to see her. He was probably concerned that she was so late since Claire prided

herself on always being on time. In the entire year and a
half they'd known each other, she hadn't been late even
once. It was a lesson she'd learned at an early age from
her father. After being told to meet him at five o'clock one
evening after an elementary-school event, Claire had daw-
dled, enjoying a conversation with one of her teachers.
She'd been out at the curb at four minutes past five, only
to see the familiar family car driving away without her.
Fortunately, she'd been able to get a ride home with a
friend, but her father had made his point. Five o'clock
meant five o'clock. Period.

So, it made sense that Bryan was surprised to see her
racing down the aisle with mere seconds to spare. Claire
stretched her legs and leaned back in her seat. It had certainly been a less-than-optimal beginning to their first vacation together, but she vowed that it would get better from
here. It was going to be such fun, she thought, a smile
playing on her lips. A part of her almost hoped the weather
wouldn't cooperate. It would be nice to snuggle up together
in front of the river-rock fireplace in their room. They'd sip
wine and talk about something other than work for once
while the logs crackled away. Outside, it would be cold and
rainy, but in their room, she and Bryan would be cozy
and—

Just then, the seat belt sign went off and Claire heaved
a sigh of relief. Standing up, she set her laptop down on
her seat and prepared to bolt to safety. Now was her chance
to run up to the first class cabin to talk to Bryan and leave
someone else to tend to the human whirlwind in the next
seat.

At that thought, she made the mistake of glancing over
at the little tyke. His big brown eyes looked at her forlornly,
as if she were abandoning him. He blinked up at her, tears
starting to form in his eyes.

She looked over at little Billy's mother, who had taken
advantage of Claire's departure to claim even more of
Claire's seat for her own. There was not going to be any
last-minute reprieve from that corner.

She thought fast. What could she do to occupy the kid's time until she got back? She ran through the list of things in her purse that a toddler might find amusing, but didn't think he'd be entertained for long with a tube of Clinique Air Kiss lip gloss, her emergency supply of tampons, or her business card collection. What did she have that might work as a diversionary tactic? Her gaze fell on her laptop. Billy had been fascinated by it ever since she'd taken it out of the case. She was sure there must be games on it somewhere. That might keep the little fella entertained. Besides, what could he do to it in the few minutes she'd be gone?

"Do you want to play on the com-poo-ter?" she asked, imitating the mommy-speak she'd overheard other women using on children and feeling like an idiot.

Billy cheered up instantly, clapping his chubby, toddler hands in a gesture that Claire guessed meant "yes."

She leaned over, picked up the computer, and put it on Billy's tray table. It took her a few moments to find the Solitaire game, but was happy to see the bright colors holding Billy's rapt attention when she started the program. She showed him how to use the track ball to move the mouse, but didn't bother explaining the finer points of the game. Even she, with her limited knowledge of children, knew that was probably a bit much for a three-year-old's comprehension. When she left, he was happily clicking away and chortling as the cards moved around on the screen. Congratulating herself on her brilliant idea, Claire picked her way up to the front of the plane, squeezing past the beverage cart that was now on its way to the rear of the aircraft.

She ignored the accusing stares of the first class passengers and staff as she pushed open the curtain separating the aviation elite from the common folk back in steerage. She had to admit, the bathroom-to-passenger ratio alone was enough to make her long for first class, not to mention the free drinks and extra legroom.

Claire noticed Bryan's head was leaning awfully close to his next-chair neighbor and pushed aside the thought that with all the extra room up here, he didn't need to be getting quite so cozy with his fellow passenger.

"Bryan, I'm so glad you didn't have the same trouble I did. Somehow, my reservation got canceled."

Bryan's head abruptly swiveled around and Claire noticed the flush of color on his cheeks. Obviously, he was taking advantage of the free booze up here. Glancing at the tomatoey-looking beverage Bryan's neighbor was holding, Claire briefly wondered if the flight attendant would be nice enough to get her a Bloody Mary too, but from the frowning looks she was getting from the blue-suited attendant, she decided not to press her luck.

"Claire, I left you a—" Bryan's words were interrupted when the plane suddenly bucked upward.

She hadn't expected the violent turbulence and pitched forward as the seat belt sign blinked on once again. Claire tried to steady herself with a hand on the headrest of Bryan's seat, but the plane hit a pocket of air and plummeted a few feet, sending her sprawling across the breakfast-laden tray tables of Bryan and his seat mate. Sterling silverware and dishes clattered. The salt-and-pepper-haired woman in the window seat screeched and scrambled eggs went flying. Low murmurs started among the other passengers; a hushed, disapproving cloud of sentiment that clearly implied this sort of thing should be expected when members of coach class were allowed on the wrong side of the curtain.

As the plane steadied itself, Claire lay motionless, wishing she could open the window and be sucked out into the atmosphere. All sound around her had ceased. She shifted, trying to extricate herself from her embarrassing position. A fork clattered to the floor and Claire flinched when the thump of it hitting the carpet broke the eerie silence that had settled over the first class cabin.

"Ma'am, you need to get back to your seat and fasten your seat belt," the flight attendant said from behind her.

Claire slid back off the laps of her fiancé and the woman in seat 3D. "I'm so sorry," she mumbled, avoiding the unnaturally bright blue eyes of the salt-and-pepper-haired woman whose breakfast Claire was now wearing.

Gooey yellow eggs dropped in clumps to the carpet and cold tomato juice laced with vodka soaked into her formerly white T-shirt. Bryan's stare was fixed on her with open-mouthed horror. Claire knew he must be embarrassed for them both at this unfortunate turn of events. She opened her mouth to apologize once more when the plane dipped again. This time, the flight attendant was more forceful, pushing Claire through the cabin with a hand on her shoulder.

As she got closer to the back of the plane, she could hear little Billy sobbing and a feeling of dread crept into the pit of her stomach. What could be wrong now?

"It broked." The boy sobbed and pointed at her laptop as Claire approached.

Claire tried to contain her panic. It couldn't be broken! How could she get any work done during the next nine days if it was broken? She couldn't live without her computer for an entire week. Who would take care of her accounts?

Clutching the laptop to her chest, she slid back into her ever-shrinking seat. She opened the top, hoping Billy was wrong and that nothing was really the matter. Maybe he had just turned the power off by accident. Yes, that was probably it. She hit the power button and her finger came away sticky. She pressed her thumb and forefinger together and pulled them apart. Definitely sticky.

Curious, she stuck the tip of one finger in her mouth.

Orange juice. Now, where had that come from?

She looked over at Billy, who had a telltale orange stain around his mouth. She touched another few keys on her keyboard. They were all sticky. She rested her forehead in her hands, trying not to join Billy in his sob fest.

"Did you spill juice on the com-poo-ter?" she asked finally.

Twin rivers of tears rolled down the little boy's face as he nodded, his big brown eyes pleading for forgiveness.

At that exact moment, Claire realized that anyone else would have known it wasn't a good idea to give a computer to a three-year-old. Why did she always have to learn this sort of thing the hard way?

And how could this day possibly get any worse?

Billy had cried himself to sleep when the plane arrived at the gate in Aspen half an hour later, and Claire had joined him in a light slumber. The bustle of activity in the cabin woke her. Blinking the sleep out of her eyes, she remained seated while people began gathering their belongings from the overhead bins. Finally, the plane emptied and Claire hauled her own bags out from under the seats in front of her.

"I hope you have a good vacation."

"Um-hmm. You, too." Claire glumly acknowledged Billy's mother's surprisingly chipper well wishes as she stepped over the still-sleeping boy and into the aisle. He looked cherubic and innocent, but Claire knew better.

She vowed to talk to the travel agent first thing on Monday. She was going to get a first class ticket home even if she had to sell her best-performing stocks to get it.

When at long last she disembarked from what she would forever after refer to as the Flight From Hell, Claire was stunned to see that Bryan wasn't waiting for her. She stopped in the boarding area, looking out over the empty chairs in disbelief. Where was he? Why hadn't he waited for her? If the situation had been reversed, she would have waited for him.

Slumping down in one of the seats, Claire looked down at her soiled clothes and gave in to her disappointment. Of course, she was capable of fending for herself; capable of dealing with the crises the past few hours had thrown at her without needing her fiancé's assistance. But it would have been nice to have a shoulder to lean on. She closed her eyes dejectedly. Her laptop bag slid off her shoulder, the strap landing in the crook of her arm. Slowly, she pulled it back onto her shoulder and took a deep breath as a

thought swept unbidden into her mind. If Bryan had been
the one who was late, she wouldn't have even boarded the
plane back in Seattle. She would have stayed at the gate
until he showed up. And she certainly wouldn't have run
off after the flight was over. She would have waited right
here for him; waited to see what had gone wrong with his
morning.

Was he punishing her for being late, like her father
would have? Claire opened her eyes and stared unseeingly
out over the tarmac. Shaking her head, she pushed away
the thought. Surely Bryan wouldn't react to her tardiness
like that. He must have become impatient waiting for her
and gone to baggage claim to retrieve his luggage, she reasoned, trying to revive her flagging spirits. Or maybe he'd
gone to make sure the lodge's van didn't leave without her.
Yes, that must be it.

Pulling herself together, Claire stood and gathered her
bags. After all, she reminded herself, Bryan wasn't the type
who could wait for long periods of time. He liked to be
doing something at all times. Sometimes, she wondered
how he managed to sit still at work, how he coped with
the countless meetings that were an integral part of his job
as an account executive at the insurance brokerage firm
where he worked.

Balancing her laptop case on the black railing of the
escalator, Claire scanned the baggage claim area for any
sign of her suitcase or her errant fiancé. A handful of children, obviously happy to be free after hours of confinement,
were running around, dodging passengers and luggage. A
dog barked as one of the children ran by its carrier. The
little girl shrieked, momentarily startled, then started giggling as she realized what had scared her. Despite her wear-
iness, Claire smiled. She wouldn't mind a little exercise
herself.

Stepping off the escalator, Claire set her carry-on bags
down on the floor in front of the conveyor belt and continued to look for Bryan as she watched for her suitcase to
come out. Since Bryan wasn't at the baggage carousel,

Claire could only surmise that her supposition was correct. He must have gone on ahead to tell the van's driver to wait for her. The crowd thinned as each piece of luggage was grabbed off the belt. When the belt finally stopped, Claire's spirits dropped. Her bag was not coming.

Claire hurried to the airline's baggage agent to file a report on her missing luggage before pulling the lodge's brochure out of the pocket of her overnight bag.

"Once you have arrived in Aspen, proceed with your luggage to the parking lot where you'll be met by a van from Hunter's Lodge," it read.

Claire heaved her bags over her shoulders, looking around for signs pointing to where she was supposed to go. Not surprised that the parking lot was as far as possible from where she was standing, Claire started the trek out of the airport. The automatic doors at the end of the baggage-claim area whooshed open and Claire was hit by a refreshing breeze. Her spirits lifted a little at seeing the overcast sky.

"Cozy fireplace, here we come," she muttered, then looked up as a dark green van sped by.

Her eyes narrowed.

The van that had just roared past had "Hunter's Lodge" painted on in bright yellow lettering. Claire shook her head in disbelief as she watched the van's license plate get smaller and smaller in the distance. HUNTR2. After the day she'd had, Claire had the sneaking suspicion that HUNTR1 would not be waiting for her in the parking lot.

Resisting the urge to sink down on the sidewalk and have a good long cry, Claire dragged herself and her bags across the street, hoping that a car and her fiancé would be waiting for her there.

The first sight of the deserted parking lot dashed those hopes. Claire dropped her bags and sat down on the warm pavement. How could Bryan have left without her? She stared dumbly at the concrete between her feet. Was he punishing her for being late, as she'd suspected? Perhaps he was angry at her for not calling all week? She knew things hadn't been going that well between them for the past few months. They hadn't been spending much time together. She'd been busy with work and he'd been busy with . . . she didn't really know what Bryan had been up to lately. That was why she'd decided to spend a large chunk of her savings on this trip. But just because their relationship was a bit strained lately was no reason for him to leave her stranded at the airport. Claire sat up straighter, righteous anger providing a measure of steel to her backbone. After all, the state of their relationship wasn't solely her responsibility.

Claire took a deep breath, trying to calm herself. Perhaps there was some other explanation for all this. Perhaps . . . uh, maybe . . . Well, she didn't know what possible reason Bryan might have had for leaving, but she wasn't going to get anywhere by sitting around feeling sorry for herself. She grabbed the cell phone out of her purse, dialed the number for the lodge, and tapped her foot while she waited for her call to be answered.

"Hunter's Lodge. How may I help you?" a cheerful woman's voice responded.

"Hello. This is Claire Brown. My fiancé and I are booked in the Rose Suite for the next eight nights."

"Yes, ma'am. Let me check the reservation. What name is it under?"

"Edwards. Bryan Edwards."

There was some rustling of paper. "Yes, I have that reservation."

"Thank God." Claire closed her eyes with gratitude.

"What can I help you with, Ms. Brown?"

"I had a problem with my luggage and was a little late getting out of the airport. It appears that your van left without me."

There was a slight pause on the other end of the line, then a deep sigh. "Are you sure?"

"Yes. I watched them drive away five minutes ago. Unless you have more than one van?" Claire asked hopefully.

"No, I'm afraid not, Ms. Brown. I'm so sorry. My

brother was driving the van and must have forgotten you. I'll have someone leave right away to get you. It will take about an hour, I'm afraid, but maybe you could get yourself something to eat in the airport?"

"Couldn't I just get a cab?"

"You could, but you'd only be saving yourself a few minutes by the time you find a driver who's willing to come out this way."

"All right, I'll meet your driver here in an hour." She paused. "Tell him he can't miss me, I'll be the one with the Kick Me sign on my back."

"Excuse me?"

"Never mind," Claire muttered, flipping the phone closed.

Chapter 2

JOHN MCBRIDE LOOKED UP FROM UNDER THE HOOD OF HIS old blue pickup as Dana Robinson, the lodge's assistant manager, pushed open the door to the garage marked "Employees Only." As the owner of both Hunter's Lodge and Outdoor Adventures, John was technically not an employee, but he doubted the shy young woman had come to argue the semantics with him.

"Hi, uh, Mr. McBride?"

"Yes, Dana?" John tried to hide the amusement in his voice at the young woman's hesitance to talk to him. He'd never done anything to frighten Dana and had no idea why she almost jumped every time he talked to her. Somebody must have told her about his former job with the FBI. That was the only thing John could think of that might intimidate the nineteen-year-old.

"Um, a lady . . . uh . . ." Dana began, obviously wishing she could avoid this discussion altogether. She swallowed and began again. "A lady just called and said that she's registered here with her fiancé until next Sunday. But Kyle didn't pick her up, and now she's stranded at the airport, and Mark's out with a group of hikers, and somebody needs to go get her." Dana took a deep breath.

"I thought we'd given your brother a checklist of passengers so this wouldn't happen again?" John asked calmly before Dana could begin stuttering again.

"Well, yes, Mr. McBride, we did. I don't know how he could have forgotten her, but she called, and she's at the airport, so I guess he did."

From the way Dana stared at her feet while she was talking to him, John thought her tennis shoes must be fascinating. "Did you make sure she's a guest here? Maybe she's mistaken and has a reservation at one of the other lodges in the area."

"Oh, no, I checked that right off." John couldn't help but notice the pride in her voice. "The reservation's under her fiancé's name, but she knew what suite they were staying in and when they were leaving and all. I guess she could have been making it up or something," she said uncertainly, peering up at him through her lashes.

"No, my guess is she wasn't making it up."

John stepped back, slamming the hood of the truck. Ignoring Dana's startled-rabbit look, he walked over to a large sink and attempted to get some of the grease out from under his fingernails. "What'd you say this lady's name was?"

"Claire Brown. She'll be waiting for you in the parking lot where we do our usual pickups."

"Okay. Thanks for handling this so well, Dana. You did the right thing," he said before pulling himself up into the truck and cranking the ignition. The engine sputtered to life and he gave a casual wave as he pulled out of the garage, noticing that Dana's face had gone red with embarrassed pride at his praise.

John drove down the deserted two-lane highway, enjoying the crisp, early fall air that filled the cabin of the truck. He didn't get into town much these days, generally relying on the lodge's general manager for any errand-running that needed to be done. His glance fell on his hands on the steering wheel and he grimaced, wishing he'd had more time to get cleaned up. He hated meeting guests looking so sloppy, but he also hadn't wanted to make Kyle's stranded passenger wait at the airport any longer than she had to.

He'd almost forgotten what a nice drive this was, with the early autumn temperatures turning the trees rich shades of red, gold, and pale yellow. The truck bumped along the quiet road and John enjoyed the momentary sense of peace. There always seemed to be so much going on at the lodge that needed his attention, not to mention all the hours he

spent keeping up all of Outdoor Adventures' other operations throughout the world.

But with the lodge's general manager off in Europe on
her honeymoon, today's errand fell to him. Laughing a little
in the silence, John recalled the happy look on the faces of
his friends when they'd announced their engagement. Their
romance had been going on right under his nose and John
never even suspected. His observation skills were definitely
getting rusty out here, he thought now, scanning the forest
as the truck lumbered along. Seven years ago he'd been
one of the best in the business at watching people and pre-
dicting their behavior. He'd been able to look at someone's
footprint and tell if that person was right- or left-handed, if
it was a male or female, if he had just eaten, and what
mood the person was in.

Now he hadn't even noticed when two people he worked
with every day walked around gazing into each other's
eyes.

A lot had certainly changed in the ensuing years. All of
it for the better, as far as John was concerned. He hadn't
thought things could get much worse than that night, six
years ago, when his now–ex-wife had told him it was over.
Fortunately, he had been right. Things hadn't gotten worse.
Delilah's refusal to stay married to someone who was, in
her words, "quitting a prestigious career with the FBI to go
out and hug trees for a living" had marked the end of a
very bad period in John's life.

Ignoring the growling of his stomach, John leaned back
and pushed thoughts of his ex-wife away. The past wasn't
a pleasant subject to think about, especially on an empty
stomach.

John leaned back in his seat and took a deep breath,
letting the wind clear his mind of the past. There was a
hint of cold in the air, a mere suggestion of the upcoming
change in seasons. A large black rain cloud slipped over
the sun, and John rolled his window up a bit to compensate
for the sudden drop in temperature. They'd probably get a
touch of rain here shortly, he thought. Nothing major, just

a typical early-season soaking to let people know that Mother Nature was warming up for fall.

Thinking about the group of guests out hiking right now, John hoped the shower would confine itself to the lower elevations. The last of his summer employees would be leaving after today's activities and John frowned, hoping that there would be enough staff around in the next month to attend to the needs of the guests. At this time of year business had historically started to slow down for them, but the August issue of *Well-Traveled* magazine had featured an article listing Hunter's Lodge as number five of their readers' top one hundred favorite places to stay. After the magazine had hit the newsstands, the lodge's phones had started ringing with people wanting to try the place out for themselves. Of course, by then, his friends' wedding plans had already been made, and even though they had offered to postpone their honeymoon, John wouldn't hear of it. He supposed that meant the blame could be placed squarely at his feet if they were shorthanded for the rest of the month.

Assuring himself they'd manage to muddle through somehow, John slowed the truck in anticipation of his turn. The first drops of rain hit the windshield just as he pulled off the highway and onto the road to the airport.

Claire hardly noticed the first drops of rain that splashed onto the back of her sweater. She waited to hear the beep on the other end of the phone and tilted her head, trying to get better reception on her cell phone.

"Rich, this is Claire again. I got cut off and I have a few more things I need you to do when you get in on Monday morning. First, please send—"

"Miss Brown?"

Claire looked up at the dark-haired stranger standing in front of her and held up a hand, indicating that she'd be done in a minute. She just wanted to finish this last message to her assistant and then she could begin to put this night-mare of a morning behind her.

"—denial letters out on the files I put on your desk last night. Next—"

"Excuse me, are you Claire Brown?" the man interrupted again.

Claire gave him a pointed look and tried to finish the message. She'd been sitting out here for over an hour now, waiting for someone to pick her up, and her temper hadn't improved as the minutes ticked by. Admittedly, Bryan should have made sure the lodge's van waited for her—and she was certainly going to let him know how she felt about that when she finally got to the lodge—but the van driver himself was also partly to blame for her current predicament. Her annoyance and frustration had been building as she sat here, all alone on the concrete, and unfortunately, it was now directed at the man standing before her. She'd had to wait for him, now it was his turn to wait for her. She'd be done with her call in just a minute, and then they could go.

"—send out initial contact letters to . . ." Claire's voice trailed off as the man turned around and hauled himself up into the cab of a battered blue pickup truck, slamming the heavy door behind him.

"Rich, I'll have to call you back." She pushed the button to end the call and started running as the man put the truck into reverse.

"Hey, wait a minute. Stop!" she yelled, racing after him.

Droplets of water slid down the back of her neck and along her spine as the sky opened up. Abruptly, the truck stopped its backward motion. Claire tried to stop her sprint toward the vehicle, but the smooth leather of her new shoes failed to find purchase on the rain-dampened pavement.

"Oof," Claire grunted, slamming into the warm grille of the truck. The force sent her sprawling, butt-first, onto the concrete. Proof once again that every action produces an equal and opposite reaction, Claire thought, rubbing her injured rear end.

Watching as a pair of worn black work boots swung out of the truck, Claire tried to struggle to her feet. The man stopped in front of her, eyeing her as if she were a lunatic.

"Are you Miss Brown? Miss Claire Brown?"

"Yes," Claire answered, pushing her wet bangs out of her eyes.

The man in front of her was tall and his thick black hair was a bit longer than she usually found attractive, but she had to admit it looked pretty darn good on him. His hair was dry so she assumed that black was his natural color. Hers, she was sure, had probably turned the unattractive dishwater-blond it always did when it got wet—which was exactly what she was right now, wet, bedraggled, annoyed, and now sore, too. The beginning of her relaxing, romantic vacation was not turning out to be anything like she'd hoped, and rather than start sobbing in front of the stranger who stood staring down at her, she chose to stick with irritation instead.

"You almost ran over me," she accused.

"I assumed you were ignoring me because you weren't the person I was looking for. And I hardly ran over you. As a matter of fact, I believe it was you who ran into me."

"Ignoring you? I wasn't ignoring you, I was trying to finish my phone call." Tired of craning her neck to look up at him, she held out a hand. "Would you please help me up? My shoes are brand-new and they don't have much traction yet."

He looked at her outstretched fingers as if she were handing him a gun and asking him to shoot himself with it. His own hands were nothing to look at, she thought irritably. At least hers were clean. Fearing that he was going to ignore her and let her flounder around on her slippery shoes like Bambi on ice, Claire grabbed his arm and hauled herself up without waiting for him to volunteer his assistance.

"Thanks," she muttered, dusting herself off.

The man nodded in acknowledgment, then said, "I'm John McBride from Hunter's Lodge. Are you ready to go?"

He continued to gaze down at her with his dark green eyes and Claire took a deep breath. This poor man had done

nothing to her except get the unfortunate assignment of
having to pick her up. None of what had happened to her
so far was his fault, she reminded herself. She picked at a
clump of dried-on scrambled eggs that was still stuck to
her khakis and lowered her eyes to the pavement.

"Yes, I'd love to get out of here. My bags are over
there."

She flipped her wet hair out of her face in an attempt to
gather her dignity. John McBride walked her around the
truck with a hand beneath her elbow. He even held the door
open for her and provided a hand to help her up into the
cab, a surprising courtesy considering their encounter so
far, Claire thought.

Having gotten her properly stowed, he came around the
other side, placed her two small bags and purse on the seat
between them, and climbed easily into the truck.

"Where's the rest of your luggage?"

Claire had the feeling the question was forced. "What
makes you think this isn't everything?"

He gave an inelegant snort and backed the vehicle out
of the parking lot. "You're a woman. That's what makes
me think you've probably got four more bags waiting for
me to pick up somewhere around the airport."

"Ha, little do you know. I only had one more suitcase."

"Had?" He raised a dark eyebrow.

"Had," Claire confirmed, fastening her seat belt with a
decisive click. "Given my luck today, it's probably on its
way to Timbuktu."

"Having a bad day, huh?"

Claire paused in the act of attempting to rearrange her
soggy hair into some semblance of order. "Yes, I am definitely having a bad day."

He merely grunted in acknowledgment of her answer,
then turned his attention back to the road ahead.

Claire pushed the headband back into her hair and slid
back against the seat, crossing her arms across her chest to
ward off the chill from her soggy sweater as she watched
John McBride out of the corner of her eye. Some women

might like his dark rugged looks, the way his navy blue shirt set off his green eyes, his tanned and muscular forearms . . .

Okay, so he was handsome. She'd admit that she had felt a little sizzle of physical attraction when he'd handed her into the truck. She was engaged, but she wasn't dead, for God's sake. And what woman wouldn't be tempted to squeeze those tanned biceps, just to see if all that muscle was for real?

She shook her head as that last thought fluttered into her brain, leaving her fingers tingling to do just that. What was she thinking? She had a fiancé waiting for her back at the lodge. She should not be considering testing this guy out like a ripe tomato at the market. Annoyed at the turn her thoughts had taken, Claire grabbed her purse and rummaged around for her square green compact. The last thing she needed today was to find herself having errant fantasies about tall, dark, and handsome men. She reminded herself that Bryan, with his white-blond hair and athletic-club-honed muscles was more her type than this rugged outdoorsman from the lodge. Feeling a bit unsettled, she focused on repairing her makeup and tried to ignore the man sitting next to her.

John maneuvered the truck back onto the highway, shaking his head at the rudeness of his passenger. Admittedly, his social skills might be in need of some polishing up, but he'd said nothing to set off the pint-sized termagant sitting in the passenger seat. If anything, he was the one who should be annoyed—she'd managed to miss the regular shuttle and made him take two hours out of his day to provide her with her own private livery service. When Dana had told him that Claire Brown had been stranded at the airport, he'd wondered why her fiancé hadn't made sure that she'd been on the van before it left. Now John began to suspect that the man had done it on purpose to get rid of her. Maybe he'd thought she'd get her snooty little butt back on the next outbound plane and leave him to enjoy his vacation.

John had met plenty of her type in his time, especially since he'd started Outdoor Adventures six years ago. There was a special breed of spoiled, self-centered women who expected the entire world to cater to their whims. These were women who'd sacrificed everything to claw their way to the top of their chosen fields. Husbandless, childless, virtually friendless, they poured every ounce of energy into making sure their own personal goals were met and didn't care how ruthless they had to be to get whatever it was they wanted. Yes, he knew a lot about this type of woman; women just like his workaholic ex-wife Delilah, whose job had always come first and everything else, including their marriage, was a far-distant second.

He slid a sideways glance at the woman sitting next to him. She had pulled something out of her purse and was attempting to fix some of the damage from the rain by dabbing powder somewhat ineffectually at the dark smudges beneath her light gray eyes. Her wet hair, now combed neatly, dripped occasional beads of water onto her stained T-shirt and dark sweater. Her khaki pants were a rumpled mess and her leather shoes were covered with mud. John couldn't help but notice how her once-white T-shirt clung to her wet skin, providing him with tantalizing glimpses of her lacy bra as she turned to put the powder back into her purse.

John barely held back a snort of disgust. Yeah, he knew her type all right, and they didn't get better on closer inspection, either.

By the time they reached the lodge, the atmosphere inside the cab of the truck could have chilled an Eskimo, and not because of the temperature war that had been raging in silence for the past thirty minutes. The two occupants of the vehicle had been pointedly ignoring each other for most of the journey, their only interaction being the subtle one-upmanship with the truck's heater.

Claire had started it. Her wet clothes were sticking to her clammy skin, making her nipples pucker painfully, so she leaned forward and inched the thermometer upward. Soon, tropically warm air circulated throughout the cabin. Claire uncrossed the arms she'd crossed over her chest, leaned back, and closed her eyes as her clothes began to dry.

Her eyes popped open a few minutes later when goose bumps broke out on her arms. She hadn't even heard a rustle of movement, but the thermostat was definitely lower than it had been a minute before. She shot a deadly glance at her seat mate, who stared resolutely out the window and refused to make eye contact.

Fine, two can play at this game, she thought. Reaching down to rummage through her purse, she "accidentally" bumped the little black knob to the right.

Five minutes passed and she started to relax again.

John reached over to fiddle with the radio and prodded the thermostat down two notches.

Ten minutes passed. Resolving not to sink to his level, Claire rubbed her hands together, then blew on them in an exaggerated attempt to revive her circulation. He didn't get the hint. Running out of ideas, she stole one from his playbook and bumped up the temperature as she turned up the volume of the radio.

It's like an oven in here, John thought as he cracked his window open to let in a little fresh air. He suspected Claire was trying to punish him for not paying attention to her during the drive by creating her own little inferno in the truck. Well, he wasn't going to be manipulated by her little tricks. He rolled his window all the way down and whistled tunelessly to the radio.

He's trying to freeze me to death, Claire thought as the cold outside air rushed into the cabin, bringing with it the scent of autumn rain. She pushed the heater up as high as it would go and pressed herself as far away from his side of the truck as possible.

When she finally spotted the lodge up ahead, Claire's first thought was relief that she would soon be rid of John McBride's boorish company. Her second thought was one

of awe as the impressive building came into view. Hunter's
Lodge was two stories of rough-hewn cedar logs stacked
tightly on top of each other. The green tile roof set off the
dark red of the logs, so rather than looking garish, the lodge
blended perfectly with the surrounding forest.

There were plenty of windows on the front of the lodge,
but Claire couldn't wait to see the back of the hotel. The
brochure had shown a view of the river through floor-to-
ceiling windows. The whirlpool tub of the Rose Suite sat
right up against the windows with a view of the river below. Claire had packed candles and bath salts in her missing
suitcase, anticipating long, leisurely soaks in that tub after
long, peaceful days enjoying the outdoors.

She put a hand on the dashboard and leaned forward as
the pickup rolled up the gravel drive.

"It's beautiful." Claire hadn't realized she'd spoken the
words out loud until John shot her a surprised glance. He
stopped the truck in front of a large set of leaded-glass
double doors that were obviously the main entrance of the
lodge.

"I'll bring your bags in," he said.

"I can manage."

"Suit yourself." John gazed across at her, his green eyes
impassive as she struggled to balance her load of belongings after hopping down out of the truck.

Claire shifted the weight of her laptop behind her, then
paused just as she was about to close the heavy door. Her
eyes met John's and, once again, she felt that unwanted
tingle of awareness tickling across her skin. She blinked,
trying to break the spell, and cleared her suddenly dry
throat. No matter that he'd tried to turn her into the human
equivalent of an ice cube, he'd still taken two hours away
from whatever he was doing to come get her. And now,
looking at the beautiful structure before her, listening to the
calls of the birds and the calming sound of the river, she
was grateful she was here at last, ready to begin that restful
vacation she'd been planning for so long.

"Thank you for the ride," she said, then pushed the door

shut, hoping all the while that whatever duties John Mc-
Bride was responsible for around here would keep him
away from her for the next nine days.

The interior of the lodge was as beautiful as the exterior,
Claire noted with delight as she walked to the small reception area. She'd been afraid the brochure pictures might
have missed showing racks of antlers mounted to the walls
or stuffed fish hanging all over the place. Instead, hanging
on the walls were tasteful landscapes, and the gleaming
hardwood floors were covered with richly colored rugs. All
that was missing from the picture was her fiancé, and she
planned to rectify that right now.

"Hello. You must be Miss Brown. My name is Dana,
Dana Robinson. Didn't Mr. McBride come in with you?"
A young woman with shining reddish-gold hair greeted
Claire, her hands twisting nervously behind the dark wood
of the reception desk.

"Yes, I'm Claire. It's nice to meet you, Dana, and no,
Mr. McBride didn't come with me. Could you please show
me up to my room? I've had a long day and I'm exhausted."

"Yes, Miss Brown. I'm, uh, I'm sure you are. But could
I ask you to wait here for just a moment?" The girl was
already sidling away. "Please have a seat. I'll be right
back."

"Wait—" Claire began to protest.

Dana nearly ran away. Claire looked down at herself,
acknowledging that she looked a fright, but not bad enough
to have scared the poor girl away. She was dirty and exhausted and she didn't want to wait even another second
to get out of her soiled clothes and sink into the luscious
tub she'd been fantasizing about for the past half hour.

Peeking around the deserted foyer to make sure she was
alone, Claire leaned over the desk. As a frequent business
traveler she'd noticed every hotel she'd stayed at seemed
to have a file with each registered guest's information on
it—including the room number they'd been assigned. The

system at Hunter's Lodge appeared to be no different. She flipped to the *E*'s, found the card for Bryan Edwards, and glanced at the handwritten number written at the top right-hand corner of the card.

Number 24, the Rose Suite. Claire sighed. It sounded heavenly. Whatever Dana needed from her was just going to have to wait.

Claire hurried up the large staircase to the left of the registration area and followed the signs to room 24, ignoring the banging of the computer case on her sore back end.

For the second time that day, Dana raced down the hall leading to the garage and flung open the door in search of John McBride.

"Mr. McBride, you have to help," she pleaded desperately just as he stepped out of his truck.

John resisted the urge to sigh at the small, everyday crises that had plagued him since the general manager had been gone. He vowed to give her a raise when she got back from her honeymoon next month. He'd never realized how many minor disasters she averted every day.

"Yes, Dana, what can I help you with?"

"It's Claire Brown. Well, actually, it's her fiancé. When he checked in, I told him that you'd gone to pick up Miss Brown and he told me that he'd called her and told her he didn't want her to come along on this vacation. He brought someone else. I saw them together when Mr. Edwards checked in, and now Miss Brown is here, and I don't think she knows, and we're all filled up, and I just don't know what to do."

John wasn't quite sure he'd followed everything Dana had said, but he figured he understood enough to know that he had a major problem on his hands.

Chapter 3

THE DOOR TO ROOM 24 SWUNG OPEN AND CLAIRE DRAGGED herself across the threshold, then stood staring in open-mouthed delight. The room was beautiful, just like the brochure had pictured it. In her experience, Claire had found that brochures tended to grossly exaggerate the benefits of a particular hotel, but this looked even better than the pictures she'd been staring at for the past two months. A king-sized bed covered with a fluffy goose-down comforter faced the fire burning in the fireplace. Two heavy oak chairs flanked the river-rock hearth. Floor-to-ceiling windows provided a view of the steadily flowing river and lush forest beyond. She couldn't wait to see the bathroom, with its giant whirlpool tub, marble floors, and gleaming brass fixtures.

Claire's carry-on slid to the floor. Oh, yes, a nice hot bath would be just the thing to make her feel human again.

Putting a hand on the bathroom door, she was startled when Bryan suddenly opened the door from the other side. He was wearing a smile on his lips and a towel around his hips.

"Hi, honey." She started to smile, then stopped when a woman appeared behind Bryan's shoulder. Her smile instantly disappeared. It was the woman from first class, the one whose scrambled eggs Claire was wearing on her sweater. "Bryan, what is going on?"

"Bryan, you said you'd taken care of her," the female behind Bryan whined.

Claire took a step backward, stumbling on the strap of her overnight bag. A sickening sense of premonition started to burn in her gut. Bryan had been distant these last few months, had claimed to be busy with friends every time she

suggested they get together. Was this the type of friend he'd
been busy with? She swallowed against the acid rising in
her throat.

"Who are you?" Claire directed the question to the salt-
and-pepper-haired woman who was pushing her way out of
the bathroom.

"I'm Cindy. Bryan's girlfriend." She was wearing neither a towel nor a smile. Claire stared at the other woman
in shocked fascination as Cindy crossed the room without
a stitch of clothing. She was well-toned and obviously did
her tanning in the nude, Claire noticed, as her mind struggled to comprehend the situation laid out before her.

"But I . . . you . . . Bryan, what the hell is going on
here?" Claire realized belatedly that she was shouting.
From the murmur of voices coming from the open door
behind her, she also realized that she was making a scene.
She never shouted or made a scene.

"Uh, didn't you get my message?" He aimed the question at Claire, but his gaze kept wandering to Cindy's firm,
bouncing breasts.

"What message?" Claire asked loudly, trying to get his
attention.

"The one I left on your phone last night."

Claire noticed Bryan shifting uncomfortably. She
couldn't remember him ever getting an erection from just
the sight of *her* without any clothes on, and her anger increased another notch.

"I didn't check my messages. I had to work late so I
could leave for this vacation. I didn't get home till after
midnight and didn't bother to check my machine."

"Well, then, don't blame me for this mess. I left you a
message and told you not to come."

"What do you mean, you told me not to come? I paid
for this entire vacation—you can't tell me not to come,"
she yelled, exhausted, confused, and getting angrier by the
second. How could he do this to her? She'd been everything
a man could want in a fiancée. She was hard-working and
loyal. She made enough money to support herself and

would never be a financial drain on the man she married.

"It was *my* birthday present." Bryan shrugged. "I should be able to bring anyone I want. Besides, I figured you knew we were over. We haven't seen each other for weeks."

Realization suddenly dawned crystal clear in Claire's eyes. She turned to nudie-girl. "Exactly when did he invite you to come along on this trip?"

"It's been over a month. Bryan kept telling me how much fun we'd have, and I just love the great outdoors. Don't you?" Cindy asked, sliding what Claire recognized as her own purple T-shirt with "Northwestern University" embroidered on the front over naked, darkly tanned breasts. It was Claire's favorite shirt, bought the day before her college graduation. She and Meg had bought matching shirts to remind them of the good times they'd had during those four years together.

She must have left it over at Bryan's house and the rotten worm had given it to his new girlfriend. Claire didn't hear anything else Cindy said. She could see the other woman's lips moving but her hearing was overpowered by a rushing sound that blocked out everything else. Bryan had been planning this for over a month, but didn't have the balls to tell her to her face. Her teeth snapped shut. He'd been avoiding her and he thought she'd just figure out for herself that their engagement was off?

"I did call," Bryan protested as the silence lengthened.

The negligent shrug Bryan gave as he uttered his lame excuse pushed her over the edge. He shrugged at her as if this were no big deal, as if this were no more important than if someone was trying to return a pair of athletic shoes that didn't quite fit. They'd been engaged to be married! It wasn't as if he and Claire had just met—they'd gone out and bought rings, had announced their engagement to family and friends, and he had the nerve to shrug her off as if that meant nothing. The bile that had been brewing in her stomach all day erupted in a flash of molten anger. She was going to rake that stupid look off his face, even if it did ruin her manicure.

"You bastard," Claire shrieked as she took the first step toward him.

And stopped abruptly as she was grabbed from behind, her head snapping back against a solid wall of human steel.

"Let me go." Claire struggled, her clenched fists held tightly at her sides by two very strong arms. She lifted a foot and stepped down hard on her captor's instep.

John grunted at the unexpected pain, then lifted Claire up so she couldn't stomp on him again. Her hair smelled fresh, like the autumn rain. The scent wafted up, distracting him from the crisis at hand. She wriggled against him as she struggled and his arm brushed across her breasts. John was astonished to find himself responding to the pressure of her body on his. His voice, when it finally came, sounded huskier than usual. "Miss Brown, if you'll calm down, perhaps we can all discuss this rationally."

"Calm down? Calm down! I'll give you calm." She lifted her foot again in preparation for a well-placed kick on the shin.

"Oh, no you don't." John's sanity returned just in time and he clasped both of her small wrists together with one hand and pushed her facedown on the fluffy, down-covered bed.

"Let me up, you big oaf," she muffled out between mouthfuls of comforter.

"Not until you've calmed down."

Claire took a deep breath and stopped struggling. "Okay, I'm calm. Now let me up."

John regarded the back of Claire's head suspiciously, then let go of her arms. She sat up, glaring at him and rubbing her wrists.

"Are you okay? I didn't mean to—"

The small fist that hit him had more passion behind it than strength, but it held enough force to take him off guard and give him a bloody nose, to boot.

She darted away as he held a hand up to his injured nose in disbelief.

"I'll kill you," she screeched, leaping across the bed for her erstwhile fiancé.

Bryan stood up, trapped in the corner next to the fireplace. He must have stepped too quickly, however, because the knotted towel at his waist fluttered to a puddle on the floor at his feet. He tripped over the towel, landing firmly against Cindy, who plunked down heavily into the chair. Claire landed on top of the heap, fists flying, crushed against several body parts that were not unfamiliar to her.

John was the first to recover from Claire's assault. Holding a handkerchief against his still-bleeding nose, he grabbed the back of Claire's sweater, pulling her off the other two.

"You're coming with me." John pushed Claire ahead of him out into the hall and she had no choice but to allow herself to be urged out of the room.

"Sorry for the disruption, folks," John said to the small crowd that had gathered in the hall as he closed the door to room number 24.

"But my purse, my bags . . . I need my things," Claire sputtered as John guided her none too gently down the stairs.

"We'll get them later."

He opened the door to an office behind the reception area, pushed her in, then followed her inside. The door swung shut with a controlled click.

"Sit down," he ordered.

Claire glared at him, but did as she was told.

"It'll stop bleeding if you tilt your head back and apply some pressure," she said sweetly, watching him dab at his nose. She'd never given anyone a bloody nose before, couldn't remember ever striking anyone, but was getting a strange, malicious pleasure out of watching his snow-white handkerchief spot with blood. Perhaps it was just that she wanted something to match her own once-white clothing, she thought, glancing down at the mess that she was wearing.

"I know how to take care of a bloody nose. It's the

guests I seem to have a problem with. Now, I believe I heard enough of what just went on up there to get the general idea of the situation," John began.

"Then maybe you can explain it to me, because all I know is that yesterday I was going on a fun-filled vacation with my fiancé and today I've been squashed, spilled on, abandoned, and, apparently, jilted." Claire felt the false bravado she'd been running on for the past hour drain out of her like water through a sieve. Her shoulders slumped with the crush of despair. She sniffed and swiped at a tear that threatened to spill down her cheek.

"I'd offer you my handkerchief, but I'm more in need of it than you are right now," John said, holding the cloth against his still-bleeding nose.

Claire sniffled again. "Thanks so much for your concern, but I'm sure I'll manage just fine without your help."

"Sure you will. And just how do you think you're going to get back to town without my help?"

"Back to town? I'm not going back to town. Just because that rat of a fiancé of mine chose to bring some bimbo on *our* romantic vacation doesn't mean I'm leaving."

"You aren't thinking of trying to win him back, are you?" John asked incredulously.

"That's none of your business." Claire glanced at him with irritation. He was so calm, sitting behind the sturdy desk. Well, why shouldn't he be calm? she asked herself. It wasn't he who'd just been dumped in such a public and humiliating manner, and it wasn't he who'd dipped into his savings account to pay for this trip in the first place. No, this guy's idea of a major vacation was probably shacking up at the nearest Motel 6 for $29.99 a night!

He continued to observe her, his green eyes seeming to take in her every movement. Claire pulled the edges of her sweater together, suddenly uncomfortable with his perusal. "Look, John, I paid for this entire trip. I've worked past midnight every night for the last month so I could get away and, starting today, I'm on vacation and I'm not leaving." Crossing her arms in front of her chest, Claire sank down on the chair opposite the desk as if to prove that she was there to stay. She was not going to let Bryan's betrayal turn her into a victim. She'd worked hard to get this time off, had done all the research and planning—not to mention the paying—and she wasn't going to let Bryan run her off. She was going to stay here at this idyllic lodge and enjoy every minute of the next nine days.

John leaned back in his chair. "According to Dana, the room was charged on Bryan's credit card."

"The only reason it's showing up under his card number is because he kept changing the dates on me. After canceling the reservation twice, I finally told Bryan to call the lodge himself once he decided when he could get the time off. He did, and had to use his own credit card when he called. I wrote him a check to reimburse him for the cost the very next day."

"That may be so, but technically the room belongs to him for the week. That means you're the one who has to leave."

"No. I need this vacation. I *deserve* this vacation. I'm not leaving."

Gray eyes met green in a silent battle of wills.

"Yes you are. The lodge is booked. We don't have one spare room to sell you. Even if we wanted to." He played his trump card matter-of-factly.

"I'd like to speak to the manager. I imagine he'll be able to find a room for me," Claire suggested.

"The manager's in Europe this week. And even if *she* was here, she wouldn't be able to sell you a room because there aren't any left to sell. There's another hotel about twenty-five miles from here. I'd be glad to give them a call and see if they have any vacancies."

"But I want to stay here. It's so beautiful . . . and perfect, just like the pictures." Claire held back a sniffle and knew she was close to an all-out pity party. She wanted the Rose Suite. She wanted long hot baths in her own whirlpool tub. She wanted rushing rivers, peaceful hikes, and delicious dinners. She wanted to stay at Hunter's Lodge.

Before she could resort to crying and begging for a room, a reddish-gold head poked through the door.

"Oh. Hi, John. I'm sorry to interrupt. I was just coming to get the schedule of this week's activities."

Claire's hope was renewed. She leaped up off the chair and clasped the other woman's hand. "Dana. I'm Claire Brown, remember?"

"Yes, of course, Miss Brown. How are you?"

"Call me Claire, please."

John cleared his throat. "Miss Brown was just leaving."

Claire's head whipped around, spearing him with a ferocious gray glare before turning back to Dana. Behind her back, John grinned. So the pint-sized shrew thought she was scary, huh? That was the first truly amusing thing he'd seen all day. He envisioned picking her up by the scruff of her neck like a spitting gray kitten, watching in his mind as her limbs flailed ineffectually at him. Yeah, she was pretty ferocious, all right. His grinning stopped as a drop of blood spilled onto his jeans. She might not be frightening, but she certainly did pack quite a punch for such a small woman. John dabbed at his nose as Claire started talking again.

"Dana, Mr. McBride here tells me that the lodge is all booked up, but there seems to have been a little mix-up and I need your help."

"Did we do something wrong?" the young girl asked, a look of horror on her face.

"No, of course not," Claire denied hastily. "The fault is all mine. Well, actually, it's all my fiancé's—or I guess I should say my ex-fiancé." She sniffed dramatically and John rolled his eyes as she continued. "You see, I bought this vacation for Bryan's birthday and I just assumed that he'd bring me along, but it seems that he, well"—John watched in amazement as seemingly genuine tears welled up in Claire's eyes—"he brought another woman. And it was hard for me to get the time off in the first place, and I was looking forward to having some time to rest. I've been working so hard lately, you see . . ." Her voice trailed off in misery.

John watched incredulously as Dana put her arms around Claire's shoulders in a show of feminine sympathy.

"Don't worry, Claire. Everything's going to be all right. Your fiancé must be an awful man to have done this to you. I think you're better off without him," Dana encouraged.

Claire sniffled. "Yes, yes, of course you're right, but now I don't have anywhere to go and I'm exhausted. It would be really nice if you could find me a room for my vacation. I mean, I understand if it's nothing fancy, but I'd appreciate anything you could do. It's so beautiful here, I would really like to stay."

"Well, we do have that room up over the garage. We never rent it out, so I'm sure we could let you stay there," Dana blurted before John could stop her.

"No," John said sharply.

"I'll take it," Claire said, wiping tears from her eyes.

Dana was looking at him as if he'd just pulled the wings off a particularly pretty butterfly. "No," he said, more reasonably this time. "That's just a storage room. No more than a closet, really. It doesn't even have a bathroom."

"She could share the employees' bath downstairs. We could even let her have it for free, seeing as how she can't get back her deposit for her fiancé's room. It seems like the least we could do," Dana offered helpfully.

"Perfect. I'll take it," Claire said again.

"Would that be okay, John?" Dana asked hesitantly.

John sighed, knowing he was beaten. He nodded.

Dana smiled happily. "Here, I'll get you the key."

John glowered at Claire's back as she and Dana left the office, chattering like old friends.

The room was awful.

It was hardly bigger than her walk-in closet at home and the small space was crowded with a single cot and a stack of boxes in the corner. There were no floor-to-ceiling windows, no stunning view of the water, no river-rock fireplace, and, worst of all, no whirlpool bathtub. As a matter

of fact, there was no bathtub at all, Claire noticed with
drooping shoulders as she tossed her overnight case on top
of the boxes and sank down on the cot.

Dana had shown her the employee facilities, which were
little more than his and hers locker rooms, with no luxurious bathtub included. She had also offered to take Claire's
clothes down to the laundry for cleaning and pressing.
Claire was grateful she'd have something to wear tomorrow
that wouldn't look as if she'd yanked it out of the rag bag,
but the last of her dreams of a romantic vacation had just
gone up in a puff of acrid-smelling smoke.

She scooted across the cot, leaned her head against the
wall, and wondered if she should just give up and go home.
There were plenty of things that needed to get done around
the house, things she never had time to do when she was
working. Claire sniffed as a tear slid down her face.

Instead of spending the afternoon relaxing with her fiancé, she was busy considering regrouting the tile in her
bathroom. This was not the romantic vacation she'd
planned. Another tear slipped down her face, and Claire
wiped it away with the belt of the thick terry-cloth robe
Dana had loaned her to wear while her clothes were in the
laundry.

Damn Bryan Edwards for doing this to her. If only she'd
made that final reservation, then he and his sleazy girlfriend
would be the ones stuck in this tiny room, and she'd be
enjoying a nice, hot soak right about now.

Claire blinked and sat up straighter in bed. Was that it?
Was her biggest concern really where she was going to be
bathing for the next nine days? What about her heart?
Didn't Bryan's betrayal hurt deeper than that?

She stared at a chip in the polish of one fingernail and
contemplated the state of her emotions. Disappointment,
yes, she definitely felt that. After months of planning, not
to mention all the hours she'd had to work to pay for this
trip, she had been looking forward to her vacation with
Bryan, thinking perhaps these perfect surroundings might
rub off on their relationship. Embarrassment and anger, she

felt those, too; anger winning out over the other emotion in terms of intensity. But heartbreak? Did she feel that?

Gazing out at the gray Colorado sky through a small rectangular window high up in the corner of the room, Claire waited for her heart to answer. Disgusted when it didn't, she turned some of her anger on herself. What kind of person wouldn't be heartbroken to be betrayed by her fiancé like this? Only a few hours ago, she was planning the wedding, and now, she was feeling . . . what? Relief? She shook her head and laughed a humorless laugh. Was it possible that work was the only thing she truly loved?

"Why not?" Claire muttered into the empty room. "At least I know I can always count on work to be there for me."

Rubbing a hand over her face, Claire decided she'd spent enough time feeling sorry for herself. Her relationship with Bryan was over, and at least she'd found out what a louse he was before they were married. She might as well turn her attention to something more productive than self-pity. She pulled her cell phone out of the purse that had been retrieved from the Rose Suite, pressed the on button, and dialed her phone.

Chapter 4

JOHN PUSHED OPEN THE DOOR AT THE END OF THE second-story hallway marked "Employees Only." Unlike other doors, this one didn't lead to a contrasting white hallway, but instead contained the same shiny, dark hardwood floors and richly colored rugs as the rest of the lodge. When he'd bought the lodge six years ago, he had taken this corner of the building and made it into a spacious three-bedroom home for himself, complete with full-sized kitchen, two baths, and an office.

He ignored the rumbling of his stomach that reminded him he had missed lunch in order to deal with the Claire Brown fiasco. He had never met a woman who could irritate him faster than this one had. Even his ex-wife hadn't been able to get under his skin as quickly as Claire. Every time he was around Claire, his hands itched to . . . Standing stock-still in his living room, John clenched his hands into fists at his side. His hands itched to bury themselves in her silky blond hair, to pull her mouth to his and silence her in the best way he knew how.

John wandered absently through the master bedroom. How could he be attracted to her? He cursed his traitorous body as if it were something separate from himself. He didn't like her type, he reminded himself, didn't like women who thought only of their careers and money. There were plenty of other women around, women who had their priorities straight. Women with ripe, lush bodies, not snobbish, pixie-sized sprites who delighted in irritating him.

He turned on the water in the sink of his bathroom, bypassing the bar of floral-scented soap his mother had left the last time she'd visited for something that felt more like sandpaper. The froufrou soap that Mary Jane McBride insisted he keep on hand for her infrequent visits went unused the majority of the time. The sandpaper soap worked better at getting the oil out from under his nails and didn't leave him smelling like some slick Wall Street type, besides.

As he came out of the bathroom, a furry head popped up from the back of the couch, sad brown eyes eyeing him soulfully.

"Jack, how many times do I have to tell you, you're not allowed on the couch?" A quick pat to the head negated any effect the scolding might have had. The dog swallowed as John scratched the soft spot just under his ear.

"Oh, and I see you've got company," John said, noting the golden-striped cat nestled comfortably against the golden retriever's belly.

"One of these days, I'm gonna get tough with you two." The dog laid his head back down on the couch, closing his eyes with a sigh. John doubted the retriever was even the slightest bit worried that he'd make good on his threat.

He walked into the kitchen he'd remodeled with cherry cupboards and ceramic tile countertops and pulled a beer out of the fridge. He didn't usually drink in the middle of the day, but felt justified after his bout with the exasperating Claire Brown.

He'd just taken his first swig of the chilled, malty brew when the phone jangled. Swallowing hastily, he picked the black cordless phone up from its cradle.

"Hello, John, it's Mom."

"Hi, Mom. I was just thinking about you and your sweet-smelling soap empire." John envisioned his mother in her usual habitat; sitting at her elegant desk high up in her fancy New York office, surrounded by all manner of fragrant soaps and cosmetics. That's probably where she was, he guessed, even though it was Saturday. Workaholics like Mary Jane McBride rarely spent an entire weekend without going into work at least once.

"You must have been comparing my products to that gritty stuff you like again. I keep telling you, John, if you'd use that oatmeal-and-ginger soap I left for you, your hands will never be the same."

"That's what I'm afraid of," John said dryly. "How am I ever going to get people to believe I'm a rugged out-doorsman if my hands are soft as a baby's bottom?"

Mary Jane laughed. "I suppose it would be hard to con-vince people that you're capable of keeping them safe out in the wilderness without the calluses to prove it," she con-ceded.

John took another sip of his beer, then cradled the phone between his ear and shoulder as he rummaged through the refrigerator for something to eat. "So, to what do I owe the pleasure of your call?"

"I just found out that I've got to be in Colorado for a meeting on Monday. I was thinking I might take a few days off and come visit. If I'm not intruding, that is."

"Of course you're not intruding." John grimaced into the mouthpiece. It was going to be a busy week with the lodge booked up and short-staffed to boot. Now it looked as if he'd have to entertain his mother in addition. "How long will you be staying?"

John sensed her hesitation.

"Well, honey, I was thinking I'd take the whole week off. Maybe return to New York early the next week?"

An entire week? He'd never known his mother to take more than a day or two off from running her cosmetics company. There was definitely something going on here. John pulled some sliced turkey and lettuce out of the fridge and proceeded to make himself a sandwich. "That's fine, Mom. I'm afraid I won't be able to take any time off, but there are plenty of things to do around here to keep you busy while I'm at work."

"Oh, don't worry about that. I'm looking forward to tak-ing advantage of some of the activities you offer. It's been a long time since I've been outside for more than a few minutes . . ." Her voice trailed off.

Probably since before Dad had died eight years ago, John thought silently. He missed Hunter McBride, too, but swallowed the sentiment along with a bite of his sandwich as he changed the subject to something less painful. "So, how's Delilah doing these days? Married life agreeing with her?"

"She's fine, John. She and Luke make a wonderful couple."

John grinned at the long-suffering sigh he heard from the other end of the line. His mother hated discussing John's ex-wife with him. "I'm sure they do. What did you get them for their wedding, a bank?"

"No, I got them a beautiful set of Irish table linens. Now that she's remarried, I wish you would stop needling the poor girl. It's been six years since the divorce, after all. It's time you got over it," Mary Jane admonished.

"Yes, Mother." He was over it, had been almost since the day they broke up, but since Mary Jane had promoted Delilah to COO a year ago John couldn't help but try to get some mileage out of it. He found the fact that his ex-wife was now running his mother's company amusing, even if Mary Jane didn't.

"You're impossible. I've got to go. I'll see you on Monday." Mary Jane sighed again before hanging up.

"Well, Jack, it looks like we've got company coming." The yellow dog's tail swept the kitchen floor and his big brown eyes met John's expectantly. John pulled off a chunk of his sandwich, and tossed it into the air. It disappeared before it had traveled even a foot from his hand. Patting the top of the dog's head, John headed back out to finish the work he'd started earlier that day on the cantankerous pickup.

Claire tightened the belt of her borrowed robe and rubbed her sore ear. After an hour of calls, her arm ached from holding the phone and her left ear was hot. She flipped the mouthpiece closed and pulled her laptop out of its bag. Since she could hardly wander around the great outdoors wearing only a bathrobe, she figured she might as well get some work done. Then, when she got her clothes back, she could take some time off and enjoy herself.

She hit the power button on her computer and looked around for a phone jack, thinking to deal with her e-mail first. A quick survey of the room confirmed that no jack existed. Praying that her computer would boot up after its dousing with little Billy's orange juice, Claire crossed her fingers and went in search of a telephone outlet.

Opening the door of her room, she peered down the hallway. There were no guest rooms down this short hall, only a door marked "Employees Only" about fifteen feet away at the end of the hallway.

Claire couldn't believe her luck when she spotted a phone jack directly across from her door.

"At least something's going right today," she muttered, turning her attention back to the laptop, which was waiting patiently for her to log in. Without watching the screen, Claire began typing her user name then looked up when the computer started beeping at her.

"No, no. Damn it." The user name space was filling up with *b*'s.

She tried prying up the offending key, cursing her short fingernails when she failed to get a grip on the *b*. The beeping was driving her crazy. Claire pawed through her computer bag looking for something, anything, that would make the noise stop.

Ah, a paperclip, that would do it. Claire uncurled the wire from its usual shape and stuck an end under the plastic key. The beeping stopped, and Claire tried again. This time, it was the *w* that stuck.

Sighing, Claire turned off the computer. This was not good. She couldn't survive the entire week without her laptop. On average, she received over a hundred e-mails a day. If she couldn't check her mail, she'd come back to almost a thousand unread messages. It would take days to get through all that, and it wasn't as if the rest of her work would wait while she got caught up.

She needed to fix this problem. Running the nail of her

left index finger across her teeth, Claire wondered how in the world she'd be able to get someone to repair her computer way out here. It wasn't as if computer technicians made house calls. And she certainly wasn't handy with . . . Hmm. Handy. That was it, she needed a handyman, somebody who was good with machinery, someone who was used to taking things apart and fixing them. An image of grease-stained fingernails flashed into her head.

John McBride. Yes, she would ask him to help. And what if he refuses? she asked herself. He obviously didn't hold a very high opinion of her, and she couldn't blame him, especially since she'd given him a bloody nose. But she needed to get her computer repaired, and if he refused, well, then, she'd just have to appeal to the man's ego. In Claire's experience, that usually worked. She could flutter her lashes and ask nice just as well as the next gal.

Claire picked up her now-silent computer and wandered downstairs in search of John McBride. She stopped at the reception desk downstairs and asked Dana if she knew where Claire could find him.

Dana looked at her in surprise. "He's in the garage, I think."

Thanking her, Claire followed Dana's directions down a darkened corridor, and pushed open a door marked "Employees Only." Claire blinked. She had just entered a different world. The world outside the door, the one most guests saw, was hushed and peaceful. Gleaming cherry hardwood floors covered with oriental rugs muffled footsteps and conversation. Expensively framed art hung from richly painted walls. Solid eight-paneled doors outfitted with shiny brass doorknobs shut out the activity in the rooms beyond. But behind the door marked "Employees Only," it was not quiet or soothing. The walls in the employee corridor were painted bright white, in stark contrast to the dark hardwoods used elsewhere in the lodge. Claire could hear the clattering of dishes from around the corner and assumed that way led to the kitchen. She stepped into the hall, letting the door close behind her and making the transformation complete. She turned away from the kitchen noises and pushed open another door that she correctly guessed would lead her into the garage.

Her toes curled as she stepped out onto the cold concrete floor of the cavernous, four-car garage.

"Hello?" she called out.

For the second time that day, John lifted his head out from under the hood of his truck. What in the hell was Claire Brown doing in here? And why was she wearing a bathrobe? He briefly considered hunkering down behind the front tire, then followed his impulse. Whatever it was she wanted, she could find somebody else to bother. He was determined to finish the tune-up he'd started that morning. With his mother coming in two days and all the summer employees leaving today, if he didn't get it done now, it would probably be another month before he had time to get to it again.

He heard Claire's footsteps coming closer and moved backward silently, intending to hide behind the pickup. His feet tangled in a pile of rags he'd tossed on the floor, and he lost his balance. Claire came around the front of the truck just as his rear end came into contact with the concrete.

"Didn't you hear me? And why are you sitting on the floor?"

John emptied his lungs with a deep sigh. This was not turning out to be a good day. "What do you want?"

"Now, John, is that any way to talk to a guest?" she asked sweetly.

Strangling was a punishable offense in Colorado, much as it was in the other forty-nine states, John reminded himself as he gazed at the white-robed figure in front of him. From this perspective, she looked like a blond angel. Too bad he knew the opposite was true.

She must have read the murderous intent in his eyes, because she toned her insincere smile down a bit. "Actually, I was wondering if you could help me with my computer."

"Your what?"

"My computer. My laptop." She held it out to him, as if he'd never seen one of the things before. Unfortunately, he had. As a matter of fact, the darn things were the bane of his existence. They just didn't make any sense, if you asked him, although the rest of the world didn't appear to agree. I mean, how the hell was he supposed to know that control-alt-something saved something, while shift-F-something-else would delete it?

"I know what a computer is. What makes you think I can help?"

Claire shuffled her feet on the concrete floor, and John's gaze shifted to the bare legs poking out from under her robe. She had slender ankles. And pretty feet, the toes not too long, her nails neatly filed and polished with a surprisingly bright red. Her skin had a golden hue, as if she'd tan well, but he could see the blue veins running across the top of her foot. He looked back to her face. She also had beautiful skin, and for one strange moment he had the urge to reach a hand out and touch her bare foot.

Apparently unaware of the direction John's thoughts had taken, Claire continued her plea for help. "I don't think it's anything electrical. Some juice spilled on it earlier and the keys are sticking. I thought maybe you'd know what to do."

He'd always been a sucker for a damsel in distress, especially one who asked nicely for his help. Getting to his feet, John dusted off the back of his jeans. "I can probably manage to figure out how to clean it up for you but I can't promise it'll fix the problem."

"I'd appreciate anything you can do."

John set the black plastic case on the wooden workbench that ran the entire length of the garage. Popping open the top of the computer, he leaned across the counter for one of the small screwdrivers hanging neatly from the pegboard-covered wall.

Claire leaned back against the pickup, surreptitiously admiring the view of John's blue-jean-covered backside. Considering herself somewhat of a connoisseur of these things, she had to admit it was one of the finer specimens she'd observed. It was nice and full, not too flat—tempting her once more to try the squeeze test. It was that whole ripe-tomato thing all over again. Claire shook her head at that, then pushed a lock of hair behind her left ear. What was it with her and produce today?

Clearing her throat, Claire shifted her gaze away from the room's other occupant. "So, how long have you worked at Hunter's Lodge?"

"I've been here since before the lodge opened. Coming up on six years now, I guess," John answered, without raising his head from his task.

"What do you do besides work on engines and taxi the guests?" she asked.

"Well, sometimes, they let me out long enough to change a lightbulb or fix the plumbing. Nothing that would tax my mental capacity too much, though."

Claire covered her grin with a cough. When he wasn't being obnoxious, John McBride could almost be considered charming. Placing her chilled left foot behind her right knee to warm it up, she watched as he methodically popped the keys off her laptop with a screwdriver and placed them in neat rows on the surface of the workbench. If she'd undertaken this project herself, she probably wouldn't have even thought about keeping the keys in order. She would have dumped them all in a pile, not planning on how she'd get them all back in the right place once she was finished. Congratulating him silently on his foresight, she watched him meticulously swab each key before placing it back in its rightful place.

Tilting her head, Claire observed how patiently he went about the job. He worked slowly, as if time meant nothing to him. She could almost feel her blood pressure lowering as she watched his tanned fingers replace the keys on the keyboard. Tension seeped out of her shoulders as she continued to watch him, leaning up against the blue pickup truck.

Must be the altitude, Claire reasoned. Maybe the thin air

was making her brain cells function slower than usual. Or perhaps it's because you're imagining those same strong fingers roaming unhurriedly over your body, a mocking voice inside her head suggested.

Claire shivered, then rubbed at the goose bumps on her arms as she pushed away that last thought. You've just been jilted, and you are *not* attracted to the lodge's handyman, she chided herself.

"Are you almost done?" she asked, her voice sounding cross as it echoed in the large room.

The glance he shot her held more than a tinge of amusement. "Why are you in such a hurry to get back to work? Isn't this supposed to be your vacation?"

"I happen to have a job with a lot of accountability."

John's green eyes darkened with anger at her implication. "Oh, and what is it you do for a living? Are you working on a cure for cancer? Healing sick children?"

Claire drew herself up to her full five feet two inches. "I'm the account coordinator for some of the most prestigious accounts in my company. It's a very important position." Claire tried not to wince as the pompous-sounding job description hit her own ears. But what she did *was* important, she reminded herself, keeping her back pressed straight against the cold truck. Just because she didn't save lives didn't mean her work had no value.

"Since you're such a key player, I'm surprised you can afford to be away from work for an entire week. Why don't you go pack up and we'll have you back to the airport in no time? I'll even drive you there myself."

"As I told you before, I am not leaving. I paid for this vacation, and nothing, and no one, is going to make me leave." Stomping over to the workbench, Claire grabbed her computer out from under John's clenched fingers. If she hadn't been so angry, she might have been frightened by the tightly restrained violence she saw in his emerald-green eyes. As it was, she was tempted to poke him in the middle of his broad chest with the computer he'd just fixed for her.

"Um, excuse me?" A timid voice from the doorway interrupted their heated showdown. As one, Claire and John turned toward the door.

"Yes, Dana?"

The younger woman's gaze shifted nervously between John and Claire. "A guest just called down and asked if I could baby-sit her little boy for about half an hour. I know you're busy, John, but I was wondering if you could watch the front desk until I get back?"

Claire noticed John slowly unclenching his fists, and tried not to admire that he didn't turn his anger toward her onto Dana. Never before had she met a man who had her swinging from visions of violence to admiration in the space of mere seconds. She didn't know which she wanted more; to bloody his nose, or to bury her hands in his thick dark hair. For a woman who usually knew exactly what she wanted, it was really a very frustrating experience.

"Yes, of course. I'll be right there," John said, interrupting her contemplation of deeds.

Seeing her chance for a clean escape from the confrontation, Claire took a hurried step away from John. "Just a second, Dana. I have something I want to discuss with you."

John let her go, using the time alone to get his temper under control. He shouldn't have let Claire's disparaging remarks get under his skin. After all, the annoying workaholic meant nothing to him. What did he care that she was so wrapped up in her own idea of success that she'd end up spending her entire vacation holed up in her closet-sized room with her phone and her computer for companions?

That was fine with him. As far as he was concerned, the less he saw of Claire Brown, the better the next nine days would be.

Claire kept her fingers crossed as she turned on her laptop, then entered her user ID and password at the prompt. Waiting for the awful beeping that would tell her a simple cleaning hadn't been enough, she heaved a sigh of relief when no discordant noises met her keystrokes. She was back in business.

She glared at the computer screen, trying to forget John McBride's insulting tone when he asked about her job.

As an account coordinator for two of her office's largest accounts, as well as several smaller ones, Claire was responsible for making sure each client's insurance claims were processed according to their expectations while also ensuring Allied's resources were used efficiently so each account was profitable.

Her employer, Allied Adjusters, was the largest claims adjusting firm in the world. In the time she'd worked for Allied, she'd been promoted from a claims adjuster, who processed individual claims, to a junior account manager and then, a year ago, to account coordinator. She was one of the youngest people to ever get promoted to that level.

Claire prided herself on being proactive, on taking the initiative, and she had performed well for both herself and her clients. Her clients consistently showed improved performance and she had one of the highest profit margins in the company. As a congratulations present for her last promotion, she'd bought herself a brand-new, champagne-colored Lexus. Every morning on the way to work, with the heady smell of new leather tingling in her nostrils, she felt an overwhelming sense of accomplishment; as if that elusive element, success, were sewn into the supple tan fabric with each sturdy stitch. She routinely worked twelve-hour days, often on the weekends as well as during the week, but that feeling, the knowledge that she made a difference, that the company needed her, made it all worthwhile.

She frowned. Who was John McBride to imply that her work wasn't important? It was. She made sure that people's medical bills got paid after an injury or illness. Without her, claimants might not receive regular paychecks after an accident; some of them might not have been able to return to work without the innovative programs she'd helped to implement at their companies. Blowing a stray lock of hair out of her face, Claire straightened her shoulders. To heck with John McBride and his opinions, she cursed as she double-clicked the icon to start her e-mail program.

Then her shoulders slumped as a line of new mail marched into her in-box. Thirty-six new e-mails. How could she have thirty-six new e-mails on a Saturday? When she'd left the office last night, the last thing she'd done was clean out her in-box. She sighed and leaned back against the wall, balancing the computer on her thighs as she perused the list.

One of the messages caught her eye right away, and not because of the urgent red flag blinking next to it. Instead, it was the sender's name that made her open it with haste. It was from Anthony Gallagher, the son of Allied's founder, and heir apparent to the presidency once his father retired.

Thinking that it must be some sort of broadcast message to all Allied employees, Claire opened the message and found instead that it was addressed only to her. Her heart did a flip in her chest like a fish at the end of a hook.

"Stay calm . . . Breathe in . . ." she chanted to herself, attempting to keep the blood from pounding out of her veins.

The message was short and to the point. Her boss, Art Engleheart, had been admitted to the hospital this morning to undergo emergency bypass surgery. Mr. Gallagher had asked the Western Region VP who could act as a temporary replacement while Art was recuperating, and was told that she, Claire Brown, was the best candidate. Would she be able to handle the increased workload for the next eight weeks? The company would be glad to provide her any necessary clerical assistance, et cetera, et cetera.

"Oh . . . oh . . . Breathe in . . ." Claire repeated to herself as she read the message again, delight warring with the fear that she wouldn't be able to perform up to the expectations of senior management.

Her boss, one of the senior-most account coordinators, handled ten of Allied's most prestigious accounts and reported directly to Anthony Gallagher. Success in his position, while lucrative enough on its own, could lead to some of the top positions in the corporation. Now, Claire, at thirty-two, had been recommended to take over Art's position, however temporarily.

Her fingers were unsteady on the computer keys as she tapped out her answer. She'd do whatever she could to ensure that Art's tradition of excellent service continued in his absence. She'd call Art's secretary on Monday to get a list of all appointments he'd scheduled for the upcoming month, and she'd call each of his clients right away to notify them of Art's condition and give them a number where she could be reached.

She read her response over at least five times before screwing up enough courage to hit "send." Then she double-clicked into Allied's client-service system and downloaded contact information on Art's clients so she could begin making her calls.

While the list was downloading, she reached into her purse for her cell phone. Hitting the power button, she cursed when the "no signal" message appeared. Darn, it had worked earlier. Pointing the antenna around the room, she soon gave up. Sometimes, technology could be as big a curse as it was a godsend. She chewed on the inside of her cheek and pondered the situation.

This wouldn't be a problem if her fiancé—no, make that ex-fiancé—hadn't stolen the room that rightfully belonged to her. There would be a regular phone in the Rose Suite, just waiting for the use of paying guests. Bryan could sit next to his fireplace and chat on his phone as long as he liked, while she was crammed into this—

Struck by a sudden idea, Claire glanced down at her watch. It was half past seven o'clock. Right about the time people would be heading down to the luxurious dining room for a predinner cocktail. Her stomach grumbled as she realized she'd had nothing to eat all day, but she ignored the hunger pangs and concentrated on her plan. Why shouldn't she borrow the phone from the Rose Suite? After all, she had paid for the room, so why shouldn't she feel free to enjoy the amenities that went along with it?

Her mind made up, Claire poked her head out of the glorified closet that was her room and crept out into the main second-floor hall. She continued on when she saw that no one was around.

Sneaking down the hallway, she jumped when a loud creak sounded as she stepped on a loose board. Chiding herself for being ridiculous—it wasn't as if she were stealing national secrets here—she strode more confidently, slowing as she reached the door to room number 24.

Bryan and his little hardbody fling were probably settled comfortably in the room she'd paid for by now, she thought, her anger rising. Looking up and down the hall to make sure she was the only lurker, Claire put an ear to the door.

Nothing.

They were probably down enjoying a nice steak dinner, just like Claire would be doing if she wasn't stuck with only a bathrobe to wear. Covering her hand with the over-long sleeve of her robe, she reached out and touched the doorknob.

She half expected the brass knob to burn her hand or the heavy door to squeak loudly as she swung it open, but neither happened. The door opened smoothly, quietly, and Claire discovered that, whatever else they might have done to while away the last few hours, Bryan and Cindy had not gotten around to unpacking.

The bed was in complete disarray, giving her a clue as to what Bryan and Cindy might have spent the last few hours doing. Her nose wrinkled with disgust—that didn't bear thinking about. The floral-patterned down comforter was lying in a heap on the floor and the sheets were a twisted mess. Claire resisted an inexplicable urge to make the bed, to restore order to the messy room. Instead, she spied her target on the nightstand and quickly pulled the phone cord from the jack on the wall. Tucking the phone under her arm, Claire turned to leave the room with her booty, then stopped when her gaze landed on a small bag on top of the dresser near the bathroom door. Claire guessed it was the fling's overnight bag.

An evil idea popped unbidden into her brain.

"I wonder how well Bryan will like nudie-girl without makeup," she whispered gleefully. He'd always been a stickler about Claire wearing makeup, even on the weekends when they were planning to just hang around and do nothing.

She remembered the first time he'd invited her to go to the gym with him. She'd met him at her door at 7 A.M. wearing her old, comfy sweats, her hair in a ponytail, her face devoid of makeup. She went to her gym every day dressed exactly the same way and Bryan's reaction had stopped her cold.

"Why aren't you ready yet? I told you I'd pick you up at seven," he'd said impatiently.

Claire looked down at herself, wondering if she'd made a reality out of her favorite nightmare and forgotten to put on her pants.

No, she saw with relief that she was fully dressed.

"What do you mean? I am ready."

"Like that?"

"Like what?"

"You look like a slob," he said bluntly. "I mean, look at you. Did you salvage those clothes from Goodwill? Your hair's a mess. And where's your makeup? Didn't you even look in the mirror this morning?"

"No, not really. I thought we were just going to work out."

"We were, but you can't go to my gym looking like that. I have to go. We'll talk about this later." He'd roared off in his white convertible, leaving Claire staring after him feeling as if she'd been trapped in her second-worst nightmare, the one where she spent the night having her father, her boss, even former grade-school teachers scold her for not being able to do anything right.

"Your shoelaces are not tied correctly. We'll have to hold you back a grade," her kindergarten teacher said.

"Another zero percent on your test," her eighth-grade biology teacher said.

"All of your clients are losing money for the company. And three of them went bankrupt because you let their claims costs get out of control," her boss said.

"Can't you do anything right, Claire?" Her father gazed down at her sternly.

As nightmares went, it ranked right up there with showing up naked for work. And now her boyfriend had joined the fray, Claire remembered thinking as she shut the door on the cold November morning. Bryan hadn't invited her to work out with him again and Claire didn't push it, convinced that she didn't want to go to a gym that she had to dress up for, anyway. She'd learned her lesson though and had always made sure to be properly made up and attired whenever she and Bryan were going somewhere.

Claire arrived back in her room, clutching Cindy's makeup bag under one arm and the telephone under the other. Blinking into the tiny space, she suddenly regained her senses along with her bearings. Looking down at the bag in her hands, Claire chastised herself for her petty larceny. It wouldn't take long for Cindy to realize her bag was missing. She shook her head. That was the problem with evil impulses, they didn't stick around long enough to get you out of the trouble they invariably caused.

"Gosh, I wonder whose room they'll search first?" Claire muttered as she sat down on the bed and put her forehead in her hands.

She was going to have to take the bag back. She got up from the bed and pushed the phone she'd liberated behind the stack of boxes for safekeeping.

Holding the small bag behind her back, Claire started her second trip back down the hallway. Just as she reached the door to room 24, the elevator bell let out a loud *ding*.

Claire didn't pause to think, she just turned around and ran as fast as she could in the opposite direction, heading for the door marked as an exit. Unlike the door to Bryan and Cindy's room, this one creaked when she pushed it open. As it closed, Claire crouched down below the small cut-out window, her heart racing.

She stayed that way for a full five minutes, her nerves still rooted firmly outside in the hall. Then, holding her hair away from her face with one hand, she slid her back up the wall and peeked out into the corridor. An elderly man was exiting the elevator with another couple. There was no way she was going to risk returning the bag again, but she certainly couldn't take it back to her room. She was going to have to dispose of the evidence elsewhere.

Looking around, Claire noticed she was in a whitewashed stairwell that she presumed would lead outside. Once again, the evil impulse grabbed her. That's it, I'll dump the bag in the river, she thought with malicious glee as she padded barefoot down the cold concrete steps. Opening the door on the first floor, Claire discovered that the stairwell did indeed lead outside, and she wished she'd had the foresight to put on her shoes as the cold night air turned the ground to ice under her feet.

Thinking only of how she was going to abandon her loot, Claire didn't notice the decisive click of the door as it closed behind her until it was too late. She stopped in her tracks and sighed. Without even testing it, she knew she was locked outside, wearing nothing but her bathrobe and a thin pair of white lace panties.

She could hear the reporters now, questioning her father after her death from an attack by a wild grizzly: "Mr. Brown, did your daughter have a habit of exposing herself in the wilderness?"

"Mr. Brown, were you aware that your daughter is a platinum-status shopper with Victoria's Secret?"

"Mr. Brown, can you tell us why your daughter came on a lengthy vacation with nothing to wear but lip gloss and a pair of hiking boots?"

She could see her father burying his face in his hands to hide the shame, as if to say, "I always knew that girl would come to a fast end."

Claire sighed and tested the door out of sheer morbid curiosity. It didn't open.

She sighed again, knowing she was trapped. She'd have to get rid of Cindy's bag, then get back into the lodge through the front door. Hopefully, no one would notice her unusual entrance.

Picking her way carefully to the riverbank, Claire peered over the edge. The river itself was about twenty feet away, down a fairly steep bank and across a rocky bed. There was no way she was going to climb down there in the rapidly dimming light, especially not with bare feet. Raising Cindy's bag over her head, she wondered if her Guerrilla Yoga classes had toned her arms well enough that she'd be able to hurl the pack all that way. She mentally gauged the distance, testing the weight above her head.

There was no way it would make it. She lowered the bag. It would probably end up on the riverbed, easily seen by anyone who bothered to look out the floor-to-ceiling windows facing the river. Besides, even if it did make it into the water, throwing Cindy's bag with all its contents into the river would be pollution.

"It's not as if the stuff is biodegradable," Claire muttered, trying to come up with a plausible Plan B.

She wasn't going any farther into the woods, not wanting to make her previously imagined bear scenario any more of a possibility than it already was. She looked around for inspiration, which hit just as the first rays of moonlight glinted off an object propped up against the side of the lodge.

"Here's my first real bit of luck today." Claire picked her way gingerly back toward the shovel leaning against the dark cedar wall. She'd bury the darn thing and be done with it.

John was washing up the last of his dinner dishes when he saw a woman dressed in white standing on the riverbank. At first, he thought he might be imagining the apparition. Moonlight reflected off of the woman's pale golden hair as she stood, silently watching the water rush by. She seemed to be pondering something, perhaps wrestling with a mournful memory.

He often stood at the river's edge, too. Whenever he felt troubled, he found the continuous force of the river helped to clear his mind, to bring him peace. When he'd first come to the lodge after his divorce, he'd spent hours there, fishing or just watching Jack chase an errant log downstream. That time had helped heal the rift in his soul that the combination of his job, his failed marriage, and his father's untimely death had brought. Watching some other broken soul now, John felt a sense of empathy for the unknown woman.

As he dried his hands on a dish towel, the woman raised something above her head, as if intending to fling the object into the rushing water. She stopped, her arms suspended above her head. John wondered if it was some painful memento that she wanted, needed, to part with but, at the last moment, found that she just couldn't let go. She lowered her arms.

She was too far away for John to see clearly. Something about the way she moved seemed familiar, but before he could figure it out, she ducked around the corner.

Had she decided that she couldn't part with whatever it was that she had been holding?

She came back into view carrying the bundle in one hand and what appeared to be a shovel in the other. Setting her parcel down on the cold ground, she started to dig. A small pile of dirt grew slowly at her feet as she worked. It seemed to be taking her a long time to dig a hole large enough for the bundle, and John considered going out into the cool night to offer assistance.

Leaning against the cherry cupboards, John continued to watch the woman from his kitchen window. He decided against an offer of help. He figured this was a personal matter, and whoever the woman was, she probably needed to be alone for this healing ritual.

At long last she dropped the shovel and turned back to the bag on the ground. Pulling something out of the pack, she shook it over the hole she'd dug, then continued methodically emptying the pack of its contents in an obvious ritual of exorcism. Whatever demons or dreams she was burying must indeed be painful, John thought, shaking his head sadly.

As she patted down the last shovelful of dirt over her sad memories, John was struck with the urge to find out who she was. He wouldn't let her see him, wouldn't let on that he'd witnessed her touching ceremony, but at least he'd know the identity of the mystery woman.

Quickly pulling his work boots on over thick wool socks, John gently nudged Jack and the cat out of the way of the door, where they lay in their usual heap.

"You two sleep too much," he muttered.

Jack's tail thumped the hardwood floor in response.

John's mind ran quickly over the layout of the lodge, searching for a hiding spot. At the top of the staircase there was a cozy alcove where guests could sit and chat, or read, with a nice overview of the main lobby. It would be the perfect spot, and he could easily angle a chair so he wouldn't be seen. He moved hurriedly down the hall to take up his place.

"Ouch," Claire yelped as a sharp, pointed rock slid like a knife into her heel.

She hopped around on her uninjured foot to keep her balance. Her feet already ached from stomping on the shovel, and involuntary tears came to her eyes as she pulled the jagged stone out of her foot. She blinked back tears, but not before two fat drops made tracks through the film of dirt clinging to her face after her sweaty bout with manual labor.

"Think of this the next time you have an uncontrollable urge to do something bad," she scolded herself as she picked her way, limping, to the lodge. The cedar steps felt smooth beneath her tender feet as Claire reached the entrance. She was struck again by how beautiful it was, the reddish-brown logs rising two stories into the surrounding forest. Even from the front of the lodge, she could hear the rushing river beyond, the sound soothing in the quiet moon-lit night. Pausing with one hand on the polished brass door handle, Claire suddenly realized that she'd hardly noticed the lack of noises she was accustomed to hearing. Turning to face the trees, she listened for any sounds of civilization, smiling when nothing reached her ears but the rhythmic sounds of the forest. Having never been much of an outdoor person, she couldn't begin to guess what sort of creatures made the sounds she heard. She supposed it didn't matter, the music would continue whether she knew the source or not.

It was so . . . peaceful. She took a deep breath of night air, enjoying the tranquillity of the moment before pulling open the heavy leaded-glass doors that marked the main entrance of the lodge.

John peered around the side of his chair as a gust of cool air entered the lobby. He caught a glimpse of the white-shrouded wraith through the heavy cedar railing at the top of the stairs. She limped slightly as she tiptoed through the foyer.

She stopped on the bottom step and John willed her to look up. As if hearing his unspoken wishes, she glanced up, one foot on the first stair. Light gray eyes locked with dark green and she immediately stopped, poised for flight like a wild animal caught in the glare of headlights.

John's eyes narrowed menacingly. Obviously it wasn't some sort of loving ritual he'd witnessed. She'd probably been burying chopped-up bits of some business rival—maybe someone who had beat her to the last cup of coffee or something equally heinous.

He watched her chin come up defiantly as she resumed her ascent up the stairs. It was only as she gained the top stair that John realized why she had been limping. The fool wasn't wearing any shoes.

"What the hell were you doing outside? You're practi-cally naked," he growled, not stopping to explore the reason for his anger.

"What, are you the night watchman as well as the handy-man?" Her voice dripped with its usual measure of saccha-rine.

As he clenched the armrest, John's knuckles turned white with the effort to not get up and shake some sense into the annoying, headstrong woman. He stood up, hoping that his extra foot of height would intimidate her as he prowled toward her.

"Look, lady, I'm not going to just sit back and watch you do something stupid and injure yourself. I know your type. You'll turn around and sue the lodge for your own recklessness."

Claire fumed at his unfounded accusation. He had no idea what kind of person she was. If she'd been injured out there . . . well, she knew whose fault it was that she'd been unable to control her own impulsive urges. As a claims adjuster, she'd seen her share of people who sued compa-nies for accidents of their own making. As a matter of fact, she had a reputation for hiring investigators to tail suspi-cious claimants and for not paying a wrongful claim even if the legal costs in the short term were higher than the claimant's demand. There was no way she'd have held the lodge accountable for her actions this evening if something had happened because of her impetuous actions.

But not for a million dollars would she tell John Mc-Bride that.

"Yeah, and I've got a great lawyer, too, so you'd better keep a sharp eye out. I bought a brand-new Lexus last year and there's room in my garage for a matching convertible," she purred, watching a flaming red tinge creep up his throat.

Claire thought she might have taken her act too far when John reached out and clamped a viselike grip on her upper arm. The look in his eyes had turned from menacing to murderous, and while she wasn't going to admit to being frightened, she did take a step back when he took one for-ward.

His voice, when it came, had lowered to almost a whis-per. "You will not do anything that would adversely affect

the lodge and the people who work here. Do you understand?" He gave her a shake. Claire tried to wrench her arm
free, to no avail. "I will not allow some self-important
workaholic to come in here and put these hardworking people out of their jobs because you won't take responsibility
for putting yourself in danger. Don't you realize that we're
in the middle of a forest here? Where do you think you are,
Disneyland?"

"Let go of me." Claire struggled harder as he continued
his tirade, pushing her back until she was pinned against
the wall at the top of the stairs.

"You're leaving tomorrow if I have to drive you all the
way back to Seattle. Do you understand?"

Okay, so she was ready to admit that he had her a little
intimidated, but what was he going to do? Slug her? Push
her down the stairs? She gathered her courage. "I'm not
leaving. I worked hard so I could take this vacation and
I'm staying. You can't make me go, and if you try, I *will*
sue you—for kidnapping and assault. God knows I'm going
to have the bruises tomorrow to prove it." She looked pointedly at the death grip he had on her arm.

John looked down, as if just realizing that he was touching her. He released her arm immediately.

"You're leaving. Tomorrow," he said quietly and he
turned to leave.

"Like hell I—" Claire started to follow him, not willing
to concede defeat, when her foot stepped into a puddle of
something slippery. In the split second before she fell, she
realized that the cut on her foot had been dripping blood
while they argued, forming a scarlet pool right where she
stood.

John turned at Claire's first startled cry, but wasn't fast
enough to catch her before she tumbled. By the time he
reached her, she was in a heap at the bottom of the stairs.

Chapter 5

"CLAIRE? CLAIRE, CAN YOU HEAR ME?"

Claire held back a grimace. Of course she could hear him. She'd fallen down the stairs, not had a bout of scarlet fever.

She almost opened her eyes, but stopped herself as a plot formed. He wouldn't make her leave if she was injured, would he? He'd probably feel just a little bit guilty that she'd been hurt. She'd seen the way he reacted when she pointed out he was hurting her arm. Certain she could milk this for something, Claire groaned softly and allowed her eyes to flutter open.

"Where am I?" she whispered hoarsely.

"You just had a little fall."

She heard the concern in his voice and knew she had him.

"Lie still for a minute, just take it easy," John instructed. "How many fingers do you see?"

He held up two fingers. Claire blinked, as if trying to focus her eyes. She didn't want to push this too far, however, and didn't want to make him think she was injured seriously enough to need a hospital. "Two," she answered.

"And now?" he moved his hand back, still holding up two fingers.

"Still two."

"Good. Can you feel this?" He tapped the bottom of her uninjured foot.

"Yes. You're tickling me."

"Can you wiggle your toes?"

He went through an inventory of body parts, gently bandaged her bleeding foot with a handkerchief, then asked

if she could sit up. Her next groan was for real as her
injured body protested the movement.

"Where does it hurt?" His concern too was genuine and
Claire felt a small twinge of guilt that was forgotten when
she felt a sharp pain in her right side.

She drew in a sharp breath as the pain knifed through
her. "I think it might be my ribs."

"Here, let me look at them."

Claire put up a protective hand as John reached out to
push her robe aside. "No, I'll be fine," she said.

"I need to see if something's broken," he insisted.

"I'll do it myself. Just tell me how to check."

"Look, Claire, I'm just going to make sure you're all
right. Stop making a big deal out of this."

She felt a blush creeping out of nowhere. "Can we do
this somewhere a little more private, then?"

John looked pointedly around the deserted lobby, then
must have decided it wasn't worth the argument. Before
she could protest, he lifted her in his arms.

"Put your arm around my neck," he ordered.

Claire would have protested then, but she was too
stunned to form any words. Instead, she did as she was
told, sliding her arm around the back of his warm neck.
Her fingers touched the ends of his thick, dark hair. She
would have expected it to be coarse, but instead it was
surprisingly soft to her touch. Bryan was a stickler for getting his thinning blond hair trimmed off the nape of his
neck. Obviously, John McBride didn't feel the same com-
punction, since his black hair touched the collar of his dark
blue shirt.

Why did he have to be so difficult and yet so incredibly
attractive at the same time? Claire pondered the question
as she rested her uninjured ribs against his firm chest. She'd
never felt such a strong physical response to a man before,
and cursed the fates that it had to happen with this particular one.

Perhaps if she'd felt this way about Bryan, he wouldn't
have felt the need to cheat on her. Her eyes widened at the

thought. Their sex life had been sporadic and . . . well, yes, she admitted, it had been lacking in anything closely resembling passion. She had started to think that maybe she just wasn't capable of the kind of passion her best friend, Meg, kept insisting was part of any successful relationship. Maybe it was simply her nature to feel more excited about work than another living being. So, why was she feeling such an intense attraction to the dark-haired man who carried her with such gentleness across the lobby?

Claire sighed, inhaling the scent of him. He smelled of an intoxicating mixture of outdoors, hard work, and spicy cologne. She would have figured him for the Old Spice type but the scent he wore was exotic, and expensive, too, she guessed. Surreptitiously, she slid her fingers deeper into his dark hair as he walked with her over to the elevator.

Thinking the fall must have made her light-headed, Claire enjoyed the feel of being held in John's strong arms. She'd never been held like this by a man, and she was amazed at how small and feminine it made her feel. It wasn't as if Bryan were a weakling, but she'd never felt like this with him, as if he would protect her, take care of her, shelter her from the dangers that lurked in the big bad world.

Claire mentally shook herself as the elevator doors slid open on the second floor. It was as if the elevator bell had woken her from a strange, yet oddly appealing, dream. What in the world had she been thinking? She didn't need some man to protect her. She was a strong, capable woman, perfectly able to handle the world without some man around to take care of her. She moved her hand abruptly out of John's hair, then groaned as the sudden movement caused another sharp pain in her ribs.

"Stay still, we'll be there in a second," John chided.

The door to room 24 flew open just as they approached. Claire sighed, wondering if this nightmare of a day was ever going to end.

Cindy's giggle preceded her as she stepped out into the hall right in front of them. Bryan was right behind her, laughing as she swatted at the hands he had planted at the front of her skimpy blue bikini.

"Oh, hi," Cindy giggled.

Bryan didn't bother removing his hands from Cindy's round, full breasts as he addressed himself to John. "We're going for a dip in the pool," he said unnecessarily.

"Claire fell down the stairs. I'm just making sure she's all right," John explained, although neither Bryan nor Cindy had asked.

"Oh. Well, we'll see you later." Bryan shrugged before pushing Cindy in front of him down the hall.

"I'm fine, thanks for asking," Claire muttered sarcastically at her ex-fiancé's retreating back.

John had to laugh at that as he passed Claire's door and continued on down the hall. If nothing else, at least she had a sense of humor.

"Are we going to an infirmary?" Claire asked

John shook his head, then pushed open the door at the end of the hall with a foot. He watched Claire's eyes widen with surprise as he carried her into the living room with its high ceilings and river-rock fireplace.

"It's beautiful. Do the owners live here?"

"Um-hmm," John answered vaguely before lowering her gently onto the couch.

"Are they here now?"

"Yep. Here, lie back so I can check out those ribs."

"They don't mind you just barging in like this?"

"No, we're very close." John choked back a grin. "Now, sit still." He pushed her back against the soft pillows of the couch.

Claire crossed her arms protectively across the front of her robe. "Can I borrow a shirt?"

By the blush spreading across her cheeks, John guessed that meant she wasn't wearing a bra. His palms started to tingle. That meant there was almost nothing between him and the small, round breasts that had been rubbing against his chest moments before. He'd been crouching down in front of her but that position became suddenly uncomfortable.

"Yeah, I'll go get something," he muttered, before fleeing to his bedroom.

What is wrong with you? John asked himself, rummaging through a dresser drawer for a shirt. He met a lot of women in his business; a lot of women with great bodies, he added. Women who loved the outdoors as much as he did. So why was his body so insistent about getting aroused around *this* woman? He didn't even like her, and there was just too much variety out there to waste time with someone whose company he couldn't possibly enjoy outside the bedroom.

It must have been too long since the last time, he reasoned as he pulled a button-front chambray shirt out of the drawer. That was the only explanation he could come up with as to why his body kept getting hot and heavy for the bitchy Miss Brown—it was lack of sex, that was all.

He returned to the living room with the shirt, an Ace bandage, and a load off his mind. "Here, put this on." He tossed her the shirt and turned his back.

Claire fumbled with the knot at her waist, then slid the robe off her shoulders. She hurriedly slipped the soft blue shirt over her head, sniffing at its familiar smell. She briefly surmised that John and the mysterious owner of the lodge must wear the same cologne.

John turned around as Claire pulled the bottom of the shirt over the top of her thighs. She winced as the tugging motion sent pain shooting through her torso.

"Okay, let's have a look at you." He unbuttoned the middle two buttons of the shirt she'd pulled on over her head. Claire tried to ignore the gleam in his dark eyes as she sat back and closed her eyes. His fingers were cool against her warm skin and she started to relax, then inhaled sharply as he pressed against a particularly sore spot. Involuntarily, she pushed herself back into the pillows to escape his probing hands.

She opened her eyes, blinking back tears of pain. "You found it."

"I'm sorry. I have to see if there are any broken ones."

"I know." Taking a deep breath, she allowed him to continue.

At least she wasn't a screamer, John thought, continuing to feel along Claire's rib cage. Her skin felt like that fancy soap of his mother's, smooth and creamy white against his darker, tanned fingers. The back of his hand brushed the bottom swell of her breast. Claire resolutely kept her eyes closed, but John noticed the hardening of her nipples as they poked through his shirt. Apparently, he wasn't the only one affected by this inexplicable attraction.

He continued his examination, gently unbuttoning the shirt as he went. Her breathing was becoming shallow as he ran his hands down her back, searching for any tender spots. She was smaller than he'd envisioned, and softer, too. His touch changed from probing to caressing as he slid his fingers from her shoulders down to the swell of her lower back. It was like dipping his fingers into a slow-moving creek, crystal-clear water flowing against his fingertips. John wondered if the rest of her felt this way, and let one hand wander to her well-toned legs to find out.

He nudged Claire up against the back of the couch with his hip, bringing his jeans-clad thighs up beside her naked ones. Her soft gray eyes opened, fixing on his with a slightly dazed look. He felt her fingers playing with the hair on the back of his neck, just as she'd been doing when he had carried her up here. It was turning him on just as much now as it had earlier.

It had been too long since he'd felt the soft skin of a woman against him. John groaned, unable to stop himself as his hands slid farther up under her shirt, caressing all that silky skin.

Claire wanted him to kiss her; wanted to feel his hard lips on hers, wanted to feel the touch of his tongue against hers. She parted her lips and watched as his head started lowering to hers. She was so lost in what they were doing that she almost screamed when the jarring ring of the telephone sounded right behind her. John seemed as dazed as she was, and didn't make a move to answer it.

"Aren't you going to get it?" she asked, her voice husky.

"No, that's what answering machines are for."

John cursed modern technology for the interruption. Ten more minutes and he'd have been well on his way to being one satisfied guy. His hand stilled on Claire's soft skin as the machine picked up, and his fingers tightened involuntarily as the message was broadcast into the room in clipped, businesslike tones.

"This is Delilah. Your mother told me yesterday she's planning to visit you next week. I'm worried about her. She's seemed . . . I don't know . . . despondent, lately. I think she may be lonely. Anyway, I thought you should know."

The voice paused, the tone changing from concerned to sarcastic. "Oh, and by the way, thank you so much for the wedding present. *The Joy of Sex* is one of Luke's favorites and, God knows, after being married to you, I can use all the tips I can get."

The message ended as the caller hung up.

"Ouch," Claire yelped at the sudden pressure on her sore ribs.

"I'm sorry," John apologized, leaping up off the couch.

Claire was too stunned to move at first. Why had this Delilah's message bothered John so much? Was John in love with her? Was that why he'd been so affected by the woman's message? Whatever the reason, it was evident that John's previous passion had been disconnected with the end of the other woman's phone call.

Taking care not to jar her bruised ribs, Claire slowly buttoned the borrowed shirt and gathered up the thick terrycloth robe. She walked to the door while John stood looking out at the fireplace. Opening the door, Claire almost hoped that he would call her back, then told herself she was glad when he didn't.

Her own closetlike room was exactly as she'd left it; her

cot-sized bed in disarray, her small overnight bag stuffed in a corner, her computer sitting on the bed. Locking the door of her room, she slumped down on the bed. It took awhile to find a comfortable position and Claire wondered if this was her curse for initially trying to fool John into thinking she was really hurt. She knew she'd feel battered in the morning and wished she could have taken a long, hot soak in the tub she was supposed to be sharing with her fiancé.

Instead, she'd been humiliated, once again. Rejected by two men in one day. That was a record, even for her. Claire laid her head down on the cot, exhausted and dispirited.

What had possessed her to allow John McBride to take advantage of her like that? What kind of fool was she to open herself up to a man who had nothing but dislike for her? If the phone hadn't interrupted them, she didn't know how far she'd have let things progress. Never in her life had she slept with a man she'd known for less than a few months, much less twenty-four hours. Bryan's defection must have hurt her more than she'd thought. Was she simply trying to prove that someone found her attractive?

She didn't think that was it; she felt fairly certain that Bryan's betrayal was more of a blow to her pride than anything. Why, then, had she run straight into the arms of John McBride? He was attractive, yes, but it was obvious that he didn't like her at all, and he had been awfully quick to push her away when he heard another woman's voice.

A tear slipped out of the corner of her eye and Claire wondered what she was doing wrong to make men keep treating her as if she were disposable; as if she were in their lives to be used and discarded. Bryan had played along with their engagement, stringing her along for no apparent reason except that he wasn't man enough to break up with her in person. He'd even blamed her for not figuring out that he was through with their relationship, as if she should be able to read his mind. Of course, he'd kept up the charade until she paid for the whole vacation—the first class tickets, the romantic suite at the lodge, the scheduled activities—

all the while knowing he didn't intend to bring her with him.

To make matters worse, this wasn't the first time something like this had happened to her. Sniffling, Claire wrapped her arms around herself, being careful of her sore ribs, and stared at the wall. She'd been engaged once before and caught her first fiancé with another woman, too. She shifted restlessly on the bed, lying on her back now, gazing out the small rectangular window on the opposite side of the room.

She had a good job. She worked hard. She took care of herself, dressed well, and had good personal hygiene. She was intelligent, well-read, and . . . and she couldn't stop crying. Obviously, there was something wrong with her, and every man must be able to sense it immediately because, even in the throes of passion, John McBride had been automatically turned off by her at the sound of another woman's voice.

"In the shower of life, I guess I'm the cold water," Claire said quietly before closing her eyes and crying herself to sleep.

John stood outside the door, listening to the telltale sounds of Claire's hiccuping. He laid a hand silently on the solid door, pausing for a moment before turning away. She probably wouldn't appreciate his concern. Besides, they didn't even like each other, John reminded himself. So what was the point? Better to let whatever strange thing had just happened between them die a natural death. He turned away and went back to his own door, heading for his bedroom.

Thank God, Delilah's voice had yanked him to his senses, or who knew how far he would have let the situation go with Claire. It had been his ex-wife's voice, her businesslike tone, that had deadened his desire like the spray from a cold shower. Delilah had always been self-centered, with no thought to anything except money—a trait he hadn't recognized when he'd asked her to be his bride. And, like Delilah, all Claire seemed to care about was work.

"We don't need another one like that, do we, Jack?" He patted the big dog's head and sat down on the bed to pull off his boots.

In answer, the dog looked at John with sad, brown eyes.

John rubbed a hand across the top of the dog's head. "Stop looking at me like that. Okay, I'll admit it. I'm sorry if I made her cry. But it probably wasn't me she was shedding tears over anyway. She's not the type to cry over a man. She's probably just upset that her room doesn't have its own fax machine, that's all."

He quickly divested himself of the rest of his clothes and crawled under the sheets. Jack hopped up onto the foot of the bed and ignored John's halfhearted rebuke to get down. John rolled over onto his right side and punched his pillow. He did not want to have a soft spot for Claire Brown, refused to believe she wasn't the hard-hearted workaholic he believed her to be. He punched his pillow again. Convinced that his assessment was right, John vowed to do everything he could to stay out of Claire's way for the next week, then he rolled over again and told himself firmly to go to sleep.

Chapter 6

CLAIRE HAD NO IDEA WHAT TIME IT WAS WHEN SHE awoke the next morning. If she had been able to move any part of her body without causing extreme pain, she might have checked her watch, but since even the smallest movement caused her to groan, she decided to stay right where she was and not move an inch.

She was still lying in bed about an hour later, staring at the wall and enjoying the smell of her borrowed shirt when a knock sounded at the door. Playing dead seemed like a good idea, since there was no way she was going to move.

"Claire. Uh, Miss Brown? It's me, Dana. I have some breakfast for you, and your clothes, too."

Immediately, Claire's stomach rumbled. She hadn't eaten at all yesterday, and just the mention of food had her salivating. Groaning, she pulled her aching muscles into a sitting position. "Just a second, Dana."

She stood up and the soft shirt fell in place to the top of her knees. This was as presentable as she was going to get, at least until she had a chance to take a shower and brush her teeth. Gingerly, she unlocked the door and pulled it open.

Dana, looking the picture of youthful good health, bounded in and set the tray down on the end of the bed. Claire hadn't realized how hungry she was until the smell of bacon assaulted her nostrils. Without waiting for an invitation, she plopped down on the cot and took the lid off a heaping plate full of bacon, ham, and scrambled eggs. A smaller plate laden with toast and jam sat off to the side and Claire greedily grabbed a piece off the top of the stack and bit off a large, butter-soaked portion.

"Thank you so much, Dana," she said around a mouthful of bread. "I'm starving."

"Didn't you get any supper? I brought up a tray last night but you weren't here so I assumed you got something to eat at John's."

"At John's?" Claire listened with half an ear as she forked some scrambled eggs into her mouth. Now that she was up and moving, the pain in her ribs didn't seem so bad. Or maybe she was just so hungry the pain was taking a back seat to her stomach.

"I . . . I heard about Mr. McBride carrying you up to his place last night."

Claire chewed her second bite of toast thoughtfully, watching a blush creep into the younger girl's cheeks. "I slipped down the stairs and John brought me upstairs to make sure nothing was broken," she said slowly as realization dawned. "So that's John's place. I assume that means that he owns the lodge?"

Dana stopped in the middle of unpacking a laundry bag full of clothes and looked at her curiously. "Of course. Didn't you know that?"

"No, but I do now," Claire muttered. So John was "close" to the owners, was he? She supposed he hadn't outright lied to her, he just hadn't told her the truth after she'd jumped to the conclusion that he was the lodge's handyman. Claire sighed. What did it matter? It was just one more humiliation added to the dozens of others she'd suffered in the past twenty-four hours. Besides, maybe she could use the information to her advantage. His suite of rooms had looked every bit as beautiful as the Rose Suite, and she'd bet he had his own whirlpool tub. Maybe her vacation wouldn't be so bad after all.

She turned her attention to the neat stack of clothing Dana had placed at the foot of the bed. "Hey, what's with all the clothes?" she asked, munching another piece of bacon.

"John brought them down this morning and asked me to

bring them to you. So you won't have only one outfit to wear until your clothes get here, he said."

"How thoughtful of him," Claire murmured dryly as she picked up a pair of sweatpants that were neon pink and at least three sizes too big.

Dana, oblivious to the undertones in Claire's voice, cheerily chatted on. "Yeah, I didn't even think to go through the lost-and-found box to see if there was anything you might be able to wear. Isn't Mr. McBride considerate?"

Claire raised her eyebrows at that but declined to answer. Instead, she asked, "So where is the wonderful Mr. McBride this morning?"

"He had to lead the sunrise hike because the general manager's on her honeymoon. Speaking of which, I have to go back down and cover the front desk. I just wanted to bring you these clothes."

"Thanks, Dana." Claire watched the door to her room close, a thought brewing in her mind. At last, the fates had smiled down on her. With John out leading the sunrise hike, his rooms would be empty for hours. After what had transpired between them last night, Claire would be glad if she could completely avoid him for the next eight days, but the lure of a hot bath was too strong.

"Whirlpool tub, here I come," she muttered under her breath, shoveling the last forkful of scrambled eggs into her mouth.

Breaking into John's place had been easy, especially since he hadn't bothered to lock the door. Dana had mentioned that the sunrise hike would last until noon, so Claire figured she'd help herself to the use of his bathing facilities. After all, it was his fault she'd fallen down the stairs and ached all over. And it wasn't as if she were stealing or anything, she reasoned, stepping into the filled-to-the-rim whirlpool tub. She was simply availing herself of the lodge's amenities; the same amenities she'd been promised by the lodge's glossy brochure.

Lying back, Claire sighed in ecstasy as the jets pulsed

heated water against her aching muscles. The big yellow dog who'd followed her from the living room pushed his cold nose against the hand resting on the tile ledge supporting the tub. She patted the dog's head as he watched her with his soulful brown eyes.

"Good thing you're not a watch dog."

The dog thumped his tail in response.

She hadn't spotted the dog last night, and wouldn't have figured John McBride as the kind of guy to have pets. But when she'd popped her head into his front door, she'd found the dog and a tiger-striped cat cuddled together on the couch.

"Even he must get lonely for companionship sometimes, huh, dog?"

A lick was her only answer as she closed her eyes and let the hot, pulsating water work its magic. At eleven-twenty, she decided she'd pushed her luck far enough. The soak had felt wonderful, and even more wonderful was the peaceful view of the river rushing by as she relaxed.

After toweling herself dry, Claire put on a minimal amount of makeup, then hunted through the drawers for a blow-dryer. Unable to find one, she ran a comb through her wet hair and left the dishwater-blond strands to air-dry. She wiped down the countertop, checked carefully to make sure the tub was clean and the floor dry, tossed her damp towel into the dirty-clothes hamper she'd spotted in the bedroom, and was back in her room at eleven-forty-five.

Since her body felt completely battered, Claire decided to spend the day working to give it a rest. Tomorrow would be soon enough to get involved in the myriad activities offered by the lodge.

She sat down on the narrow bed and pulled her computer onto her lap. As she powered up the laptop, she organized her thoughts of how best to handle her boss's accounts during the coming weeks. She opened the list of Art's clients that she'd downloaded yesterday before her foray into petty larceny, and decided the first order of business was to contact each client and their corresponding insurance

broker to let them know she had a handle on things. Of the
ten accounts that were now her responsibility, six were bro-
kered through Bryan's firm, Unity Risk Services. She was
surprised to find that four of the accounts were handled
directly by Bryan's father, Robert Edwards. Claire was sure
Robert didn't oversee the day-to-day servicing of his accounts—he was the head of the Seattle office and wouldn't
have time for that—but it wasn't often that an office head
was so involved with his clients that he was listed as the
primary contact.

Shrugging, Claire composed e-mails to all ten clients.
Robert Edwards's workload was none of her business, but
making sure she did the best job for her new accounts was.

"All right everybody, that was a great hike." Kyle Robinson's enthusiasm reminded John of a high-school cheerleader. With the general manager and, as of yesterday, the
remaining summer staff gone, John had needed an extra
pair of hands and eyes on the lodge-sponsored excursions.
Kyle had eagerly volunteered and John was beginning to
realize that what Dana's younger brother lacked in matur-
ity, he made up for in energy.

The usual group size for the excursions ranged from
eight to twelve guests, and safety was John's first concern.
If a guest got injured on the trail, it was his job to ensure
that there was enough experienced help to lead the entire
group back safely. Sprained ankles were a common occur-
rence, since many guests weren't accustomed to walking
on anything more challenging than a sidewalk.

Preferring to act more as a technical advisor on the trips,
John would rather leave the guest-relations side of the business up to someone else. It wasn't that he didn't like people, John thought as Kyle continued his warm-down
speech, encouraging guests to indulge in a soak in one of
the lodge's hot tubs to ease any aching muscles. Instead,
he enjoyed being able to concentrate on their surroundings
rather than having to tend to someone's blistering corn or
itchy bug bite.

"Remember, folks, we also have a sunset hike today for any of you who still have the energy." The majority of the group groaned as Kyle cheerfully finished his speech.

The evening hike was more like a walk, really, but John couldn't blame the group for their lack of enthusiasm about it. They'd just completed a six-hour trek, including a leisurely stop for breakfast and a dip in a natural hot spring. That was more exercise than many guests had in a week, much less one morning.

"Is Claire all right?" Bryan Edwards's question intruded on John's thoughts.

Bryan and Cindy had been two of the morning's hikers. Although the brochure said the trip to the hot springs included a "clothing-optional" swim, John had never led a group where all the guests didn't bring their swimsuits. Until today, that is. Bryan and Cindy had shed their clothes at the first mention of the swim and now John had a hard time looking at either one of them without picturing them naked. He was glad none of the other hikers had followed Bryan and Cindy's lead. The last thing John wanted was to start envisioning all the guests naked every time he turned around.

The general manager had put the "clothing-optional" clause in the brochure as a joke, never dreaming that anyone would take it seriously, but John planned to go up to his office right now and change it. It was hard to keep a straight face when he kept picturing the other man's pastywhite ass climbing out of the hot springs.

He focused his eyes on a tree just over Bryan's right shoulder before answering the question. "Yes. She's a bit bruised up, but it's nothing serious."

"Good." Bryan casually put an arm over Cindy's shoulders. "I wish she hadn't come here, but I'm sorry she got hurt."

John noticed a small flash of jealousy in Cindy's eyes as she folded herself closer to Bryan. Something arrogant in the other man's voice had John fighting a wave of irritation. It wasn't as if Claire needed John to defend her, but even he had to admit it had been awfully low-down of her former fiancé to dump her like he had. Even worse, his own behavior hadn't been what anyone, including his own guilty conscience, would call exemplary. John gritted his teeth.

"Claire will be fine," he said abruptly, then turned on his heel and headed toward the lodge.

"Geez, what's up with him?" John heard Bryan mutter. Cindy's response was an unintelligible murmur as he let himself into the lodge.

Robert Edwards propped a hand on one of the spotless windows of his home office with its view of downtown Seattle and contemplated the e-mail message he'd just finished reading.

Claire Brown, his son's fiancée, was taking over the claims handling for his most important accounts. This was the first he'd heard of Art Engleheart's medical problems and he cursed himself for not establishing a better notification system for situations like this. He should have known about Art's health problem before it got this serious. If he had known, he might have been able to influence the outcome rather than being presented with a fait accompli.

As it was, it seemed that he was going to be stuck with Allied's choice of Miss Brown. At least for the moment.

He wondered what sort of a claims adjuster she was, then figured there was one way to find out. Turning toward the phone on his solid mahogany desk, he dialed the number his son had given him when he'd left for vacation, not noticing the fingerprints he'd left behind on the windows.

It took a moment for the call to go through and Robert impatiently unwrapped one of the sugar-free sourballs he kept in a glass jar on his desk.

"Hunter's Lodge. How can I help you?" a woman's voice answered.

"Please ring Bryan Edwards's room," Robert said, popping the apple-flavored candy in his mouth.

"I'm sorry, Mr. Edwards isn't in his room right now. Could I take a message?"

"How do you know he's not in his room? You didn't even try putting the call through," Robert challenged.

"Well, I just saw him walk into the dining room with his girlfriend," the youthful-sounding woman answered hesitantly.

"Oh." Robert moved the sourball to his left cheek and swallowed the saliva collecting in his mouth. "Could you get him on the line, then? This is his father and it's a bit of an emergency."

"Yes, of course. Just let me put you on hold for a moment."

Robert waited, thankful the lodge didn't have any of that repetitive advertising to listen to while on hold. The corporate office of Unity Risk Services had forced him to use a message on his office's phone system. The corporation had spent millions of dollars on a new ad campaign and, no matter how successful the Seattle office might be on its own, corporate insisted there were certain standards which had to be enforced, without exception. Robert had no choice but to comply.

"Bryan Edwards."

Robert had just moved the slowly disintegrating ball of candy under his tongue when his son picked up the phone. Being careful not to swallow the slippery treat, he responded, "Bryan, it's your father. What do you think of this news about your fiancée?"

"What news? And what fiancée? If you're talking about Claire, we've broken up."

"Broken up? When did this happen? You should have discussed it with me first, Bryan." Robert put the sourball between his teeth and bit down, shattering it into tiny sugar-free shards.

"Look, Dad, I know you thought Claire and I made a good match, but you were wrong. She's boring. All she ever talks about is work."

Robert crunched the tiny bits of candy and contemplated

how best to proceed. He knew his son, his only child, was
a bit of an idiot—he took after his mother that way. But
he was malleable and he didn't ask a lot of questions. For
now, that was enough. Robert got back to the original purpose of his call.

"Did you know, then, that your ex-fiancée has been assigned all of Art Engleheart's accounts for the next two
months?"

Bryan sounded less than interested when he responded
with, "No."

Robert shook his head and tried not to sigh. Didn't
Bryan see the potential implications of this turn of events?
Was he really that feeble-witted? It was hardly a question
he could pose to his progeny, so he went with "Haven't
you been checking your e-mail?" instead.

"I'm on vacation," Bryan answered defensively.

"Yes, Bryan, I know. But Claire's on vacation too and
she seems to be keeping up with her work."

"I told you, Dad, that's all she does. Work, work, work.
It's like she's the goddamn Energizer Bunny or something."

Robert did sigh at that, then reached for another sourball.
"All right. Just answer me this, then you can go back to
your vacation—do you think it's possible that your ex-
fiancée will discover our arrangement before Art gets
back?"

"Hell, no," Bryan answered immediately. "She's so buried with her own accounts, there's no way she can take on
the extra responsibility and have time to do any digging.
She already works eighty-hour weeks and can't keep up.
This is going to bury her."

"Hmm. Well, I certainly hope you're right," Robert con-
ceded before hanging up.

They might literally have to bury someone if his son
was wrong.

Dinner at Hunter's Lodge was a casual affair. Most guests
had spent their day outside, hiking, horseback riding, fishing, or taking leisurely walks on the marked walking paths.

Guests at the lodge could choose from a variety of packages to fit their lifestyles. The package Claire had chosen for Bryan's birthday present was the most expensive. It included all meals and regularly scheduled activities, as well as a special two-day whitewater rafting trip as a culmination of the vacation.

Claire flipped through the magazine she'd brought with her as she waited for the waiter to bring her the chardonnay she'd ordered. She didn't mind eating alone. She'd brought a pad of paper to scribble down any thoughts she might have after spending the day working. But she *did* mind having to watch her jerk of an ex-fiancé and his bimbo girlfriend practically making out on the couch in front of the fireplace in the dining room.

"No doubt they've taken advantage of the all-expenses-paid outdoor activities, courtesy of my bank account," Claire grumbled, violently stabbing a tomato from her salad.

"It's already dead."

Claire's arm jerked at the unmistakable voice of the lodge's owner and accidentally came into contact with her water glass. John caught the tumbler before it toppled over, stopping the action mid-disaster.

"I'm beginning to wonder if you can be trusted around liquid refreshments," he drawled. "Yesterday it was—what? Tomato and orange juice?"

Claire eyed the glass in his hand, wishing she could upend it over his head through force of will. Why did so much sheer male attractiveness have to come in such an arrogant package?

"Looks like your telekinetic powers aren't working," he said with amusement, pulling out the other chair at her table.

"Oh, please, do have a seat," Claire offered dryly.

"Don't mind if I do." John leaned back, stretching his long legs so she had to pull her own feet back under her chair to avoid contact with him.

Claire eyed him irritably, then shrugged, accepting the

fact that there was nothing she could do to displace his considerably larger frame. So much for her hopes of not seeing the lodge's owner again this week.

She chewed on a piece of lettuce and tried to pretend that she wasn't glad to see him. He'd replaced his usual blue jeans with a pair of charcoal-gray slacks and a short-sleeved shirt patterned in geometric shapes of gray and black. She had to admit he looked incredibly handsome tonight. The colors of the shirt showed off his tanned skin to perfection, making his deep green eyes stand out like the emeralds on her mother's favorite ring. Feeling drab in comparison, Claire couldn't help but long for the brand-new wardrobe that, according to the airline, was currently missing in action. One of her favorite missing pieces was a light yellow denim dress that brought out the gold tones in her hair, and looked quite good on her, if she did say so herself. Instead, as her own sort of private joke, she'd chosen to wear a hideously ugly pair of cream-colored poly-ester pants with flared legs and giant flowers printed all over the legs. A particularly ugly brown daisy was placed in an unflattering position right on the crotch, with a match-ing bright orange one plastered across the seam of the butt. Her brown sweater complemented the ensemble quite nicely.

"By the way, I suppose I should thank you for sending up those clothes. I'm particularly fond of these pants," she said, standing up to model. She turned around with one hand on her hip and gave John an over-the-shoulder pose.

"Nice." John grinned and Claire figured her original sup-position was correct. He had picked out the worst clothes he could find.

Claire sat back down and resisted the urge to roll her eyes. If he had hoped she'd run back home just because of an ugly wardrobe, he was very much mistaken. The waiter arrived with the wine she'd ordered and John declined an offer for one of the same.

She took a sip of chardonnay, then carefully replaced the glass on the table. "So, is there some reason you're favoring me with your company, or did you just run out of other people to torment?"

"Actually, I came to ask how you're feeling, but I can see that you're doing much better today."

"I am feeling better, thanks. As a matter of fact I'm planning to jump right in tomorrow with the sunrise hike."

John frowned at her from across the table. "It's a six-hour trip. Are you sure you're up to it?"

"Of course," she said breezily. "I take yoga at the gym so I'm sure I can handle it."

"A six-hour hike is hardly the same as assuming the lotus position for thirty minutes every day."

Claire took another sip of wine, forcing a neutral expression onto her face. She actually worked out for an hour every day, finding that the stress-reducing benefits of exercise were addictive. She vowed to tell her Guerrilla Yoga instructor about John's condescending lotus-position comment when she got back to Seattle. Nathan, a former Navy SEAL, and hardbody *extraordinaire* would definitely find it amusing. Claire speared another tomato from her salad. Besides, when she'd signed up for the hike, Dana had assured her it was well suited for beginners as well as experienced hikers, so she was sure she'd be fine. She'd spent all day working, resting her battered muscles, and she did feel almost recovered. She had a couple of ugly bruises on her rib cage, but they only hurt when she touched them.

"Well, you should be okay. There are a couple of places where you can get a ride back to the lodge if you can't keep up," John assured her.

Claire did roll her eyes at that. He must think she was a total wimp. "I'll keep that in mind."

Her dinner arrived at that moment and John excused himself, saying he had other dinner plans. He took a step away, then stopped.

"By the way, Dana tells me that your fiancé—"

"*Ex*-fiancé," Claire interrupted.

"Ex-fiancé," John continued, acknowledging her correction with a mocking nod of his head. "Your ex-fiancé's girlfriend reported one of her bags missing. You wouldn't happen to know anything about that, would you?"

Inhaling the aroma of the roasted chicken and vegetable pasta she'd ordered for dinner, Claire pasted an innocent look on her face. Eyes widened, she answered, "Me? Of course not. Why, I've been cooped up in my little room all day, doing my best not to get in anyone's way."

"Um-hmm. Well, it seems the bag in question went missing sometime last night. About the same time you were outside doing God knows what, I might add. I never did get around to asking what you were doing out there." John eyed her expectantly.

She had to think fast. What plausible lie might work? Uh . . . damn . . . she couldn't think of a thing. She was just about to give up and blurt out the truth when John's next words stopped her.

"I happened to be looking out a window last night, and I could have sworn I saw you bury something that appeared to be about the same size as a woman's makeup bag. But by the time I had a chance to look around this afternoon, I couldn't find the spot again. I got to thinking that maybe I had just imagined the whole thing about you and the shovel."

"Yes, you must have imagined it," Claire mumbled, looking down at her plate. So John was willing to cover for her, was he?

"Yeah, that's what I thought." He leaned close, a lock of dark hair falling over his forehead. Claire looked into his mesmerizing green eyes and felt her pulse leap as his hand brushed over hers. His mouth was so close, she was tempted to lean just a fraction of an inch closer to touch her lips to his. "Of course, it helps that it rained this afternoon. You can thank Mother Nature for covering your tracks." His soft breath stirred a wisp of her blond hair, tickling her neck.

Patting her hand, John stepped back, breaking the spell he'd cast over her. He waved lightly as he left, off to join whoever it was he was meeting for dinner. Watching him go, Claire felt a momentary pang of—what? Not jealousy, she assured herself. No, it was just that she was enjoying not being alone, had even briefly forgotten all about Bryan and his girlfriend getting friendly in front of the fire. That was all, she decided, thoughtfully chewing a bite of her now-tasteless dinner. Glancing over at the blond and salt-and-pepper heads cuddled together on the sofa, she waited for the anger and the hurt to start gnawing at her. Instead, she felt only embarrassment and irritation that her ex-fiancé had so easily taken her for a fool.

Turning to look out the window at the river beyond the dining room, Claire marveled at how she'd ever convinced herself she cared enough for Bryan Edwards to agree to their charade of an engagement. She also wondered why Bryan had consented to it, as well. It was obvious his feelings for her didn't run very deep, either, or he would have been able to resist having an affair with another woman while they were still engaged. Perhaps they'd simply moved ahead in their relationship according to someone else's predefined plan. Claire knew that Bryan's father, Robert, had encouraged the engagement; she had heard Robert congratulate his son several times since they'd made the announcement. Was it possible that Bryan was just going along with his father's wishes?

Claire spread butter on a slice of chewy sourdough bread as she pondered the possibility. Bryan was an account executive at the insurance brokerage firm headed by his father and Claire wondered if Bryan had inherited the job rather than worked for it. If that were true, it made sense that Bryan might feel obligated to go along with his father's wishes to repay Robert for providing his son with a lucrative career for so many years.

Robert Edwards was a well-respected man in the insurance community. Claire had only met Bryan's father a few times, but there was something about him that made the tiny blond hairs on her arms stand on end whenever he was around. She had decided early on that he was the kind of guy you never wanted to get into an empty elevator with.

But she figured she must be alone in her thinking, because under Robert's leadership, the Seattle office of Unity Risk Services had become one of the most successful insurance brokerage firms in the country. They almost never lost an account to a competing broker, Bryan's accounts included.

Since she'd found out today that two of Art's accounts were handled by Bryan, she was interested to see how he compared to other account executives. Some AEs monitored their accounts' claim activity diligently to ensure their customers' money was being properly handled. This route usually led to more work on the AE's part since both the claims adjusters and the clients themselves had to be educated about the best way to handle their insurance claims. Other AEs didn't monitor claims costs and were ignorant about the entire process in general. Claire was interested to find out which category her ex-fiancé fell into. She was honest enough to admit, at least to herself, that some part of her wanted to find that he fell into the latter category; that he was not doing the best job he could for his clients. It would be satisfying to her bruised ego if she could point out to Bryan's clients things that their AE should be doing to help contain their claims costs. Inevitably, they'd want to know why Bryan hadn't been providing them with these types of services all along. Perhaps it was petty of her to feel this way, but after the way he'd treated her, she felt justified in being a bit of a poor sport.

After all, all's fair in love and—

Claire's thoughts were interrupted by a commotion at the entrance to the dining room. "Oh, no," she gasped aloud, her eyes widening with horror.

"Billy, honey, come back to Mommy." Claire recognized the sleep-deprived woman from the plane as the tot ran into the room filled with diners.

"Yummy, yummy, yummy." Little Billy stopped at the table where an older gentleman and two teenaged girls were eating and peered at the food on their plates.

"Hi, there, little guy," Claire heard the man say in a friendly tone of voice. She wanted to yell a warning at the poor man; to tell him to hold on to his wallet before the kid sucked him dry. But she restrained herself. As far as she was concerned, it was every man for himself.

Claire opened the magazine she'd brought, holding it out in front of her face like a shield and sliding down in her chair, hoping to avoid detection.

"Me gotta new toy." The toddler plopped a red and white plastic fire truck into her lap. Claire sighed. Well, at least she had a means of escape this time, she thought, lowering her magazine.

"Yes, Billy. It's very nice. Now, why don't you go to your mommy like a good little boy?" she suggested hopefully.

"My daddy gived it to me." Little Billy proceeded to run the vehicle around the white linen tablecloth, making his best fire engine noises.

"That's great." She signaled frantically for her waiter as Billy started using her legs as his own personal transportation system. This kid was like a cat; he seemed to sense the one person in the room who was the most uncomfortable around him, and then homed in on that person like a bee to hairspray. Billy ran the truck along the back of her chair as she signed the bill and grabbed her purse in an attempt to make a quick getaway.

Her hand stilled as she heard a burst of masculine laughter from across the room. Looking up, she saw John entering the dining room with a beautiful brunette on his arm. The woman's sleeveless red dress set off her shining cap of short brown hair to perfection. She was smiling up at John, her brightly painted lips turned up at something he must have said.

Claire frowned. How nice that he could be charming and amusing to everyone except her, she thought, pushing out her chair. Without looking where she was going, she backed up, intent on getting out of the dining room before John or his beautiful date spotted her.

Her hip came into contact with something soft, and her

heel with something hard. It only took a split second for Little Billy to start wailing.

Glancing heavenward, Claire prayed for patience as she turned her attention to the boy. "I'm sorry, Billy." She reached a hand to the ground to help him up.

Billy screeched. "My twuck," he bawled.

Claire looked down at her feet. The fire engine was now a jumble of mixed-up red and white plastic pieces.

"Oh, damn," she cursed, remorse filling her voice. Well, she knew how to fix this problem. He'd certainly taught her well enough during their three-hour flight here. Rooting around in her purse, Claire fished out a five-dollar bill. "Here, I'm sorry." She offered him the money.

"Claire, what are you doing?" John asked from beside her, aghast.

"I accidentally broke his truck so I'm paying him for it," Claire explained.

"What good is money to a three-year-old? Don't you know anything about children?"

"You don't understand," she started to protest.

"No, it's you who don't understand, Claire. Money can't fix everything," John said before turning his back on her. He bent down into a crouch and helped Billy to his feet. "Hey, there, son. Are you all right?" he soothed.

Claire sighed. There was no way she was going to win this fight.

"Forget it. Good night," she muttered, deciding to quit while she was behind. It seemed as if the occupants of the entire dining room watched her exit with disgust.

Chapter 7

AS THEY ALWAYS DID, CLAIRE'S EYES POPPED OPEN ONE full second before the alarm went off.

She reached out a hand and smacked if off just as the first jarring ring sounded. Flinging off the warm blanket she was comfortably cocooned in, she pushed herself out of bed.

Claire didn't consider herself a morning person, exactly. She didn't leap out of bed each morning, thrilled to greet a new day, but when the alarm sounded she got out of bed immediately. She didn't hit the snooze button two or three times.

She didn't even hit it once.

When her alarm went off, she turned it off and got out of bed.

"Because that's what you're supposed to do when the alarm goes off," she muttered, slipping the thick terry-cloth robe over the borrowed shirt she'd worn to sleep in last night.

This was a concept she never had been able to get through to her old college roommate, Meg. To Meg, the shriek of the alarm clock was merely a suggestion that she start thinking about getting up in, oh, say the next hour or so. Meg was exactly the type of person that Claire's father was referring to when he complained "Those kids have no concept of a work ethic. They show up whenever they feel like it, take breaks whenever they want. Why, when I was their age I was working eighteen hours a day . . ."

Claire couldn't remember the rest of his speech. Didn't want to anyway. After graduation, Meg had gone to work for a small software company in Washington State. It was one of the few companies at the time that didn't care what time of day their employees started work, as long as the job got done. And now, ten years later, Meg's stock options at the formerly small computer company had made her a multimillionaire.

Without bothering to tie the belt of her robe, Claire slung her overnight case over her shoulder and pawed through the pile of lost and, unfortunately, found clothes, looking for something suitable to wear for this morning's hike. It was a toss-up between the neon-pink sweats and a pair of navy blue shorts with gold piping. She chose the sweats, thinking the shorts might not be warm enough this early in the morning.

She stacked a red, white, and blue plaid flannel shirt on top of the bright pink sweatpants and added a tattered T-shirt imprinted with a faded photo of the heavy-metal band Def Leppard on the front.

Her bare feet made no sound on the hardwood floor as she headed out of her room and down the hall. The employee showers were on the first floor. Claire looked longingly at the door to John's suite, wishing she could use the luxurious bath facilities there. But not wanting to chance that they were already occupied, she headed downstairs. There was no way she was going to jeopardize any future whirlpool bathing experiences for one private shower. She pushed open the hallway door leading to the showers, and was struck once again by the contrast of the stark white walls to the luxuriously appointed public rooms outside as she headed off to get ready for the day's activities.

"Make sure all the packs have towels."

"They're on the checklist," Kyle protested.

"I know, but it never hurts to double-check."

John heard Kyle's sigh, but the younger man started rechecking the backpacks. John knew he was being overly cautious, but he also knew that, ultimately, it was his responsibility to make sure every guest had the necessary equipment to enjoy the day's excursion.

"I'll meet you out front in half an hour." John left Kyle

with the backpacks and headed to the kitchen in search of some coffee. He let himself into the lodge, wiping his boots on the mat as he entered a hallway.

Rounding a corner, he collided with something—or rather someone—soft.

"Oh, it's you," Claire said, steadying herself against his chest.

John took in her disheveled appearance, her blond hair in disarray, lightly tanned bare legs visible beneath his favorite shirt. The instant attraction he felt for her annoyed him. Why couldn't he get it through to his body that his mind didn't like this woman? Especially after how she'd treated that little boy last night. What kind of woman offered money to a three-year-old after breaking a favored toy? She obviously knew nothing about children; she probably knew more about how the Dow Jones Industrial Average was calculated than how to deal with people.

"What are you doing running around half-naked?" he asked irritably.

"I'm on my way to the shower. I didn't feel that it was necessary to dress up for the occasion," Claire answered, eyeing him as if he were a particularly disgusting bug she'd like to squash.

"Who said anything about dressing up? I'm just suggesting you might consider not wandering around in public without any clothes on, that's all."

John watched as Claire opened her robe wider and looked down at the shirt that fell almost to her knees. "I have more clothing on than your date did last night. Besides, if you hadn't let my ex-fiancé and his bimbo girlfriend steal the room I paid for, I'd be in my own bathroom right now and we wouldn't be having this discussion."

What was this about his "date" with Gina, the lodge's chef? If he hadn't known better, he might suspect that Claire was jealous. The thought filled him with a perverse sense of satisfaction, and something egged him on. He couldn't remember ever wanting to cross verbal swords with a woman, but he couldn't seem to stop himself from goading Claire Brown.

"So it's my fault you can't hang on to a man?" he said, without thinking.

Claire's intake of breath came with a hiss. Clutching the edges of her robe, she took a step backward, bumping against the white-painted wall. "You bastard."

John raised his eyebrows in surprise, but not at her curse. He had only meant to taunt her, to get under her skin the way she kept getting under his. But the second the words left his mouth, he knew how wrong the comment was. The urge to spar with Claire immediately deserted him, leaving remorse in its wake. He took a step toward her, his sense of guilt swelling when she refused to look up at him, staring at the buttons of his light green shirt instead. "I'm sorry. I didn't mean that," he apologized.

A sniffle was her only response, and John felt even more like a heel. Putting two fingers under her chin, John lifted her head. Seeing the pain in her light gray eyes, he almost wished he hadn't met her gaze. She had just lost her fiancé in a public and humiliating way and all he could do was rub salt in the wound. "I really am sorry. Your fiancé—"

"*Ex*-fiancé," she interrupted, blinking rapidly.

"Sorry. Your ex-fiancé is an asshole, and my comment was uncalled for. Forgive me?" he asked softly, resisting the urge to rub his thumb across her full bottom lip.

She shrugged, still looking miserable.

"You'd better go take that shower or you'll be late for the hike." He stepped aside, giving her a little push toward the women's shower room as if she were a child. John watched her go, then headed toward the kitchen, still feeling as if he'd just cut the whiskers off a little gray kitten.

Claire still felt confused forty-five minutes later as the group of hikers assembled in the lobby of the lounge. Just when she had John McBride classified as a real jerk, he had to go and surprise her. His remorse about hurting her feelings had certainly seemed genuine, although if he was really a nice guy, he wouldn't have made that comment about her not being able to hold on to a man in the first place.

Claire sighed. And men were always saying that women were hard to figure out.

Shaking her head, she surveyed the small group of people gathered for the hike. She had to stop herself from groaning aloud at seeing the woman from the plane standing next to a man Claire hadn't seen before. Little Billy stood, quietly for once, next to the man who Claire assumed was the boy's father. He was about six feet tall with dark brown hair just beginning to recede from his forehead. From the stern expression on his face, Claire guessed this family vacation had not been his idea.

Her observation of the crowd ended when the front door opened and John strode into the lobby followed by a young man who had the same facial features as Dana. All eyes turned toward John, and Claire marveled at his ability to immediately get everyone's attention without saying a word. It wasn't John, however, who addressed the group. Instead, it was the young man who had followed John in who addressed the gathered crowd.

"Good morning, everyone. I see some new faces this morning. My name is Kyle Robinson and I'm going to lead today's hike along with John McBride." Claire heard a hint of pride in the boy's voice as he continued. "We'll have plenty of time to get to know each other this morning, but let's start off with some introductions. Why doesn't everyone say their name and let us know your level of hiking experience? Mr. Isler, would you start us off?" Kyle nodded toward an elderly gentleman who sat with two teenaged girls.

The older man introduced himself and his granddaughters as George, Lisa, and Heather Isler. Claire studied George Isler as the other hikers introduced themselves, wondering at the hint of sadness that seemed to hang over him. Claire guessed that the girls' parents had gone away on a second honeymoon and asked George Isler to take care of their daughters while they were away. Maybe the girls just missed their parents, and that's why they looked so forlorn, sitting together on the couch.

Claire shrugged, turning her attention to the woman from the plane, curious to know what the woman's name was after all this time. The man did all the talking, introducing them as William and Peggy Weber, with their son, William Junior.

"You mean Billy the Blackmailer," Claire muttered under her breath. William and Peggy were probably high school sweethearts, taking a vacation in an attempt to rekindle whatever romantic feelings they might have once felt for one another—without much success, it would seem.

Claire introduced herself, adding that she was a beginning hiker. The only one in the group who admitted to having any wilderness experience was Mr. Weber. He claimed that he ran marathons, was a proficient rock climber, and was currently in training to hike to base camp at Mount Everest. Claire had thought she and Bryan were mismatched in the physical-activity arena, but William and Peggy Weber were obviously even further apart on the divided-interest scale. As Mr. Weber continued to regale the group with his accomplishments, Claire began to almost feel sorry for his wife, who looked more uncomfortable the more her husband talked. She wondered if she was the only one who noticed Peggy and Billy slipping away as William Weber finally stopped his self-serving diatribe.

After the introduction, Kyle started a talk about safe hiking practices. Claire settled back into one of the comfortable chairs to listen when the obnoxious giggle that had plagued her for days made her sit bolt upright. Dreading what she would see, she turned, then stifled a groan.

"Hi, everyone. Sorry we're late. We got, uh, caught up in something." Cindy giggled as she and Bryan made their way over to the group in the lobby.

I'd like to catch you up in a net and drop you off a cliff, Claire thought, eyeing the annoying woman. She turned her head and locked gazes with John. The amusement in his eyes told her he'd accurately read her mind. Claire coughed to cover a laugh as he raised his eyebrows in mock surprise at the murderous gleam she knew must be evident in her gaze, then refocused her attention on Kyle's spiel.

"Don't hesitate to let us know right away if there's anything that's bothering you. You'd be amazed at how many people will suffer through hours of pain when they don't have to. We do this every day and know a lot of tricks that can ease most of the problems you'll encounter on a trip like this."

John took over. "Besides what Kyle's already told you, I want you all to remember the most important rule of hiking, which is to stay on the trail at all times. If, for some reason, you want to explore something off the trail, let us know. It's easy to get lost in even the most familiar of forests. I've found people who took no more than two steps off the trail and were unable to find their way back, so just make sure this doesn't happen to you.

"We have packs outside for each of you. The contents of each pack is identical, so you don't have to worry about taking the wrong one. Let's get geared up and get moving." With that final message, John herded the group outside.

Claire fell into step behind Mr. Isler and his granddaughters, hoping she'd be able to avoid all contact with Bryan and his giggling girlfriend for the next six hours as she slid her cell phone into a bright blue backpack. Slipping the pack over her shoulders, she turned at hearing John's polite but firm tone.

"Mr. Weber, you can leave your own pack here. We've taken care of everything."

"I prefer to bring my own, thank you."

Watching John's jaw clench, Claire was happy to see his annoyance directed at someone other than her for a change. She watched the exchange between the two men curiously.

"All right," John said evenly, turning to Kyle. "Kyle, can you go over the checklist with Mr. Weber to make sure his pack has everything we require?"

"Sure thing, boss." The younger man pulled a rumpled sheet of paper from his front pocket and went down the list with Mr. Weber. "Do you have water?"

"Of course," William Weber replied.

John leaned up against the wall of the lodge, crossing his arms over his chest.

"Great." Kyle kept going down the list. "How about bug repellent? A towel? First-aid kit? Sunscreen? Flare gun? A flashlight?"

Claire saw the satisfied gleam in John's green eyes as Mr. Weber was forced to answer no four out of six times.

"A flashlight? Why in the hell do I need a flashlight? This is a day hike," William protested at the last question, a ruddy flush spreading across his face.

John stepped in, rescuing Kyle from the older man's anger. Pushing himself away from the wall, he stopped directly in front of William Weber. "Mr. Weber, I've been doing this for a long time. I'll agree that there's a ninety-nine-point-nine percent chance you won't need a flashlight, or a first-aid kit, or many of the other things in your pack. But I'm not willing to bet your life on that point-one percent chance. Are you?"

Claire chewed the inside of her cheek, waiting for Mr. Braggart to respond. What could he say to save face now? John's argument had been so reasonable that William Weber would look like a fool if he insisted on taking his own backpack now, but he'd lose the testosterone battle if he didn't. Claire hid a smile. Yes, it was quite a dilemma. Who knew that having a penis carried such a burden with it?

William Weber was the first to break eye contact. Without acknowledging John's question, he propped his own heavy-looking pack against the lodge, exchanging it for one of the lighter daypacks the lodge provided.

"Guess yours is bigger," Claire muttered under her breath as John stopped to adjust the straps of her pack for her. She was rewarded by the gurgling sound of a man choking on his own laughter.

"Okay, everybody, let's go," Kyle said cheerfully with a wave of his arm.

The group set out across a wooden bridge that spanned the river.

Grinning, Claire fell into step at the end of the line where John had taken up position. "That was very well done of you," she commended. "Have you ever thought about trading in your pliers for a CEO's suit?"

"No, thank you. I'm happy enough with the simple life I lead."

"Hmm." Claire wasn't yet ready to call his bluff. "I can see why you insist on providing the backpacks. You're very thorough."

"I aim to please." John shot her an amused glance, and Claire felt a blush creep into her cheeks. An irritable John McBride she could handle, but an amiable John McBride was a different animal entirely. Claire tried not to stare at the wicked light in his emerald-green eyes; resisted the itch in her fingers at the temptation to trace the little lines next to his mouth when he smiled at her.

In an attempt to regain her senses, she tried to focus on something, anything, else. She tried thinking about the cool morning breeze as it caressed her skin. She looked down at John's strong, tanned hands. They were capable hands, his fingers thick and roughened, not at all like her ex-fiancé, whose hands were soft and well-manicured. At the sudden recollection of how those work-roughened hands had felt against her flesh the night she'd fallen down the stairs, Claire felt her nipples start to rub against her shirt.

Distracted, she tripped over a rock on the trail.

"Are you all right? Are your ribs okay?" John's steadying hand on her arm kept her from falling.

"I'm fine, thanks," Claire muttered. This was ridiculous. She was mooning over the guy like some lovesick teenager, and they didn't even like each other. She had to put an end to this, and soon, or she'd be in a full body cast by the time the week was over.

Straightening, she pulled ahead of John, trying to put some distance between them.

"What a nice outfit. That color looks great on you," Cindy gushed as she and Bryan passed Claire on their way to the front of the line.

Claire looked at the other woman in disbelief. Cindy had on a new-looking dark blue nylon sweatsuit with a sparkling white T-shirt, which brought out the color of her unnaturally bright blue eyes. In contrast, Claire's neon-pink sweatpants had holes in both knees, her T-shirt was stained, and the red, white, and blue shirt she wore to top it all off looked like someone's idea of a patriotic tribute to America in one hundred percent cotton flannel. Claire shook her head at the retreating back of Bryan's new girlfriend. Was it possible for someone to be so insincere? How could Bryan not see what a phony she was?

The worst of it was that Bryan had chosen Cindy over her. Wincing, Claire remembered John's words earlier this morning. *"So it's my fault that you can't hold on to a man?"*

The barb had found its mark then and came back to nibble at her now as she trudged past aspen trees whose leaves were just beginning to turn gold. At thirty-two, she had been engaged twice and both times her fiancés had left her for other women. Before two days ago, she would not have believed it could happen to her again.

Cool morning air lifted the ends of her hair and Claire pulled the loose strands into a makeshift ponytail as she trudged along behind the group of hikers. She'd been twenty-six the first time, and a junior account executive at her father's insurance brokerage firm. Her parents were overjoyed when she'd announced her engagement to Craig Knight, a tall, sandy-haired charmer who was her father's uncrowned golden boy. Her parents always threw a lavish Christmas party at their home in Greenwich, Connecticut, and, that year, the celebration was twofold, encompassing both the upcoming holiday and the engagement of the boss's daughter to his heir apparent.

Claire remembered the night as if it had happened yesterday, rather than six years ago. It had started out magically, with a light snowfall dusting the bare skeletons of the trees and covering the sculpted boxwoods surrounding the house, making them look like giant snowballs. Her mother, always the perfect hostess, decorated the entire house with pine boughs draped in royal blue and gold to match the enormous Christmas tree standing in front of the floor-to-ceiling windows in the living room.

Claire knew that not everybody's Christmas trees were the product of weeks of careful planning. She'd spent one Christmas with Meg's family when they'd been at Northwestern together and Claire hadn't been able to fly home for the holidays. The Brewers' Christmas tree was overloaded with ornaments crafted by Meg and her four siblings throughout the years. There were ceramic picture frames holding photos of the children dating back twenty years, Styrofoam balls and pinecones decorated with sequins and ribbon, and plaster molds with the imprint of tiny hands forever trapped in the fragile clay. As Mrs. Brewer had lovingly unwrapped each ornament, Meg and her family played the "I remember" game, reminiscing about what had been going on in their lives when a particular treasure had been crafted.

After that Christmas with Meg, Claire asked her mother where her own handcrafted ornaments were, and wasn't surprised to hear they'd all been thrown out. After all, Claire thought, gazing at the beautifully decorated, color-coordinated marvel in blue and gold before her, none of the crude, childish objects would ever look right on one of the Browns' elegant Christmas trees.

Claire had to admit that this year's decorations were beautiful, and a nice change from the usual red and green. Her mother had even had the gardener string golden lights throughout the yard, and their soft glow on the white snow lent a magical feel to the evening. She wouldn't have been surprised to see a sleigh, complete with horses decked in blue and gold, in the backyard, but figured her mother had drawn the line at animals that might leave unsightly droppings to ruin her perfect Christmas-party vision.

"Claire, your father's ready to make his speech," her mother's soft voice interrupted Claire's reverie.

"Thank you, Mother. Do you know where Craig is?"

"No, dear, I haven't seen him. Why don't you go find him while I make sure the caterer has enough champagne out for the toast?"

"All right," Claire murmured. Her ice-blue heels clicked softly on the worn cherrywood floors as she left the noise of the living room.

She didn't find Craig on the first floor and wondered what on earth he could be doing upstairs, when common courtesy would dictate that all guests stay on the main floor.

There were five bedrooms on the second floor, all with their own baths. She climbed the stairs, careful to tread on the carpeted runner instead of the slippery hardwood steps. Turning right at the top of the stairs, Claire hesitantly poked her head into her parents' room.

"Craig?" she inquired softly.

She glanced around, then quietly closed the door. She'd never felt comfortable coming into her parents' room, even as a child, and was surprised to discover that her mother had redecorated since the last time she'd intruded on their sanctuary.

A hasty search of the three guest bedrooms uncovered nothing. Claire paused at the final door. This room, the one farthest away from her parents' at the end of the upstairs hallway, had been hers for the first eighteen years of her life. She'd been shocked upon her first visit home during college to find that in the three months she'd been away, her mother had boxed up all her personal belongings and turned her bedroom into another guest room, explaining that they'd had extra guests over Thanksgiving and needed a place for them to stay.

"After all, dear," she remembered her mother saying,

"your father and I can't have people staying in a bedroom covered with stuffed animals and posters of half-naked teenagers, now can we?"

Claire supposed she was glad her mother had bothered to box up her things rather than just throwing them away. However, just to be safe, she'd taken the boxes with her when she'd gone back to school after the holiday was over.

She didn't like coming here now, didn't like that her eighteen years of occupancy had been so thoroughly wiped out. She'd stayed in this room on her infrequent visits from college and disliked the cold feel of its newly painted pale green walls and dark, heavy furniture.

Now, hearing a noise from inside, Claire opened the solid, eight-paneled door and stood staring with shocked horror at the scene in front of her.

Her fiancé was standing, his hips propped against the low mahogany dresser as a dark-haired woman in a short black skirt and white blouse crouched on the floor in front of him.

Claire gasped in shock.

Her fiancé opened his eyes at the unexpected sound.

"Craig, Claire, what's going on up here?" her father's voice rumbled, and he pushed past her as she stood frozen in the doorway.

The woman on the floor turned around in surprise at the obviously unexpected audience. Her unbuttoned blouse had come loose from the waistband of her skirt and she hastily pulled the open edges together to cover the breasts that had been freed from her bra.

Craig fumbled for his zipper in a near-comical attempt to hide the evidence of what had just occurred.

"Yes, I'd like to know what's going on here, too." Claire crossed her arms across her icicle-blue dress, her entire body going suddenly cold. Craig's soft brown eyes met hers and Claire clearly read his plea for help. Her lip curled in revulsion. They weren't even married yet and he was cheating on her with the hired help.

"I can explain—" Craig began.

Claire's father held up a hand as if to physically block the words coming out of Craig's mouth. "There's no need for any explanations, Craig. I believe the situation is perfectly clear."

Claire waited for her father's cutting temper, which she had been on the receiving end of many times, to shred Craig into bite-sized pieces. She waited for her father to tell Craig that, not only was the wedding off, he could clean out his desk besides. She waited for the righteous anger on her behalf, waited for her father to stand up to the man who had just betrayed his only child in such a demeaning and contemptuous way.

She waited for something that was never going to come.

"I expect you to get yourself straightened up and be downstairs in five minutes. Our guests are waiting for my speech." He turned to leave, stopping when he saw the caterer's server out of the corner of his eye.

"You, young lady, can consider yourself dismissed," he said tightly.

Until that moment, Claire's brain had been frozen with outrage at the situation. How could her father let Craig get away with this type of behavior? What was happening was incomprehensible to her. "Father, what are we going to do?" she asked, bewildered.

Sumner Brown turned his steely gray eyes to his daughter. "Do? About what?"

"About the engagement. Everyone's expecting you to announce it tonight."

"Yes, and that's exactly what I'm going to do."

"I . . ." Claire sputtered, then took a deep, calming breath. "I can't marry Craig now. Not after this."

Her father's eyes bored into hers. Claire almost stepped back from the intensity of his gaze. "Claire, it's time you grew up and realized that life isn't one big fairy tale. You and Craig are a perfect match, although I would expect him to practice a bit more discretion in the future." His disapproving gaze moved from his daughter to his future son-in-law.

Claire looked at her father incredulously. Apparently, he not only expected her to go through with this farce of an engagement, he condoned Craig's tomcat behavior.

"No," she said forcefully, anger welling up deep inside. "No, I won't marry that cheating rat." She waved a hand at her fiancé, who seemed to have regained his composure quite nicely and was leaning against the chest of drawers with his arms crossed smugly across his chest.

Her father reached out and grabbed her bare arm, his fingers tightening against her soft flesh. "You'll do it, by God. The firm is going to stay in the family and I've chosen Craig to succeed me when I retire."

Claire turned to her father, unable to believe that, in this day and age, he expected her to abide by his decree. She drew herself up to her full height of a not-so-impressive five feet two inches, anger pushing her to do something she had never done before in her life—defy her father. "Well, then, you and Mother had better get busy producing another daughter to marry him off to, because I refuse to marry a man who's cheating on me even before we say 'I do.' "

She yanked her arm out of her father's grip, attributing her success to his stunned state. Her arm throbbed where he'd grabbed her and she resisted the urge to rub it as she turned to leave. No sense in ruining the drama at this point.

She was halfway down the stairs when her father's raised voice reached her. "If you take one more step, you're fired. Do you hear me? No more cushy job where you're protected from the real world because you're the boss's daughter," he said derisively.

Claire stood stock-still at his threat, her mind racing. She'd worked at the firm for the past two years, ever since she'd completed her MBA. If she'd been a man, she knew she would have started as a full-blown account executive, but she'd had to start as an administrative assistant. She'd tried to convince herself it was because her father had wanted her to learn the business from the ground up, but deep inside she knew it was because he didn't want to admit her into his inner circle of male cronies. She'd worked hard, staying late every night for two years, and had earned a promotion just last month to junior account executive. Now he was threatening to take it all away, as if her hard work meant nothing.

Claire realized at that moment that it wasn't that her hard work meant nothing, it was that her value as an heir-producer meant more.

Well, she refused to live her life as her father's brood mare. Without looking back, Claire continued down the stairs.

Her father's raised voice followed her and a small crowd gathered in the foyer to see what the fuss was all about. Her mother stood watching her silently at the bottom of the stairs as her father continued to rain threats down on her. "Fine, then, consider yourself fired. Don't bother to come in and clean out your desk, I'll have my secretary do it for you." He paused. "Oh, and don't think you can count on any inheritance from me. I'll be calling my attorney tomorrow morning. Do you hear me?"

Claire noticed her hands were shaking as she reached into the hall closet and freed her pale gray coat from the hanger. Placing the coat over her arm, she picked up the small beaded silver purse she'd bought especially for this evening. She met her mother's disapproving gaze as she pulled on the cold brass doorknob, and knew instantly that she'd get no support from that corner.

Claire hadn't looked back as the heavy front door closed behind her.

"Okay, everybody, let's take a break." John's deep voice intruded on her memory, startling her back to the present. "We'll have a full breakfast set up for you at the hot springs so why don't you grab a cup of coffee, tea, or hot chocolate and just relax for a minute? And let us know if anyone's boots are rubbing or if your pack is uncomfortable and we'll do what we can to fix the problem."

Claire gratefully accepted a cup of coffee from one of the two lodge employees manning a small beverage stand in the clearing.

The back of her neck started to tingle and, without turn-ing around, she knew that John was behind her. Feeling raw from the recent attack of memory, Claire wished she could just slip away for a moment. Her eyes burned with the sting of unshed tears and her throat felt tight. John McBride seemed to have the uncanny ability to read her emotions from just looking into her eyes, and she didn't want him to see that he'd hit a bull's-eye with his poison comment this morning. He had been one hundred percent correct—she wasn't able to hold on to her fiancés, wasn't woman enough or satisfying enough to keep them from straying, and the knowledge of her failures in her personal life was pinching her heart more than her new hiking boots were cramping her feet.

"Are you enjoying the hike?" John was so close that his breath stirred the wisps of hair on the nape of her neck.

She felt goose bumps involuntarily rise on her arms, and knew if she turned around now, he'd see the hurt and pain radiating from her eyes as if someone were holding a mirror up to her emotions for all to see. Instinctively, she knew she needed to give herself some emotional distance.

Claire grabbed a packet of sugar she didn't want and shook it to move the crystals to the bottom. Closing her eyes briefly, as if by doing so she could pull a shade down over her thoughts, Claire took a deep breath. Unable to avoid it any longer, she turned to face him, cloaking her pain behind an armor of disdain.

"So far it's been rather unspectacular, don't you think? I mean, I was expecting to see bears or maybe a mountain lion or two at least." She emptied the pack of sugar into the paper cup filled with coffee and watched as his eyes narrowed.

"I mean," she continued, "for what we're all paying I would have expected a little more adventure. You know, scary rope bridges, wild animals—that sort of thing."

Claire almost cringed at the superficial words, but she couldn't seem to stop herself. All she wanted was for John to go away and leave her alone with her misery. She congratulated herself on her tactic when John gave a disgusted snort and walked away.

"Maybe I should give acting a try," she muttered, taking a sip of her too-sweet coffee.

"Pardon me?"

She hadn't realized that Mr. Isler was standing so close by. "Nothing. So, how are you and your granddaughters enjoying your vacation?" she asked, hoping the older man hadn't heard her obnoxious comments to John. She'd succeeded in getting rid of him, but now she felt lower than slug slime. She sipped her coffee, trying not to grimace. There was no doubt about it, she was a coffee purist. As far as she was concerned, coffee shouldn't contain cream or sugar or chocolate or any other exotic flavor that some marketing whiz tried to fob off as the "new and improved" version. Coffee should be hot, fresh, and black. Period. But the hot brew was helping to ease the tightness in the back of her throat, so she continued to drink it.

"I think I'm having a better time than the girls are," George Isler replied.

"Don't they like the great outdoors?"

"I think, like you, they were expecting it to be a little more dangerous. They're used to playing video games with more excitement than this," he said wryly.

Claire blushed, realizing that he must have overheard her conversation with John. She considered explaining herself, then decided it was too much to share with a stranger, even one as seemingly nice as George Isler. "It is beautiful here, though," she said instead, looking around. They'd stopped in a clearing bounded by a small brook and surrounded by trees that, in mid-September, had just begun to change color. It was a riot of greens and golds, set off by the mottled white bark of the aspen trees.

"What strikes me most," Claire said after awhile, "is how quiet it is. I live and work in the city and I guess I'm used to the sounds of civilization at all hours of the day or night."

"I've always believed that I do my best thinking when

I'm out in the woods. Maybe it's because there's nothing else to focus on, or perhaps the silence outside gives me the opportunity to listen to myself, I don't know. But I always feel like I know myself better after a walk in the woods."

Claire understood exactly what George Isler meant. She hadn't given her breakup with Craig much thought over the last six years, but she'd realized this morning that her feelings about the whole episode were largely unresolved. She almost wished it wasn't quite so quiet here; she wasn't sure she wanted to deal with issues that had been buried for so long.

In a move that startled even herself, Claire reached out and squeezed Mr. Isler's weathered hand. "Is that why you brought the girls here? So they'd have the chance to learn something about themselves?"

George laughed without humor and nodded. "Hopefully, they won't see through my ploy. They think I just brought them here to get them away from their friends for a few days."

Claire was surprised by her sudden insight. She didn't consider herself to be a particularly empathetic person. She saw George glance over to where the girls were sitting, apart from the rest of the group. They weren't talking and, for some reason, Claire thought they seemed to be surrounded by an air of sadness.

"I know I'm a lot older than they are and that causes a communication gap, but I always try to do what's best for them."

Claire hesitated. She didn't want to pry, but it seemed that he wanted someone to talk to. "You can tell me to mind my own business, Mr. Isler, but where are the girls' parents?"

"Oh, please call me George." He glanced at the girls again, and Claire could clearly see the pain etched on his face. "Their parents, my son and daughter-in-law, died in a car accident a year ago. The girls have been living with me ever since, but I've long since realized that I don't know the first thing about raising children."

"But you had a son," Claire protested.

"Yes, but I'm sorry to say that my wife gets all the credit for raising him. Like most men of my generation, I spent the majority of my life at work while my wife handled all the child-rearing responsibilities," he said wryly.

"I'm sure your wife is a great help now, then."

"My Elizabeth died nine years ago. So it seems I'm on my own in this."

"I'm so sorry, George." Claire held on to his warm hand compassionately.

"Thank you, dear. I don't know why I told you all that," he laughed self-deprecatingly. "There's no reason to feel sorry for me. I wanted to take care of the girls, maybe in some way to make it up to my son for missing so much of his childhood." He squeezed Claire's hand, then the contact was broken. "Looks like we'd better get packed up again," he said as Kyle's cheerful voice announced that they were ready to move on to the hot springs.

Claire shouldered her pack, trying to shake off the sadness that had seemed to flow from George Isler to her. Sighing, Claire wondered why life had to be filled with so much unhappiness as she took up her position near the end of the line of hikers.

Chapter 8

AS THEY NEARED THE HOT SPRINGS, THE SMELL OF SIZ-
zling bacon had the hikers moving a little bit faster and
Claire hastened to catch up. Glancing at her watch, she was
surprised to see that it wasn't yet ten o'clock in the morning. Her fingers started to tingle with the desire to call her
assistant back at the office, but her stomach insisted on
being taken care of first.

Since she'd been last in the line of hikers, Claire was
also the last person through the breakfast line. With her
plate loaded up with pancakes she found, to her dismay,
that the only place left to sit at either of the two picnic
tables was right next to Bryan and Cindy. With a sigh of
inevitability, she trudged over and sat down, hoping it
would be a quiet meal.

"I just love your hair color. Where do you get it done?"
Cindy gushed as Claire sat down, dashing Claire's hopes
for a silent feast.

"It's natural," Claire responded shortly, grateful at least
that Bryan was deep in conversation with William Weber.

"Oh, my gosh. You're so lucky. Mine's natural, too, of
course," she babbled on, patting the short cap of salt-and-
pepper curls that should have made her look old, but somehow didn't. "I tried fighting the gray when I was younger,
but then one month I let it go too long and, you know, I
realized that the silver with my jet-black hair looked really
good."

Could the airhead routine be an act, Claire wondered, or
was it really possible for someone to be so full of herself
that she'd be discussing her hairdressing secrets with, not
just a perfect stranger, but someone whom her boyfriend
had been engaged to only two short days ago? Whether it

was an act or not, Claire had to almost physically restrain herself from reaching out and clapping a hand across the other woman's mouth to shut her up. Instead, she decided to see what had transpired after Cindy realized her makeup bag was missing. Assuming the same phony inflection in her voice as she'd heard in Cindy's, she said, "Oh, but I could never go without makeup like you. I'd just feel so, I don't know, so naked."

Cindy reached out and put a hand on her forearm. Claire had to stop herself from recoiling. "You know, I felt the same way. But my makeup bag got lost and here I am, stranded in the wilderness with no eyeliner, no foundation, nothing! I tell you, I was in a panic. But then Bryan said the sweetest thing." She leaned toward Claire conspiratorially.

"What'd he say?" Claire asked, hoping that what Cindy took as sweetness was something nasty in disguise.

"Well, he told me that he never liked his girlfriends to go without makeup, that he'd even refused to take you to his gym one morning when you showed up at the door looking like you'd just crawled out of bed. But he told me that he thinks I'm so beautiful that makeup only detracts from my looks."

Claire muttered something unintelligible while Cindy continued chattering on, tuning the other woman out as she processed the hurt. It all came back to the same thing. Why couldn't she find someone who loved her enough to say that he thought she looked great, with or without makeup?

She sighed despondently and took a bite of her syrup-soaked pancake as she leaned her head on one elbow.

"Are you going to swim in the hot springs?" Cindy's voice intruded on Claire's thoughts.

"Uh, no. I didn't bring a suit."

Cindy giggled. "Well, neither did I."

Then she was definitely not going to go in, Claire thought silently, resisting the urge to roll her eyes. Was Cindy clothing-challenged? Was she a suppressed nudist? Had she had some kind of damaging childhood experience

involving apparel? Could that explain why she seemed inclined to flaunt her naked body at every opportunity? The
woman obviously needed professional help, Claire concluded as she scooped up the last forkful of pancake and
tried not to watch her ex-fiancé and his new girlfriend strip
down to nothing before sliding into the warm water of the
springs.

Shuddering, Claire turned away from the scene at the
pools and rummaged through her backpack for her cell
phone. The meter showed a low-strength signal, which
wasn't surprising, but Claire figured she'd give it a try anyway. Wandering to the edge of the clearing, she dialed her
assistant's phone number, tilting her head to get the best
signal. She could barely hear the ringing on the other end,
so she pressed the phone to her left ear and stuck a finger
in the other ear to help her hear better.

Damn, his voice mail was picking up. She pressed zero
for the operator.

The voice on the other end of the line was faint, but
Claire thought she recognized it as Allied's receptionist.

"Hello. Barbara? This is Claire. Claire Brown. I'm trying
to reach Rich, but I got his voice mail. Could you page
him for me?"

Claire assumed the receptionist answered in the affirmative as the faint strains of Muzak piped into her ear, then
groaned as Rich's voice mail message started again.

"Rich, this is Claire. I need to talk to you. Give me a
call on my cell as soon as you get back to your desk," she
instructed before hanging up, vowing to try him again if he
didn't call back within thirty minutes.

Looking up, Claire suddenly realized she'd wandered
behind the hot springs. Several brightly colored garments
were strewn about the rocks as Bryan and Cindy cavorted
in the pools, their attention on some sort of game of grown-
up tag. The all-too-familiar sight of Bryan's silk boxers
mingled with a pair of black thong panties had an evil light
going on in Claire's head again. It was the same devil that
had possessed her the other night when she'd pilfered

Cindy's makeup bag, and the urge to commit another crime was strong . . . too strong to resist, as it turned out. Before she knew what she was doing, Claire reached out and grabbed the offending attire. Clutching the material between her thumb and forefinger, Claire held the garments out in front of her like week-old garbage and stepped back into the forest.

After three steps, her sanity returned.

"Oh, no, I've done it again," she wailed into the thick underbrush.

At that moment, her cell phone rang. Claire set her stolen goods on top of a bush, then flipped open the mouthpiece of her phone.

"Hello."

"Claire? This is . . . Returning your . . ."

She couldn't make out all the words, but guessed it was Rich.

"Rich? Is that you?" She tried tilting her head and plugging her ear again to get better reception.

"Claire! Claire, where are you?"

This voice came over loud and clear. Damn it, why did John keep insisting on interrupting her phone calls? Claire turned her back to the clearing, spying Bryan and Cindy's underwear where she'd set them seconds ago. She couldn't let John see the evidence, and didn't have time to return them to their rightful owners. Well, she figured, there was nothing else she could do. Kicking the bush, she watched the slips of black and paisley silk drop into the shrubbery as if they were the evergreen's breakfast.

"Just a second, Rich," she said, then covered the mouthpiece with one hand. "I'm over here," she called out.

John appeared before her, as if he'd been magically transported to her. "What the hell are you doing out here? Didn't you listen to anything I said this morning?"

Claire sighed. Apparently, she was going to spend her entire vacation getting chewed out by Grizzly Adams here. She uncovered the mouthpiece, meeting John's furious green-eyed glare as she ended the call to her assistant. "I'll have to call you back, Rich. It seems I'm overdue for another lecture right now."

Claire watched as the muscles around John's jaw clenched, and waited for the verbal lashing to begin.

John took a deep breath in an attempt to rein in his anger. This was exactly the type of guest he hated to see at the lodge. She had absolutely no respect for nature, and too much confidence in her own survival instincts. He read about her type every week, foolish people who went out into the wilderness unprepared for the experience, ending up lost or, all too often, dead. Reminding himself that he was in this business to help educate people like Claire Brown, John forced himself to relax.

"You know, Claire, as much as you may not believe this, I really don't want to see you get hurt during your vacation. I take my responsibility as a guide seriously because people's lives depend on how well I do my job. I wasn't kidding when I told you that I've seen people get lost after taking no more than two steps off the trail. I did some volunteer work with Search and Rescue a few years back, and it really wasn't pleasant having to find hikers who froze to death ten feet from help.

"Now, I'm not able to spend all my time watching out for you. There are other guests who need my attention. So, if you decide to ignore our rules again, I'll see to it that you're back on the first flight to Seattle before you can say 'Starbucks.' You got it?"

As verbal lashings went, she'd give it a nine-point-nine. He'd made her feel childish, petty, stupid, and irresponsible, all in less than sixty seconds.

"I'm sorry," she mumbled, "I could hear everyone from here, and I guess I just wasn't thinking."

John's hand under her elbow was his only answer to her apology as he guided her back to the clearing, where the rest of the hikers were gearing up for the return trip. Even Bryan and Cindy's frantic search for their underwear failed to cheer her up.

Taking up her usual spot near the end of the line, Claire

tried to ignore her feelings of guilt and enjoy the scenery. They were taking a different route back to the lodge, this one with a bit more incline than on the way out to the springs. Claire's thigh muscles started to burn as she pushed herself up the hill, silently thanking Nathan for the strengthening exercises he took the Guerrilla Yoga class through every day. The class was billed as a relaxation method for the chronically stressed. She'd become addicted to it on her first day after hearing Mr. Tough-Guy Yoga Instructor shout "Go to the happy place" while delivering a kick powerful enough to knock out a grown man. Something about it appealed to her sense of humor, she supposed, stopping for a moment to catch her breath.

"Are you doing all right? Your ribs bothering you?" John caught up with her, and she was disgusted to notice that he wasn't even breathing heavily.

"No, I'm fine," she panted. "I just needed to stop for a—"

Claire winced as the telltale ringing of her cell phone interrupted what had started out as a pleasant conversation. Reaching an arm over her shoulder, she tried fishing the phone out.

"Here, let me get that for you."

Later, after she'd had time to reflect, Claire realized she should have suspected something of his intent by the overly helpful tone of John's voice. However, she didn't think anything of it now, and turned her back to him for assistance as the ringing continued. She watched as John freed the black phone from her pack, then waited dumbly, her hand outstretched, as he took a step toward the edge of the trail and raised his arm.

Realizing his intention a split second too late, Claire stood transfixed in horror as John hurled her ringing phone over the cliff.

Her feet, which had been rooted to the ground seconds before, suddenly gained wings. Racing to the edge of the cliff, Claire stopped mere inches from the drop-off, watching her beloved cell phone plummet toward the ground.

"Get back from there." John's voice sounded rough in Claire's ears.

"You've destroyed my phone." She continued to stare at the bottom of the canyon in disbelief.

"Uh-huh. Now, get back from the edge of that cliff."

Her head whipped around, eyes narrowed, all thoughts of her previous remorse lying in pieces on the ground with her shattered telephone. "How dare you! That phone was my property and you had no right to take it."

John raised his eyebrows. "*You're* giving *me* a lecture on theft? That's rich. After you get back over here, perhaps you'd like to tell me where your fiancé's—"

"Ex-fiancé," she shouted, crossing her arms over her chest and refusing to budge.

"Yes, maybe you'd like to tell me where a particularly personal item of your ex-fiancé's ended up this morning? We can discuss it right after you get back on the trail."

His repeated request—no, make that order—to get away from the edge of the cliff finally sank in to Claire's brain. Why was he so concerned with where she was standing, and why was he standing at the edge of the trail as if his feet had turned to concrete? A sudden suspicion wiggled into her consciousness. Was it possible that Tarzan here was afraid of heights?

"If you want me to get back on the trail, why don't you come over here and make me?" she taunted. She thought her guess might have been incorrect when John took a step toward her. Fortunately, she resisted the urge to take a step backward, since that move would have had her tumbling down the steep incline.

"I'm not playing games with you, Claire. Get over here now."

He stopped a good five feet from her and issued his command. Claire felt a glimmer of satisfaction in having her suspicion proved true. Her mouth turned up in a gloating smile. "Okay, Mr. Audubon, whatever you say."

She started to take a step forward when her foot slipped on some loose rocks. The unaccustomed weight of the pack on her shoulders threatened to pull her backward over the cliff. Struggling to regain her balance, her arms started cycling in the air as if she were a human windmill. Her last thought before she was slammed up against something very hard, her breath whooshing out of her lungs, was that she was really starting to dislike this vacation.

John pulled her back from the edge.

He could feel his own heart racing wildly, thumping against his chest where he held Claire's head crushed against him.

She would have gone over. His mind conjured up an image of her broken body lying at the bottom of the cliff and his hand tightened in her silky hair. His heart continued pumping too much blood too quickly through his veins.

"Uh, John?" Claire asked, after a moment.

"Yes?" He felt the adrenaline changing to something else as she stirred against him, her soft breath caressing the skin at the open neck of his shirt.

"I can't breathe."

He loosened his grip, but not by much. She looked up at him. Her gray eyes held a touch of remaining fright, and something else; something that was probably mirrored in his own eyes, John guessed. Attraction. Pure, physical, animal attraction to a member of the opposite sex.

Her lips were so close, and the desire to taste her was too strong to resist. He lowered his head, intending to just brush his mouth over hers, but his good intentions flew over the cliff as their lips met and his heightened emotions exploded. He buried his hands in her hair, caressing the back of Claire's neck as she pressed her hips against his. He felt himself get hard as she rubbed against him like a hungry cat. Cool mountain air tickled his stomach, and he realized her fingers had untucked his shirt from the waistband of his jeans.

Sliding his lips across her cheek, he kissed the tender skin just under her ear, and nipped her earlobe lightly. She rewarded him with a muffled groan as he slipped his hands inside her ragged T-shirt, running his hands up her rib cage and barely brushing the sides of her breasts. John tried to move his hands lower, to get his hands on the firm backside he'd been watching all morning, but the straps of her backpack got in his way.

He was in the process of sliding her pack down her arms when a familiar voice interrupted, "Um, John? I, uh, came back to check on you. Are you guys all right . . . I mean, uh . . ." Kyle's embarrassed stutter trailed off.

John kept Claire pressed tightly to his body as he raised his head. The entire group of hikers were gathered, of course, and he wondered how long they'd been there, watching the free peep show. "Yes, Kyle. We're fine. Why don't you go on ahead, and we'll catch up in a minute?"

"A minute? Boy, he works fast." John heard Bryan Edwards's snide comment, and briefly considered finishing the job Claire had started two days ago. He decided the other man wasn't worth the effort, and turned his attention back to Claire, who had her nose buried in his chest.

"I'm not going to apologize for what just happened," he said softly. "We're two consenting adults and it's obvious we're attracted to one another, although for the life of me, I can't figure out why."

"Well. That certainly makes me feel better." Claire pushed away from him, awkwardly reshouldering her pack. She felt the combined heat of embarrassment and anger creep up her face as she turned to rejoin the hikers. Once again, she'd made a fool out of herself in front of everyone. She felt like an incompetent laughingstock, as if all of her actions were being controlled by some evil puppeteer, whose only intent was to see how much humiliation Claire could take before she cracked.

A firm hand grabbed her arm, forcing her to stop.

"Look, Claire, it was just a kiss. It's not worth getting upset over."

"You're absolutely right. It was nothing," Claire said, then yanked her arm out of John's grip, continuing on alone to catch up with the others.

Chapter 9

JOHN STARED UNSEEINGLY AT THE REPORT SITTING IN front of him and attempted to will away his thoughts of how it had felt to have Claire's lithe body pressed against his. He also tried to reconcile himself to the fact that it was most likely never going to happen again. In trying to ease her embarrassment at being caught in the act by Kyle, he'd said the wrong thing. You didn't tell a woman who'd just given you a kiss that made you forget where you were that it was no big deal.

He shook his head, attempting to rid his mind of thoughts of Claire, and refocused on the report.

"What's wrong with these expense numbers?" he muttered to himself after a moment. Something wasn't right, but he couldn't quite put his finger on what it was.

"I don't know, would you like me to take a look at it for you?"

John's head jerked toward the doorway in surprise. He'd been so engrossed in his thoughts, he hadn't heard the footsteps approaching him.

His mother looked impeccable, as always, her trim body clothed in a tailored ivory pantsuit with matching shoes and purse, a pale pink silk blouse unbuttoned casually at the neck, and a string of pearls at her throat. John felt sloppy in comparison, even though he'd changed into clean clothes after the morning hike. Somehow, she always made him feel dirty and rumpled, like a seven-year-old who'd been out playing in the mud.

"Hello, Mom. I didn't hear you come in."

Mary Jane McBride watched her son come toward her to give her the obligatory peck on her cheek. Although she knew she was biased, she'd always thought he was one of the most handsome men she knew. Turning her cheek to receive his kiss, she briefly considered adding a hug to their normal ritual greeting, then gave up the idea with a soft sigh.

"I wasn't sure you'd be home so I let myself in with the key you gave me. I hope that's all right."

"Yes, of course. I was just working."

"Well, don't stop on my account. I can get myself settled in. Which room shall I take?"

"Whichever one you prefer. They're both made up for guests." John shrugged, then leaned back in his chair, his green eyes pinning her to the spot. "So, you never did tell me why you're taking time off from work."

Her son seemed to have the uncanny knack for looking right into her eyes and finding whatever weakness was lurking there. Mary Jane blinked, then turned her head to look out the window at the light blue sky filled with wispy puffs of clouds before answering. "We just completed a rather stressful buyout and I was hoping to relax for awhile. But if I'm going to be in your way, I can make other plans."

John's chair squeaked as he brought it upright. "No, don't be silly. You won't be in the way at all. I'm just surprised that you're able to stay for so long."

"Yes, it's not often that I get a whole week to call my own. I'm really looking forward to it," she said cheerfully. "Well, I'll let you get back to work while I get settled in. And I really would be glad to help you with those expense numbers."

John muttered something noncommittal and Mary Jane knew that he wouldn't take her up on her offer. With a shrug, she crossed the living room and poked her head into the first bedroom. Both of the guest rooms faced the river and shared a bath, so it really didn't matter to Mary Jane which she chose. In the end, she decided on the one farthest away from her son's room. She didn't know if John had a girlfriend right now, and she figured there were some things a mother just didn't need to hear.

The room she chose was tastefully decorated in peach

and green. She'd been impressed the first time she'd seen the finished lodge, glad that it was rustically elegant rather than tacky rustic. She'd been afraid that some decorator would come along and dress the place from head to toe with the mounted heads of dead animals and bearskin rugs. Mary Jane smiled ruefully as she removed her clothes from her suitcase, placing them neatly in the hand-painted cedar armoire.

Her unpacking completed, she sat in one of the heavy armchairs facing the windows and watched the river meander by, enjoying the first real moment of quiet she'd had in a long time. She'd acknowledged long ago that her son did not need her help. Even though she had started her own cosmetics company almost thirty years ago and built it into one of the largest and most successful companies of its kind, John had not once asked her for her help in setting up or running his own company.

When he'd first started Outdoor Adventures, right after he and Delilah separated, Mary Jane suspected his reticence to ask for her help might be due to her continued employment of his soon-to-be-ex-wife. Rationally, she knew that the fact that John and Delilah were divorced shouldn't have any bearing on her decision to employ, and promote, her ex-daughter-in-law. Emotionally, however, she knew that John had every right to resent her for her apparent show of loyalty to his ex-wife.

Looking out at the cloudless sky, Mary Jane sighed. John had never said anything to her about how he felt about her continued relationship with Delilah, but, then, had she really expected him to? He had always been so much closer to his father. They'd both shared a love for the outdoors that Mary Jane didn't quite understand and never felt part of. Mary Jane had loved her husband completely, accepting his great love of nature just as he did her involvement in the world of business. Still, she'd always been envious of the close relationship between father and son. Sometimes, when she came home from a particularly long business trip, it would have felt good if her son expressed any sort of

feelings that he'd missed her. Instead, he treated her po-
litely, answered all her questions about school and sports
and Boy Scouts, but never once did she feel that he wished
she wasn't gone so much.

Sometimes she'd watch them, father and son, heads bent
together over some project or another, and she felt—what
was the word?—superfluous. Yes, that was it. As if she
could just disappear and they wouldn't even know she was
gone.

She knew Hunter's sudden death from a heart attack had
hit John hard. Mary Jane remembered Delilah mentioning
at the time that John was finally taking his job at the FBI
more seriously, was really starting to put in the effort that
would lead to a promotion. And then one day, John called
her on her personal line at the office and told her that he
and Delilah were getting divorced, that he had resigned
from the FBI, and that he was going to be virtually un-
reachable for the next few months. Just wanted to let her
know. Don't worry about anything. I'm leaving tomorrow
morning and I'll call you later.

Then he was gone. And she was his mother, so of course
she worried. Every day for months she worried, wishing
that he could share what he was feeling with her; that he
would ask for her advice, that they could share their pain
at losing her husband and his father. Instead, they each dealt
with their pain in their own way, each taking their own
route to the same place.

John had returned months later—he just showed up on
her doorstep one night as if he'd never been gone. And she
looked into his dark green eyes, eyes that were so much
like his father's, and she wanted to hug him tight, tell him
how much she loved him, and scold him for being away
for so long and not calling her more often. But instead she
just invited him in, offered him a drink, and asked him how
he was as if he were some stranger and she was merely
making polite small talk at some damned cocktail party.

He'd looked happy, though, and seemed more comfortable around her, as if perhaps he were more comfortable

with himself, too. Then he told her that he'd put together a new business venture, something that would let him combine his love of the outdoors with his need to make a living, he'd said dryly.

She'd listened to his idea and offered to help him find backers, put together a business plan, do a market study. And was hugely disappointed to find out that it was already done. He didn't need her help. She shouldn't have been surprised. He never had.

The little clock on the nightstand chimed four o'clock. No, her son didn't seem to need anyone's help, least of all his mother's. She held back another sigh.

"You've come here to relax and enjoy yourself. Now, stop whining, and get on with it," she scolded herself.

Picking up the high heels she'd discarded earlier and stacking them neatly in the armoire, she proceeded to change out of her business attire and into her relax-and-enjoy-yourself clothes.

What seemed strange to her now was that while her son never seemed to need her help, she had come running to him with one of the biggest decisions of her life hanging over her head. She wished she could talk to John about it, but the timing just hadn't seemed right. She hoped the solitude would help her make her decision. The offer to sell Mary Jane Cosmetics was a fair one, but was she ready to quit? What would she do with her time, if not work?

She stopped with a hand on the doorknob and considered the question that was troubling her most, the one she hoped to find an answer to somewhere in the Colorado wilderness.

"Without work, who am I?"

Mary Jane closed the door behind her, leaving the whispered question to echo in the empty room.

Claire's ribs ached as she tugged off the hideous pink sweats she'd worn for the hike and changed into a pair of blue nylon running shorts with gold piping down the side. She would have liked to curl up in John's bathtub with a good book and a glass of wine, but that would have to wait

until after he'd left on the sunset hike. She'd checked out
his schedule by looking at the sign-up sheets down in the
lobby. He was leading the sunset hike tonight, a one-day
whitewater rafting trip tomorrow, the hot springs and sunset
hikes on Wednesday and Thursday, then the final overnight
rafting trip on Friday and Saturday. She'd noticed that he
was also leading one of the horseback-riding tours. Now,
with her sore muscles, she almost wished she rode, anticipating how nice it would be to let the horse do all the work
for once.

She would have liked to avoid John McBride entirely
for the rest of her vacation, but wasn't about to spend the
next six days holed up in this tiny room. Besides, now that
she'd had time to reflect, she'd decided to agree with him.
After all, what was one little kiss between consenting
adults? If he wasn't going to be embarrassed by their public
display of lust, then why should she? She'd just do her best
to try to forget that it had ever happened and make sure it
didn't happen again.

Tossing her patriotic flannel shirt onto the boxes in the
corner of her room, she pulled on another tattered T-shirt,
this one with Garth Brooks's likeness on the front. Since
she was planning to spend the afternoon sitting on her bed
working, she figured she'd save her one decent outfit for
dinner. The clothes Dana had brought up to her didn't leave
her with a whole lot of choice in terms of her attire.

"You're not here to win a fashion contest," she admonished herself, shoving the pile of lost-and-found clothes off
the end of her bed with one red-polished toe.

"Good thing, because I'd lose hands down," she muttered in disgust as she fished her stolen—uh, scratch that,
she thought, commandeered, yes that was better—her commandeered phone out from under the bed. Stretching the
cord out into the hallway, Claire plugged one end into
the jack on the wall and dialed the toll-free number for the
airline.

After the usual maze of electronic greetings, Claire finally got through to what she hoped was a live person in

the missing-baggage department. The man asked for her claim ticket number, which she read off from the stub stapled to her itinerary.

"Well, let's just take a look-see in our computer and see what we can find out about your missing suitcase."

Claire imagined the man waving his hands over the monitor as if it were a crystal ball. With her luck, it was probably more like one of those fortune-telling eight balls she'd played with as a kid; the one whose only answers seemed to be "No Way" and "Ask Me Again."

"Hmm. You say you were on a flight out to Colorado?"

"Yes. On Saturday."

"Hmm."

Claire counted to ten and waited for the man to say something a bit more helpful than "hmm."

"It says here your bags are in Bombay."

"Bombay?" Claire's voice came out in a squeak. Clearing her throat, she started again. "Do you mean Bombay, India?"

"Yes, ma'am. That's what my computer says."

Resting her forehead in one hand, Claire forced herself to continue. "Well, I'm glad my luggage is enjoying a round-the-world trip, but I'm in Colorado. Could you tell me when I might expect to see my suitcase again?"

"Hmm."

The man paused, and Claire took a deep, calming breath.

"We'll do our best to get it to you by Wednesday."

Claire thanked the man and hung up, grateful that at least she'd have her own clothes before they left on the final rafting trip on Friday.

With that chore done, she unhooked the phone line from the telephone and plugged it into her laptop, ready to get down to business. After dialing in to the Allied network, she double-clicked the icon to connect her to the Internet. Her mouth turned up a bit at the corners as she contemplated her first task.

She was going cell phone shopping. If John McBride thought he could thwart her so easily, he was in for a big surprise. As she surfed to the electronics section of the Web site, she wondered if Amazon.com would agree to bill him for the charge. Probably not, she guessed, but it would be worth a try.

Her eyes widened like a kid at the toy store as the selection of phones danced across her screen. It had been two years since she'd bought a new one, and there were all sorts of new features available now that hadn't even been dreamed of two years ago.

Wireless Internet.

E-mail Compatibility.

Electronic Calendar With Automatic Alarms.

Global Satellite Positioning.

An option that would turn the display into a mirror for sixty seconds so she could pretend to check her messages when she was really checking to see if she had spinach stuck in her teeth. Wow. That was cool.

Her breathing quickened. If she hadn't known better, Claire thought she might be on the verge of an orgasm. In the silence of her room, she snorted at that thought. If she was thinking about orgasms and cell phones in the same breath, perhaps she was spending way too much time with her work.

She clicked on the model with the most goodies per dollar, then discovered that she had to enter a credit card number in order to get it shipped. She'd done some strange things these last few days, but she was not going to stoop to outright theft of someone else's credit card. Instead, she pulled out her own American Express and figured, if nothing else, she'd send John a bill after her vacation was over. In the meantime, she needed a cell phone now. She paid the extra for express shipping—although since it was Sunday that meant that she wouldn't get it until Tuesday—then thought about doing some electronic retail therapy while she was in a shopping mood. It seemed silly, though, considering she'd spent a small fortune on the clothes that would be here the day after tomorrow.

Instead, she closed her Internet connection and turned

her attention back to work. She'd take care of e-mails first, then voice mails, then continue working on the comparative analysis she'd started yesterday. She wanted to see how Art's accounts compared to hers, then see if she could spot any trends in his accounts that could help her focus on suggestions for improvements.

With the data she'd downloaded yesterday, she had already done an overall account comparison. Claire was almost disappointed when six out of ten accounts showed comparable results to hers, which meant that it would be hard for her to make any noticeable difference in the few months she'd be helping out. Oddly enough, all four accounts that showed worse results than she had expected were handled by Robert Edwards, Bryan's father. She had no idea why that was the case and wanted to look closer at each one to see if she could find the answer. However, all that was going to have to wait until after she'd finished with the day-to-day issues that plagued her existence.

Watching with dismay as her mailbox filled up with unread messages, she figured it might be awhile before that time came.

After recalculating the figures from the faxed report, John still hadn't figured out what was wrong with the expense numbers from the operation in Hawaii. And he was not particularly happy about it.

Instead of continuing to brood over it, he hoped this could all be solved with one simple phone call. He picked up the phone to call the office on Kauai and was met with a strange screeching sound. Hanging up, he tried again, but still wasn't able to get a regular dial tone. He switched over to the line he used for faxes and that seemed to be working fine. As he left a message for the office manager, he wrote a note to himself to have the phone company check out his main line as soon as possible.

Who was it who said that technology was supposed to make their lives easier?

Whoever it was, John thought as he hung up the phone, should be tossed over the cliff with Claire's cell phone.

Chapter 10

AS MUCH AS SHE PRIDED HERSELF ON BEING ABLE TO FIG-
ure things out for herself, Claire decided it wasn't worth
spending her entire vacation staring at charts and numbers
that made no more sense now than they had two hours ago.
She was ready to admit defeat. She couldn't figure out why
the four accounts handled by Robert Edwards had claims
costs that were so much higher than her boss's other accounts. So, rather than spending any more time with it this
afternoon, Claire figured she'd just give up and call Robert.

It wasn't only pride that kept her from calling her ex-
fiancé's father. There was something about Robert that gave
her the creeps. But, she told herself, one phone call certainly wasn't going to kill her. So she picked up her commandeered telephone and dialed the number for Unity Risk
Services in Seattle.

Robert's assistant put her on hold and Claire listened to
Unity's canned advertisement. The announcer's voice could
best be described as unflaggingly chipper—an incongruous
tone for something as dull as insurance, Claire thought with
a smile.

"Robert Edwards." A serious voice interrupted the insurance brokerage cheerleader's rah-rahing.

Claire cleared her throat, straightened her shoulders, and
reminded herself she was a capable grown-up. Besides, it
wasn't as if Robert were *her* father, she told herself, forcing
her most professional voice. "Yes, Robert. This is Claire
Brown. How are you?"

"Fine, fine. How can I help you?"

She opened her mouth, then shut it again. She really
didn't know the best way to broach the subject. Cursing
herself for not thinking this through before calling, Claire

stalled with, "You got my e-mail that I'm going to be working on Art Engleheart's accounts for the next few months while he's recuperating from surgery?"

"Yes."

Rats. That hadn't worked very well as a stall tactic. What could she say? Robert, I know you're a successful executive but can you tell me why your accounts are all screwed up? Right. Very smooth.

"Um. Yes. Well, I've been working to familiarize myself with Art's accounts these last few days." She paused, hoping Robert would start talking and give her time to think.

He didn't.

The silence lengthened, so Claire had no choice but to jump right in. "Okay. So I've been doing a lot of work, comparing average payouts of all Art's accounts to see if I could spot any areas for improvement. I've found that four of your accounts have much higher claim costs than I would have expected. Is there any reason you can think of for this?"

This time the silence was on Robert's end. Claire chewed on her index finger and shifted positions on the bed while she waited for a response. She wasn't always the best at being tactful. She knew that was something she had to work on if she wanted to continue to climb the corporate ladder. Which she did. Of course. Why else was she working this hard, if not to get promoted?

The question made her uncomfortable so she switched fingers and continued waiting.

"You know, Claire, it's difficult for me to offer any insights without the benefit of having your data in front of me. I'm sure there's some reason for these anomalies, one that would be evident to me if I could just see the same information you're looking at. Why don't you send me something, and I'll give you a call once I've figured it out?"

Claire frowned at the smooth tone of Robert's voice. There was no reason she couldn't print out the graphs she'd produced and fax them over. Except, of course, she didn't have a printer. She'd spied one in John's office, but she was barely going to have time to take advantage of his bathtub before he returned from the sunset hike, much less hook up her computer to his printer, print the graphs, and get them faxed. If she had to choose between a long, leisurely soak and a session at the printer . . . well, she *was* on vacation, after all.

"It will be tomorrow afternoon before I can get them off to you," she said finally.

"Why don't you e-mail them to me?" Robert suggested.

Claire hesitated. Her file included data from clients of other insurance brokers, information she didn't feel comfortable sharing with Robert Edwards. In order to clean it up, she'd have to spend hours moving data from one file to another and she didn't want to spend her entire vacation working. He'd just have to wait until she had a chance to get to it. She glanced at her watch. If she didn't get off the phone soon, she'd miss her opportunity to borrow John's tub. That thought made her decision easy.

"It's not like this is an emergency," she said. "It'll just have to wait until tomorrow."

With Robert's good-bye ringing in her ears, Claire logged off her computer, then groaned as she sat up and pressed her back to the wall behind the bed. She rubbed her upper arms, which ached from hunching over her laptop for hours, then groaned again as she moved her legs from their cross-legged position. Her left foot was tingling, a sure sign that all the blood was gone from it and, sure enough, the ten thousand tiny stinging bees told her that circulation was now being restored.

She wriggled her toes, grimacing against the odd pain, then stood up.

John would have been gone for an hour now, leading the so-called sunset hike, a two-hour stroll that ended just as the sun was going down. Even she, who admittedly knew very little of the rules of the outdoors, knew it would be foolish to go for a hike during the darkness unless it was absolutely necessary. John McBride didn't seem like the foolish type. Pig-headed, stubborn, and obnoxious maybe,

Claire thought as she stretched her aching muscles, but not foolish.

He also had a great bathtub, an amenity she intended to avail herself of before he could come back and catch her in the act. Claire quickly gathered up her toiletries and some clean clothes. The way she figured it, she had just under an hour to enjoy soaking away the soreness of her muscles and she intended to enjoy every moment of it.

She locked the door to her tiny room, hoping that John hadn't started doing the same. The knob turned smoothly in her hand and Claire sent up a silent thanks for the unsuspecting nature of Mr. McBride.

"Hi, dog." She patted the retriever's familiar golden head as he greeted her at the door, his tail wagging.

As she passed the kitchen, she briefly considered foraging for a glass of chardonnay to make her bathing experience complete, but rummaging around in his refrigerator seemed like too much of an invasion of his privacy, even for her. Besides that, she thought as she turned the hot water on full power and tempered it with a tiny bit of cold, she didn't want to take any chances on being discovered.

Shedding her clothes, Claire stepped into the mounting tide of hot water, wishing she'd been able to find some scented bath salts in the entirely masculine bathroom.

"It just figures that a man wouldn't think about such things," she said to the dog as he padded into the bathroom. "But at least the jets work," she muttered, pushing the button to turn on the bubbly, whirlpool effect.

She figured she had twenty minutes to just relax, then she'd have to shampoo her hair, get washed up, and get herself out of there. Claire patted the dog's head and closed her eyes as the soothing jets pulsed water over her sore muscles.

"Uh, hello there."

Claire's eyes flew open at the woman's greeting and she scrunched down into the tub, burying herself in frothy water up to her nose.

"I'm sorry, I didn't mean to startle you." The woman eyed her curiously.

Claire considered sliding all the way underwater, then figured that she would have to come up for air sometime anyway. "Yes, uh, hello. I wasn't expecting anyone."

"I'm John's mother, Mary Jane McBride. He obviously didn't warn you that I was coming to visit."

Claire tried to hide a blush, hoping that the bubbles from the jets were sufficiently hiding her naked body. She wasn't sure any of Miss Manners's columns had covered meeting someone's mother while you were naked in that someone's bathtub, but if she had, Claire was sure she must have missed it. She couldn't offer more than a hand in greeting or Mrs. McBride would get quite an eyeful, but she didn't want to be rude.

"Don't worry, dear, considering the circumstances, we can shake hands later," Mrs. McBride said with more than a hint of good humor.

Claire laughed, the tension of the moment gone. "Thank you, I was just wondering what Emily Post would suggest in a situation like this."

"I'm sure there's a rule for it somewhere." Mrs. McBride's bright blue eyes crinkled at the corners as she smiled. She was a beautiful woman, with the most perfect skin Claire had ever seen.

"Now, what's your name, dear? I'm afraid John didn't tell me any more about you than he told you about me. You'd think he could have at least warned me that he had a new girlfriend," she protested. "I thought you were an intruder."

Claire briefly considered not telling the whole truth to John's mother, who seemed genuinely happy to find that her son had a new girlfriend, even one he hadn't told her about. But good sense prevailed. After all, it would only take one moment of seeing John and Claire together for his mother to realize that there was nothing between them. Well, nothing except a strange attraction that they weren't going to do anything about, she amended silently.

John's mother continued to watch her quizzically.

"To tell you the truth, I am an intruder," Claire said sheepishly.

"Pardon me?"

"I'm not your son's girlfriend. My name is Claire Brown. I'm a guest here at the lodge and . . . well, it's a long story. Suffice it to say that my room didn't come with bathing facilities so I'm borrowing your son's."

"Oh." Mrs. McBride sounded disappointed, and Claire was almost sorry she'd told the truth.

"He doesn't even know I'm here," Claire told her conspiratorially, then added with a laugh, "As a matter of fact, he doesn't even know that I know he's the owner of the lodge."

"What?"

"Let's just say that your son and I got off on the wrong foot and if this were a three-legged race, one of us would have a broken leg by now."

Mrs. McBride smiled. "That doesn't surprise me. John's just like his father that way. Once he has his mind made up about something, it takes an awful lot to get him to change it."

"He's not the only one. I've been known to exhibit my own stubborn streak at times, as well," Claire admitted ruefully, then added with a hint of panic, "His father's not here, is he?" It was bad enough to be sitting here naked in front of a woman; she didn't need any more humiliation heaped on top of the situation.

"No, dear. His father, my husband, Hunter, died eight years ago," she said.

"Oh, I'm so sorry." Claire didn't know what else to say. The other woman's pain was easy to read on her face. "Hunter," she mused softly. "Did John name the lodge for his father?"

"Yes." Mary Jane smiled sadly. "They were so close, and as alike as two peas in a pod. Even their voices sounded the same. Sometimes, even now, when I talk to John he'll say something just the way his father did and—" Her voice broke off.

Claire didn't stop to think. She grabbed her towel off the ledge and, as best as she could, wrapped it modestly around herself before crossing the room to put an arm around Mrs. McBride's shoulders. She muttered something soothing as the other woman blinked back tears.

It was a moment before John's mother regained her composure and Claire could almost see the physical change in her as she did. Shoulders straightened, head came up. "I'm so sorry. I never do that," she apologized.

Claire leaned back on the edge of the bathroom counter and crossed her arms over her chest. "If I'd been married to someone that I loved for decades and he died, I'd miss him every day. I don't think there's any weakness in that. Your husband was lucky to have found someone who loved him that much. Given my track record, I doubt I'll ever find anyone who ever feels that way about me."

Mary Jane gratefully accepted the change in conversation. "That's ridiculous, my dear. Why, you shouldn't have any trouble finding someone wonderful."

"Oh, my problem isn't finding them," Claire said with a self-deprecating grin. "My problem is keeping them."

John's mother raised her eyebrows at that, but didn't answer.

Claire looked up at the clock on the wall and grimaced. So much for her leisurely soak.

"You should finish your bath." Mary Jane obviously read her concern. "John said he'd be back just after six-thirty so you've got less than half an hour till he gets home."

Claire smiled. "Thank you. I'll go back to using the employees' shower after this. I just couldn't resist a nice, hot bath."

"Nonsense. You can come over whenever you like. We'll keep it our little secret."

Claire smiled. Too bad Mary Jane McBride's annoying son wasn't anything like his charming mother.

* * *

John took a deep breath of cold, clean air and listened to the chattering of birds as they warned each other of the approach of alien wildlife.

When he'd started Outdoor Adventures six years ago, he had never dreamed how wildly successful the idea would be. It seemed that there were lots of people who enjoyed being pampered while participating in some kind of physical activity. He'd started out with three excursions: whitewater rafting in Colorado, bicycling in Kauai, and sailing in the Caribbean. Each excursion mixed the pleasure of being outdoors with luxurious sleeping arrangements, gourmet meals, and the knowledge that all the details would be taken care of by Outdoor Adventures. There had been a few bumps along the way, but within their first year they'd been written up in no fewer than ten national magazines, and business continued to double every year.

After he and Delilah separated, John decided he wanted a base of operations somewhere away from the noise and distraction of the city. Since most of his business dealings were done by phone, it didn't matter where his office was physically located. As soon as he'd seen it, John knew he'd found the perfect spot for Hunter's Lodge, named in honor of his father, who'd had so much to do with John's love of the outdoors. The grounds were perfect, with plenty of places to put hiking trails, easily accessible quiet fishing spots, and spring-fed pools at the far corner of the property.

It had taken him awhile to get used to the peacefulness of his surroundings. Although he'd spent quite a bit of time in the wilderness in his former career as a tracker with the FBI, it hadn't exactly been conducive to his peace of mind. It made a huge difference to him now, knowing he could enjoy the surroundings without having to be on the lookout for signs of death.

"If you would lose some weight, Peggy, this wouldn't be so hard for you." William Weber's words sliced through the chill Colorado air; a well-honed arrow aimed carelessly, thoughtlessly, at its target.

John blinked, startled out of his reverie by the other man's voice. He'd let Kyle take the lead on the sunset hike, preferring to follow along behind to take care of any stragglers. Now, he pulled his attention to the couple walking in front of him.

"Mr. Weber, why don't you take your son and go on ahead? I don't mind staying back here with your wife. To tell the truth, I'm a bit tired myself after the hike this morning." John took a step forward on the trail, stopping at Peggy Weber's side. The rest of the group was quite a bit farther up the trail and it was obvious that William Weber wasn't happy lagging at the end of the line with his wife.

John tamped down his anger at the look of disgust William Weber shot his wife before hauling Billy up in his arms and picking up his pace to reach the other hikers.

"William's a leader. He just can't stand to take things slowly," Peggy mumbled, looking down at her shoes.

William's an asshole, John thought, but kept it to himself. The evening hike was supposed to be a leisurely, even romantic, walk to view the golden-orange sunset as it splashed over the distant mountains. It was not intended to be a race to some imaginary finish line; no prizes were given to the man who reached the turnaround point first. Reminding himself that the Webers' relationship was none of his business, John changed the subject. "There's a breathtaking view of the valley right around the next corner. With the light clouds we've got this evening, the colors should be incredible."

They spent the next half hour meandering along the trail, chatting idly about the native flora and fauna as John waited for the group to reach the turnaround spot and start heading back toward him. When he saw the hikers returning, John wasn't surprised to see William Weber in the lead, the others following at a more unhurried pace.

Something nagged at John at the first sight of William striding confidently toward them; some niggling sense that something wasn't quite right. But what was it? Mr. Weber wasn't limping, he seemed physically fit, so what was wrong?

Trying to shake off the disturbing feeling, John turned to Mrs. Weber, ready to suggest they turn around and start heading back. It was the sight of the small blue and green jacket thrown casually over Peggy's arm that stopped him. Turning back to watch the line of hikers near, John searched for a glimpse of Billy as William Weber approached.

"Mr. Weber, where's your son?"

William Weber squinted his eyes, then blinked as if coming out of a trance. "Huh?"

"Your son, Mr. Weber. Where is he?"

"William, where is Billy?" Peggy echoed, her voice rising anxiously.

Mr. Weber looked back at the trail, as if expecting to see his son trotting along with the other hikers. "I . . . uh . . . I don't know. He was walking right next to me a minute ago."

"Billy?" Peggy called, walking quickly toward the group of hikers. "Billy, where are you?"

"Mrs. Weber, I need you to stay calm. We're going to find your son." Laying a hand on Peggy's shoulder, John turned to the assembled group. "Who was the last person to see Billy?"

Amid the mutterings of the hikers, John noticed the downturned head of one of George Isler's granddaughters. Giving Peggy's shoulder a reassuring squeeze, John walked over to the girl, stopping right in front of her.

"Hi, there. Lisa, isn't it?"

The girl looked up at him, nodding. John looked into her dark brown eyes and saw the unmistakable glint of fear and shame she was trying to hide.

"Did you see Billy, Lisa?"

She hesitated, and John looked over to see Mr. Isler watching his youngest granddaughter. "Lisa?" John asked again.

Her eyes started to fill with tears and she tried to blink

them back. "Yes, I saw him. He . . . he was bugging me, you know, whining that he was tired. He wanted me to pick him up, but I—" She choked on a sob.

John waited silently for the girl to continue.

"Lisa, what did you do?" Mr. Isler asked quietly.

Tears streamed down her face and she refused to look at her grandfather as she finished. "Oh, Grandpa, I just left him there on the trail. He's probably going to die, and it's all my fault," she wailed.

No, John thought, his own fear rising. Not another missing child. The picture of a small blue tennis shoe seared into his brain. Caked with dirt, the laces untied, sitting by itself on a carpet of decaying leaves. Two feet away, a tiny foot.

He shook his head. No. It wasn't going to end like that. He wouldn't let it happen again.

"Lisa, this isn't your fault. Now, I need you to stay calm and help me. Can you show me where you last saw Billy?"

Her straight brown hair brushed her chin as Lisa nodded.

"Okay. Kyle, keep everyone here for now. I'll let you know if we need to send someone back to the lodge for help. Mr. Isler, can you come with us?"

"I'm coming, too," William Weber interrupted.

John looked at Billy's father coldly. "No, you're not, Mr. Weber. Stay here with your wife." John met the other man's gaze straight-on, unblinking. Too many people around a search site only made matters worse; evidence destroyed by careless footsteps, witnesses distracted, the possibility that the person helping would also become lost. He wanted Lisa's grandfather to come along to help keep the girl calm and focused, and he didn't need anyone else's assistance, especially the man whose responsibility it had been to watch Billy in the first place.

Herding George and Lisa Isler back down the trail from where they'd just come, John watched William Weber out of the corner of his eye to make sure the man stayed put. After a slight hesitation, William stopped, obviously deciding it was best to do as John had ordered.

The forest swallowed the sound of their footfalls as they walked, the only sound reaching John's ears that of Lisa's occasional sniffles. They'd walked at a fast clip for about fifteen minutes when Lisa stopped suddenly.

"Here. This is where I told Billy to go find his mother."

"Are you sure, honey?" George Isler asked.

Lisa looked down at the tops of her green canvas sneakers. "Yes, I'm sure. Heather wasn't feeling good and she sat down on that log for a minute." She gestured to a moss-covered tree that had fallen at the side of the trail. "I stayed with her, and that's when Billy asked me to pick him up." Lisa raised tear-soaked eyes to John's steady gaze. "The poor kid was tired and all he wanted was to sit in my lap for awhile until his mom could catch up. I left him here all by himself."

John swallowed, mentally counting the minutes the boy had been missing. A lot of bad things could happen to a small child out here, lost and alone. But Lisa Isler didn't need to know that, not yet. "I need to know where to start looking for Billy. When you left, was he headed back down the trail?"

Lisa sniffed, a fat tear sliding down her cheek. "No. When Heather and I got up, he went over to the log and pulled himself up where we were sitting."

"Okay. Now, I want you two to stay right here. Try not to move around until I get back, I don't want any evidence blurred if we can help it."

"All right," George Isler agreed, putting an arm over his granddaughter's shoulder comfortingly as she laid her head in her hands and started crying in earnest.

Walking slowly, John looked carefully around the base of the log, hoping to find a small footprint in the soft earth. At least Billy was the only child on the hike, so it would be easy to tell his prints from everyone else's. Crouching down, John studied a slight indentation in the ground—a small oval with the familiar waffle-tread of children's shoes. Following the trail that Billy had left behind, John tried to quiet all thoughts of anything besides finding the next track. His feelings of sympathy for Lisa, his anger at Billy's father, and, most of all, his fear that he'd find another little boy lying forever still on the ground; all had to be ignored so he could concentrate on the task at hand.

"Billy?" John called, pushing aside some brush. There was a different sort of print here, a round indentation in the leaves that covered the ground and a slight skid from the soles of the small shoes. Billy must have slipped on the slight incline and fallen backward. A set of prints away from the slide showed that the boy had gotten to his feet, wandering farther off the trail.

John picked up his pace as the early evening air dipped a few degrees. It was going to get dark soon and, although he had a flashlight in his pack, following the boy's trail would get much more difficult in the waning light. Besides, Billy's mother had the little guy's coat, and he was probably starting to get cold by now. John called out for the boy again. He should have thought to get the jacket from Peggy, but everything except finding the boy had fled his mind.

Clenching his teeth, John continued scanning the ground for the trail. Memories crowded into his head; another forest, another boy. His last case before resigning, the one that had haunted him for the past six years.

He reached the edge of a clearing and stopped in his tracks.

No, it couldn't be.

Reaching out to steady himself, John felt the cold, smooth bark of the aspen tree under his palm. He closed his eyes, hoping the vision would be gone when he opened them again. He opened his eyes to the same scene he saw regularly in his nightmares.

The boy was lying facedown in the tall grass, hands curled up around his face, blue-jean-clad legs hugged tightly against his stomach.

John felt his knees weaken and involuntarily took a step backward, away from the clearing, away from his haunting memory. He watched as a golden leaf fluttered down from

one of the trees overhead, falling softly toward the boy's
body. It landed right next to one curled-up fist.

The boy's eyes flew open.

John released the breath he hadn't realized he'd been
holding. "Billy?" His voice was unsteady, clouded with
fear.

"I cold." Billy sat up, rubbing his eyes sleepily.

Willing his fumbling fingers to work properly, John un-
shouldered his backpack and rooted around for the extra
sweatshirt he'd packed for the hike. "Here you go, son.
Let's get this on you and get you back to your parents."

The sweatshirt draped past the boy's ankles when John
pulled it on over Billy's head. He picked the boy up and
Billy wriggled against his chest.

John tried not to clutch the child too tightly as he tried
to shove back the terror of the past. The inadequacy of his
own inner strength clawed at him, like it had every day
since his first case with the FBI. Others he worked with at
the Bureau had come to terms with facing death on a regular basis, but he had never been able to quiet the nightmares that plagued him every time he was forced to find
another lost soul. It was important work, he knew. Often,
finding the body provided clues that led to the conviction
of the killer, but John hadn't been able to live with the
trauma of the job and had quit.

Retracing his footsteps, he inhaled the clean scent of the
child in his arms. How many others might he have saved
if only he had been better at his job? If only he had been
strong enough to deal with the pain, there might be one, or
ten, or hundreds, of lives he could have saved.

But Delilah had been right. He couldn't hack it, and the
guilt gnawed at him like a hungry wolf.

John emerged from the forest with the boy in his arms
and pain wrenching at his heart.

"Is he all right?" George Isler asked.

John nodded, unable to push words past the dryness in
his throat.

"Can I hold him?" Lisa asked.

John let her take him, knowing the burden would help to alleviate some of the girl's guilt at leaving him alone.

The return to the lodge was made in a celebratory mood, although John didn't share the guests' overall sense of triumph at the return of the Webers' son. Catching Kyle alone a few hundred yards from the lodge, John said quietly, "From now on, you and I are on the buddy system where Billy Weber is concerned. Whenever he's along on one of our trips, we need to take turns being responsible for his whereabouts. Agreed?"

"You got it, boss. I don't want to go through *that* again. I was pretty scared that something might have happened to the kid back there."

"Me, too, Kyle. Me, too."

"Would you mind terribly if I didn't join you for dinner tonight, Mom?"

Mary Jane stood in the doorway of her son's office, noticing the glass of scotch balanced on a stack of papers beside him and the blank way he stared at his computer screen. She wanted to ask him what was wrong but, instead, she said, "No, of course not, dear. I'm used to having dinner alone."

John took a healthy swallow of his drink, then turned back to his computer.

As she let herself out into the hall and headed downstairs, Mary Jane felt sadness hanging heavy on her shoulders. She and John could be polite strangers instead of mother and son, she thought sadly, rounding the corner to the dining room.

"Hello there, Mrs. McBride." Claire's greeting interrupted Mary Jane's thoughts.

"Oh. Hello, Claire. I didn't hear you coming."

"Good, then I guess that spy training is finally paying off."

Mary Jane smiled at the younger woman. She liked a girl with a good sense of humor. After working with Delilah all these years, she had to admit that was one thing

John's ex-wife didn't have. She was all business, all the time. But Claire was a different sort altogether. Mary Jane wondered how Claire and John had gotten off on the wrong foot, and decided now was as good a time as any to find out. "Would you care to join me for dinner? My son has left me to my own devices this evening, and I'd enjoy the company."

"I'd love to. Maybe you can fill me in on the news I heard about Billy Weber's rescue this evening." Claire looped her arm in Mary Jane's as she led the way into the dining room.

"What's this about a rescue? John didn't tell me a thing," Mary Jane protested, taking a seat at a table near the crackling fire.

Claire shook her head and Mary Jane watched the firelight pick up the gold tones in the younger woman's hair. "It just figures, doesn't it? Whenever there's a good story to be told, men just clam up. They can talk for hours about stupid things like football or trucks, but give 'em something interesting to chat about, and they get laryngitis." She paused. "I heard from Dana Robinson that a little boy got lost during the evening hike and your son found him," Claire continued as she shook out her linen napkin and placed it neatly in her lap.

"So that must be why he wasn't feeling up to taking me to dinner," Mary Jane muttered absently.

"Pardon me?"

Mary Jane looked into Claire's lively gray eyes, wanting to share her feelings with someone. It had been so long since she'd had someone to talk to, and Claire Brown seemed like a nice girl. It was the good humor and lack of any hint of maliciousness in Claire's gaze that decided it. "Did you know that John used to be with the FBI?"

Claire's eyes opened wide with surprise. "No. What did he do?"

"He was a tracker. It was a skill he'd learned from his dad, and when he graduated from college, I think he wanted to find a job where he could use his talents, and not be stuck in an office. The FBI used him to look for missing persons where foul play was suspected. He got called in on all sorts of cases—child abduction, kidnapping, even searching for criminals."

"Why'd he quit?"

Mary Jane's response was delayed as a waiter came to take their order for drinks. Both she and Claire asked for glasses of white wine. "I don't know all the details," Mary Jane continued once the waiter had left. "But I accidentally interrupted an argument between John and his ex-wife, De-lilah, just before he resigned. I don't remember the exact words, but Delilah said something like 'I don't know why you let it bother you so much. It isn't as if you killed the kid.' Hunter once told me that John's job involved search-ing for dead bodies more often than not, so my guess is that John led a search for a missing child, and found the child dead."

"How awful."

"Hello, Miss Brown." Both women looked up, startled at the interruption.

"Oh, hello, Mr. Isler," Claire said, turning to John's mother. "Mary Jane, this is George Isler and his grand-daughters, Lisa and Heather. This is John's mother, Mary Jane McBride."

As she greeted the Islers, Mary Jane noticed the group looked decidedly unhappy. "Would you like to join us for dinner?" she offered, looking at Claire for approval at the intrusion.

Claire nodded vigorously. "Yes, please do. We won't take no for an answer," she added, leaving to fetch some chairs from a neighboring table.

"We'd love to, wouldn't we, girls?" Mr. Isler encour-aged. The girls nodded, but Mary Jane didn't think they really cared one way or the other. They were very pretty, both with shoulder-length brown hair and dark eyes that hinted of a deep sadness. She turned to George Isler, a stocky man she guessed to be around her age. He had a full head of silvery-gray hair and brown eyes that mirrored the look of his granddaughters.

As they all sat down, Mary Jane pushed aside worry for her own son and wondered what secrets were hidden in the hearts of this family.

Chapter 11

THE FIRE DANCED MERRILY IN THE FIREPLACE AS JOHN sipped a glass of cabernet.

His mother had gone off to bed right after she'd come back upstairs from dinner, claiming exhaustion from a long day of traveling and a slight case of jet lag. He took a sip of his wine, feeling agitated and not knowing what to do about it. If Jack hadn't been sleeping peacefully on the rug in front of the fire, he might have taken the dog for a moonlit romp to relieve some of his own nervous energy.

Leaning back on the couch, John stretched his legs out in front of him, his worn boots resting on the gleaming hardwood floor. Restlessly, he picked up the magazine he'd abandoned moments before, trying to concentrate on the article he'd been staring at for half an hour now. But instead of words, he saw pictures. Flashing images of those he had been too late to save. How many had there been?

Tens? Hundreds?

What did it matter? Even one lost soul was too much.

If he'd been better, faster, maybe he could have saved them. He should have trained longer, should have—

John's head jerked up as the shrill of the telephone interrupted his darkening thoughts. He hurried to answer it before it could wake his mother.

"Hello?"

"John? It's Calder Preston. From the Bureau."

John had recognized the voice immediately, but he had no idea what Calder would be calling him for now. "Yes, of course. How are you?"

"Good, thanks. I wasn't sure if you'd remember me after all these years."

"Sure I do," John answered. Hell, a job like that wasn't

easy to forget, even though he'd tried hard to erase the memories. "I heard you got transferred to the Computer Crimes Division."

"Yeah, and promoted to run the department last year. I'll take tracking cybercrooks over real bad guys any day of the week."

"I don't blame you. Congratulations." John had always respected Calder Preston. It was good to hear that the other man had found his niche at the Bureau.

"Thanks."

"Well, I'm sure you didn't call just to give me the news about your promotion. What's up?"

"No, I didn't call to talk about my job. I heard some gossip around here today that I thought you might be interested in. I tried calling earlier, but your phone's been busy all day."

"Yeah, I called the phone company. I think there's something wrong with the line," John answered absently. What in the world could Calder have heard that would have anything to do with him now, six years after John had resigned from the Bureau?

"Derrick Washington turned eighteen today and the state of Tennessee has released him."

John froze. Blond hair, red blood, blue tennis shoes, gold leaves. He shoved the picture back where it had come from and blinked, clearing his throat. "What does that have to do with me?"

"Word on the street is, he's been talking about you."

John was silent, staring out the window into the utter darkness of the forest beyond.

"Seems Derrick made friends with one of the guards, and for the last few weeks, all he's been talking about is you. The guard called the Bureau." Calder paused. "I talked to the guy this morning, just to make sure it wasn't some kind of hoax."

"And?" John asked.

"And the guard says that he caught Derrick writing your name on a pad of paper. He asked Derrick what that was all about, and Derrick said something like, 'He's the guy who put me away. I'm gonna get in touch with him when I get out of here.' Guard said he doesn't think he means you any harm, but to my way of thinking, it never hurts to be careful."

"Thanks for the warning."

"You're welcome, John. I just thought you should know." He paused again and John could hear the discomfort in his former colleague's voice as he continued. "Take care of yourself."

"I will. Thanks again."

John slowly replaced the phone on its cradle and went back to the couch, the magazine he'd been pretending to read forgotten as he stared blindly at the dancing flames in the fireplace.

The child was crying.

Sobbing.

Asking for his mother.

"Shut up, kid. Your fucking mother's dead," someone shouted.

But he didn't shut up.

He cried harder.

John couldn't see him, could only hear his cries.

Golden leaves were falling.

Falling all around him.

They were red and gold and his first thought was about how pretty it was in this forest.

If only the boy would stop crying.

"Shut up, kid!" the voice screamed.

So much anger. So much hatred.

So much pain.

It started to rain.

The leaves were becoming wet, heavy.

He tried to walk through them, had to get to the boy.

But the leaves were falling heavier now.

They were past his knees.

He couldn't step over them.

He tried to wade through them but their stems pulled at him, slowing him down.

The boy's cries were growing softer.

He wouldn't give up. Couldn't give up.

He fell, his mouth filling with blood.

The leaves had veins.

The leaves were bleeding.

He was drowning.

Drowning in blood.

The boy stopped crying.

John woke up, panting, gasping for air.

He bolted upright, panicked eyes moving across the room. He saw the river reflected in the moonlight, the dog curled up at the foot of the bed, the cat in a ball beside him.

He took a deep, calming breath, just as he'd been told to do, and fought down his anger and fear. It wasn't getting better. The nightmares were coming less often, but they were just as intense.

He turned to the empty pillow beside him, wishing it were a warm body instead. The loneliness was an ache inside him. It wasn't just a need for sex. He longed for that connection between two people who understood each other. He'd had it with his father, knew his parents had had it; believed, or at least convinced himself in the beginning, that he and Delilah had it.

But he'd been single now for almost six years. He wanted, needed, someone to talk to, someone to hold. He got out of bed, pulling on an old, comfortable pair of jeans. Jack looked up as he passed, gave him a wide-mouthed yawn, then went back to sleep.

John stepped out into the hall, walking the few steps to Claire's room.

He put his palms against the door, as if just being this close would be enough. The door felt warm and he rested his forehead against it for a moment, trying to clear his head. There was an undeniable attraction between them, something stronger than he had ever felt, pulling him to her. But would it be enough? Was sexual attraction the only thing they had in common? And how long did they have to find out? She would only be around through the weekend. Six more days. Was he really interested in yet another affair that had no hope of a future?

No.

The despair threatened to overwhelm him. He was tired of trivial relationships that meant nothing once they were over. He wanted something permanent. Something that would last beyond someone's vacation. He wanted a lifetime, not just a week.

He turned, then froze as the door behind him opened.

He turned back.

She was framed in the doorway with moonlight streaming in from the small window in the corner of her room. She wore his shirt. It was rumpled, as if this were not the first night she'd worn it to bed. Her blond hair was messy, tousled and sexy.

"I heard something," she said sleepily.

"It was me. I'm sorry I woke you."

"I wasn't asleep." She smiled.

"Why did you open the door?"

She looked up at him. Her light gray eyes collided with his and he felt the intensity behind her gaze. "I knew it was you."

"How?" he asked, taking a step toward her.

She took a step forward, closing the gap between them. "I could smell you." She lifted up the collar of the shirt she wore and sniffed, closing her eyes. She smelled man. Spice. Something unique that belonged only to the man standing a hair's breadth away.

She opened her eyes. He didn't touch her. She sensed he was waiting for something.

Permission perhaps?

The same urge that had made her open the door to him spurred her on. She touched his forearms, running her fingers lightly over the smattering of black hair that covered his skin. Her hands explored his shoulders, the taut muscles of his back. She pulled him into her room, closing the door behind him.

As their eyes met, Claire saw something in the dark green depths that made her feel oddly protective of the strong man standing in front of her. Sadness. Loneliness. She understood, knew exactly what it felt like to have only yourself to rely on when all you wanted was to curl up in someone's arms and feel comforted by their strength.

Well, she was lonely, too. And tired of sleeping with her laptop; although, being brutally honest with herself, she'd have to admit that cuddling up with her computer had provided her with more warmth than either of her ex-fiancés ever had. It had been a long time since she'd been made to feel like anything more than an obligation that needed to be satisfied. Just for tonight, she wanted to know that someone found her desirable.

John lowered his mouth to hers, his lips touching hers lightly, fleetingly.

His hands skimmed the length of her arms, down to her fingertips and back again. It felt so good to be touched, to be caressed as if there were no hurry to get this over with. Claire sighed, then deepened the kiss, opening her mouth against his.

John groaned, his hands against her back pulling her even closer. Claire could hear the pulse of hot blood pounding in her ears and wasn't sure if it emanated from her body or John's. The rough material of John's jeans rubbed against her thighs as she pressed herself against him. His hot breath tickled in her ear, sending shivers of sensation tickling across her skin.

"Mmm. That feels good." Her eyes fluttered closed as his lips traced the line of her neck, unhurriedly, the tip of his tongue touching here and there as he went.

Claire put her hands on his tight butt and pressed him into her. There was nothing like the feel of a nice, firm male butt in your hands, Claire thought as she felt his erection against her stomach. And nothing like knowing she had aroused that sort of . . . well, arousal in him. She ran her hands across his hips and up his naked back. He had very smooth skin for a man. Her fingers tingled as she slid them up into his hair.

John backed her up a step and captured her mouth again. His hands in her hair felt so good, like he was pinning her there to make sure she wasn't going to escape. His tongue teased hers and it was Claire's turn to groan. Kissing just wasn't enough. She'd never felt so aroused, so fast. She knew, could feel, that she was ready for him.

And he had barely even kissed her.

She was ready. It was time to make sure he was, too. She pulled back a bit so she could move her hands to a more strategic area of his body, somewhere that would guarantee his readiness in the next few minutes.

"Where do you think you're going?" John growled, taking a step forward, pressing the backs of her legs against the bed.

Claire giggled, then remembered that she was *not* a giggler. But John hadn't seemed to mind so she let it go. Instead, she raised her arms around his neck, curling a strand of his soft dark hair around her index finger. "I'm not going anywhere," she assured him, just before his mouth came back down on hers.

When he finally eased back, she dropped her arms back to his waist. She pulled open the top button of his jeans, then popped each one in succession, enjoying the peep show. It didn't take long to realize he was buck naked under his jeans.

John must have caught her staring at him. "I sleep in the nude," he said, an amused light in his emerald eyes.

"What if there's a fire?" Claire pictured him racing around the lodge with nothing but a bucket of water and giggled again. She couldn't help it.

He worked open the top button of her, or rather, *his* shirt with a smile playing on his lips. "Good question. Guess I never thought of it that way."

Two seconds later, Claire had stopped thinking about it, too. She'd stopped thinking about everything except the feel of John's work-roughened thumbs skimming over her nipples. She'd never felt that her breasts were particularly sexy, they were too small for that. But now she revised her opinion. John certainly didn't seem to be having a problem with them, and every pass of his fingers increased the pressure building up inside her.

She felt, heard, her breaths starting to come in pants, as if she couldn't get any air past the desire burning in her throat. She wanted to be in control again, wanted to know that she had the same power over him as he had over her. Even knowing she'd probably never see John McBride after her vacation was over, she wanted him. Now. Without any more foreplay. She was ready. He was ready. And if she stopped to think about what she was doing, she probably wouldn't have the nerve to go through with it.

She pulled off her light blue silk panties and pulled the shirt off her shoulders, then glared at him defiantly. She knew her body wasn't perfect. She was too short, her breasts were too small, and she wasn't curvaceous like John's date last night had been. But if he was turned off by her, she'd rather know it now, before things went any further.

John looked into her eyes. And smiled. "So that's how it's going to be, huh?"

She nodded.

"All right, we'll do it your way this time." He peeled off his jeans in one smooth movement.

They stood facing each other for the space of a heartbeat.

She was beautiful, her tousled hair reflecting the moonlight like a halo, standing before him like some naked, pint-sized Nordic goddess. "Come here," John said softly, holding out his arms. She stepped closer, fitting against him perfectly. He ran his hands slowly, tenderly, through her golden hair, feeling the strands of silk slide through his fingers. His hands moved lower, cupping her firm breasts, teasing her small pink nipples into hard little points. He groaned as she rubbed her distended nipples against him with a catlike purr.

The fear and anger of his nightmare weren't gone, but they were retreating, bit by bit, with each touch, each whisper of breath against heated skin. It's only sex, he reminded himself, then his thoughts shattered into a million fragmented pieces when Claire pushed him down onto the narrow bed and, without a moment's hesitation, took him inside her.

It took her body a minute to adjust to the intrusion, but the tightness felt good. She didn't remember ever making love with this kind of intensity. Claire looked down into John's glazed eyes. The sadness she'd seen in them earlier was gone, replaced by a desire she knew was mirrored in her own eyes. She was thankful for whatever it was that had brought him to her door, glad she could help ease his pain just as he was erasing her loneliness.

With a smile, she ran her fingers up the taut muscles of his stomach, letting him slide almost out of her. He groaned and tried to push himself back inside. Claire laughed, enjoying being in control. John gave her a mock growl, the mighty lion taming his lioness, then spanned his hands across her back.

Claire heard herself moan as John took control. Rolling them over awkwardly on the narrow cot, he pressed into her. This was even better, she thought, as he increased the tempo of their heated bodies colliding with one another. Their breathing quickened together. Faster breaths, as if there weren't enough oxygen in the tiny room to share. John murmured something into her ear, but Claire couldn't concentrate on what he said. Her fingers slid across the smooth skin of his back as she wrapped her legs around his waist and pressed herself into his thrusts.

Just the sound of his breathing in her ear was bringing her to the point of climax. Higher and hotter. Faster and farther. She couldn't wait any longer. The pressure behind her eyes exploded. All thoughts fled her brain, her mind turned black, and she moaned with an intensity she had never felt before.

Feeling the convulsions of her muscles against his erection, John came with a helpless groan, pulsing into her until, at last, he subsided and collapsed on top of her in a drained heap.

Chapter 12

WHAT HAD HE DONE? JOHN QUESTIONED HIMSELF, ANgrily shoving first one leg then the other into his jeans.

His hair, wet from a recent shower, rained droplets of water down his back as he yanked on his shirt. He knew Claire wasn't the right woman for him, knew she'd be gone from his life in less than a week. But he hadn't been strong enough to walk away from the temptation she offered, and she had felt so right. She'd felt so good, in fact, that he'd wanted her again almost immediately and sanity hadn't returned until he'd left her sleeping, curled into a ball like a well-fed cat.

He had sneaked back across the hall at 4 A.M. like some kind of thief, sliding into the tangled sheets he'd left hours before and staring at the ceiling for another hour before giving up any attempt at sleep. He glared at himself in the mirror, his dark shadow of a beard and bloodshot eyes giving him a sinister look.

Why did he continue to feel this intense physical attraction for Claire, even now after his body had been sated? What fatal flaw in his character kept him coming back to women whose only motivation was monetary success?

Years ago, he'd told himself he didn't want a woman like his mother, someone who had always been more interested in business than her own family, but then he'd married someone just like her. Then he'd faced the ultimate betrayal when Delilah had walked away just when he'd needed her most.

And now there was Claire. He couldn't get her out of his mind, her soft hands running over his body, those stormy gray eyes that had seen into his soul and eased his pain. But she was just like his mother, just like Delilah, driven to put her career ahead of everything else in her life.

He frowned at his image in the mirror. One night of sex, as good as it may have been, wasn't worth all of this. It had been a mistake, but now it was over. They were two consenting adults indulging their bodies in some sexual recreation, and that was it. It hadn't meant anything to Claire, he told himself, and it meant even less to him. She didn't care about him. She cared only about her computer. Her cell phone. Her work. He was just a sexual diversion, someone to replace the fiancé who'd deserted her on her romantic vacation. Well, that was fine. He had his work, too. He certainly didn't need somebody like her in his life.

John slammed out of the bathroom and out of his suite, neglecting to shave. The black shadow on his face matched his mood as he stormed into the hallway and past the door to Claire's room, giving it an angry look.

"All right, everybody, if you'll just give me your attention for a minute, I'll explain today's routine," Kyle Robinson announced.

Sitting in one of the oversized chairs in the lobby, Claire gnawed on her left index finger and shot John a sour look from under her lashes. She'd woken up to find he'd pulled the old Invisible Man routine on her. The realization that she'd been used and discarded like a dirty tissue hadn't improved her usual lack of morning cheerfulness.

She supposed she shouldn't have expected him to be there when she woke up. After all, she was looking for the same thing he was, right? Just a night of comfort in someone's arms, that's it. No strings, or emotions, attached. Just some good, old-fashioned sex to prove to herself that her ex-fiancé's defection hadn't beaten her. Right. That's all she'd wanted.

She looked over at John again, noticing the dark stubble on his chin. He looked dangerous, as if their encounter hadn't improved his mood at all, either. Claire felt a brief pang of . . . tenderness? Ruthlessly, she shoved away the remembrance of the pain she had seen in his eyes when she'd opened the door to him last night. He had obviously been more interested in her body than in any sympathy she might have mistakenly believed he needed. He hadn't wanted anything more from her than the proverbial roll in the hay. After he got what he wanted, he'd deserted her.

Well, that was just fine, she told herself. She'd forget about him, too. She'd forget about his strong arms, and how they'd felt so good wrapped around her while she faded off to sleep. And the silky feel of his legs entwined with hers, she'd forget about that, too. And the feel of his mouth on hers, his tongue doing delicious things to her skin. Forgotten as if they'd never happened.

Uh-huh.

Cursing silently, Claire wrapped her arms around herself. Damn. Why'd he have to go and awaken these feelings inside her, then abandon her as if last night had meant nothing? Kyle continued his spiel as Claire hugged herself, trying not to cry as she dreamed up a multitude of painful, torturous punishments for a certain haggard-looking man.

"We'll get everyone suited up outside. John and I will hand out wet suits, helmets, booties, and rain gear. Then we'll all get on the bus for the half-hour drive up to where we'll put in the rafts. We'll do our safety talk there and go over the techniques you'll be using on today's trip. After our morning run, we'll pull out for lunch right about noon. If there's anything you want to take along that you want to keep dry, I suggest you load it in these two containers that the lunch crew will take to the pull-out site. I can guarantee that anything you bring with you on the raft will get wet— and that includes cameras, sunglasses, and yourselves."

The group of guests gathered in the lobby laughed.

"We'll end up right back here at about 4 P.M. Any questions?"

No one said anything so Kyle herded everyone out the door to get their gear.

Claire looked around as people spilled out onto the lawn. It appeared that the same people were coming rafting as had attended yesterday morning's hike, including George

Isler and his granddaughters, William and Peggy Weber, and Bryan and his obnoxiously phony girlfriend.

Claire watched with distaste as the latter couple moved from line to line as if they were joined at the hip. What were they going to do next, dress each other? she wondered with disgust as Bryan tested the tightness of Cindy's helmet for her.

"Shoe size?" John asked sharply.

Claire hadn't realized she was at the front of his line. She glared at him. "Six."

He roughly thrust a set of rubber booties and a helmet at her.

She took the offending items and said in a saccharine voice, "Well, it looks like somebody got up on the wrong side of the bed this morning." She batted her eyelashes then turned to go.

His rough voice stopped her in her tracks. "No, I just got up in the wrong bed, period."

Claire blinked around the sudden burning in her eyes and turned back, pasting a fake smile on her face. "As I recall, there's one part of your body that certainly didn't raise any objections."

She turned and walked away before he had a chance to verbally knock her down again.

As victories went, it was a little hollow, she thought, getting in line behind the Webers to take one of the brightly colored wet suits Kyle was doling out.

"I hope they have one that's big enough for you."

Claire's head popped up at the insult, belatedly realizing that William Weber's comment hadn't been aimed at her. She watched as Peggy's neck turned red under her ponytail.

"I'm not that big," Claire heard her protest quietly.

"Look around, Peggy, you're the largest woman here. I didn't mean it as an insult. I'm sure they're just used to catering to a much more fit crowd than your typical house-wife."

Claire cringed at the man's hurtful words. Peggy Weber certainly wasn't in top physical shape, but she didn't de-

serve her husband's insults. Claire had felt a certain irritation with Peggy herself back on the plane when the other
woman had slumbered through the entire flight, but after
watching the disrespectful way the woman's husband
treated her, Claire supposed she couldn't blame the poor
woman for needing a momentary respite from the stress of
her daily life. She wondered where Mr. Weber had been
during the flight. Had he been sitting elsewhere so his wife
would have to deal with their three-year-old terror herself,
or had he traveled separately, perhaps using work as an
excuse to travel to the lodge alone?

Claire waited for Peggy to defend herself, to ask her
husband what shape his own body would be in if he'd been
the one to bear children, the one who probably never got
a minute to himself between feeding, bathing, nurturing,
and cleaning up after their little tyrant all day. But he was
probably the kind of guy who expected his wife to have
the kid in bed by the time he came home from work or
golf or whatever. He probably had no idea how much effort
she put into raising his family, and if it was he who was
responsible for taking care of Billy, he'd probably still be
in great shape because he'd make that a top priority, pushing his family way down on the list, no doubt.

She hated men like that. Claire pulled the bright red
rubber wet suit on over the baggy swimsuit she'd chosen
from the lost-and-found pile.

As she leaned against a tree for balance, her gaze fell
on Bryan and Cindy and she held back a laugh. Cindy was
surreptitiously checking out the rear view of herself reflected in one of the lodge's main-floor windows. Bryan
was doing the same thing with his own reflection, each of
them eyeing themselves in their own faded blue wet suits.
With a mocking smile, Claire wondered if they'd specifi-
cally asked Kyle to give them blue suits to match their eyes.

She felt a sudden lightening in her heart. If she'd married Bryan Edwards, they would have ended up just like
William and Peggy Weber. Appearances were so important
to Bryan that he wouldn't have been able to stand it if she

gained an ounce, much less the twenty-five pounds or more she'd likely gain if she ever got pregnant. And she couldn't quite picture Bryan helping out with the domestic chores to give her a chance to keep up with any sort of exercise routine.

But Bryan and Cindy were perfect for each other. Claire shook her head, pulling up the cold metal zipper of her wet suit. They were both so self-centered that they didn't resent the effort it took to keep their bodies looking in tip-top shape, and neither one probably had any interest in ever having children, since that would take energy away from themselves. Funny, she and Bryan had never even talked about having children. She hadn't yet started feeling the infamous ticking of her biological clock, but she'd just assumed that Bryan would want at least one child after they were married.

She sent up a silent prayer of thanks that Bryan had dumped her, glad that one of them had realized their mistake before it was too late. Then she swallowed her prayer as she watched Cindy pull *her* favorite T-shirt on over her wet suit. Claire gritted her teeth. She wanted that shirt back. It was hers. She didn't care anymore that Cindy had taken her worthless ex-fiancé, but her favorite college T-shirt was another matter.

Keeping an eye on Cindy, waiting for her chance to get back what was rightfully hers, Claire dropped a bundle into one of the dry storage containers and made her way to the bus. Bryan and Cindy got on in front of her and took two seats near the driver. Claire walked down the aisle and took a seat near the middle of the bus, then looked out the window just in time to see Mary Jane running out of the lodge, her blond hair perfectly coiffed. She stopped in front of her son, obviously apologizing for being late.

Claire rested her chin in one hand and watched John's hard, lean body as he talked with his mother. With her shirt safely stowed on the bus, albeit attached to a salt-and-pepper-haired tramp, her thoughts turned back to more important things. John's defection that morning had hurt, more than she cared to admit, but she supposed she'd hardly done anything to make him like her. He had been cranky this morning, but what if she were to make an effort to stop annoying him? When he wasn't trying to get her on a plane back to Seattle, he had actually shown that he could be nice, even charming on occasion. Claire stared out the window of the bus, waiting for the rest of the guests to climb aboard.

Claire watched as John straightened from his task, his gaze wandering over the guests. Suddenly, he turned, his dark green eyes meeting hers through the window of the bus. For a moment, their gazes locked and Claire felt her pulse quicken before he turned away.

If John McBride could affect her so strongly after only one glance, he was definitely worth a little effort on her part.

"We'll be going through several Class Four rapids and one Class Five today. It's our goal to keep everyone in the rafts at all times, but you need to know what to do in the unlikely event that you end up in the water."

Claire's helmet felt uncomfortably lopsided. Listening with one ear to John's safety talk, she leaned her paddle up against a nearby tree and unclipped her chin strap, then took it off so she could readjust the length.

"Miss Brown, could you please pay attention?"

Claire raised her head. The entire group had turned to stare at her at John's admonition. Her cheeks flamed with an angry blush, and her earlier vow to make an effort to be pleasant went up in a blaze of temper. She waved her hands with a flourish. "Yes, of course. Please do go on."

Crossing her arms over her chest, she leaned back against the tree indolently, her helmet dangling at her side.

The glance John shot her before he continued was full of annoyance so Claire brought a hand up and contemplated her rapidly deteriorating manicure. So much for trying not to annoy him. His jaw tightened and Claire guessed that he was some dentist's dream—no doubt he'd grind his molars into dust before the week was out.

"So what do you think you should do if you fall out during the trip?" John ignored her posturing and addressed the question to the group at large.

Claire figured this was a trick question and kept her mouth shut.

"Swim to the side?" George Isler offered. That would have been Claire's guess, too.

"Get into 'River Position,' " William Weber announced authoritatively.

"That's exactly right, Mr. Weber. Let's explore why you shouldn't try swimming to the side, because that's the most common assumption people make, and believe me, your first response when you hit forty-degree water will be to try to get out of it as soon as possible."

A few people chuckled.

"There are a couple problems with that," John continued. "First of all, you're going to be in water that's moving downstream very quickly. In order to get to the side, you're going to have to swim across that current. Now, you might think you're strong enough to beat that, and many of you probably are, under normal circumstances, but remember, you're going to be using your muscles all day. Whitewater rafting is a rigorous sport and you shouldn't underestimate how taxing it is, especially considering that just being in the water itself is going to sap your strength.

"But even if you are strong enough to swim to the side, there's another reason why you don't want to try. This is a fast-moving river and there's all kinds of debris that gets caught up in it. If you're concentrating on getting to the side and swimming across the current, the full length of your body is exposed to anything that just happens to be hurtling down the river. You won't see it until it hits you, and I don't know about you, but I don't want to get broadsided by a tree going twenty miles an hour."

More chuckles from the crowd.

"So if you're not supposed to swim away, you might

ask what it is you're supposed to do." He paused for effect. "Mr. Weber alluded to the River Position and he was absolutely correct. River Position protects you from being a giant bull's-eye until we can fish you out. If any of you are into Zen training, you can think of River Position as allowing you to become one with the river," John said wryly.

"Here's what you do. First of all, don't panic. Next, point your feet downstream so you can see where you're headed. Then, bend your knees and lift your rear end up so you don't hit every rock between here and the lodge. Finally, hold on to your paddle with both hands across your chest, like this." He demonstrated, laying the bright yellow plastic oar across his chest.

"You can use your paddle to push things away from you." He extended the paddle and pushed away an imaginary log. "And it also extends your reach, so you can hold it out for me or Kyle in a rescue attempt."

Claire wondered how much damage the plastic would do to his thick head and the thought brought a smile to her lips as John continued his lecture.

"River Position is very important, so remember: one, don't panic; two, feet downstream; three, bottoms up, knees bent; and, four, hold on to your paddle." John made the group repeat the steps a few times.

"Okay, good. Now that I've explained about River Position and told you not to try to swim to safety, I need to tell you the one exception to the no-swimming rule. I mentioned before that this is a powerful river. And like any powerful river, it has the tendency over time to erode its banks and take over more of the forest, upending trees in its wake. At the root end of the tree is its root ball, which is to be avoided at all costs. I don't want to scare anyone, but I want to be clear about the dangers of getting trapped in a root ball—we can't tell from looking at the exposed part of the root structure what lies beneath the surface of the water. If you see that you're heading toward one of these, I want you to forget River Position and swim like hell away from it. Everybody got it?"

There was a general murmur of acknowledgment.

Claire had a sudden vision of being trapped within the tentacles of some long-dead tree, its strong weblike roots holding her underwater while she gasped for air. Shuddering, she shook off the creepy thought. Looking around, she sensed that perhaps she wasn't the only one visualizing a similar fate.

Kyle called out raft assignments and Claire was dismayed to learn that she was going to be stuck in John's boat.

"Wonderful," she mumbled, "he'll probably throw me out at one of the root balls."

As she walked to her assigned raft, Claire heard the unmistakable sound of somebody crying.

"I can't do this."

"Now, there's a surprise," William Weber said sarcastically. "I don't even know why you bothered to get out of bed. You should have just stayed at the lodge, ordered room service, and watched TV all day. Or, better yet, you should have just stayed home with Billy where you belong."

Claire watched in openmouthed horror as Peggy Weber's husband stomped off, leaving his wife in tears. She took a step toward the other woman, then stopped in surprise when John walked over and put a comforting arm over Peggy's shoulder.

"Hey, I told you, I didn't mean to scare you with my root-ball story."

Peggy sniffed, then sent him a watery smile. "I guess I'm just not very adventurous."

John laughed. "I'd lay odds that seventy-five percent of the people here right now want to back out but are too proud to say so."

"I doubt that."

"Look, Peggy—do you mind if I call you Peggy?" He continued as she nodded her consent. "Well, Peggy, I've been doing these trips for six years now, and I think I've learned to read people pretty well. They show up here laughing and talking, but I can feel the tension. And it gets worse after our little safety talk, once they realize there's a very real possibility that one of them could fall out of the raft and they'll have to remember what we've told them.

"It's normal, and actually very smart, to be afraid. I'm always more nervous about the cocky ones, the people who don't realize that getting down the river safely has nothing to do with strength or swimming ability—it has to do, first of all, with doing everything you can to keep your butt in the raft."

Peggy laughed and Claire could see that she was relaxing. Damn it, why did John have to keep redeeming himself? And why was he so nice to everyone else, and so mean to her? Claire leaned back against the tree, waiting to see if John was able to convince Mrs. Weber to overcome her fears.

"It also has to do with respecting the power of nature and using what we've taught you to keep yourself safe."

"I don't know . . ."

"Tell you what, why don't we make a deal? The first part of the day is more calm so we get a chance to make sure everyone's got their paddling down right before we hit the tougher part of the river. Why don't you give it a try this morning and then, if you don't like it, you can leave with the lunch crew and be back at the lodge with your son before one? Want to try that?"

Claire watched as Peggy Weber looked into John's clear, green eyes. Whatever she read there must have reassured her because she nodded slowly.

"Good." John squeezed her shoulder reassuringly. "I'll be really surprised if you leave at lunchtime."

He smiled down at Peggy and Claire felt a pang of envy. All he ever seemed to do was glare at her. It would be nice to be on the receiving end of that smile occasionally, she thought wistfully, pushing herself away from the tree.

"Kyle, we have a slight change in seating arrangements. I'm going to put Lisa and Heather in your boat and I'm going to take William and Peggy Weber."

"Why, is there a problem?"

"No, I just want to keep an eye on Mrs. Weber."

"No problem, boss. Are we ready to go?" he asked eagerly.

"Yep, let's take off."

John organized his group and waited for Kyle to shove off. Once the other raft was moving, he'd push off so his boat could serve as the rescue boat if Kyle had trouble.

As everyone took up their positions, John glanced at his mother, wondering again why she had decided to join them. She'd never been keen on outdoor activities, usually leaving John and his father on their own. He shrugged as people claimed their spots. She was a grown woman, and if she decided she wanted to learn to river-raft, far be it from him to dampen her desire. After all, wasn't that why he'd started Outdoor Adventures in the first place, to expose the great outdoors to people who wanted to enjoy new experiences?

William Weber raced to grab a front position in the raft but was beaten out by George Isler and Mary Jane. The front positions had the best views and, in John's opinion, got the best ride. He was glad someone else beat Mr. Weber to the punch.

William grabbed a seat in the second row and Peggy Weber sat in the back of the raft next to John, behind her husband. Bryan and Cindy took the second row, sitting across from each other. Claire took the last seat, right in front of him, and John wished belatedly that he'd put her in Kyle's boat instead of his. As she wriggled to find a comfortable position, he realized that no matter how irritated he was with himself, he couldn't seem to shake his attraction to Claire. The bright red wet suit she wore clung to her body, outlining the small breasts he'd cupped in his hands early this morning. He closed his eyes, fighting his desire, knowing he was going to have to spend the entire day resisting his attraction to her, especially given the clinging nature of the wet suits.

Kyle waved to him to let him know everything was fine in his boat. John wished he felt the same optimism as he stepped into the cold river water and gave the raft a push.

Pulling his mind back to his job, John showed everyone how to wedge their feet under the inflated tubes of the bench seats or along the inner wall of the raft. "Contrary to what you might think," John said as the raft began its journey down the river, "you don't sit with one foot in the raft and one foot out. If you did, you'd be assuming the River Position the first time we hit a bump."

"But this feels so unnatural," his mother said, trying to position her feet comfortably.

"I know. You do get used to it, but you'll definitely feel some discomfort for awhile. To make it even worse, I need you to sit on the farthest outside edge when we're paddling. That way, you'll be using the stronger muscles of your backs and upper arms when you paddle, rather than your forearms and wrists. Let's give it a try. Forward paddle."

John watched with amusement as the group clumsily paddled, oars clanking together. Every trip followed the same pattern.

"Okay, stop. Let me give you a tip. Left side, you need to follow George's lead, right side, you're with my mother. They set the pace. So, Bryan, when George puts his paddle in the water, you should put yours in. Your strokes should mirror his. Cindy, you should follow my Mom. Claire, you follow Cindy and so on. Now, forward paddle again."

"That's better," John said after a moment of watching the group pull together. "Now we're going to practice a maneuver called 'high side.' We'll probably have to do this at least once today. This move comes in handy when you're running the rapids."

John explained the physics of raft versus rock and how they'd need to put all their collective weight against a rock if the raft got stuck, even though common sense might tell you to get as far away from the rock as possible.

"Our weight against the rock will counterbalance the current trying to pull the raft under. So if I yell 'high side right,' everyone on the left side of the raft get to the right side immediately. I'll only need to do this if we're in danger of capsizing, so speed is much more important than form on this one.

"Let's give it a try. High side left," John called.

Claire slid over to the left side of the raft and sat down behind William Weber. After a moment of bumbling and tripping, John laughed. If this had been for real they'd all be floating down the river without a raft by the time everyone got into position. "That was good for a first try, but remember you're going to be doing this move under extreme pressure. Water will be pouring into the raft and we'll have less than three seconds to get ourselves off the rock or we're all going to be assuming the River Position sans raft. Got it?"

Heads nodded in unison.

"Let's try it again. High side right," John shouted.

Claire yelped as William Weber slammed into her. Instinctively, she recoiled. The move threw her off balance and she slid off the slippery rubber toward the water. She felt herself slipping, but couldn't seem to do anything to stop her momentum until, with a sudden jerk, she was yanked back in the raft.

"Thanks," she muttered, pulling herself up off the floor of the boat.

"Any time." She met John's amused gaze with as much dignity as she could muster.

"That was much better," John praised the group, "but try to make sure you don't push anyone out of the raft if you can help it."

"Sorry about that. I guess I don't know my own strength."

Claire looked at William Weber coolly. It hadn't been just the force of his body slamming into her that had pushed her off balance. She'd recoiled because she'd felt the unmistakable groping of his hands on her breasts—that was what had almost sent her over the edge of the raft. From the amused way he was looking at her now, Claire was convinced that the placement of his grabbing hands hadn't been an accident.

She nodded, acknowledging his mocking apology, then turned her attention back to the river.

"That wasn't so bad, was it?" John asked.

"It was great. Thank you so much for encouraging me to go." Peggy Weber smiled up at him engagingly. "I can't wait to do this afternoon's run. You said there are even more rapids than this morning?"

John laughed as Peggy leaned toward him enthusiastically. She was hooked. "Yep. Rapids are rated on a scale of one to six, with six meaning that no sane person would run them. We've got one Class Five rapid coming up near the end of the afternoon and three Class Fours."

It was almost time to get everybody back in the boats. He made a mental note to commend Gina and the rest of the cooking staff on a great meal. They'd brought pots of homemade beef barley soup, crusty bread and butter, and plenty of oatmeal raisin cookies for dessert. The group of rafters probably didn't even stop to consider the amount of work Gina had gone through to research the best sources of nutrients that would keep their energy levels up this afternoon, but John knew, and he appreciated her efforts. Now, warmed and relaxed, the guests chatted about this morning's events, ready to move on to the next leg of their adventure.

John stretched his shoulders, grinning as he recalled Claire's near-dunking in the river this morning. Never before had he met a woman who could irritate and arouse him in the same moment. He looked around for the familiar blond cap of hair and frowned when he didn't see her. Telling himself that he was only concerned because it was his job to ensure the safety of all the guests, he checked around the clearing where they'd stopped for lunch.

Since the clearing was on his property, he'd been able to build a lavatory facility for guests to use during the lunch break. It was possible that Claire was there, but he walked into the woods around the perimeter just to look anyway.

Surely she wouldn't have been foolish enough to wander into the forest again after yesterday?

The cooking staff had set up a table to hold the food for lunch. They'd hauled the supplies in with two pickup trucks from the lodge, which were parked off a forest service road just past the clearing. John glanced at the trucks and turned back to the clearing, but stopped when something dark caught his attention.

John watched as William Weber, wearing a black wet suit, approached the first truck and peered in. From where he stood, just inside the forest, John's view was blocked by the other truck. He heard the first vehicle's door open and wondered what the other man was doing. He moved closer for a better look, his rubber-soled feet moving silently over the forest floor.

Claire's half-eaten sandwich sat perched on a paper plate on top of the blue vinyl dashboard of the truck. Her fingers lay still on the keyboard of her laptop and the sounds of her even breathing echoed in the silence of the cab.

Feeling guilty that she was falling behind in her workload, she had put her computer in the dry storage and planned to steal some time during lunch to work. She'd hoped to find somewhere quiet to get some work done and the trucks were far enough away from the clearing to provide some peace as well as a comfortable seat.

Unfortunately, the truck had electric windows and the keys weren't in the vehicle. It was a sunny day and the temperature inside the cab was right around seventy-five degrees, just warm enough to increase the somnambulant effect that Claire didn't need after her late night. She'd only been working for about twenty minutes when she made a bargain with her heavy eyelids, the one about being able to close her eyes for "just a minute," then she'd feel revived and ready to work again.

That had been over thirty minutes ago.

Claire awoke with a start as she heard the soft click of the door closing. She looked around, momentarily disori-

ented when she saw William Weber sliding across the
bench seat, then realized she'd fallen asleep in the truck.

"Have a nice nap, Sleeping Beauty?"

Blinking drowsily, Claire glanced over at William.
"What are you doing here?" she asked, pushing herself
against the passenger-side door.

"Just came to see if you might be interested in an, uh,
an extracurricular adventure," he answered, eyeing her
breasts suggestively.

Claire pushed out an irritated breath. "Forget it. You're
married and I'm not interested."

"Are you sure?"

Claire reached for the door latch, only to find that he'd
locked the doors. She pressed the unlock button, but nothing happened.

"Don't you just love those child locks?" William pressed
himself against her side and slid his arm over the back of
the seat.

"Unlock this door right now," Claire ordered, the first
stirring of fear in her stomach. He was stronger than her,
undoubtedly. The truck was parked far enough away from
the clearing that someone would have to come looking for
them to see them. And for all her time spent with Nathan's
Guerrilla Yoga class, she wasn't sure that she could fight
off a determined man in such close quarters. But lunch was
scheduled to be over soon. Surely John would realize that
two of his guests were missing and come looking for them
soon? Just stall, she told herself, pressing against the
passenger-side door.

"Now why would I want to do that, when we're so cozy
here?"

"Mr. Weber, this is ridiculous." Claire kept her voice
calm. "I'm not interested in having an affair with you."

He twirled a lock of her hair around his finger and put
his other hand on her knee.

Claire was wondering if she was strong enough to brain
him with her laptop when he jerked her hair, forcing her

head up. His lips crushed over hers, his tongue jammed into her mouth.

Claire bit down on his probing tongue, knowing she'd hit her mark by the coppery taste of blood in her mouth.

William recoiled furiously, opening his mouth on a curse.

The door behind her was flung open and, since she'd been pressing herself against it with all her weight, she tumbled to the dirt, her laptop landing with a thud beside her.

"What the hell do you think you're doing, Weber?"

Sitting up, Claire spat out the awful taste of blood and drew her sleeve across her mouth to erase the feel of William's unwanted advance. Her savior stood over her, looking like a warrior god as he glared at William Weber who had wisely chosen not to remove himself from the protection of the vehicle. John's hint of beard looked even darker against the black collar of his wet suit, Claire noticed, waiting for him to yank William out of the truck and pound on the miserable cur like any avenging hero should.

"Claire, get back to the others," John ordered quietly without looking down at her.

"But . . ." she sputtered, wanting to stay and watch William Weber get his comeuppance.

"Now," he ground out through gritted teeth.

Claire glared up at the man sitting in the cab of the truck nursing his injured tongue. Well, if John wasn't going to confront the creep, she would. "If you ever touch me again, William, I'll have you arrested for attempted rape. Do you hear me?"

William remained silent as Claire pulled herself up, slapping the dirt off her bright red wet suit before picking up her computer. She'd been right to be worried about William Weber, but she hadn't had any idea that he would have tried forcing himself on her like he had. She wondered if he would really go so far as to attempt rape, but wasn't about to put herself in the position of finding out.

What bothered her more was that John seemed to think

he'd been interrupting something between her and William Weber. She didn't know what she'd done to earn his dislike, especially since he'd been the one who came to her room last night, not vice versa. Of course, she thought miserably, she certainly hadn't turned him away. Maybe that was why he thought she was sleeping around like a cat in heat. After all, she'd invited his advances after only knowing him for a few days. So why wouldn't she be just as willing to have sex with anyone else who asked?

She slowly returned to the clearing and replaced her computer in the plastic container before joining the rest of the group at the raft. How was John to know that she'd never felt that instant attraction to anyone but him? He couldn't know that she could count the number of lovers she'd had on the fingers of one hand, that before last night she hadn't realized how incredible making love could be, or how vulnerable it could make you feel afterward.

Claire sighed. She supposed she should be happy. As awful as this vacation had been so far, it couldn't possibly get any worse.

"Look, McBride, she's been coming on to me since the beginning of the week. I figured when she sashayed past me after lunch, she was giving me the signal that she was ready for something to happen between us."

"What the hell are you talking about, Weber?" John forced his voice to remain calm, to not lash out with the anger that was building up inside him as he watched the other man's eyes dart to the clearing.

"I'm sure you know what I mean. I heard her fiancé—"

"Ex-fiancé," John interrupted.

"Yeah, whatever. I overheard Bryan and Cindy talking about how you took her up to your room the other night. So I figured, hey, she's obviously interested in getting a little action on her vacation. Why not get a little myself while I had the chance?" William Weber shrugged nonchalantly.

The shrug did it, telling John that William Weber didn't give a shit about anyone but himself. Although the two men were about the same size, John spent his life being physically active, while William only played at it in his spare time. Added to John's actual physical strength were the strength of emotions he didn't want to explore at the moment.

In one lightning-quick motion, John grabbed the front of William's wet suit by the zipper and hauled the other man out of truck, slamming him back against the vehicle with unrestrained force.

"You touch her again, Weber, you so much as brush past her, and I'll kill you. You got it?" he asked quietly, eyes narrowed to angry slits. Seeing the fury in the other man's eyes, John waited for William to take a swing at him. He wanted the other man to start something, would have relished the release of tension the physical violence would bring.

But, like a typical bully, William apparently only chose to pick on targets he thought were weaker than himself. "Yeah, I got it. Now, let me go," he mumbled.

Forcing his fists to unclench, John dropped the front of William's wet suit, leaving the other man standing by the trucks as he strode back to the clearing.

The seating arrangement had shifted for the afternoon leg of their journey. William Weber had snagged one of the coveted front seats and Bryan took the other. Somehow, Claire had gotten stuck sitting behind William, and she forced herself not to glare at the back of his head, imagining a target right where the beginning of a bald spot was. After John had rejoined the group at the boat, she'd hoped to see William come limping back from where the trucks were parked with a black eye, a few missing teeth, or a bloody nose, at least.

I mean, really, she thought, shooting John a look of disgust, *even I'm capable of giving somebody a bloody nose and I'm not some hotshot ex-FBI agent.* She snorted, turning her attention back to the front of the raft. John had probably clapped the other man on the back in a male bonding ritual before sharing a guy's-locker-room version of his own experience with her.

She shoved that painful thought away and tried to concentrate instead on the scenery; the sparse trees at the edge of the riverbed, the call of the birds as their habitat was intruded upon by a big yellow raft, the purple of Claire's shirt squashed between Cindy's perky butt and the rubber raft.

Claire's eyes narrowed. The Babe-o-the-Month was sitting on Claire's favorite shirt, crushing the white block letters.

She had to get it back. But how?

John had slipped into *National Geographic* mode, droning on about the native plants and animals in the area. While she was sure his discussion of trees and rocks was fascinating, Claire had pretty much tuned him out. But now, listening to his deep voice explaining the intricacies of the mating habits of trout, the evil impulse whispered something in her ear.

Pointing in the general direction of the treetops, Claire made sure she had a good grip on her paddle and muttered loudly, "Is that an eerie side white?"

"An eerie side white?" John repeated questioningly, raising his voice above the sound of the water.

Later, after Claire had had plenty of time to dissect her plan in minute detail, she would admit that she should have ignored the evil impulse. But it had seemed like such a good idea at the time. Once again, that was the problem with evil impulses. They never sounded quite as good once you had time to reflect upon them.

Unfortunately, however, her good judgment was slumbering at this moment, so at John's words, which sounded suspiciously like the "high side right" they'd practiced earlier that morning, the overeager rafting crew leaped as one across the raft and landed atop their raftmates on the right side of the inflatable boat. Claire hadn't meant to unseat

Cindy. Again, later—much later—she actually felt that she had done the other woman a favor. After all, had Cindy been sitting on the slippery T-shirt once they entered the rapids, she would surely have ended up in the drink. As it was, she still ended up in the drink, but John made easy work of sprinting to the head of the raft and fishing her sputtering form out of the slower-moving water.

As John rushed by on his rescue mission, Claire surreptitiously slipped her bright yellow oar into the cold water and snagged her Northwestern T-shirt before it could float away. She pulled the sopping wet purple shirt out of the water, and was then plagued by a new question. Where in the heck was she going to hide the darn thing now that she had it? She could hardly slip it on over her wet suit. Cindy might not be too bright, but Claire guessed even she might catch on to that.

Cindy had been hauled back into the boat by now, and was making the most of the attention being bestowed on her by the other passengers. She fluttered her lashes over her sky-blue eyes. "Oh, thank you, John. You saved my life."

Claire rolled her eyes to the top of her head and resisted the urge to stick her finger down her throat in a juvenile "gag me" gesture. Instead, she moved back to her seat and looked around the raft for a place to hide her recovered loot. Finding nothing that looked suitable, and figuring she had only seconds before the commotion died down, Claire hastily unzipped her wet suit and stuffed the T-shirt in.

She felt her nipples pucker instantly as the almost-freezing shirt made contact with her warm breasts. John turned at that exact moment and Claire yanked her arms up and crossed them as nonchalantly as possible against her chest. Tilting her head, she attempted an expression of angelic innocence, noticing that John's face was red. She chalked it up to exertion, and thought perhaps that Cindy must be heavier than she looked.

"What the hell were you talking about back there? Eerie sided what?" His voice came out in a low growl.

Claire kept her right arm crossed against her still-cold chest and used her left to point backward in the general direction of the treetops they'd just passed. "It was some sort of bird's nest. I thought I remembered the name from one of my guidebooks." She kept her gaze steady on John's flashing green eyes.

He watched her for a moment, his gaze intense, then said, "All right, everybody back to their seats." As he passed her on the way back to his seat at the rear of the raft, Claire could have sworn he muttered something to the effect of "Guidebook, my ass" but she didn't stop him to ask for clarification. Instead, she hastily zipped her wet suit back up, shot Cindy a saccharine smile, and wedged her right foot up against the side of the raft.

Chapter 13

"WE'RE APPROACHING A RAPID CALLED THE BOULDERS." John's voice broke through the silence. The atmosphere in the raft had changed subtly in the past half hour, becoming quieter and almost tense.

"Forward paddle, everyone," John commanded.

Claire gasped as a paddle full of frigid water hit her in the face. It was the third time in the last thirty minutes that William Weber had managed to hit her with a face full of water.

"Stop it," she said, loud enough for him to hear.

"Stop what?" William turned and asked indolently.

Claire's fingers tightened on her paddle.

"Claire, did I tell you to stop paddling?"

She hadn't realized that she'd lifted her oar out of the water until John chastised her. It was no use arguing with him, especially as they approached their first real white-water. She waited for William's oar to go in the water in front of her, then mimicked his stroke.

"After the Boulders, we're going to hit the only Class Five rapid on this stretch of the river. It's called the Three Bears, and not because of any of the wildlife in the area. There are three obstacles that we have to go between or over, two giant rocks and a root ball. Now, we'll want to hit it so we go between the rocks and avoid the root ball at all costs, but sometimes it just doesn't work like we plan it. If we have to go over the rocks, well, I guess you guys will just get to practice your high side technique for real this time.

"But first we've got to get through the Boulders." John's voice had risen over the sound of the water and, as they turned a bend in the river, Claire could see why.

They were heading into a narrow, watery alley flanked on one side by boulders reaching up ten, sometimes fifteen or twenty feet. The other side of the alley was made up of a rocky cliff.

Claire watched as Kyle's raft entered the alley where the compressed water was moving twice as fast as at other parts of the river. Behind her, she heard John's mother gasp as the first raft momentarily hung up on a submerged rock. Water started pouring over the rock and into the raft.

"High side right, high side right," Claire heard John mutter, then looked back to make sure he wasn't talking to them.

Kyle got his rafters into proper position and, like magic, the raft righted itself and flew off the rock toward the cliff wall. Claire watched as the people in the first raft scurried back into position and started paddling furiously to avoid getting hung up on the cliff. Kyle's boat careened lightly off the rocky face of the cliff and slid out of the Boulders. Even from the distance, Claire could hear the other boat cheering, gloating over their successful battle with Mother Nature.

"All right, gang. We're going to do the same thing, minus getting stuck on the rock in the middle. Just keep in mind, we're going to hit the Three Bears about two minutes after we get out of this, so stay alert.

"Let's go!" he shouted.

Claire could actually feel the adrenaline course through her body as she braced her feet against the raft and leaned out over the water. It was easy to see how you could get addicted to this, she thought, digging her paddle into the river at John's command.

She felt the raft pick up speed as they entered the narrow alley. John kept them heading straight for the rock.

"We're gonna hit it," Claire said aloud to herself, paddling furiously.

"Right side backpaddle," John shouted just as Claire was sure they were going to hit the boulder.

The raft slid around the rock like an egg yolk sliding out of its shell.

"Right side forward, left side back." John changed commands as they rocketed toward the cliff.

They bounded off the wall and popped out of the canyon like a rubber band being shot from a slingshot.

"Great job, everybody. High five." John raised his oar to the center of the boat.

With much whooping, everyone else did the same, clapping their paddles together noisily. John let them savor the moment, then, as the next set of rapids came into view, said, "Okay, we're coming to the Three Bears. Paddles in the water. Forward paddle, everybody."

Claire's adrenaline rush was doused as she got another faceful of near-freezing water. Without thinking, she stood up, shaking the water out of her eyes and sputtering.

"I told you to knock it off," she yelled.

"Sit down," John roared.

Claire looked back to the rear of the raft, startled by the ferocity of his tone.

It was as if the river had been waiting for him to make a mistake, waiting for its chance to show off its power to the mere mortals who dared to brave its mighty force. In the split second he took his attention from the rushing river, they hit the top of a partially submerged rock.

Standing, Claire's center of balance was too high to counterbalance the sudden movement of the raft. Without the advantage of her toeholds to keep her inside the boat, she plunged into the churning river.

John watched Claire tumble into the river as the raft wrapped around the rock and was trapped, water pouring in at hundreds of gallons per second.

"High side left," he yelled, knowing he had to get them off the rock or they'd all be facing the next rapid without the protection of the raft.

Bryan, Cindy, and his mother leaped over to the left side of the raft and the boat, its right side almost totally submerged, pushed them up higher against the rock.

For tense seconds, John prayed the raft wouldn't flip, trapping them all underneath. But then it shook loose, releasing them as if some giant magnetic force field had suddenly been turned off.

John saw the unmistakable orange of Claire's life vest bobbing farther down the rapid, but something didn't look right.

"Forward paddle. Forward paddle," he shouted urgently. They had to catch up with her.

The rafters paddled furiously.

John's heart stopped. "Oh, my God."

George Isler had obviously seen the same thing John did because the older man looked back at him in horror.

Claire was floating, facedown in the water, straight toward the tangled roots of the overturned tree that made up one of the Three Bears.

"I'll get her," George shouted.

"No." John made the decision in a split second. "Come back here!" He yelled hasty directions as the older man scrambled over the bench seats.

"Stay off the rocks if you can, just have everyone paddle as hard as they can until you're out of it. Use your oar to push yourself off any rocks. Tell Kyle to wait for us at the bottom."

George Isler nodded solemnly.

"Forward paddle," John heard the other man yell as he jumped into the frigid water.

The swiftly moving current grabbed at him, trying to pull him away from the downed tree and toward the rocks. John swam across the current, ignoring his own advice about becoming a target for debris and staying away from root balls.

Claire's helmet bobbed into his line of vision and John kicked viciously, trying to put every ounce of muscle into each stroke.

He raised his head again.

Damn it, where was she?

His eyes scanned the water line. She must have hit the

tree roots by now. He grabbed one of the roots sticking out of the water to hold himself in place as he searched for a glimpse of her bright red wet suit.

He pulled himself along, frantically looking beneath the water for her. He took a step and something soft brushed against his leg. He felt around, unable to see anything in the churning water.

An arm. He grabbed and pulled. Her life jacket had caught on the branches.

John reached down to his ankle and released his knife from its scabbard. Feeling his way, with fingers numb from the cold, he slid his knife under the fasteners of her life jacket and yanked upward.

He freed her arms from the jacket and brought her to the surface of the water.

Her skin was pale, her lips almost blue from lack of oxygen or the cold or both. He didn't have time to get her to the bank of the river, twenty feet away.

John turned his back to the river to shield her from the current and braced her back against a thick root. Holding her nose closed with one hand, he tilted her head back and blew warm, life-giving oxygen into her lungs.

He waited the space of a heartbeat, then did it again.

"Breathe, damn you!" he yelled, pushing his own air into her again.

She coughed weakly, then sucked in a huge breath. Her arms spasmed and she pushed against him as her eyelids fluttered open.

"I'm going to be sick." She turned her head and John held on to her as her body purged itself of the river's contribution.

She was crying when she turned back to him and her teeth were chattering from a combination of cold and shock.

He wanted to wrap his arms around her, to share the heat of his body with her. He also wanted to shake her and curse her for being so foolish, for nearly getting herself killed. But both things were going to have to wait. They had to get out of the water and back to the rafts before they both ended up with hypothermia.

"Claire, we've got to get out of the river. We're going to have to swim over to the bank. Do you understand?"

She continued to gaze at him, tears sliding out of her soft gray eyes to mix with the river.

He gave her a little shake. "Come on, Claire, we've got to get you out of here. Can you manage to hold on to my shirt?"

He started unbuckling his life jacket, wincing as the cold water of the river hit his wet suit without the protective layer of orange. Slipping his arms out of the life jacket, he put it around Claire and tightened the buckles as far as they would go. He worried that it was so loose it might just slip over her head, but it would be better than nothing.

She still hadn't answered him, but she was following his movements with her eyes.

"Claire, listen to me. I'm going to do all the work. All you have to do is hold on to me. All right?"

She still didn't answer, so he cut the Mr. Nice Guy crap. "Do it!" he yelled. "Grab the back of my wet suit."

She blinked. He turned around, waiting to feel her grip on him.

She grabbed his shoulders with both hands and he plunged back into the river.

John felt her kicking, trying to help as the river dragged them downstream. It seemed like an eternity before they reached the riverbank and John was able to get firm footing in the rocky shore.

Exhausted, he pulled himself up onto the sun-warmed rocks, then pulled Claire up after him. Wrapping his arms around her, he rested his chin on her hair, trying to stop the chattering of her teeth and the frantic thoughts of his own mind.

She could have drowned. If she'd been any place but right at the base of the root ball, he wouldn't have been able to save her. She would have drowned.

John fought the nausea rising in his throat. Since he'd

started Outdoor Adventures, he'd never had a guest come so close to dying, thought he'd escaped death when he quit his job as a tracker. The fact that he hadn't, that death had snuck up behind him and tried to take someone—no, he interrupted, not just someone, but someone he had started to care about—made him furious. Death had no place in his new life, he wouldn't allow it. He tightened his hold on Claire and shook his fist at death. He'd won. This time.

"John, are you all right?" Kyle called, rounding a bend and seeing them lying on the rocks.

Slowly, John released his grip on Claire and sat up, wincing as he felt a pain in his ribs. He hadn't felt anything at the time, but something must have hit him when he was looking for Claire. Something heavy, he thought, touching the sore spot on his side.

"I'm fine. Give me your jacket, will you?"

Claire stared fixedly ahead as Kyle unzipped his nylon windbreaker and handed it to John. He put it on over her borrowed life jacket, rebuttoning the jacket with three distinctive snaps.

Now that the crisis was over, John's emotion channeled itself in a different direction. First, he'd saved Claire from William Weber's advances and then he'd saved her from the river. Didn't she care at all what happened to herself?

His fists clenched at his sides as the anger raced through his body like a piece of bad meat, turning his insides to liquid. He'd only known Claire for four days, didn't believe in love at first sight, and didn't even like her sometimes, but he felt an actual, physical pain at the thought of something happening to her. He didn't like it, didn't want to feel this way, and he resented Claire for her part in it.

"How is she?" his mother asked quietly from beside him.

His fear and anger rose up inside him like bile. "She's fine," he answered loudly. "Foolish and irresponsible, but fine."

Mary Jane gasped as her son turned on Claire and continued his tirade. "Your actions endangered not just yourself but everyone else on that raft, do you understand?"

He grabbed her arms, his coldly controlled voice worse than if he were yelling. "You owe an apology to everyone on this trip for your behavior. Do you hear me?"

He watched as her eyes began to fill with tears. She blinked them back, then turned to the entire group of rafters who had assembled on the riverbank. "I'm sorry I put everyone in danger. I just didn't think. I'm—" She stopped and John watched as she took a deep breath and swallowed convulsively. "I'm glad that everyone's okay."

She turned back to John, her gray eyes appearing huge in her pale face. "Can we go now?"

It was a somber group that pulled in at the riverbank next to the lodge.

Kyle's boat beat John's to the pull-out spot and his guests had hoisted the raft onto their shoulders and were loading it onto a trailer as John's boat drifted in. Unlike Kyle's group, who filled the air with their talking and laughing, the rafters in John's boat were a subdued bunch, no doubt owing to the tension emanating from their guide.

John jumped out of the raft as soon as it hit the bottom of the river and held it steady as the crew disembarked. It only took a moment to get the raft stored, then everyone began the tedious chore of getting out of their equipment. This was John's least favorite part of the rafting trips. They'd seen the last rapid half an hour ago, and while the river had still moved them along at a good clip, the adrenaline high from running the rapids was long gone by the time they pulled in at the lodge. Without the energy surge, people started feeling the cold that came with floating down a river of frigid water in sixty-something-degree weather.

He could almost hear Claire's teeth chattering from twenty feet away as he watched her unsuccessful attempt to unfasten the buckles of the oversized life vest with fingers numbed by the cold. John started toward her, then quickened his step as William Weber walked nearby.

Claire took a step backward, bumping into John's chest.

"Go help your wife, Weber," John snarled, without spar-ing a glance at the other man as he pushed aside Claire's trembling fingers and unsnapped the first fastening of her life jacket.

"I was just on my way to do that," William protested innocently, giving John a wide berth.

John waited to hear William's retreating footsteps before meeting Claire's gaze. He'd expected to see anger there at his interference, expected her to tell him that she was perfectly capable of dealing with William Weber herself. Instead, he was dismayed to see nothing besides bone-wearying defeat.

"Give me your hands," he ordered.

She did, putting her small fists in his. They were like two balls of ice in his hands. It was no wonder she couldn't get her buckles undone. He uncurled the fingers of her right hand and placed them between his, rubbing gently to put some heat back into her flesh. Her hands were small and soft, and he continued to massage life back into them. She had a blister just forming on her left hand from the unaccustomed friction of the oar against her skin.

"We've got to get you out of the wet suit," John said briskly.

He tossed the life jacket to the ground and turned back to find her fumbling with the heavy zipper of her wet suit. Her fingers were shaking and her teeth were chattering again. John felt an urge to pull her into his arms, to comfort her, to transfer his strength to her through a physical connection. The urge was so strong, he had to force himself to take a step back, to put some distance between himself and this woman who had him caught in the spell of an irresistible physical attraction.

He gave himself a mental shake. There were other guests he needed to tend to, equipment that needed to be taken care of, and here he was, thinking only of stripping Claire naked and making love to her right here and now, despite the presence of a dozen other people.

"Here, I'll get it." John tried for a businesslike tone as he pulled down the zipper of her suit. He raised his eye-

brows questioningly when a purple T-shirt dropped from
the front of her wet suit onto the ground, but Claire just
gave him a tired shrug so he ignored it. He peeled her out
of the damp red rubber like a banana, leaving the suit on
the hard-packed dirt as he tugged the black booties off her
chilled feet.

"I'll be right back." He took her booties and wet suit
and deposited them in the appropriate piles before grabbing
an oversized towel from the pile they'd had waiting for
their return, intending to help Claire get dried off. He turned
around to where she'd been standing, only to find her gone.

He looked toward the lodge and saw her disappear
around the corner. He took a step forward, intending to
follow her, when Kyle's voice halted his progress.

"Hey, John, can you give me a hand with these wet
suits?"

John grunted, wishing for once that he could abandon
his responsibilities, could say to hell with the wet suits, the
helmets, the rafts, the other guests. Just this one time, he
wanted to follow Claire into the lodge, lock her into his
suite, make sure she was warm, and get rid of that defeated
look that was lurking in her beautiful gray eyes. He paused
for a split second, desire warring with dependability, then
turned back to his responsibilities, taking a load of dirty
wet suits from Kyle's arms.

"I sure hope the next trip is more challenging." William
Weber's superior tone stopped John in his tracks.

Water from the suits dripped onto the dry grass at his
feet. John turned to the other man, biting back a retort when
he saw that William's arm was around his wife's shoulders.
"There are more Class Five rapids on the longer trip, plus
a Class Six we have to hike around. So far, nobody's complained that it's too tame," John replied, trying to keep the
ice from his voice.

"Good. I can't wait to go. How about you, honey? Are
you sure you're up to it? It might be dangerous." William
nudged his wife's shoulder.

John watched the life in Peggy's eyes drain out at her

husband's mocking tone and clenched his teeth. He'd been brought up to believe that the best way to resolve conflicts was not through the use of force, but by talking about the problem and trying to understand the other person's point of view. But John figured that his father would've made an exception for a worm like William Weber. This guy deserved to be knocked down a peg or two, and John would be glad to be the guy to do it.

Peggy Weber mumbled an appropriate response and meekly followed her husband back to the lodge.

John shook his head with disgust as he hauled his load of wet suits up to the station they'd set up to wash all the equipment. Turning the suits inside out, he pinned them up on a heavy clothesline where they could be hosed down with soap and water and left to dry in the pale sunshine.

"Don't you think you were a little hard on Claire?"

John grimaced as his mother came and sat on the bench he'd pushed up against the wall. She'd pulled a light yellow sweatsuit on over the swimsuit she'd worn for the rafting trip. Her makeup had worn off during the day, but her skin glowed from exertion and fresh air and, John realized with a start, she looked pretty and much younger than her fifty-six years.

"Mother, I'm responsible for the lives of everyone that we take out on these trips. Claire not only endangered herself, she endangered everyone else on that boat. It could have been a disaster." He turned and clipped another suit onto the nylon line.

His mother didn't say anything for a long moment, and he almost thought she'd left when he heard her softly spoken response behind him. "Would you have been so harsh if it had been someone else who'd fallen out? What if it had been one of George's granddaughters? Or Peggy Weber? You seem to have a soft spot for her. Would you have humiliated her like you did Claire?"

John's hands stilled on the clothesline as he stared unseeingly at the river.

He barely heard his mother's footsteps across the yard as she walked away, not waiting for his answer.

"So, did you girls have a good time today?"

Freshly showered, John stopped to chat with the Islers, who sat in the lobby, sharing a pot of hot cocoa. He smiled as the girls excitedly reenacted the entire trip. It had obviously been worth a day away from video games to them.

"Yeah. I wish I'd been the one to fall in. That would have been so cool," Heather, the younger granddaughter, said.

George Isler groaned. "I'm glad it wasn't you; I'd have had a heart attack."

"But Grandpa, you were great, the way you guided the other raft down that rapid," Lisa said proudly.

"Yeah, you were all, like, 'backpaddle, backpaddle.'" Heather imitated her grandfather. "We could hear you even from our own raft."

Watching them, John realized that something good had come out of the day's trip. The girls seemed more talkative, less withdrawn than they'd been before.

"It sounds like I know who to call if I ever need another river guide." John clapped a hand on Mr. Isler's shoulder, then left as the girls looked at their grandfather with new respect.

As he walked to the kitchen to check on things there, his mother's words came back to him. Would he have been as harsh if it had been one of the girls who had fallen in the river and almost drowned? What if it had been Peggy Weber? Or even her husband?

He mentally put himself back in the river, the frigid water rushing past, lapping at his back, and instead of seeing Claire's pale, lifeless face, he replaced her small form with Peggy Weber's. Did his heart give that same jolt as it did every time he'd thought about how close he had come to losing her?

His vision cleared.

No, he would not have reacted the same. He would have

been frantic, certainly, no matter who had fallen in, but he would have seen it as the accident it was. He wouldn't have felt the same panic, that awful sense of terror, if it hadn't been Claire whose life was in danger.

His mother had been right, and he owed Claire an apology.

He immediately changed directions and let himself back out into the lobby. Taking the stairs two at a time, he hurried down the hall to her room.

"Claire?" he called, knocking on her door.

There was no answer from inside the room. She was probably ignoring him, he thought wryly as he knocked again.

"Come on, Claire, open the door. I need to talk to you."

There was still no answer.

John rattled the doorknob, expecting it to be locked, and was surprised when it turned easily in his hand. He took one look inside the room and knew that she was gone. The computer case and overnight bag that had littered the floor last night were missing. The lost-and-found clothes that had been piled up on the cardboard boxes were now neatly folded in a stack on the narrow bed with a beige telephone sitting next to them.

"Damn," John cursed, slamming the door shut as he backed out of the empty room. Where could she have gone?

He opened the door to his suite, absently patting Jack on the head as the dog greeted him at the door. Picking up the phone in his office, he pushed the button for the front desk.

"Hello, front desk," Dana answered on the second ring.

"Dana, it's John. Did you see Claire leave the hotel?"

"No. I've been here ever since you guys got back and I haven't seen her."

John hung up the phone, then tapped his fingers on the edge of his desk thoughtfully. She could have taken one of the lodge vehicles to get back to town. If she'd left right after they'd gotten back, she'd be there by now. He wasn't sure if there were any flights leaving for Seattle this time of night but, knowing Claire, if there wasn't a flight out of town tomorrow morning, she'd probably drive the thousand-plus miles back home just to get away.

He sighed, knowing it was his fault she'd left and wanting her back.

"Come on, Jack," he whistled, gathering up his car keys. "Let's go for a ride."

Chapter 14

"THANK YOU FOR DRIVING ME TO THE AIRPORT, MARY Jane." Claire watched the lodge disappear in the passenger-side mirror of Mary Jane's rented white Mercedes.

"You're welcome," She paused. "I love to drive but, living in Manhattan, I don't ever get a chance."

"Do you like living in the city?" Claire wrapped her arms around herself, still unable to fight off the chill that had seeped into her bones. Before she'd left the lodge, she'd pulled some extra shirts on over her head, but nothing seemed to be working. So much for the layering effect, she thought, trying to stop her teeth from chattering. Glad to have the conversation focused on something other than herself and her misery, Claire settled back into the heated seat of Mary Jane's luxury car.

"Not really. I moved my business to New York when John's father died. We were originally based out of Denver, but it seemed that I was spending half my time on planes flying to New York. With Hunter gone, there wasn't any reason for me to stay in Colorado, so I decided to make the move. My company was much smaller then, so there weren't as many people to move and, frankly, all of my key people were excited about moving to New York."

"What about John? How did he feel about you moving two thousand miles away?"

Mary Jane shot Claire a sideways look. She'd noticed the way her son had barely let his eyes stray from the pretty blonde, had seen the desolate look in his eyes after he'd pulled her from the river this afternoon. For six long years, she'd waited to see her son open his heart to someone else and, today, she'd finally seen her first glimmer of hope.

That was why she'd interfered when she'd noticed Claire

standing in the hall with her bags. The younger woman was determined to leave and Mary Jane guessed she'd even take one of the lodge's vehicles to do it. So, rather than letting her only hope drive right out of her son's life, she figured she'd take a chance and perhaps be able to convince Claire to stay. And if she couldn't, at least she'd know what hotel the woman was staying at just in case her pig-headed son came to his senses and wanted to know.

"John was married to my chief operating officer at the time and they moved to New York with the company."

"Funny, your son doesn't strike me as the big-city type," Claire said, trying to picture John walking around the streets of New York. She conjured up a weak smile at the image of him standing in the middle of a wide sidewalk, wearing a wet suit and holding a bright yellow oar, surrounded by suits. Talk about a fish out of water, Claire thought.

"That's an understatement." Mary Jane laughed. "At the time, though, he was traveling so much that I don't think it mattered a great deal where his mail was sent, as long as there was an airport nearby. Delilah, on the other hand, loved New York from the very first day."

Claire opened her mouth to ask another question about John, then stopped herself. What did it matter, she asked herself glumly, since she was never going to see him again? She looked out the window at the passing trees, wondering why she felt saddened at the prospect of never seeing John again. Admittedly, the sex had been good—no, great, she corrected—but they'd hardly had what could be termed a relationship. They'd bickered, fought, made love, he'd saved her life, then scolded her as if she were some sort of errant schoolgirl, but these were hardly the type of things one built a lasting relationship on. She, for one, was tired of getting dumped almost at the altar. And she was beginning to wonder what it would feel like to have someone honestly love her; not love her father, or her job, or her salary, but actually love *her* for who she was.

Maybe it was her near-death experience on the river that

afternoon, the startling epiphany she'd experienced while
lying on the riverbank, being crushed by the weight of
John's body, that her death wouldn't really matter to anyone. Her mother would cry, of course, because that's what
she'd be expected to do. Her father would shake his head
sadly at the gravesite, then would promptly go back to the
office. Her college friend, Meg, would truly grieve for her,
but after awhile it would be more of an afterthought, the
kind of sadness she'd feel once a month or so when she
picked up the phone to call and realized that Claire would
no longer be there to answer.

It wasn't that Claire wished misery on people. She simply wanted someone to love her so much that her absence
in his life would *matter*. She wanted to love someone so
much that she'd be willing to make more time in her life
for him. Both of her previous fiancés had encouraged her
to work increasing hours. They'd enjoyed the money, and
the freedom they got from having a girlfriend who was
always at work.

Her life was empty, and she kept trying to fill the void
with more work, more responsibility, more money. She
worked harder and harder, waiting for the accolades to
come, waiting for the one moment when she felt as if she'd
done enough to win the approval of her bosses, her co-
workers, her clients, and her father.

But it wasn't working. Her job had taken over her life.
She woke up during the night, worrying about something
that she needed to get done the next day and couldn't get
her mind to stop racing and let her go back to sleep. She
had a chronic rash on her wrist that hadn't gone away for
over a year. Her doctor had prescribed lotion for it, but it
wouldn't go away. She glanced down at the red patch on
her left wrist. She usually caught herself scratching the red
welts absently two or three times a day, but it hadn't bothered her at all since she'd come to Colorado. As a matter
of fact, two-thirds of the red patch had started to heal, she
noticed as she pulled the sleeve of her sweater back down

over her wrist. She was stressed out, overworked, and still it wasn't enough.

Claire closed her eyes, then opened them again but the scenery was still the same. One tree after another after another, an entire forest out there rushing past as she sat cocooned in a speeding car, like life passing her by while she waited for something that was never going to happen. It had to stop. She had to stop racing toward a goal she could never reach.

She looked over at John's mother, suddenly realizing that she was being watched. She pulled her thoughts back and blurted out the question she'd been thinking about a few minutes before. "Why did John and his ex-wife split up?"

There was a long pause. "I'm not sure exactly. I know things weren't going well between them. They were both working too hard, and I think my son always believed Delilah was too much like me," Mary Jane answered finally.

"How so?"

Mary Jane met her gaze and Claire could see the sadness in the older woman's blue eyes.

"I wasn't around for most of John's childhood," Mary Jane confessed. "I was too busy trying to build my business. I used to tell myself that it didn't matter, that John and Hunter didn't really need me around. They were very close, you see. Even when John was a baby, he seemed to prefer his father to me. I think I was jealous." She laughed without humor.

"You only had one child?" Claire asked softly, knowing what it was like to feel excluded from your own family.

"Yes. Hunter and I tried to have more children, but . . ." She shrugged, her voice trailing off. "I tried to do all the right mommy things. I volunteered at John's preschool, was head of the PTA, baked cupcakes for Cub Scouts. I did all the other things a good homemaker should do, but by the time John was in kindergarten, I was bored out of my mind. I'd spend all week doing things that revolved around John. Then he and Hunter would go camping almost every weekend and I wouldn't know what to do with myself."

"Why didn't you go with them?"

Mary Jane laughed with genuine amusement. "Oh, I did at first, but then I realized that my idea of roughing it was when the hotel we were staying at didn't have twenty-four-hour room service."

Claire shared in Mary Jane's mirth. "Me, too. I love being here at the lodge where there are hot showers and they feed you gourmet lunches."

Mary Jane stopped laughing and looked at Claire strangely. "My God," she said as realization dawned. "I'd never thought about it before, but John's built his entire business around people like me."

"So maybe he realized that not everybody likes the idea of eating freeze-dried food and going without bathing for days on end," Claire said wryly.

Mary Jane chuckled. "I know I didn't, though God knows I tried. It didn't seem to matter to Hunter, but I'm sure we would have had an even better relationship if we'd enjoyed more of the same activities."

"Do you really think so?" Claire continued hesitantly. "I mean, I always thought that if you really loved someone, you loved them because of who they are—not despite it. It doesn't sound to me that you loved your husband any less because he liked to spend his time outdoors."

"No, of course I didn't," Mary Jane agreed.

"Well, then, why do you think that he could have loved you more if you'd tried to make yourself over into Mother Earth?"

"I'd never thought of it like that, but I suppose you're right," Mary Jane said slowly.

A comfortable silence filled the leather interior of the car.

"I still miss him," Mary Jane said softly, almost to her-self.

"I'm sure you do." Claire laid a sympathetic hand on the older woman's arm. "Do you ever go out with other men?"

Mary Jane shot her a shocked look. "Of course not," she protested.

"Why not? You were what—forty-five?—when your husband died?"

"Almost fifty."

"So you have a good twenty or thirty years ahead of you. Don't you ever even think about it?"

Mary Jane fiddled uncomfortably with the knobs on the radio.

"I'm sorry, I wasn't trying to pry," Claire said into the silence, expecting Mary Jane to drop the subject.

"No, that's all right," she was surprised to hear Mary Jane say. "I have been thinking about it lately. Quite a lot, actually."

Claire watched an embarrassed blush climb up the other woman's cheeks, and guessed that she hadn't talked to anyone about her feelings.

"It's just . . ." Mary Jane hesitated, then began again. "I'm lonely, I guess. When Hunter was alive, I knew I could pick up the phone, day or night, and he'd be there. I miss that feeling, knowing that I had someone else to depend on. I didn't realize how much I valued his opinion until recently. I haven't told anyone yet, but I recently got an offer to sell my business. It's been so hard, trying to make the decision without having anyone to talk to about it. I suppose that's made me miss the companionship even more than usual."

"So why don't you do something about it? You're intelligent and attractive; I imagine there are plenty of men who've asked you out. Unless I misread the look in George Isler's eyes last night at dinner, I would guess he's interested."

Mary Jane's blush deepened. "Well, yes, I thought so, too, but I can't imagine *dating* at my age. Besides, I think it would hurt John terribly if I did."

Ah, so here was the real issue, Claire thought. "Have you talked to John about it?" she asked, knowing what the answer would most likely be.

"I couldn't. I already know what he'd think—that I must not have really loved his father if I could bring myself to date someone else," Mary Jane answered dispiritedly.

"It's been a long time since his father died. Do you really think John expects you to live alone for the rest of your life?"

Mary Jane sighed. "I don't know. I just don't think I could talk about this with him. We're not exactly close," she said ruefully.

"How often do you see each other?" Claire asked.

"Oh, five or six times a year, I'd say."

"Sounds to me like you're closer than you think. I don't see my parents at all."

"Not even at Christmas?" Mary Jane asked incredulously.

"Especially not at Christmas." Claire shrugged as Mary Jane looked askance at her. "Don't ask, it's a long story. Suffice it to say that I refused to do something my parents wanted me to do so they decided they don't want to see me anymore. We talk on the phone a couple of times a year, but it's been years since I've been back home."

"How awful."

Claire nodded her agreement, then let the subject drop. "Perhaps you and your son are closer than you think. You should at least broach the subject with him. I'm sure you know him better than I do, but I can't believe that he'd want you to live alone for the rest of your life."

Mary Jane looked up into her rear-view mirror and hid a smile. She might have the chance to bring it up sooner than Claire expected, if the vehicle bearing down on them was being driven by who she thought it was.

"You may be right," she acknowledged, easing her foot off the gas pedal. She'd been driving well under the speed limit since they'd left the lodge, hoping Claire wouldn't notice or, if she did, that she'd blame it on Mary Jane's advancing years. It appeared that her plan had worked, she thought with a touch of satisfaction as John's sleek midnight-blue Jaguar pulled behind her and flashed its lights.

"Oh, dear, I think that's John now," Mary Jane exclaimed with what she hoped was just the right amount of surprise in her voice.

Claire twisted sharply in her seat.

"Are you sure? Where's his pickup?"

"I'm pretty sure that's the sports car he bought a few years back."

"Damn. I don't suppose we could outrun him?" Claire asked hopefully, eyeing the boxy interior of the sedan.

Mary Jane coughed back a delighted laugh. Now here was a woman with some spirit.

"No, I think he'd catch us," she agreed solemnly with Claire's supposition.

"Maybe he just wants you to get some milk and bread from town," Claire muttered.

"Uh-huh." Mary Jane nodded as she eased her car to the side of the road. She was perfectly certain John hadn't sped after them to ask her to pick up groceries.

Her son was out of his car and striding toward them purposefully before her own car had even rolled to a stop. Mary Jane pressed the lever to roll down her window and bit her bottom lip to keep from laughing as John came to a halt beside her door.

"Hello, Mom."

"John." She nodded.

"Claire, could I see you for a moment?"

"Guess I was wrong about the milk," Claire muttered under her breath.

"Looks like it," Mary Jane agreed.

"Claire?" John's voice warned.

"Yes?" she answered, meeting his stormy green eyes.

"Could I have a word with you in private?"

Claire crossed her arms over her chest. The look in his eyes was dark, murderous even, although why he should be angry at her for leaving she couldn't begin to guess. He'd treated her like a giant nuisance from the minute they'd met. She would have thought he'd be delighted to see the back of her. Perhaps he was angry because she'd encroached upon his mother's vacation? By the look of his fists clenching and unclenching at his sides, she wasn't about to step out of the car and find out.

"I think anything you have to say, you can tell me from right there."

Claire noticed the wicked gleam in his eyes the second before he opened his mouth. "The sex last night was great. I would even say incredible, except for the fact that I kept worrying that one of us was going to end up on the floor at any moment. But, other than that, it was—"

Claire was out of the car before he could finish. Dashing around the front fender, she clapped a hand over his mouth.

"Shh," she hissed in his ear.

John winked at his mother behind Claire's back, then let her lead him away from the Mercedes.

Claire released him when they got out of earshot of his mother. He leaned against the hood of the dark blue sports car, lazily crossing his legs out in front of him. "So, you chickened out, huh? Decided to throw in the towel because of one little mishap? I thought you were tougher than that."

"No," Claire denied defensively, "I just figured it was time to go. My work's piling up on me, and after today's episode, I think I've had enough of the great outdoors."

John was quiet for a moment, pondering how best to approach the problem at hand. As usual, he decided on the direct approach. He'd often found the truth was disarming.

"I'd like it if you'd stay," he said quietly.

Claire looked up at him as if she suspected a trap.

He held out his hands, palms up for surrender, and gave her a wry smile. "No tricks, Claire. I find myself incredibly attracted to you, although I'm not exactly sure why."

"Gee, thanks," she said.

"I guess what I'm trying to say, and not doing a very good job of it, is that I'd like the chance to get to know you better and that can't happen if you leave now."

Claire looked off into the forest.

John didn't want to give her time to ponder every aspect of the request, he wanted her gut reaction instead. He reached out and pulled her toward him. Tilting her chin up, he saw the uncertainty in her light gray eyes.

"Why don't you give your vacation one more try? If you go back to Seattle, you'll just spend your entire vacation working. You don't really want to do that, do you?"

She shook her head imperceptibly, and he knew he'd won.

His lips brushed hers in a soft, fleeting kiss. Even that smallest point of contact sent heat through him. He felt himself responding and shook his head over his lack of control over his own body when it came to Claire. He lifted his head at the crunch of gravel as his mother turned her car around and headed back to the lodge, giving them a serene smile and a little wave as she passed.

"Come on, let's go home." Putting an arm around her shoulders, John led Claire around to the passenger side and opened the door for her to slide into the supple beige interior.

"Mary Jane, come and join us," George Isler offered as she hesitated in the doorway of the dining room.

Straightening the pleat of her neatly tailored ivory-colored slacks, Mary Jane walked to the Islers' table. "Are you sure you don't mind?"

"Of course not." George stood, gallantly pulling out a chair for her to sit down. Mary Jane held back a sigh. It was these small courtesies she missed the most. Having someone pull out her chair, or open a door. Those were the things she hadn't realized made a good relationship until they were gone.

She noticed Lisa Isler staring at her and pulled herself out of her reverie. "Did you girls enjoy the rafting trip?" she asked, including both girls in the question.

"Um-hmm" and "Yes" were their brief responses. Mary Jane had forgotten what it was like having a conversation with teenagers. Rule number one was, ask open-ended questions so they'd be forced to answer with something other than monosyllables. She tried again.

"What was your favorite part?"

"Definitely when Claire fell in," Heather answered.

Ah, now they were getting somewhere.

"I'm sure she didn't enjoy it as much as you did," George said, his brown eyes sparkling.

"Are you all planning to go on the longer trip on Friday?" Mary Jane asked.

"Yes, we are. And you?" George asked.

Mary Jane met his eyes. She hadn't given it much thought until now, and answered without thinking. "Yes, I believe I will go."

Heather Isler leaned forward. "It must have been fun doing all this cool wilderness stuff with your son when he was growing up. My parents used to—Ow! Why'd you kick me, Lisa?" the younger girl asked her sister.

"Why don't you just shut up about Mom and Dad, Heather?"

Mary Jane saw tears start to well up in Heather's eyes and wondered what in the world was going on here.

"I'm sorry." Pushing back her chair, Heather ran from the dining room, tears streaming down her cheeks.

George Isler stood up. "Heather," he called, just before she ran out the door. He turned to his older granddaughter. "Lisa, that was uncalled for. Your sister hadn't done anything wrong."

Lisa stood up; a tall, willowy girl with her grandfather's dark eyes. "They're dead, Grandpa. And it just makes it worse that she has to talk about them all the time. I'm sick of listening to her whining about them."

Before George could respond, Lisa pushed her chair back from the table and walked away, leaving her grandfather staring at her sadly.

Mary Jane sat quietly for a moment, not knowing what to say as the other diners turned their attention from the scene at the Islers' table back to their own dinners. "Would you like to talk about it?" she asked finally.

George turned to look at her, his eyes showing his surprise at finding her still there. "I'm sorry you had to witness that." He sighed, taking his seat. "I thought things were getting better, but obviously I was wrong."

"I'm guessing it was the girls' parents who died?"

He turned to look out the window at the dark forest outside the lodge, and Mary Jane wondered if she'd been too prying. "It was my son and his wife," he said quietly after a moment. "They'd been to a dinner party at a friend's house, had a little too much to drink, and lost control of their car on the way home. It happened about a year ago, and we all still miss them."

"Of course you do. And I can see why Lisa might be angry. I'm sure she feels as if they caused their own death, as if they abandoned their family on purpose."

George closed his eyes. "I'm sure she blames them. Heather just misses them. She and her father were very close. Lisa's older, was spending more time with her friends, but it still hit her hard."

"If I were Lisa, I'd probably be mad at myself, too, for knowing that I can't get that lost time with my family back now that they're gone."

"I never thought of that." He met her eyes, surprise evident on his face. "No wonder she lashes out at everyone," he muttered.

"What about you, George? How are you coping with the loss of your son?" Mary Jane asked softly.

"Me . . . I'm fine." George cleared his throat, dropping his gaze to the fresh flowers in the center of the white linen tablecloth. "It's been hard, of course, but I'm surviving."

Mary Jane reached out and covered George Isler's weathered hand with her own. She couldn't imagine the pain he must be feeling, having to deal with the loss of his child. Looking down at the hand she clasped, she noticed he wasn't wearing a wedding ring. Did he have a wife helping him through this difficult time? She couldn't bring herself to ask, to pry even further into his personal life.

"Do you think it would help if I talked to Lisa? I'm a

stranger, and maybe she'd feel more comfortable sharing her burden with someone she didn't have to face across the breakfast table every day," she said instead.

"I couldn't ask you to do that."

"You didn't ask. I offered. I'd be happy to do it if you think it would help."

George let out a deep breath. "In that case, I'd love it if you'd try. Heaven knows, I don't seem to know what to do to make her feel any better."

"All right, then. Where do you think she might have gone?" Mary Jane stood up, ready to take charge.

With a small smile, George Isler put a hand under her elbow. "I always have liked women of action."

Mary Jane looked up at his handsome profile through her eyelashes, feeling a prickle of awareness where his strong hand rested on her arm as they walked out of the dining room. It looked as if Claire was right—George Isler *did* seem interested in her. Mary Jane shook her head and held back a sigh. If only she knew what to do about it.

"This is an awfully nice car for a handyman," Claire said, wondering if John would rise to the bait.

"I borrowed it from the owner of the lodge," he answered, smoothly shifting gears on the powerful car.

"Sure you did. I hate to tell you this, but I've known who you were since Sunday morning."

John just shrugged and Claire rolled her eyes. After all this time, she'd hoped to get a better rise out of him than that. Men, she snorted, patting his dog's cold wet nose as he pushed his head up over her shoulder.

"Jack, lie down," John ordered.

"He's fine. Aren't you, puppy?" Claire cooed, looking into the sad eyes of her new friend.

"He's a pest," John said fondly. "And he's hardly a puppy."

"He's a nice dog, and he's not bothering me. I've never had a dog."

John took his eyes off the quiet two-lane road for a moment. "Never? Not even as a kid?"

"Nope. My parents didn't like pets of any kind."

"Hmm." That one word conveyed what he thought of people who didn't like animals. Claire silently agreed with him. "So why don't you get one now?" he asked.

"Easily said by someone who lives in a giant pet paradise. I live in a townhouse with a tiny backyard in the middle of a city."

"City people have pets," John protested. "I'm sure you have parks where you could walk a dog."

Claire wrinkled her nose with distaste. "Oh, sure, and you have to walk around with those little plastic bags to pick up the poop. No, thanks."

"I know exactly what you mean." John laughed, turning his warm green eyes on her.

Claire noticed the sadness was gone, at least for a moment, from his clear emerald gaze. Smiling, she leaned over and traced the lines of laughter around his eyes, something she'd wanted to do for days.

He wrapped a hand around hers, bringing her fingers to his lips. He nipped the soft pad of her index finger, sliding the sensitive flesh across his bottom lip. Claire groaned as he slid his tongue around her finger suggestively, then cursed the demise of bench seats as she realized she couldn't move closer to him without straddling the gearshift. John continued to tease her fingers, sliding them slowly in and out of his mouth.

Claire let her head fall back against the soft leather, her hair sweeping across her cheek as she reveled in the sensations John's teasing mouth was eliciting from her body. Never before had a man bothered to touch her like this. Usually, it was right to the breasts, as if she were some sort of milk cow, or even worse, a direct grab between her thighs, as if all it took to get her in the mood was a second or two of groping.

No, this was definitely much better, Claire thought, hearing her own labored breathing in the quiet interior of the car.

"That's it, I can't take anymore." John groaned, pulling the car off into the grass-lined shoulder of the road and cutting the engine. Unsnapping his seat belt, he leaned over the center console and hauled her to him.

Claire laughed as she awkwardly rearranged her legs to straddle him. "You should have brought the truck," she said as her head bumped the top of the car.

"I needed something faster," John said, pulling her lips to his.

His tongue continued its earlier teasing with her mouth instead of her fingers, as his hands started tugging at her shirt. Or rather, shirts.

"How many of these things do you have on?" he asked, trying to get his hands on her silky skin.

"Five. Don't give up yet," Claire urged, capturing his mouth in hers.

Successful at last in getting one hand against her skin, John put the other on the back of her head, taking back control of the kiss as his tongue caressed hers. He slowed the pace, sliding his fingers up and down her back as his mouth mated with hers.

Claire moaned as the blood began to pulse between her legs, starting an ache that needed to be fulfilled. Rubbing against him, Claire felt John's hardness through his jeans. She wanted to touch him, touch all of him.

Without breaking the kiss, Claire slipped her fingers between their bodies, pushing open the buttons of his shirt as she caressed downward. She slid her hands over the taut muscles of his chest, reveling in the feel of the thick hair that covered his skin and her feeling of power as he groaned against her mouth.

Reaching down, she undid the top button of his jeans, then slid open the zipper. She tried to back up, to give him enough room to get his pants off, but she inadvertently banged against the steering wheel. A loud honk followed

her rear end's collision with the horn, startling her eyes
open.

From the back seat, Jack barked at the unexpected noise
and pushed a curious nose up over John's shoulder.

Claire couldn't help the giggle that slipped from her lips
as she leaned back against the steering wheel. When the
dog licked John's face, her giggle turned to outright laughter. She laid her head against John's shoulder, hugging him
tightly as her shoulders continued to shake with mirth, tears
pouring out of her eyes.

"This is not the reaction I was going for," John said
wryly, rubbing her back.

"I'm sorry." Claire's voice was muffled, her nose buried
in his chest. "I can't seem to stop laughing."

Man and dog looked at each other. Women, John
shrugged, who could understand them?

Jack nodded his agreement, then curled up on the back
seat for a nap as the sleek car's engine purred to life and
carried them back to the lodge.

Lisa Isler was busy tossing stones into the river when Mary
Jane found her.

The orange glow of sunset was just beginning to fade
into the horizon as Mary Jane sat down on the bank and
watched the girl below. Gray stones, worn to a smooth
roundness by years of pounding water, made a distinctive
plop as they broke the surface of the river.

When John was a boy, he used to be a stone-thrower,
too. She recalled a favorite picnic spot near the lake where
she and Hunter would take him, then spend hours watching
their son picking out the best rocks for skipping. John had
always been patient, even as a child. She'd often marveled
at his ability to stay focused on a task while other children
had the attention spans of . . . well, of children.

Her lips curved up in a smile. Lisa Isler, on the other
hand, was not carefully choosing perfect, flat stones that
would skip easily off the surface of the water. Instead, she
heaved anything she could lift into the rushing river, as if

a chunk of her misery could fly away with each hurling motion.

With the sun's disappearance, the early fall air started to cool down rapidly, but Mary Jane didn't want to disturb Lisa's ritual yet. A little chill wouldn't hurt her, but keeping all that sadness and anger bottled up inside would.

A handful of rocks went into the river, then Lisa sat down abruptly on a boulder, putting her head in her hands. Mary Jane could hear the muffled sound of the girl's sobs, and picked her way across the slippery rocks toward her.

Without saying a word, she laid an arm over Lisa's shoulder, wincing as the small bones shook beneath her.

"I'm sorry," the girl sobbed. "I didn't mean to hurt Heather."

"Shh. I know you didn't," Mary Jane soothed.

If anything, Lisa's crying increased. "I just can't believe that Mom and Dad are gone. Why did they have to be so stupid and selfish?"

Mary Jane didn't have any magic answers, so she just hugged the girl as she cried. "I know it hurts, Lisa. It's perfectly natural to be angry at your parents for leaving you and your sister. I'm sure you probably feel sad, too, that you didn't get to talk to them one last time, to tell them how much you loved them."

Sniffling, Lisa raised her head, her dark brown eyes puddling over with tears. "I miss them so much." A fat tear dripped off the end of her nose. Mary Jane pulled a perfume-scented handkerchief out of her pocket and handed it to Lisa.

"I'm sure you do. They must have been wonderful people to have raised you and your sister so well."

Lisa nodded miserably. "They were great."

"But?" Mary Jane sensed there was something more Lisa wanted to say.

The quiet sounds of the night closed around them as Lisa looked out into the darkening forest. From somewhere nearby, a frog croaked, the rough deep sound unmistakable among the softer sounds of the crickets' serenade and water lapping against its banks.

"We had a big fight the night they . . ."—Lisa swallowed—"the night of the accident. Mom didn't want me to go out with my friends that night. We were just going to go to the movies and hang out at the mall, but they told me I couldn't go. Right after Mom and Dad left, I—"

She started crying again, and Mary Jane finished her sentence. "After they left, you went out to meet your friends, figuring your parents would never find out." So that was the problem. Like most kids who have to deal with tragedy at a young age, Lisa probably felt that her own misbehavior had caused her parents' accident. As if God were punishing her for doing something bad by killing her loved ones. "Oh, honey, just because you disobeyed your parents' order doesn't mean you had anything to do with their accident."

"I know, but I just can't help feeling that if I hadn't snuck out that night, my parents would still be alive."

Mary Jane hugged the girl tighter, knowing there was nothing she could say, nothing she could do that would make the pain go away. Instead, she remained silent and rocked the girl in the fading twilight, whispering comforting words to her as she cried.

"It looks like you're having a bit of a problem with your expenses," Claire said, eyeing the report sitting on top of John's desk as she absently tapped in the fax number Robert Edwards had given her.

John leaned back in his leather-upholstered chair and eyed her curiously. "How do you know that?"

As the fax machine gobbled up the first page of her stack of charts, Claire picked up the report and began studying it. It looked like a standard variance report, revenues this quarter versus revenues last quarter, expenses year to date versus expenses for the same period a year ago. The usual type of thing corporate offices loved to spend their time creating.

"We get similar reports at Allied." Claire shrugged and handed the report back to John. "The expense figure shown for the current quarter is twice what it was the same quarter last year without a corresponding increase in your revenues. Either you're in the process of a major expansion, or something's wrong."

Claire sat down in the chair across from John and waited for her fax to finish going through. She hid a smile as John raised his eyebrows at her. She'd majored in finance. What did he expect, that she'd giggle and tell him she wasn't good with numbers?

"That was very good, but I'd be even more impressed if you could tell me why it's off. I left a message with the head of operations in Kauai but haven't had the chance to talk to him yet."

"Kauai, hmm? Tell me, is your head of operations new?"

"Yes. I just transferred him from—"

"Japan?" Claire interrupted, biting the inside of her lip to keep from smiling at John's incredulous stare.

"Yes. How'd you know?"

"Just a guess. I'll bet I can tell you what the problem is." She leaned back and crossed her arms over her chest, nonchalantly swinging one leg over the other.

John leaned back in his own chair and crossed his arms, mimicking her stance. "Shoot," he said.

"In Japan, if you want things to run smoothly, it's perfectly acceptable, if not encouraged, to, uh, grease the wheels of commerce, if you know what I mean."

"No, I don't know what you mean."

"There's no moral stigma in Japanese culture against accepting cash and other gifts to help smooth business relations. While we might consider it bribery, in their culture it's considered honorable and courteous. When an executive is transferred to the U.S., he may not realize it isn't necessary to offer these types of incentives to other businesspeople."

"If that's the case, why are people accepting the bribes? Hawaii's not Japan, after all."

It was Claire's turn to raise her eyebrows. "If you were offered thousands of dollars to do something you already intended to do, wouldn't you take it?"

"No, of course not," John protested, uncrossing his arms and leaning forward.

"Me, neither." Claire shrugged. "But there are lots of people out there who wouldn't turn down a little extra cash if it was handed to them. From your manager's perspective, he hasn't done anything wrong. It's really just a matter of educating him about American business practices."

"So how do you know about this?" John asked.

"I've handled several accounts with Japanese owners. Let's just say I could have bought myself a bigger house but chose to educate my new clients instead."

The fax machine beeped and spat out a confirmation that her report had been sent to Bryan's father. Claire reached for the piece of paper, not bothering to hide her satisfied grin.

John's hand snaked out across the desk and caught her wrist.

"You think you're smart, don't you?"

Claire's skin tingled where he touched her and a shiver of awareness radiated up her arms when she met his darkening gaze. "Yes, I do," she answered, her voice husky as she leaned toward him across the expanse of smooth wood.

"I've always liked smart women," John said, meeting her in the middle.

Chapter 15

"HAS ANYONE EVER TOLD YOU, YOU HAVE BEAUTIFUL feet, Miss Brown?"

Claire laughed. "Stop it, John. That tickles."

Early morning sunlight streamed in through the small window of her room, painting a silvery glow around John's head as he rested his head against the foot of her bed, his fingers playing lightly with her toes. He'd invited her to his room last night, but Claire didn't feel comfortable sleeping with him while his mother was visiting. He'd laughed at her quaint values, but hadn't protested. Instead, he'd spent the night with her in her room.

"Why don't we give my room a try tonight?" he suggested now, between placing light kisses on the balls of her feet.

"Mmm," Claire murmured, leaning her head back on her pillow. She'd never realized how turned on she could get from having someone touch her feet. Looking into John's eyes, she realized she wasn't the only one who was getting pleasure out of this. She ran a hand slowly up the inside of his leg.

"I mean, it's not like she doesn't know what's going on," John cajoled. "Besides, I'm always afraid I'm going to end up on the floor when we're rolling around on this tiny bed."

"Your fear doesn't seem to be affecting your performance any," Claire laughed.

He nipped her big toe lightly. "Sure it is, I'm even better when I'm not worrying about tumbling out of bed every time I move," he teased.

God help me, Claire thought. If he was any better, she'd be dead by Sunday. "I don't know. I just . . ." She broke off, trying to stop the heat she could feel creeping into her cheeks.

"You just what?"

"I know this is stupid, but I just can't stand the thought that your mother might hear us." She lost her battle with the blush.

John laughed. "Well, you did get kind of loud last night—"

Claire yanked the pillow out from under her head and leaped across the bed. Straddling his hips, she smothered him with a faceful of feathers.

He came up smiling and tossed the pillow to the floor. With his hands on the borrowed blue shirt covering her back, John pulled her down to rest on his chest. Claire tangled her legs with his, sliding her smooth calves against his rougher ones. Unlike her, John didn't seem to be bothered by his own nakedness. She had never been able to sleep in the nude, had always felt that this meant she wasn't as sensual as other women who did, but it didn't seem to matter to John. He seemed to want her whether she was naked or not.

"If I promise to make sure my mother doesn't hear us, will you agree to sleeping in a bigger bed tonight?" he asked, tracing lazy circles on the backs of her thighs with his fingers.

"How are you going to do that?"

"I don't know. I'll think of something."

"Okay, you've got a deal." Claire couldn't resist the urge to run her tongue across his chest.

John groaned. "Stop it. I've got to get up."

Claire grinned. "Feels like you already are."

"That's not what I meant." John grabbed both of her wandering hands in one of his and pushed her back onto the bed. His kiss was intended to be light, quick, but she met his mouth eagerly, and it was several minutes before he pulled back.

Claire watched with unabashed interest as he pulled on his jeans and combed his fingers through his disheveled hair. He was certainly a fine specimen to behold, she thought, wishing he'd forget his responsibilities and come back to bed.

"You sure you don't want to come along?" he asked, pausing at her door.

The warmth in his emerald eyes was almost enough to convince her, but she had formulated a plan yesterday when she'd agreed to come back to the lodge, and she needed the morning free to accomplish it. "No, I'm going to laze around here today."

"All right, then I'll see you tonight."

He left with a smile, sucking all of the air out of her room when he went. He'd told her he was going to be gone all day. After the morning hike, he had to help with an afternoon horseback ride, then go out again for the sunset hike.

She hadn't expected to miss him.

Claire sighed. Now there was a man who could tempt her into giving up work.

She blinked, suddenly sitting up straight. Where in the world had that thought come from? She wasn't giving up work, for heaven's sake. She was just going to try to get things in order so she wouldn't have to lug her laptop around for the next three days, that was all. She just didn't want to have to worry about her computer out there in the wilderness. It had nothing to do with John McBride, no matter how good a lover he was.

The cellophane wrapper crackled loudly in the quiet of his office as Robert Edwards untwisted it to release the piece of candy trapped inside. He popped the sugar-free, cherry-flavored ball into his mouth, then pulled a stapled report out of his briefcase and studied the top page.

Claire had blacked out the names of the other accounts before faxing the graphs to him, but it really didn't matter. Her findings were clear. Of the ten accounts she'd been assigned, four of them—the only four accounts that he, himself, was directly responsible for—had much higher than average claim costs.

She didn't know why—at least, not yet—but she was looking to him for answers. That was a good sign that she didn't suspect anything. Again, not yet.

Robert swallowed, then rolled the sourball around on his tongue and stared at the opposite wall of his richly furnished office. He grimaced. He hated the picture his wife had chosen, an abstract with muted colors of teal and aquamarine with deep, jarring slashes of scarlet oozing out like knife wounds. He would have preferred something nautical. Tall ships or seascapes. But Nancy and her fancy interior decorator had insisted on refurbishing his office, and he hadn't wanted to make a scene so now he was stuck with the ugly picture staring at him every day.

Holding on to the report, he swiveled around, putting his back to the bleeding painting as he watched a ferry chug peacefully across Puget Sound. From his office on the seventy-fourth floor of the Columbia Tower, he could see for miles in every direction except east, across Lake Washington. Normally, the view calmed him, even when the rain poured down and he couldn't see past West Seattle, much less across the Sound to the majestic Olympic Mountains on the peninsula. Usually, just knowing that he had one of the most impressive offices in the most prestigious building in Seattle was enough to fill him with a sense of well-being.

He didn't feel peaceful today, however. Bryan had been wrong about Claire. She obviously wasn't as buried with her own work as Bryan had suspected since she'd already had time to figure out that something was amiss with Robert's accounts. He should have known his son's opinion couldn't be trusted.

The problem was, he didn't know what to do about it yet. He had to think up a plausible reason why his accounts were different from the others she'd been given. In the meantime, he needed to make sure that Claire Brown didn't know any more than what she'd already told him. As much as he hated to depend on his son, Bryan was his only hope.

Shaking his head with disgust, Robert crunched down on the last remaining shards of his sourball and swiveled around in his chair. He picked up the handset of his phone and dialed the number for Hunter's Lodge. This time when he asked for Bryan, the girl put him right through. Robert tapped his fingers impatiently as the phone rang three, four, five times.

"Hello?" came the sleepy response when the phone was finally answered.

"Bryan? It's your father."

There was a loud thunk on the other end of the line and some shuffling before Bryan responded. "Oh. Hi, Dad."

"What was that noise? And why is there an echo on the line? Is there something wrong with the phone?"

Bryan yawned loudly into the phone. "I was just putting down the toilet seat so I could sit down. There's an echo in the bathroom, there's nothing wrong with the phone line."

"In the bathroom? Why are you talking to me from the bathroom?" Robert wrinkled his nose with distaste. Really, there was such a thing as too much information and his son had just crossed that line.

"This is the only phone in the room, that's why I'm talking to you from here. Why are you calling so early?"

Robert squelched the urge to ask why the only phone was in the bathroom. He knew he'd only get an asinine answer in response. Instead, he answered his son's question with, "It's ten o'clock there. I'd hardly call that early."

"I guess we overslept. We were, uh, up late last night."

Robert heard some female giggling, then the sound of water and knew he only had a moment before he lost his son's attention completely. Rolling his eyes heavenward, he sighed. "Bryan, listen to me," he said sharply. "I need you to keep an eye on Claire. Do you hear me?"

"Uh, yeah. Keep an eye on Claire," Bryan repeated absently.

"Tell me if she asks you any questions about my accounts or if she does anything out of the ordinary. Can you do that for me?"

"Sure, Dad. No problem. I've, uh . . . yeah. Bye."

With that cryptic uttering, the phone went dead. Robert stared at the instrument in his hand, then shook his head and replaced the receiver back on its cradle.

It was time to start formulating Plan B.

Amy Anderson, a thirty-four-year-old female, was one sick chick, Claire decided, squinting at her computer screen.

Ms. Anderson had filed claims for back problems, carpal tunnel syndrome, and a knee injury, all in the past January. That was odd enough in itself, but what confused Claire even more was that Ms. Anderson was claiming workers' compensation benefits from each one of the four accounts Claire was reviewing.

"How could she work at all four companies at the same time?" Claire muttered to herself, stretching out across the narrow bed in her room.

It was just as well she'd stayed here to work. Claire sighed, unconsciously nibbling on the end of a finger. She'd had over a hundred e-mails and half as many voice mails when she'd checked in after John left this morning. She'd ordered breakfast from room service, dealt with all the pressing issues, and had about two hours left to get back to analyzing her boss's accounts before John returned.

After summarizing each account's claims by month, day of week, time of day, and type of claim, she still hadn't spotted any trends that would explain why their numbers were so out of whack. Robert hadn't called her back with any information yet and her last resort was to see if any of the accounts were having trouble with a single claimant filing multiple claims. This would mean that the clients and claims adjusters were possibly allowing workers to file fraudulent claims.

She'd seen it happen with other accounts. Some weekend warrior would come in to work and blame his strained back on the job, rather than the fact that Mr. Sedentary had

simply overdone it on yard work or a friendly game of
neighborhood football. If that claim was allowed to go
through the system, it didn't take long for that employee
and others to figure out how easy it was to get paid for
doing nothing. Just show up to work for a few hours, pretend you'd been injured on the job, and voilà, you could
sit at home getting paid to watch Oprah all day.

Thinking this might be the problem, Claire had sorted
the claims by employee name, but hadn't found an unusual
number of claims by the same employee at any of the companies. Then she had accidentally resorted her data again,
removing the subtotals by company so that all four clients'
claims data were mixed in together.

That was when she discovered Ms. Anderson and her
multiple injuries. Claire double-checked the woman's Social Security number just to make sure they weren't really
four different Amy Andersons, but all four claims showed
the same number.

Claire scribbled Ms. Anderson's Social Security number
on her notepad, then decided to dial into her company's
database of claims information that would tell her if this
woman was a known abuser of the workers' compensation
system. She'd used the service almost daily when she was
an adjuster to check on claims that didn't seem quite right,
finding that claimants filing fraudulently would quite often
use the same medical history over and over again. And why
not? Claire thought scornfully as she logged into Allied's
mainframe, some of them made quite a good living by
claiming they'd been injured at every job where they were
fortunate enough to be hired.

She entered Ms. Anderson's Social Security number at
the prompt and waited for the search engine to scan the
database.

Claire blinked with surprise when a message popped up.

"Twelve records found. Do you want to continue?"

"Twelve records!" Claire exclaimed, hitting the yes button. Most people, in their entire lifetimes, wouldn't file
even one claim, but it wasn't unusual in labor-intensive

companies to see the same claimant two, or even three, times if the employee worked somewhere long enough. But twelve claims was unheard-of. This Ms. Anderson was obviously defrauding her employers, Claire thought angrily as she clicked on the first of Amy Anderson's records.

The claim was dated in March, eight years ago. As Claire read through the details of the case, she frowned. Eight years ago, Amy Anderson had worked at an aircraft manufacturing plant. In March of her seventh year of employment, Amy, along with three other employees, was involved in a freak accident when the scaffolding she'd been standing on fell, dropping her the equivalent of three stories to land on the hard concrete floor of the plant.

The families of all four employees sued the aircraft company for wrongful death when it had been discovered that there were numerous entries in a maintenance log regarding the scaffolding equipment. The company had refused to replace the equipment, and it was obvious they would have been found negligent if the case had gone to trial. The claim was settled out of court a year later.

Puzzled, Claire looked up from her computer screen. If Amy Anderson had died eight years ago, why had eleven more claims been filed under her Social Security number subsequent to her unfortunate death?

She pulled up a copy of the settlement check and was surprised to see that it was mailed to a Mr. Scott Anderson at an address in Colorado. Then she went through the computer files for the other claims and wrote down the dates of each claim and the address where each claim check was being sent. The claim dates were scattered throughout the past six years. They were all the same types of claims, debilitating injuries where a claimant could expect to receive disability payments throughout her entire life. The address for each check was the same, a post office box in Seattle. The only thing that was different was the name of each employer.

Setting her alarm to ring in an hour, Claire decided to

check her list of claimants to see if there were any more claimants like Ms. Anderson. As she scrolled through her data, her scribbled notes took up more and more space on the yellow lined pad.

Chapter 16

"CLAIRE?" JOHN CALLED, KNOCKING ON HER DOOR.

Just like yesterday afternoon there was no answer from within.

"Claire?" he called, knocking again. He rattled the doorknob, but, unlike last night, the door was locked. She must be somewhere around, John thought, disappointed that she wasn't in her room.

He'd spent the afternoon on the trail ride, wishing he were back at the lodge. Even as a boy he'd never taken to horses, preferring to hike rather than fight with some thousand-pound animal who seemed to want to do nothing but eat all the time.

As soon as they'd arrived back at the lodge, he'd checked the sign-up sheet for the sunset hike and found that only Cindy and Bryan were planning to go, so he let Kyle lead the hike by himself. Since he had another full day tomorrow and they had to leave early Friday morning for their final rafting trip, he figured this was his last opportunity to be alone with Claire before Saturday night when they returned to the lodge.

He had stopped asking himself what it was about her that kept him coming back for more. She was smart, funny, and sexy as hell. Now, if only he could convince her to give up her office equipment for awhile, they just might be able to enjoy themselves until she went back home. The thought wrenched something in the vicinity of his heart, and he pushed it away. He wasn't going to worry about that now; he'd rather concentrate on enjoying the next few days.

That thought didn't cheer him up either as he let himself

into his suite, noticing absently that Jack wasn't at his usual
greeting spot just inside the door.

"Must be napping on my bed," John muttered, then
stopped, cocking his head. It sounded as if the water were
running in one of the bathrooms, but he knew his mother
wasn't here. He'd just seen her down in the lobby playing
cards with George Isler.

Suddenly, he remembered the call he'd received from
his ex-colleague at the Bureau. If Derrick Washington was
on his way to pay John a visit, it was possible that he could
be here by now.

John glanced around, searching for any signs of forcible
entry. He clenched his jaw as he wondered again where
Jack was. Jack was almost twelve years old and spent most
of his day curled up with the cat who'd adopted John a few
years back. Even if a burglar did break in, Jack was more
likely to greet him with a friendly wag of the tail than with
any show of ferociousness. He'd kill the bastard if he'd
hurt the old dog, John vowed, slipping his gun out of its
usual hiding place in the silverware drawer in the kitchen.

The unaccustomed weight of the gun felt heavy in his
hand. There'd been a time, not that long ago, when it was
the absence of a gun that felt odd and not the other way
around. Last month, when he'd taken it out to practice, John
had been thankful that it felt strange, had even thought
about getting rid of the weapon. Glad now that he hadn't,
John followed the sound of running water. It came from
the master bathroom and John wondered if Derrick was
trying to lure him into a room with only one entry and exit
point. Running several scenarios over in his mind, John
thought Derrick would have been smarter to confront him
out in the living room where the younger man would have
multiple means of escape if something went wrong.

Of course, not all criminals were smart. John crouched
down to peer into the master bedroom. This one could be
cocky enough that it would never enter his head that he
could possibly make an error and end up on the receiving
end of a bullet instead.

From his position in the doorway, John didn't see anyone in the bedroom, so he slid through the door as quietly as he could, checking around the bed to make sure no one was lurking there. John warned himself this could be a trap. Derrick could be trying to lure him into the bathroom with the running water and was planning to come up behind him, cutting off his exit route and—

The sound of running water stopped abruptly. Derrick couldn't have turned off the water if he wasn't in the bathroom.

John crouched again by the doorway of the bathroom, knowing that Derrick would probably aim at where he expected John's head or chest to be..

Slowly, he peered into the bathroom, then sat back on his heels, shaking his head with a mixture of disgust and relief. Standing up, he quickly shoved the gun into the top drawer of his dresser, then leaned against the doorjamb of the bathroom, crossing his arms over his chest.

Jack stood up, wagging his tail in greeting but not moving out from under Claire's hand where it lay on his head.

"Some guard dog you are," he admonished, meeting the dog's friendly gaze.

Claire gasped and opened her eyes at the familiar, yet unexpected voice. She slid down farther under the water, thankful that Mary Jane's bubbly bath gel hid her from John's view.

John raised his eyebrows at her modesty and wanted to ask if she thought there wasn't an inch of her body he didn't already know after their latest bout of lovemaking. But he considered himself a gentleman, so he held his tongue.

"Jack, out," he ordered, patting the dog's head and closing the door as the wagging tail disappeared.

He freed the top button of his shirt.

"What are you doing?" Claire asked, watching from the tub as more of his chest became exposed to the humid air in the bathroom.

"You look so comfy, I thought I'd join you," he an-

swered. Pulling off his shirt, he sat down on the edge of
the tub to pull off his boots.

Claire appreciatively watched the muscles of John's
back as he moved. He had the lean, firm body of somebody
for whom physical activity was a part of daily life, not the
built-up, sculpted muscles of someone who worked out at
the gym. Biting her bottom lip, she sat up and slid her
warm, soapy arms around his stomach, pressing her breasts
into his back.

The hard muscles of his stomach tightened under her
hands, and she could feel the rumble of his groan under her
cheek.

He turned and lifted her out of the water in one smooth
movement, settling her wet body on his lap.

"I'm dripping all over you," Claire protested, laughing.

"I'll dry," he growled, and captured her mouth in his.

Claire wound her arms around his neck, burying her fingers in his thick, dark hair and pressing her body against
his.

He rained kisses down her neck, raising goose bumps
on her arms.

"You smell good," he breathed into her ear, gently
kneading the muscles of her back with his strong hands.

Claire giggled, pressing a moist kiss just below his ear.
"You smell like horse."

"And to think I never really enjoyed horseback riding
before this," John growled, tumbling them backward into
the hot, soapy water. Warm water sloshed over the rim of
the tub and onto the marble floor.

Claire shrieked at his sudden movement, laughing when
she realized he was still wearing his pants.

"Here, let's get you out of those wet things." She leered,
wiggling her eyebrows up and down.

"Be my guest," John offered, leaning back and laying
his head on the rim of the tub.

Laughing, Claire fumbled with the top button of his
jeans, watching his eyes darken with desire as she slowly
eased down the zipper of the wet cloth.

It was odd, Claire thought, as she dropped his sopping pants onto the bathroom floor, she'd never realized making love could actually be fun. Then all thoughts of amusement fled as John took her breast into his mouth, teasing her nipple with his hot tongue.

"So, my mother knew all about your sneaking into my bathtub, did she?" John asked, lazily winding a curl of blond hair around his finger.

"Um-hmm," Claire acknowledged sleepily, twining her legs with his under the covers of his king-sized bed. She knew she needed to get up soon and get dressed for dinner, but a strength-sapping lassitude held her fully in its grip.

"I guess I know where her loyalties lie. She didn't say a word to me."

"Your mother's nice."

John snorted. "You're just saying that because she went along with your little conspiracy."

Claire bit his chest playfully. "Of course that helped, but I really do like her." She wondered if Mary Jane had broached the subject of dating with her son. Thoughtfully chewing the inside of her cheek, Claire wondered if the older woman would appreciate Claire's interference. Maybe John would take the suggestion of his mother's renewed love life better if someone else brought it up. She was just deciding how best to open the conversation when she heard a door open and close, followed by the sound of female laughter.

Glancing at the open door of John's bedroom, Claire yelped and slid all the way under the covers.

"John? Are you here?" she heard his mother call.

"Uh, just a minute, Mom." Claire heard the amusement in John's voice, muffled as it was through the blankets. She pinched his naked thigh.

He lifted the covers up, exposing her to the cooler air of the room. "Can't hide in here forever. We have to go out sometime for food."

"I don't have any clothes." Her voice came out in a squeak.

"Well, now, that's an interesting dilemma. Did you walk in here naked?" John grinned.

"Of course not. My clothes were sitting on the floor next to the tub and they're all soaking wet now, thanks to a certain someone who decided to join me in the bath."

"All right, all right. Don't get your panties in a twist— Oh, sorry, guess you don't have any panties to get twisted, do you?"

"John, are you in there? I've brought George Isler's granddaughters up for awhile. I hope you don't—"

John popped his head outside the covers, grinning as Claire plastered herself to his side. He leaned back against the headboard, enjoying Claire's predicament. "Hi, Mom. Sorry, I forgot to shut the door. Guess I'm used to living alone."

His mother stood in the doorway of his room. She raised an eyebrow at the curious movements under the covers.

"Don't worry, Mom. That's just Claire trying to hide. Ouch." He lifted up the covers again. "If you pinch me again, Claire, I'm going to shove you off the bed, and then where will you be, flopping naked on the floor like a trout on the hook?"

"You think this is funny, don't you?" Claire hissed, her cheeks a delightfully flaming red color.

"Yes," John answered thoughtfully. "Yes, I guess I do." He popped his head out again, meeting his mother's amused blue eyes. "What about you, Mom? Do you think this is funny, too? I mean, there's a woman hiding in my bed, and she doesn't have any clothes on at all."

"None at all?" Mary Jane played along with his game.

"Nope, not a stitch."

"Well, then, I'd have to say that it would depend on the perspective of the person you're asking. I mean, you might think it's funny—although I'm assuming you're not wearing much more than poor Claire—and I might be able to see the humor in the situation. But I'll bet that Claire is probably not going to find this amusing in the least." Mary Jane made her final determination.

Claire's blond head popped out from under the covers. "Thank you, Mary Jane."

"You're welcome. Now, why don't I let you two . . . uh . . . finish up whatever it is you were doing, then you can come out and join us?"

"How embarrassing," Claire muttered as Mary Jane closed the bedroom door.

"Hell, that was nothing. Just think if she'd come home ten minutes earlier."

John laughed when Claire groaned and buried her head in her hands.

"Come on. I'll let you borrow some more of my clothes. It's a good thing you're leaving in a few days or I might run out of things to . . ." His voice petered out as he realized what he'd meant as a joke wasn't funny.

The hurt in Claire's gray eyes told him that she agreed with his assessment.

"Damn it, Claire, I'm sorry. That wasn't what I meant." Getting out of bed, John ran an agitated hand through his hair.

"It's fine. Can you just get me some clothes?"

Shit. Why had he said that? He wasn't looking forward to Sunday when she'd get back on a plane and fly out of his life, probably forever. But what did he want? Did he want her to stay?

No, surely he wasn't ready to make a lifelong commitment to a woman he'd known for less than a week, a woman who had the same workaholic tendencies he'd sworn he'd never live with again. So why did the thought of never seeing her again bother him so much?

John pulled open a dresser drawer and hauled out a pair of navy blue sweats and a light gray polo shirt and tossed them to Claire before extracting blue jeans and a green flannel shirt for himself. She was silent as she pulled on the borrowed clothes, then headed to the bathroom to gather up the soggy things that were still strewn about the wet floor.

"Here, let me throw these things in the wash," John offered, holding out his arms for the load she was carrying.

Claire handed over the dripping mess, then went back to mop up the trail of water on the slippery floor. Watching her, John sighed, not knowing what to say to erase the tension that had come between them at his insensitive comment.

He followed her out into the dining room, where his mother had covered the table with pots of creams and lotions and was holding court like a queen with her loyal subjects.

"It's never too early to start wearing moisturizer," Mary Jane said, holding a yellow bottle out to the elder Isler girl.

"Hello, Claire. John." George Isler stood up as they entered the room. "Your mother offered me one of your beers; I hope you don't mind?"

"No, of course not, George. Hello Lisa, Heather." John nodded to the girls, who continued eyeing his mother's wares with all the enthusiasm of the recently converted.

He could hear his mother continue her explanations of this potion and that as he loaded the wet clothes into the washing machine, added a cupful of detergent, and started the machine. Jack padded into the laundry room, stopping in the doorway so John could rub his head. Leaning against the doorjamb, John watched the scene in the other room: the teenagers listening intently to his mother as they explored the contents of each container, his mother happily sharing her considerable knowledge of the cosmetics industry to her rapt audience, George Isler looking relaxed for the first time since he'd come to the lodge; and Claire . . . Claire standing apart from the rest of the group, looking beautiful and sad.

"I've got to be going," he heard her say from across the room.

"Oh, we were going to see if the kitchen would send up

a pizza. Are you sure you don't want to stay?" his mother asked.

"No, thank you. I'm not hungry." John barely heard Claire's mumbled reply before she turned and walked away. She left the room without looking back.

Refusing to meet his mother's curious gaze, John opened the back door and ushered Jack down the stairs and out into the still night.

Chapter 17

CLAIRE DOODLED GEOMETRIC SHAPES ON THE NOTEPAD ON her lap and listened to the rain pelting the small window in her room. She hadn't slept well, had missed the warmth of John's body, his heavy arm thrown over her shoulders.

She gnawed on the end of her pen, then looked down at the pad of paper.

"Ugh," she groaned, wrinkling her nose with disgust. The top sheet was full of little black hearts and arrows she'd unconsciously drawn while staring at the opposite wall. Ripping the piece of paper off the pad, she crumpled it into a wad and tossed it across the room.

Restlessly, she shifted positions on the bed and reminded herself it was just as well that John wasn't there. She knew their relationship, such as it was, couldn't last. She had a job back in Seattle where she was needed. Looking at her notes reminded her of that. And his place was here, at the lodge he'd built and named for his father, with the river and the wilderness that were so much a part of him. He hadn't asked her to be a part of that world. All he'd wanted was a few days out of her life and she'd agreed. Why not? They were consenting adults. She was entitled to a satis-fying sex life, just like anybody else. It had certainly been satisfying while it lasted. There was no denying that.

So why was she so disappointed that it was over?

She sighed and her stomach growled, reminding her that she'd missed dinner last night.

"Might as well go down and get something to eat," she muttered, pulling on a pair of lime-green sweatpants and the tattered Def Leppard T-shirt. She'd called the airline again first thing this morning. Her suitcase was supposed to have been delivered yesterday, but it was missing in action again. Apparently, she was doomed to spend her vacation looking like a reject from Goodwill.

Bringing the pad and a pen with her so she could take notes over breakfast, Claire opened the door to her room.

And ran smack into Bryan.

She stepped back hastily. "What are you doing?" she asked.

Bryan's face turned splotchy red. "Nothing. I was just, uh, exploring."

Claire narrowed her eyes at him, wondering what he had really been doing loitering outside her door. Then she shrugged. Whatever he was doing probably had nothing to do with her. Why had she never realized how weird he was before this? She could almost thank Cindy for saving her from making one of the biggest mistakes of her life. Almost. She was glad it was over, but there was a limit to her generosity. She was human, after all.

Turning, she closed and locked her door, ignoring Bryan as he followed her down the hall. As she passed room 24, Cindy bounded out, wearing orange-tinted goggles and a barely there, bright blue bikini.

"Hi, Claire. Great day for a dip in the pool, don't you think? I just love the idea of going swimming in the rain," she gushed cheerfully.

Claire fought the urge to roll her eyes back in her head. "Yes, I'm sure it will be delightful. Why are you wearing goggles?" she asked, unable to stop herself. Cindy looked ridiculous.

"I can't wear my contacts in the pool. All that chlorine, you know. But my vision is terrible so I have to wear these prescription goggles instead," she explained, then turned to Bryan. "Did you decide to come swimming with me, sweetie?"

Bryan mumbled something and the pair took off down the hall.

Claire stood rooted to the spot, in front of the door to the room that was rightfully hers. Once again, that evil impulse reared its tantalizing head and whispered hot, tempting words in her ear.

Ever since she'd first seen Cindy on the plane, Claire had wondered if those too-bright blue eyes were for real. Tempting as it might have been in the beginning, however, Claire could hardly have stuck her fingers in the other woman's eyes to see if she was wearing colored contacts. Now, the answer was right there in front of her, not ten feet away, calling to her, urging her to discover the truth.

If someone, someone with a cool head and an ounce of reason, had stopped her just then and asked her if it really mattered, Claire would have gained the upper hand over the evil impulse and admitted that it didn't. She didn't want Bryan back. He and the blue-eyed bimbo deserved each other and, even if her fling with John was flung, she was glad that things had turned out this way.

Unfortunately, no one was around to intervene so Claire found herself, a split second later, once again turning the knob on the door to room 24 and slinking inside, her heart pounding a thousand beats a minute as it tried to catch up with her nimbly moving feet.

She snatched the contact case up from the bathroom counter and was back out in the hall in the space of two heartbeats. She pulled the door closed behind her.

Then screamed when a hand touched her shoulder.

"Claire, what are you up to?"

With a silent groan, Claire leaned her head against the cool wood of the door. She was busted. John had caught her again. Briefly, she considered slipping the contact case into her sweats for safekeeping but John's next comment stopped her.

"If you hide whatever it is you've taken, I'll do a full body search." He paused and the words fell between them, hot and thick. "With pleasure." He was closer behind her than she had thought, his breath stirring the hair at the base of her neck. His voice had gone low and husky and the mental image of him doing a long, slow search of every inch of her body had Claire's breath hitching in her throat.

So much for not caring that their relationship was over, a silent voice taunted.

She licked her suddenly dry lips, then took a small step back and closed the gap between their bodies. John's hand snaked around her waist and pulled her even closer while his mouth teased the side of her neck.

"I'm sorry for hurting your feelings yesterday. I'm not looking forward to Sunday, to when you have to leave."

His hands slid upward to cup her breasts. Claire closed her eyes, reveling in the feel of his hands on her, teasing her through the soft cotton of her T-shirt. He trailed a line of wet kisses up her neck, stopping to nip her earlobe. Her hands went nerveless at that, and she was surprised she didn't drop her notepad and pen, much less the stolen contact lenses, when John traced the line of her ear with his tongue.

Claire groaned. If she hadn't lost the power of speech, she would have told him how good that felt. As it was, she kept quiet and enjoyed the sensation as John continued whispering in her ear.

"I don't want to know what you've stolen from your ex-fiancé, but I need to put it back before we finish this. Why don't you hand over whatever it is so we can finish this up in private?"

She could only blame her next action on the evil impulse since her brain was occupied with other thoughts that had nothing to do with Bryan or Cindy or anything besides her and John, naked, engaged in an act that would not be appropriate to continue in the middle of the hall. So, without conscious thought, she palmed the contact case in her right hand, and handed John the pen she was holding in her left hand.

"You went through all that to steal a pen?" John asked.

"Yes, uh, I gave it to Bryan as a Christmas present and I wanted it back," Claire lied, glancing at the pen in John's hand, thankful it wasn't one of the ninety-nine-cent ones she usually used. This one was black with gold striping— a Christmas giveaway from Allied to all their employees.

With any luck, John wouldn't turn the thing over and see the Allied Adjusters name embossed on the cap.

John shrugged a "whatever" shrug, looked up and down the hall to make sure no one was around, opened the door to Bryan and Cindy's room, and placed the pen on the dresser near the door before pulling Claire behind him to her room.

She went willingly, surreptitiously slipping the contact case into the pocket of her lime-colored sweats as she followed John into the room and made her earlier fantasy a reality.

"Thanks for driving me here," Claire said as John steered the midnight-blue Jaguar up the paved driveway to Scott Anderson's house.

"You're welcome. I didn't have much to do at the lodge anyway, since the hikes were canceled because of this rain," John answered with a shrug and a flick of the windshield wipers.

Claire wanted to find Scott Anderson and ask about his wife, Amy. Something was definitely going on with Art Engleheart's accounts, and the coincidence of one of the claimants living in a small town thirty miles northwest of Aspen was too much for her to pass up. When she'd mentioned her intention of going into town, John had volunteered to drive her and Claire welcomed his company on the trip.

Even in the rain, it was a beautiful drive. The foothills were covered with a carpet of lush green dotted with amber, stark mountains capped with white beyond, rising up to meld with the angry gray sky. Mostly, Claire was struck by the absence of humans. There were no housing developments, no condos or townhouses, no golf courses or restaurants until they passed Aspen itself. Seattle was so crowded you could drive twenty miles in almost every direction without a break in the evidence of human population. There was something peaceful about getting away from that. Something soothing in the endless flashing of trees as the car sped past on its way to civilization. A comfortable silence had engulfed them almost as soon as they had left the lodge and Claire felt relaxed, almost in a trance, as they reentered the world of brick and concrete.

John slowed the car, then stopped in front of a light tan house with tidy blue trim. The front yard was neatly landscaped and a large, reddish-colored dog lay sleeping under the cover of the front porch.

Claire checked the wooden numbers tacked onto the house under a porch light with the address she'd written on her notepad. This looked like the place.

"You seem surprised," John said.

Claire's forehead crinkled as she looked back at the modest house. "I suppose I am. I'm not sure what I'd expected, maybe a secluded mansion with an RV or fancy car in the driveway, but not this. The payments for the eleven claims under Amy Anderson's name since her death have netted almost a hundred thousand dollars a year, easily enough to fund a bigger house in a more exclusive neighborhood. So, why settle for this?"

"I don't know. Maybe her husband can tell us." John got out of the car and Claire was astonished to see him come around and open her door for her. She was certainly capable of opening the door for herself, but it was an awfully nice gesture. He put a hand under her elbow to help her out, and Claire couldn't help but smile up at him. Something about the whole routine made her feel feminine and . . . cherished. It was a strange, and not unpleasant, experience. Claire grabbed his fingers and gave them a squeeze, then started toward the house.

The dog lifted its head when she stepped on the first stair, but it didn't bark so she felt safe in continuing on to the front door. She rang the doorbell, then stepped back and waited. It was most likely that Mr. Anderson wouldn't even be home. It was just past three o'clock, and it was possible he would be at work.

The door was opened by a handsome brown-haired man who looked to be in his mid- to late-thirties. "Yes?"

"Scott Anderson?"

The man smiled good-naturedly, "Yes. What can I do for you?"

"I'm Claire Brown from Allied Adjusters and this is my, uh, friend, John McBride," she said awkwardly, gesturing to John. He wasn't a friend, exactly, but boyfriend sounded silly, like they were in junior high school. Somebody needed to think up a better word for two grown-ups involved in a relationship, but that was an issue for another time. "I'm here to ask some questions about your wife, Amy."

Scott Anderson's stance went from relaxed to guarded in the space of a blink. Claire could feel the tension emanating from the other man when John asked, "Maybe we should come in and sit down rather than discussing this out here in the rain?"

"I'm sorry. Please come in." Scott opened the door and stood aside to allow them to enter the house.

Claire was careful to wipe her feet on the mat before stepping into the house and following Scott down a narrow hallway and into a cozy living room. He waved a hand to indicate they should take a seat on a tan and cream striped couch, then sat down on a coordinating overstuffed chair that looked as if it had come right off the page of a Sears and Roebuck catalog. It was of good quality; sturdy, but not fancy. It was the type of furniture you had when you didn't want to agonize over someone spilling Kool-Aid on it, Claire decided, looking around at the telltale signs that this room was often inhabited by children: a baseball bat propped up in a corner, a video game on the floor near the television, board games stacked on the bookshelf.

"Amy's dead," Scott said, a bitter note to his voice. "She's been dead over eight years. I don't know what you could possibly want to talk about."

"I'm sorry, Mr. Anderson. It must have been awful losing your wife, especially for the kids."

Scott leaned back in the chair and closed his eyes for a moment. When he opened them again, there was a suspicious brightness in the brown depths. "Yes. We still miss her."

Claire wished she could rewind her day like a videotape and stop it just before knocking on Mr. Anderson's door. She wished she hadn't come here and reminded the poor man of his loss. But there was nothing she could do now. She might as well finish what she'd come here to do. "I won't take much more of your time." Claire paused, searching for the best way to word her question. "I was recently assigned the oversight of several of Allied's accounts," she said in her most businesslike tone. "It has come to my attention that several claims have been filed under your wife's name, subsequent to the date of her death. I wondered if you knew of any reason why this might have happened? Perhaps your wife had worked at some of these other companies and was in the process of filing these claims before she died?"

Scott shook his head, then met her eyes. Claire was saddened by the pain she saw in them as he answered, "No, that's not possible. Amy started working at Lockmar Aerospace right out of high school. It was the only job she ever had."

"Are you sure?" Claire asked.

There was a slight smile on Scott's face this time when he answered, "We were married the day after graduation, and I think I'd have known if my wife had changed jobs. Amy worked for Lockmar until she died. The settlement they offered made it so we could move here to Colorado to be near Amy's folks. I've also been able to work part-time while the kids are in school, but it doesn't make up for the loss of their mother."

"No, of course it doesn't," Claire said. "That's all I needed to ask. I'm sorry I had to bring up such a painful time in your life."

John stood up and held out his hand. "Thank you for your time."

Claire followed suit, squeezing Scott Anderson's fingers, wishing she could pass on how sorry she was through the touch of her hand on his. "Yes, thank you. You've been a big help."

Back in the car, Claire was surprised when John reached for her hand. "You couldn't have known that he'd react that way. Don't beat yourself up for it."

She grasped John's strong fingers, thankful for his understanding. She *hadn't* known the pain would still be so fresh, even after so many years. "Thanks," she said huskily, swallowing around a lump in her throat. "I'm pretty sure he was telling the truth."

"I agree. I don't think he was lying." John kept her hand clasped firmly in his as he started the car. "Where to now?"

"Allied has a small office in downtown Aspen. I'd like to talk to one of the adjusters there, if you don't mind making another stop on the way back."

John turned to her then, his green eyes intense on hers. There was something there that Claire couldn't define, but whatever it was frightened her a bit. "Will you promise me something?"

"Um, sure," Claire said, wondering nervously what he wanted.

"Will you promise that this is the last work you do until your vacation is over? I'll bet you've spent as much time working over the past six days as you would have if you'd never left Seattle. Why don't you let it go for a few days?"

Claire opened her mouth to agree, then closed it again. This should have been an easy request to comply with, but for some reason she hesitated. What if an emergency came up? And how would she know there was an emergency if she didn't check her e-mail or voice mail? What if . . . what if . . . what if she relaxed and enjoyed herself for the rest of her vacation? Would that really be so wrong? Would the world fall apart if she didn't respond to someone's request until after she got back to the office?

She did a good job. She was conscientious and dependable. What was she trying to prove by letting work take over her life like this?

She lifted her gaze to John's. "Okay. After this last meeting, I promise. No more work."

John's smile came out like the sun peeking from behind the watery gray clouds. He leaned over the console, kissed the tip of her nose, then put the car in gear and headed back into town.

"Aspen? Why did they go to Aspen?"

"I don't know, Dad. I'm just telling you what I heard, which is that Claire and the owner of the lodge drove off a couple hours ago while I was getting myself a late lunch. I was keeping an eye on her, like you told me to, but a guy's got to eat sometime."

Robert should have known his son's sleuthing skills wouldn't be any better than his insurance skills, but he had held out the tiniest grain of hope that Bryan wouldn't botch this job. Now he swallowed that hope with the watermelon candy he was sucking on. It went down wrong and he wheezed, trying to get air back into his lungs.

"Are you all right? Dad?"

Robert continued choking while Bryan continued asking what was wrong. After a moment, Robert had his breath back. He coughed.

"I'm fine now. Stop yammering at me, I need to think."

There was a long-suffering sigh from the other end of the line, but Robert ignored it as he leaned back in his chair and contemplated the problem. He'd always prided himself on his superior problem-solving abilities and if ever there was a time to call up those skills, it was now. "I'm going to call the group together," he said finally. "I'll let you know what we decide."

He ended the call to his son abruptly, then dialed another number. "This is Robert Edwards. Meet me at McCormick's in half an hour." He left the terse message, then repeated the process three more times.

Before Bryan's call, he'd been having a good day. One of the risk managers he'd worked closely with was moving to Texas to work for one of the largest oil companies in the world. The news meant that his office would get the account, increasing their current revenues by almost fifty percent.

In other circumstances, Robert might not have been so confident that they'd get the business from the risk manager's new company. But if there was one thing he'd learned in the past ten years, it was that blackmail was an incredibly powerful tool, if used sparingly.

He straightened his red silk tie and put his glen-plaid jacket on over a crisply starched white shirt. Other offices in the country had moved toward business casual dress, but Robert staunchly refused to let his employees relax their dress code.

"If you dress like a professional, you act like a professional," he told the human resources girl every time she suggested a change.

Pulling his white cuffs down over his wrists, he opened the door to his office and breezed past his surprised secretary.

"I'll be gone for the day, Valerie. You can reach me on my cell phone if you need me," he announced, ignoring the curious glint in the woman's eyes. He didn't often deviate from his schedule and he hadn't expected to be gone this afternoon, but it couldn't be helped. The Claire Brown situation had to be dealt with immediately, before it got out of hand.

In the lobby, Robert pushed the elevator button impatiently, then pushed it again as if in so doing he could communicate his sense of urgency to whatever machinery controlled the movement of the cars. Finally, the elevator arrived and he rode it down to the fortieth floor where he switched to another elevator which would take him down to the Fourth Avenue entrance where the restaurant was located.

The bar at McCormick's was loud, even at four o'clock in the afternoon. It would continue to get louder as more people got off work, which was why Robert had chosen the place for his rendezvous. There was nothing like the anonymity of a noisy, crowded bar, Robert thought, sitting down at a table in the back facing the door so he could keep track of the comings and goings of the other patrons. McCormick's was a popular insurance hangout and he wanted to know if someone in the business came in.

He glanced at his watch impatiently, pulled a sourball out of his jacket pocket, then stopped in the midst of unwrapping it as the door opened and a woman with shoulder-length black hair, wearing a stylish black suit came in. Her skirt was short and her legs long and her entrance was watched by most of the men in the bar.

"Prompt as always, Jennifer. I admire that in a business partner." Robert stood up and placed a chaste kiss on the woman's cheek as she handed him her jacket to hang on the coat rack behind him.

"Yes, hopefully Shane won't be half an hour late like usual. I have another appointment in an hour and, unlike him, I hate to be late."

Robert nodded his agreement. He had noticed an increasing trend for people in the software industry to pay no particular attention to time, and Shane MacGrath, the risk manager for a local software firm, was no exception. Jennifer Davin, the attractive human resources manager for a national clothing retailer with its headquarters in Seattle, was the exact opposite, always arriving promptly for any of their scheduled meetings.

The door opened and two men entered, heading straight for the table where Robert and Jennifer were seated.

Ollie Tvenstrup, a pale, thin man wearing a worn short-sleeved shirt, arrived at the table first, nervously shaking hands with Robert and nodding to Jennifer. The man behind Ollie had a ruddy face and sounded out of breath as he greeted the rest of the group.

"Jennifer, I don't believe you've met Bill Webster. Bill, this is Jennifer Davin. Jennifer, Bill Webster," Robert made the introductions, then looked up to see a chubby young man advancing toward them.

Shane MacGrath must have been very worried indeed to

make it on time, Robert concluded as they all took their seats.

A waiter came by to take their order for drinks. Robert ordered tonic water with a twist. He believed that if you took care of your body, it would take care of you, so he stayed away from all manner of drugs, alcohol, even caffeine and sugar in the hopes that he'd live a long and healthy life.

By unspoken consent, the group stuck to small talk until the waiter returned with their drinks, but as soon as he was out of earshot, Shane blurted, "You told us on Monday we shouldn't worry about this Claire Brown at Allied Adjusters. So why are you calling this meeting now? It has to have something to do with her."

"Yes, it—" Robert began.

"Then how could you tell us not to worry?" Bill Webster accused, his red face darkening even more.

Robert held up a hand, as if to physically ward off their accusations.

"I never expected that Miss Brown would take her job so seriously. As a matter of fact, she's on vacation this week somewhere in the backwaters of Colorado. I had no idea that she'd be working this diligently. Even if I had known, there's nothing I could have done."

"Couldn't you have requested that Allied put someone else on our accounts?" Jennifer asked reasonably.

"Claire Brown is one of the best account coordinators Allied has, and they know it. They assigned her to your accounts without consulting me, and I already tried calling to suggest that someone else might be better since she's on vacation. The head of the region reiterated that Claire was the best person for the job, and I could hardly have insisted on someone else without arousing suspicion. Believe me, it's not in my best interest to have her poking around, either," Robert answered.

There was a general murmur of agreement around the table. Everyone here was going to be in a heap of trouble if their scheme was discovered. Robert figured that each of the people at this table took home at least an extra half-million dollars tax-free each and every year because of the deal they'd made with Robert. Although he didn't make any money directly off the deal, Robert enjoyed a lifelong commitment from every person who signed on to the scheme, making his office one of the most profitable, and least volatile, insurance brokerages in the world. His office's success brought him recognition and respect throughout the corporation, as well as generous monetary compensation year after year.

"What are we supposed to do?" Shane MacGrath's voice rose to a whine.

"We need to think of a story. Something simple and believable," Jennifer suggested.

"What, like maybe we all had the same dead people working at our companies?" Bill Webster said sarcastically.

"Don't be an asshole, I was just trying to do some brainstorming," Jennifer shot back.

"Stop it. Attacking each other isn't going to help," Robert interrupted before they started for each other's throats like a pack of hungry mongrels.

"What do you suggest we do, Robert?" Ollie asked quietly.

Robert steepled his fingers on the table. "I've been going over and over it in my mind for days and you may not like my solution," he began. "Like Jennifer, I started out thinking that there must be some story we could concoct that would explain the situation sufficiently. But if there is one, I haven't been able to think of it, at least not something a reasonably intelligent person wouldn't see through in a matter of seconds.

"We all have a lot to lose if this thing comes out." Robert paused for effect, looking around the table at each person in turn. "Jennifer, you remember what it's like trying to live on your salary and raise your children without any help from their father. Isn't your family's life better now that you can afford a full-time nanny?

"Ollie, your wife's cancer is in remission now, but can

you afford the medical bills if, God forbid, it comes back?

"Shane, you were able to buy your parents that trip around the world they'd always dreamed of and help your father retire from that awful, backbreaking job of his, right?

"And Bill, I'm sure you don't relish the thought of having to tell your wife that you have to sell your new waterfront house or the fifty-foot Ocean Alexander, do you?"

Robert looked around at the nodding heads and hoped they were going to be easier to convince than he'd originally thought.

"We could try paying her off," Bill Webster suggested.

"Yes, we could, but I don't think she'd take it. While I don't claim to know her all that well, I do recall Bryan telling me some story about her walking away from a quite sizable bribe on the basis of principle."

"Still, we could try," Shane said hopefully.

Perhaps this wasn't going to be so easy, Robert thought. He was already convinced that paying Miss Brown off wasn't going to be an option, but he was obviously going to have to work a bit harder to get the group to see the inevitable solution. "I agree. We should try to pay her off and see if she'll go away, but we need to be prepared in the event that she refuses."

"Like having a Plan B," Shane added as if they were playing some sort of war game.

"Exactly," Robert agreed, nodding his head.

"So what's Plan B?" Ollie asked.

Robert glanced around the table, looking into the eager eyes that waited for him to suggest some magic answer that would wipe away their problem cleanly and easily. For several long days he'd pondered the situation, but perhaps in the back of his mind he'd known when he'd first started the scheme ten years ago that it would ultimately come to this.

The answer was clean and relatively easy, made even less complicated because, from what little he remembered of Miss Brown's life story, she was estranged from her parents, had no siblings, no husband, and no children who might get suspicious at her sudden disappearance. All in all, he thought as everyone focused their attention on him, this was really the best solution all around.

"Would you be my guest tonight for dinner?" John asked as they pulled into the garage at Hunter's Lodge.

"Why, Mr. McBride, are you asking me for a date?" Claire fluttered her lashes and did her best Scarlett O'Hara impression.

"I think it's about time, don't you?"

"I think it would be delightful." Claire looked down at her plain khakis and grimaced. "It would be even more delightful if, by some miracle, the airline delivered my luggage."

"I don't know. I'm kind of fond of those bright pink sweats you were wearing the other day."

Claire laughed as she stepped out of the car. "You go for the sloppy look, huh?"

"Yeah, I think it's cute when a woman doesn't care how she looks around me." John threw an arm across her shoulder and planted a kiss on her neck. Claire stopped on the top stair leading up to the lodge and looped her arms around his neck, intending to exact payment for his jibe.

The door behind her flew open and Dana barreled through, stopping just before she ran into Claire. "Oh, Mr. McBride. Miss Brown. I'm sorry."

Claire shrugged at the interruption and smiled at John, then dropped her arms and turned around. "No problem, Dana."

"Did you need something?" John asked.

Dana seemed to have momentarily forgotten what she'd come for, but remembered her mission at John's question. "Yes. You have a phone call, John. He said it was important, that he's been trying to call your regular line for days but either the line's been busy or nobody's answered. Do you want me to take a message?"

John's first thought was that it was Calder Preston from

the FBI trying to give him more information on Derrick
Washington. John clenched his jaw and set Claire aside.

"Give me a minute, then put the call through to my
suite," John said, then took off for the second floor.

Dana and Claire looked at each other, puzzled by John's
strange behavior. "You'd better do as he said," Claire said,
shooing Dana back inside.

She left Dana at the front desk and trudged up the stairs
to her room, then stopped in her tracks at the sight of her
suitcase propped beside her door. A cardboard box sat on
top of her suitcase. Claire glanced at the return address. It
was from Amazon.com. Her new cell phone had arrived,
along with her clothes.

Claire set the box on the floor, then fell on her suitcase
like a parent on a lost child. Her clothes! What would she
wear tonight? The light yellow denim dress that picked up
the highlights in her hair? Or the soft gray floral skirt with
a white shell and sweater that matched her eyes?

She unlocked the door of her room, pushed it open, and
hauled her suitcase up on the bed. She was half-afraid of
opening it. What if the airline had mixed up again and sent
her *Clarke* Brown's luggage instead of her own? If she
unzipped the top and found boxer shorts instead of the
pretty silk panties she'd bought especially for the trip, she'd
burst into tears. She knew she would.

With shaking fingers, she reached out and pulled down
the zipper. Then, in one swift movement, she threw it open.

She almost wept with joy at seeing her own clothes
there.

She gathered them up, hugging them to her chest with
delight. After her joy was spent, she picked out the gray
outfit that was her favorite, added a new pair of white underwear and headed off downstairs to take a shower and
get ready for her date with John.

John wasn't in the dining room when Claire made her grand
entrance an hour later. She tried to contain her disappointment. She wanted so much for him to see her at her best,

freshly washed and unwrinkled, just so he could see that she didn't always look like a rumpled mess.

Mary Jane waved to her from a table in the center of the room so Claire shrugged off her feminine vanity and walked over to say hello. Mary Jane met her halfway.

"Can I talk to you for a minute?" she asked.

"Of course," Claire answered, following Mary Jane back out the door.

Once they got out into the hall, John's mother turned to her, and Claire could see the faint puffiness around the other woman's eyes that spoke of recent tears. Claire reached out a hand and touched Mary Jane's arm in a show of sympathy. "What's wrong?"

"I'm sorry, Claire. I didn't mean to ruin your evening. I didn't even know you and John had plans until he mentioned it to me a few moments ago. It's just . . . oh, this is so hard to talk about." Her voice broke and Claire saw tears forming in her eyes.

"Please don't cry." She put an arm around Mary Jane's shoulders.

After a moment, Mary Jane got a hold of herself and shot Claire a watery smile. "Thank you, dear. Is my mascara all right?"

"It held up just fine. I'm going to have to get some of that."

"Remind me before you go and I'll give you a free sample." Mary Jane sniffed.

Claire waited while Mary Jane dabbed a tissue under her eyes. "Would you like to tell me what's wrong?"

"I suppose I should. I didn't know you and John had plans for the evening and I had hoped he and I would have some time to discuss some things tonight. I was out all afternoon with the Islers, you see. Being with them, being part of a family again . . . it made me realize that I'm not happy just running my company anymore. So I've decided to sell. After I made that decision, I guess I felt so good about it that I . . . I . . ." She stammered to a halt, her face turning pink with embarrassment. Claire waited patiently for her to continue. "I asked George Isler out for dinner," she blurted.

Claire coughed to cover a laugh. "I see. Then you had to tell John what you'd done."

Mary Jane nodded. "I had hoped we'd have some time to talk about it. I would never want him to think I'm betraying his father's memory by going out with another man."

"What did he say when you told him?"

"Not much. He seemed upset when I came in and I probably should have waited for another time to broach the subject, but I was afraid I'd lose my nerve. He didn't appear to take the news well. He grunted at me, then told me he had to go get ready to meet you for dinner. I'm sorry if I've ruined your evening."

Claire patted Mary Jane's arm comfortingly. "Don't worry, Mary Jane. I'm sure it will be fine. You look lovely, by the way. That blouse brings out the color of your eyes just beautifully."

Mary Jane squeezed Claire's hand. "Thank you, dear. I did take extra time with getting ready tonight. I'd forgotten how nerve-wracking this dating can be."

"I know exactly what you mean." Claire laughed. "Now, why don't you go enjoy your dinner with the Islers and I'll try to cheer up your son—who happens to be stalking toward us right now."

At that, Mary Jane made a hasty escape, obviously fresh out of courage for the evening. Claire rocked back on her heels and watched John's approach. There was definitely something dangerous about him this evening. His emerald eyes were darker than usual, his expression hooded. Claire felt a tingle of excitement, her body responding to the danger coming at her full force.

She looked up into those green eyes and felt a sudden, fierce possessiveness.

Mine.

The word echoed in her head, reverberating louder and louder the closer he came. She reached out a hand as he came within striking distance and grabbed his arm, stopping his progress. Sliding her arms around his neck, she rubbed herself against him like a cat marking her territory and pulled his mouth down to hers.

He kissed her, hard and angry, and pushed her back against the wall.

Claire delighted in the freedom of letting her emotions come out in that kiss, of not feeling forced to rein in her passion for fear it might be overwhelming.

John was the first to pull back, his breath ragged as he looked down at her. Claire leaned her head on the cedar logs behind her, enjoying the bemusement in his gaze.

"What was that for?"

"You looked like you needed it," Claire answered with a sultry smile.

"Hmm," was John's only response as he pulled her along behind him into the dining room.

The first thing she noticed was the loud wailing coming from little Billy Weber.

The second thing she noticed was the strange look on Bryan's face as he stared at her intently from across the room.

And the third thing she noticed was how ridiculous Cindy looked wearing orange-tinted goggles with her evening dress.

Claire had forgotten about the stolen contact lenses, still tucked safely away in the pocket of her lime-green sweatpants. She'd have to find a way to get them back to their rightful owner. This vision was revenge enough, even for her.

Ignoring her ex-fiancé's perusal, Claire turned to John. "I didn't bring my purse down. Do you have a dollar?"

"What for?"

"You'll see." She waited expectantly.

John raised his eyebrows at her, but removed a well-worn black leather wallet from the back pocket of his charcoal gray slacks and withdrew a crisp one-dollar bill.

"Come with me," she said, then approached the Webers' table.

Peggy Weber was attempting to comfort her sobbing child, offering crayons and assorted toys from her oversized purse. William looked as if he'd like to change tables, abandoning all child-rearing responsibility to his wife. He eyed John suspiciously as he and Claire stopped in front of their table.

"Offer Billy your dollar," Claire said, turning to John and ignoring William Weber.

"What? Claire, I told you before, you can't bribe children with money."

"Just tell Billy you'll give him the dollar if he stops crying."

John shot her a look that questioned her sanity, but did as she had instructed. The crying stopped instantly, replaced by an outstretched hand.

Claire smiled as John handed over the loot.

"The kid likes cash." She shrugged in answer to John's unspoken question. "I guess he wants to get a head start on his college fund."

John simply shook his head as he led her to their table.

Claire looped her arm around John's as they left the dining room.

"You seem preoccupied. Was that phone call bad news?" she asked.

"Hmm," John answered noncommittally, steering her into the spacious lobby of the lodge. "Look, I feel like taking a walk. Why don't we call it a night? We both have to be up early for the raft trip tomorrow."

Her arm slid out from around his. Had she said something wrong at dinner? She didn't think so. John had been a bit distracted, but she'd chalked it up to his earlier conversation with Mary Jane. However, Claire knew a brush-off when she heard it.

"All right. Thank you for dinner. I'll see you tomorrow." She gave a wave and as nonchalant a shrug as she could muster, then headed up the stairs, mumbling under her breath about getting all dressed up for nothing.

Claire let herself into her room and slumped down on her bed.

What was wrong with her? Why wasn't she the type of woman that a man couldn't forget, even after eight years, like Amy Anderson had obviously been? Scott's obvious distress over his wife's death had been painful, and incredibly touching, to behold. Claire wanted someone to feel that way about her.

She'd hoped that John might be the one who would. There was no denying there was something between them. She felt more in tune with John and his moods than with any other person she'd ever known. It didn't hurt that the sex was great, too. But it was more than that, at least for her. John made her feel special, attractive and funny—unlike anyone else in the world.

Did he feel the same way about her, though?

Claire sighed.

She didn't know. And the not knowing, the self-doubt, opened a needy place in her heart that she didn't know how to fill. Except with work. Work calmed the fear, soothed the ache, quieted the voice inside her that told her she wasn't good enough to be loved like that. Like alcohol, it numbed the pain and allowed her to go on. It called to her, "Come to me, I can help." And it did. For awhile, she didn't have to think about what was going on inside her brain, inside her heart. All she had to do was focus on the numbers, write the letters, solve the problem, take on more and more until there was nothing left to do but fall into bed, exhausted at the end of the day, with no time left to feel the hurt that came from knowing that no one, not even her parents, really loved her.

Claire gritted her teeth and blinked back the tears. It was no use thinking this way. It didn't accomplish anything. It wouldn't make John, or anyone else, love her.

But everything would be all right. She had work to do.

*   *   *

Robert Edwards picked up the telephone in his home office on the second ring.

"Mr. Edwards, this is Claire Brown from Allied Adjusters. I'm sorry to be calling so late, but I have something I need to discuss with you."

Robert reached for the glass jar holding his sourballs, then pulled back. He didn't really want a piece of candy. What he wanted was for Claire Brown to go away and leave him in peace. Permanently.

"Yes. What I can do for you?" he asked.

"I mentioned to you earlier that I've taken over Art Engleheart's accounts and that I've been doing some basic data analysis and something looked strange?"

"Um-hmm. I've studied the graphs you were kind enough to fax over, but I'm afraid I don't have any answers for you yet."

"That's all right. I did some investigating of my own today and discovered some information that I wanted to discuss with you before taking the matter up with my management."

Robert leaned forward at that, a smile spreading across his face. Had Miss Brown discovered their scheme and now wanted a piece of the action? If so, that was excellent news. He reached for a sourball and pulled out a green apple—flavored one. His smile widened. Green apple was his favorite.

"I went to see the husband of one of the claimants but it's obvious he isn't involved in any wrongdoing. Then I talked with one of our adjusters in Aspen. He and I reviewed the service instructions for all four of the accounts in question and we discovered something strange."

"Yes? Go on," Robert said, leaning back in his chair and sucking happily on the candy.

"Art's instructions on the four accounts say that all claims should go through him first. That's highly unusual. An account coordinator is responsible for the oversight of an entire account, not adjusting individual claims, but there were specific instructions that Art was to get first notification of every claim. He passed most of them back to the individual adjusters, but there were some that he kept control of himself."

Claire paused and Robert waited for her to make the next leap. He wondered how much she wanted in for. Art was getting ten percent of each fraudulent claim, easily an extra quarter of a million every year. Robert had already decided he could go up to fifteen percent for Claire, but she and Art would have to decide how to split the accounts when he got back after his surgery.

"It's obvious that Art was defrauding your clients, Robert. I'll prepare a report on this issue for Allied's management after I get back from vacation, but I thought you should hear it from me first. There will be a complete investigation, of course. I just wanted to let you know how sorry I am that an employee of ours was involved in something so patently dishonest."

The sourball turned to vinegar in his mouth. Robert spat it into the wastebasket under his desk, but still the bitter taste remained.

It was the taste of defeat, but he wasn't ready for it to be over. He had worked hard to climb from his humble beginnings to this—a magnificent house overlooking the city, a luxurious car, enough money that he never had to worry how he'd pay for the next meal. He would never be ready for it to be over.

He'd worked much too hard to give it all up now.

Which meant only one thing.

It all boiled down to this: either he would lose or Claire Brown would.

The moon hung bright and luminous in the blackened, starless sky as John picked his way across the smooth stones of the riverbed. The water made a constant, soothing hum as it ran in its usual path over boulders that had stood in its way for thousands of years.

John paused for a moment, enjoying the stillness of the night air and the sounds of the forest around him. He was

comfortable in the natural world, mostly because it made
sense to him. There was a certain predictability about it.
Too much rain will cause flooding. Too much sun will
cause drought. A hungry predator will kill something to eat.

But animals, unlike humans, did not kill senselessly. An
animal would kill for food or to protect its territory, but it
would not kill just for the sake of killing.

Not like Derrick Washington and his older brother, who
had killed a teenaged convenience-store clerk and kidnapped her three-year-old son.

Derrick, barely a teenager himself, with a list of criminal
offenses two pages long, and his brother, Leon, with an
even longer history of crime, had shot the convenience-
store clerk and taken her little boy as protection before fleeing over the Tennessee state line. It had taken hours for the
police to find the boys' hideout in the forest, hours for John
to get to the scene—hours they didn't have.

John had set out immediately, but it had been too late.
By the time he'd found the abandoned child, the child was
already dead—killed not by a gunshot as John had expected
but from a fall in the dark. Later, John was told Derrick
had convinced his brother to let the boy go, hoping the
child would have a better chance at survival alone than with
the homicidal Leon.

John had found the boy's body, then led the police to
where Derrick and Leon were sleeping, hidden behind a
fallen log. John had quit his job at the FBI before the cases
went to court. He couldn't take any more pain and suffer-
ing. No more senseless death.

He hadn't wanted to hear Derrick's side of the story,
hadn't wanted the memories to return, the blond hair and
gold leaves splattered with blood where the boy had fallen.

But this afternoon Derrick hadn't offered any excuses
for his behavior. He'd called to thank John for his part in
stopping Derrick's slow slide into inhumanity. He had
known he was on the wrong path, but was too frightened
of Leon to say no. He was sorry for the trouble he'd caused,

had made his peace with God. That was all. He wasn't coming after revenge, or even absolution.

John continued his walk, weary with the weight of memories crushing him. Derrick had found his peace, why couldn't John find his? "If only" ran around and around in his mind.

If only he'd been a better tracker. If only he'd arrived sooner. Maybe he could have saved that one life, rather than discovering, once again, the horror of man's inhumanity to man.

Without realizing it, John found himself at the entrance of the lodge. As before, when the memories had been too much, he wanted to turn to someone. No, not just someone, he admitted. He wanted to turn to Claire, wanted the comfort she had brought him after the last nightmare seized him in its grip.

He took the stairs to the second floor two at a time, then marched purposefully down the hall and turned the corner.

Her door was closed and a phone line ran across the width of the hall and under the door like the tail from some giant rodent. John yanked the phone cord out of the jack, then turned and pulled open the door.

Claire looked up from her laptop, her eyes unfocused as they met his.

She was working again. Even after she'd promised him this afternoon that she wouldn't.

He had come to her, needed her, but she was busy with work.

Just like his ex-wife.

Work came first.

The anger came then, red-hot like water spewing out from a geyser. All his life, he'd come second to the women who'd mattered most. He had hoped Claire would be different. That hope came crashing down like a felled tree, desecrated and dead, lying on the forest floor.

She closed the top of the computer and rubbed her eyes. "How was your walk?" she asked, as if nothing were wrong.

John exploded. "Can't you even leave your work for twenty-four hours? Isn't anything else in your life as important to you as your job?"

Her gray eyes became instantly focused and sparkled with anger. She slid the computer onto the bed, stood up and took a step toward him. "What do you care what I do? Seems to me you're just counting the hours till I go home."

"Why shouldn't I? I get your attention only long enough for a fuck and then it's time for you to punch the clock again. Is that all you want? Someone to satisfy your sexual needs, just as long as they don't take any time away from your almighty career?"

Claire's arms dropped to her sides. "And what is it that you want, John? You made it pretty clear yesterday that you're not looking for any kind of commitment from me, either."

"You're right. I'm not looking for a commitment from you, Claire. I've already had one relationship with a woman who'd rather spend her time at the office than with her own family. I won't make that mistake again."

He tossed her the phone cord along with his parting blow, turned on his heel, and left her standing in the doorway, staring after him.

Chapter 18

"I'm sorry, son. You're going to have to take care of her. There's no other way."

"But Dad, I don't know how to kill anyone. I'm an insurance broker, for God's sake." Bryan's voice crackled through the phone lines.

The bright lights of Seattle's waterfront winked mockingly at Robert Edwards from across Elliott Bay as he leaned back in his chair, for once not enjoying the scent of the expensive leather. He could understand why Bryan was balking. It wasn't every day that he was called upon to commit murder, after all, but he didn't care for the petulant tone of his son's voice.

"You're going to have to think of something, Bryan. You're out in the wilderness; I'm sure there are all sorts of hazards around. Sharp rocks, steep cliffs, poisonous plants, that sort of thing. Just make sure it looks like an accident and don't leave behind any evidence that can link her body to you."

"I don't think I can do it. I mean, Claire was a little boring but I don't hate her or anything."

"This has nothing to do with your feelings for Miss Brown, Bryan. It has to do with money and all our reputations. She's only found out about four accounts so far, but what do you think is going to happen when she discovers all the rest? You'll end up in jail, you know. There will be no more vacations with your assistants, and no more expensive health clubs, either. Tell me, are you willing to let Claire Brown live and give up your comfortable lifestyle to become somebody's plaything in prison? You've seen the movies, you know what happens to handsome men like us in there."

Robert let the words sink in. He wasn't sure if the movies were anywhere close to the reality of prison, but he didn't want to take any chance of finding out.

The silence stretched for several seconds.

"All right. I'll do it." Bryan said, at last.

"Fine. That's the right decision. Give me a call after it's over."

His son mumbled an agreement before hanging up.

Robert continued looking out over the dark strip of water separating Seattle from the Olympic Peninsula. He had risen from a lower-middle-class background to become one of the top two percent of Americans with incomes in the seven figures. He hadn't gotten there by accident, he thought now, smoothing back a lock of graying blond hair. Always have a Plan B, that had been his strategy from the beginning.

He should have been better prepared for this eventuality, but things had been going well for so long, he had made the mistake of letting himself relax. Now, he'd do whatever he had to in order to correct that mistake.

He picked up the phone and dialed a number.

"United Airlines reservations. How can I help you?"

"Yes, I need some information on your flights to Colorado."

"Your departure date, sir?"

"Tomorrow." Robert leaned forward, committing the flight schedule to memory as a brightly lit airplane headed out over Puget Sound.

"Don't you ever go anywhere without that thing?" John asked irritably, squinting against the early morning sun.

"Hmm, just a second," Mary Jane replied absently, listening to the last of the voice mails on her cell phone.

John shot her a disgusted look, but the effort was wasted since his mother wasn't paying him the least bit of attention. He returned his gaze to the road, watching the painted lines of the highway flash by like some endless stream of Morse code—dash, dash, dash, dash.

Checking the rear-view mirror to make sure the van with the rest of the passengers was following, he slowed the truck in anticipation of turning down a gravel road just ahead. They'd been driving for a little over two hours and had another half hour until they'd arrive at the starting point for the rafting trip, thirty-five miles north and just east of the lodge. He'd planned it so they'd pull out at the lodge after two days of rafting for a welcome bit of pampering before returning to their normal lives on Sunday.

Apparently finished with whatever dire cosmetics emergency she'd been attending to, Mary Jane ended her call and stowed her phone in the glove compartment of his truck.

"It certainly is pretty up here," she observed.

"I'm surprised you even noticed," John muttered.

"I'm the CEO of a major corporation, John. I can't turn off my responsibilities at work just because I'm on vacation. I've actually done very little work since I've been here at the lodge."

The irritation that had started with Claire last night spilled over onto his mother. "What are you working on that's so important it can't wait for a week?"

Mary Jane looked at her son assessingly. She was working on selling her company, but that didn't seem relevant right now. Obviously, the fact that she'd brought her work with her upset her son, but she didn't have a clue why. He had been edgy ever since he and Claire had come back from Aspen yesterday afternoon. Was it possible that John's anger had more to do with a certain petite blonde than he cared to admit?

"Are you angry because I'm working and not paying attention to you?" she asked.

"I'm not angry, Mother," John answered, but his tone belied his words.

Mary Jane raised her eyebrows but didn't contradict him. "Well, obviously it's bothering you that I was catching up on my voice mail."

She heard his exhaled breath across the cabin of the

truck and continued to watch him as he visibly reined in his temper. He'd gotten that from his father. One of the things she'd loved best about Hunter McBride was that he almost never let anger get the best of him. Her son's voice, when it came, was much calmer than it had been moments before. "I don't understand why anyone would come on a vacation if she can't bear to get away from work. I mean, why wouldn't she stay at the office if she can't let it go?"

Mary Jane sat back in her seat, remembering Claire's comment about never seeing her family, not even for Christmas. "Well, I can't speak for everyone, of course, but I suppose that if the only place in your life that you feel needed is at your job, you might get caught in a trap where all you do is work. I think, in everyone's life, you have to know that someone or something can't survive without you. It's rubbish, of course. None of us are indispensable, but maybe we just need the illusion." She paused, struggling to reveal something of herself, even though it might make her uncomfortable to do so. For some reason, she felt that her son needed to understand what had driven her to work as hard as she had when he was young. "When you were growing up, I tried to be the kind of mother you couldn't live without, but you were always the independent type, even as a child."

"Huh?" John sent her a confused look.

"I remember taking you to kindergarten for your first day of school. All the other kids around you were crying, clinging to their mothers. It was an awful scene, and I had told myself I wouldn't make you go that first day if you were too unhappy." Mary Jane sighed, remembering that day in the parking lot, so long ago.

"And?"

"And you got out of the car and walked into the school-house as if you'd been doing it every day of your life. I don't think anything ever intimidated you."

"Of course it did," John said uncomfortably.

Mary Jane laughed, shaking her head. "Well, you never let it show. In any event, I realized that day that no matter how many cookies I baked or buttons I sewed, you were going to get through life just fine, with or without me. So, I decided to do something for myself. I got that part-time job at Nelson's Department Store selling makeup while you were at school. And you know what? I really liked it. I was good at it. It got so that women would only come in when I was working, because they knew I'd do my best to help them look better. One time, you had the flu and I had to stay home with you, and two of my customers called me to make sure I hadn't quit. I can't tell you how good that made me feel. I know it probably sounds silly, but I felt *needed,* and it was addictive. Pretty soon, you couldn't have paid me to stay away. Well, anyway, that's how it happened to me." Mary Jane laughed self-consciously, embarrassed that she'd revealed so much.

John was quiet for a long time as they bumped along the gravel road. Mary Jane smoothed lotion onto her hands as the truck finally rolled to a stop next to a flatbed trailer with the rafts tied up on it. She started to get out of the cab when her son stopped her with a hand on her arm.

"I never meant to make you feel unneeded, Mom."

"I know you didn't, dear, and to tell you the truth, I'm glad you were ready to make your mark on the world, even at five." The delicate skin at the corner of her eyes crinkled up as she smiled, then straightened out with surprise as her son leaned across the cab and enfolded her in a hug. Mary Jane hurriedly blinked back the tears that sprang up in her eyes.

"I love you, Mom. And I'm sorry if I didn't take your news about wanting to date George Isler the right way. He seems like a great guy. I was preoccupied with something else, but I should have told you that it was fine by me. I know you loved Dad, nothing can change that. But you shouldn't have to spend the rest of your life alone."

"Thank you, John. I love you, too." After he left, Mary Jane sat in the cab for a few moments, trying to compose herself.

Why hadn't he done that somewhere where she could

go and have herself a good cry afterward? she wondered,
stepping down from the truck as the van full of guests
pulled up.

She was being followed.

Claire felt the skin on the back of her neck start to tingle
as realization dawned that she wasn't alone.

It had been a long day rafting, but by the end of the
day, the feeling of the oar in her hands seemed almost like
second nature. Her arms, however, ached from the unfamiliar effort of fighting a raging river for eight hours. She'd
come down to the river to be by herself for awhile and
practice some Guerrilla Yoga moves to get the kinks out
of her arms. She had just finished her Chop the Cherry Tree
move when the sound of boots hitting gravel startled her
into turning around.

The expression in John's emerald-green eyes was un-
readable. Although she'd spent all day sitting across from
him in his raft, they'd barely spoken two words to each
other since his tirade last night.

Claire was tired; tired from the physical exertion of the
day, and tired of defending herself against this man whose
opinion of her seemed to bounce up and down like one of
those balls attached to a paddle with an elastic string. She
didn't want to fight with him. She wanted things back the
way they were when he'd played with her toes and acted
as if he might be starting to like her.

She sighed, wrapping her arms around herself protectively. "John." She nodded, acknowledging his presence
next to her on the riverbank.

"Claire."

He continued to stare at her, his steady gaze making her
uncomfortable. Claire waited for him to break the silence,
could tell there was something he wanted to say. His question, when it came, surprised her.

"Why do you work so much?"

"Pardon me?"

"Why do you work so much?" he repeated, sounding

genuinely curious, rather than angry. "Why did you bring your work with you on vacation? Why do you have so much work to do that you can't get away from it for even a week?"

Claire opened her mouth. Then closed it. It should be an easy question to answer. She worked all the time because she never seemed able to catch up, right? Well, why was there always so much for her to do? Why did she continue to take on more and more responsibility, even during her so-called vacation? She supposed it was because she knew she was needed at her job. She worked harder, was more dedicated than anyone else in her office, and her hard work had always been rewarded with more and more responsibility. It was somewhat hollow at times, but she knew she'd always have work to depend on; it was something she'd always be good at, unlike her relationships with people where she seemed perpetually doomed to failure.

John waited patiently for her answer, his hands stuffed into the pockets of his blue jeans. Claire met his gaze, searching his eyes for the anger that had been there last night, but not finding even a trace. Instead, she saw only curiosity, and an odd hint of understanding. How could he understand when she didn't?

"I don't know, John. I just . . . I can't seem to say no when someone asks me to do something. And I can't do anything only half-right. I like to do a good job." She shrugged, absently rubbing her sore upper arms.

"But why, Claire? Why is that so important to you?"

Because then maybe everyone will love me. The answer popped into her head without conscious thought. She turned her head away, looking out at the wind gently ruffling the golden leaves on the aspen trees. She didn't really believe that, did she?

Turning back to John, she dropped her arms to her sides. "I guess it makes me feel needed."

He looked out at the river, then back at her and Claire wished she could reach up and straighten the dark lock that fell across his forehead. Her eyes widened with surprise when John stepped closer and pulled her to his chest. Inhaling the clean scent of him, she buried her nose in the front of his shirt. She felt his strong fingers in her hair and wrapped her own arms around his waist.

"Can we make a deal?" The words rumbled through his chest.

Claire nodded and closed her eyes against the warm wall of his body, feeling safe and protected within his embrace.

"I promise not to bring up your work again if you can put the cell phone and laptop away for the rest of your vacation. Deal?"

"I didn't bring my laptop," she said, hoping to get points for that, at least.

"Well, that's a start. How about, when we get back to camp, I put your cell phone in my pack for safekeeping?"

Claire nodded her agreement, the idea of being totally disconnected from work oddly appealing as she stood sheltered in his strong arms. Besides, after all the time she'd spent working yesterday, she'd earned a real break.

"You never did mention what that phone call yesterday afternoon was all about," she said after awhile.

"Just something that stirred up a lot of bad memories." John's grip around her tightened, and Claire felt there was more to it than that, but he remained silent.

They stood on the bank of the river, wrapped tightly in each other's arms, until rumbling of another kind loosened John's arms. He looked down at her with a smile as she patted her growling stomach.

"Sounds like somebody's hungry."

Claire grinned sheepishly. "Sorry, I guess I am. I didn't realize how much of an appetite all this outdoor activity would give me."

"Dinner should be ready in about half an hour. Want to head back to camp?"

"Sure." Claire tried not to be too delighted at his touch as John enfolded her fingers in his, but it was a losing battle. She moved closer to him as they picked their way over rocks.

"By the way, have you noticed that your ex-fiancé has been acting strange today?"

She stopped walking, staring at him. "Yes, but I thought it was just me."

"No, he's been asking me all kinds of questions. Wanted to know if there were any hemlock trees in Colorado. Then he asked if any of the plants around here were poisonous."

"Why would he want to know that?" Claire's brows drew together in a frown.

"I have no idea. I thought you might know."

"Don't look at me. Maybe he's thinking about trying some kind of Euell Gibbons thing. Bryan always was a bit of a natural-food freak."

"Euell Gibbons?" John raised his eyebrows.

"Yeah, you know that Grape-Nuts guy who ate pine-cones and tree bark back in the seventies?"

John just shook his head at her as if he suspected she was making the guy up. "What made *you* think Bryan was acting strange?"

"I don't know. He seems to be right behind me every time I turn around. It's like he's lurking behind every tree and bush, waiting for me. I'm sure it's my imagination, but it's kind of creepy."

"Hmm. Well, I'll keep my eye on him. It sounds innocent enough."

"Yeah. I never noticed how weird he was before this trip," Claire said, tugging on John's hand as the smell of food being cooked on an open fire came wafting through the forest. As they neared the clearing, all she could think of was getting her teeth into whatever was being grilled, Bryan's odd behavior forgotten.

Robert Edwards glanced from the brochure in his hand to the impressive cedar structure in front of him. Hunter's Lodge looked just like the picture, beautiful and, even better, fantastically remote.

"I'll bet there are a million places to hide a body out here," Robert mumbled, shrugging into his lambswool jacket as he crossed the gravel driveway to the lodge.

"Good evening. How can I help you?" the girl at the front desk asked cheerfully.

Robert hoped she wouldn't recognize his voice from his earlier phone calls to Bryan. He did his best to imitate a hearty Midwest accent as he began his practiced pitch. "Hello there, young lady. I read about your lodge a year ago, and when I got sent to Colorado on a business trip, why, I just couldn't pass up the opportunity to drive on out and see the place for myself. You see"—he leaned toward the girl and lowered his voice conspiratorially—"my wife just loves all this outdoors stuff." In truth, Nancy thought opening the door between the house and the garage constituted being outside, Robert scoffed silently as he continued his speech. "She'd just love it if I bought her one of these adventure packages. But, like I said, I'd like to see the place for myself, you know, just to make sure your brochure didn't exaggerate."

"Oh, no, Mr.—"

"Smith. Al Smith from Des Moines, Iowa." Robert stuck out a friendly hand.

The girl shook his hand enthusiastically "No, Mr. Smith, our brochure doesn't exaggerate. The lodge sits on acres of prime Colorado wilderness. We have fifteen regular guest rooms plus five deluxe suites which come with separate sitting rooms, in-room fireplaces, and whirlpool baths."

Robert stopped her before the girl could get too far into her sales pitch. "My wife would be much more interested in the activities you offer."

What he really wanted to know was where Claire Brown might be during the next few days so he could plan on the best way to approach her. Unfortunately, he could hardly just come out and ask, especially since Miss Brown wouldn't be returning to the lodge after they had their little talk, and he didn't want to raise anyone's suspicions.

"We offer a variety of activities here at Hunter's Lodge. Hiking, horseback riding, whitewater rafting, swimming, and fishing are the most popular. In the winter we also offer

cross-country and downhill skiing, as well as snowshoe-
ing."

"And are all these activities included in the regular price
of a room?" Robert wondered if this line of questioning
was going to get him anywhere. He didn't know what else
to do, however. He couldn't hang out and watch for Claire
to emerge from the lodge since someone might spot him,
and it would look a bit suspicious if he was found loitering
in the stairwells.

"No, guests sign up for the activities they think they
might want to participate in and the activity leader checks
off the people who actually show up. We only charge you
for the activities you attend. We also offer an all-inclusive
package that includes all the activities scheduled during
your stay. That's the most expensive option, of course."

Robert attempted to hide his excitement. "That sounds
great. What activities are going on today, for example?" he
asked in as offhand a manner as he could muster.

The girl pulled a clipboard from a hook on the wall and
flipped a page.

"Well, today's the first day of a two-day whitewater rafting trip. And"—she flipped another page—"we have a trail
ride scheduled for early this afternoon for those people who
are still here at the lodge."

Robert wanted to grab the clipboard from her hands and
had to restrain himself by gripping the edge of the desk in
front of him. "That rafting trip sounds just like something
my wife might like. About how many people usually go on
those trips?"

The girl laid the clipboard down on the desk and Robert
tilted his head surreptitiously. His son's name was first on
the list and, there, about halfway down, was Claire
Brown's. Robert bit his lip to hide a triumphant smile.

"Fifteen people went today, including the two guides.
We can fit eight people to a raft, so attendance is limited
to sixteen." The girl finished counting names and hung the
clipboard back on its hook.

"Can you show me the route the trip takes?" Robert

pulled out the local map he'd purchased at a gas station that morning. "I want to be able to show my wife," he added.

The girl turned the map toward her and searched the multicolored paper with a small frown.

Robert dabbed at the beads of sweat on his upper lip and resisted the urge to reach into his pocket for a sourball.

"Here it is." She pointed a blue-tipped fingernail at a spot on the map. "They put in near the end of Johnson's Mill Road and follow the east fork here to where it joins up with the main river, and from there back to the lodge."

Robert followed the blue dot of her nail with his eyes.

He thanked the girl for her help, promising to call soon to make a reservation, then went out to his rental car to plan his next move.

He'd find Miss Brown by tomorrow morning and, if things went as he expected, she'd be dead by tomorrow night.

Chapter 19

"THIS TOMATO AND MOZZARELLA SALAD IS WONDERFUL." Claire directed her comment to John's mother, who was sitting a few seats away on the circle of logs that had been arranged around a cheerfully crackling campfire.

"Yes, it is. Everything we've had to eat has been great. John, you'd better make sure you're paying Gina well for all her hard work."

"Believe me, I am. Her food probably brings more guests to the lodge than anything else."

"Claire, did you know that John is a very good cook? I don't know where he got that talent, neither his father nor I had much in the way of culinary skills."

Claire smiled at Mary Jane's obvious sales pitch. John's face turned a slight red under his tan, but he didn't say anything. She couldn't help but tease him for his obvious embarrassment. "That's good to know, Mary Jane. Does your son have any more talents I should know about?"

Waiting for Mary Jane's answer, she raised a forkful of salad to her mouth, only to stop with it halfway there. How had that bark gotten into her food? It wasn't windy, and she hadn't noticed anything drifting down from the trees. She picked the debris off her tomato and ate the bite of salad before turning back to John's mother.

"Now that you mention it—" Mary Jane began, only to be stopped by her son's voice.

"That's enough, Mother. Claire will just have to discover my virtues for herself."

"All right. If you say so, dear. Although why you should be embarrassed about liking to vacuum is beyond me." She shrugged innocently.

Claire raised her eyebrows and turned her gaze to John's decidedly red face. "You *like* to vacuum?"

"No," John defended himself. "I just like clean floors, that's all."

"He never could stand dirty floors," Mary Jane agreed. Claire watched the older woman smother her smile as she continued to embarrass her son. "You should have seen him when he was little. Why, he wasn't any bigger than that old Hoover we used to have, but he'd drag it back and forth across the carpets if there was even just a speck of dust on them. He was such a good little helper."

"Mother," John warned.

Mary Jane couldn't hold back her laughter any longer. She raised her arms in supplication. "All right, dear. I'm sorry. I was just teasing."

Claire smiled and turned back to her food, only to notice another piece of the great outdoors had found its way onto her plate. What was going on here? She turned a suspicious eye to Bryan, who had seemed determined to snag the seat next to her, but he appeared to be engrossed in conversation with George Isler.

Tossing the errant twig out of her food, Claire took the last bite of steak she'd heaped onto her plate along with the tomato salad and a delicious wild-rice pilaf with mushrooms. Dessert was going to be crème brûlée, and Claire couldn't wait to taste the creamy egg custard with a cup of the strong coffee the lodge provided. What was it about food cooked outside that made it taste so good? She laughed to herself. Maybe it was all the stuff that kept falling into it, the stuff she kept throwing back out, that made it taste so good. With a smile, she leaned against John's side, rubbing her satisfied stomach with a sigh as the conversation flowed around her.

"That was really cool how you found Billy when he was lost. How did you do it?" Lisa Isler asked, directing the question at John.

Claire noticed the hesitation in John's voice. Clearly, he wasn't comfortable talking about what it was like to be a

tracker. Reaching out a hand, she squeezed his fingers. He
smiled down at her and squeezed back, then answered the
teenager's question. "Besides footprints, I look for things
that don't belong. A snapped branch too high up for some
animal to have broken it, a piece of fabric, a strand of hair.
Anything that seems out of place is a clue."

"Where did you learn all that?" Lisa asked.

"Mostly from my dad."

"John, I've heard the term 'true north' before when people talk about compass headings, but I've never understood
what it means. Can you explain it?" George Isler asked.

"I'll try." Obviously relieved that the line of questioning
had changed, John put an arm around Claire's shoulders,
and she scooted even closer, enjoying the warmth of his
thigh against hers. "The oldest, and most common, kind of
compass is magnetic. This is the sort of compass we all
built at one time or another when we were kids using a
magnet, a dish of water, and a pin. In the kind you buy in
the store, magnetized needles point in the general direction
of the North Pole using the magnetic field of the earth. The
key word here is 'general.' When you're using a magnetic
compass, you have to realize that even though the needle
is pointing north, you need to make a few adjustments to
find true north.

"There is another, more expensive, kind of compass
called the gyrocompass which is unaffected by the mag-
netism of the earth. It aligns itself with the north-south line
parallel to the axis of the rotation of the earth, thereby indicating true north. These are used mostly in airplanes or
other navigational systems where a few degrees can make
a huge difference.

"So you need to know which kind of compass you're
using to know if the needle is pointing at magnetic north
or true north."

Drowsily, Claire let the words wash over her as John
rubbed her sore right arm. If you were using that first kind
of compass and you didn't know any better, you could be
going in the wrong direction without even knowing it, she

thought. It was funny how life was like that; you could think you were making the right choices, and it was only when you got where you were going that you realized this wasn't what you had intended at all. Take her engagement to Bryan, for example. Or even Craig. In both instances, she had simply let the relationships progress along the path she had thought they should follow. Casual dating led to monogamous dating—well, at least on her part, she corrected—and that led to engagement, which would progress to marriage, kids, a dog, maybe a goldfish or two, and then what? In both cases, she couldn't remember ever consciously examining her decision to spend the rest of her life with the other person. It was as if she were doing what she thought was expected of her, hoping for approval.

And what about her job? Was that the same? She sat up a little straighter, staring into the flames of the campfire. Why *did* she spend so much time and effort on her work? Was it because she thought she was going to get to the career version of the North Pole by allowing her job to take over her life? What if she got to the North Pole and found out she didn't like it there? Wasn't it cold and lonely there, just like her life had been before John had pushed his way into her heart?

Why was she looking for the North Pole in the first place? She'd rather be in Hawaii any day of the week. And what did she mean about John pushing his way into her heart?

She glanced up at him through her lashes as he patiently answered one of the Isler girls' questions about the bears that inhabited the forests of Colorado. He was responsible, nice to children, seemed to love his mother, had a good sense of humor, drove a hot car, and was the sexiest man she had ever met. But was she in love with him? Could she imagine having little green-eyed Janeys and Johnnys with him? The picture that flashed in her mind was so vivid, Claire's breath stuck in her throat: she and John, sitting in front of his fireplace; Jack asleep at their feet; two dark-haired babies, one for each of them, in their laps; and a look of something between them that was so intense it made her want to weep. Was it love?

God, she hoped so.

"Claire? Are you ready for dessert?" John squeezed her shoulders, snapping her back to reality.

"Mmm," was all she could come up with.

His eyes, full of humor, met hers. "I couldn't help but notice the way you were eyeing those cups of custard earlier as if you'd like to stuff a couple of them in your pockets for safekeeping. Want me to cover you while you fill up your backpack? We may have to hold off the other guests, but I think together we could manage."

Claire licked her suddenly dry lips and fought the urge to throw her arms around him and never let him go. She'd be like one of those remoras, clinging to his back wherever he went. The image was enough to break the spell he had on her. She smiled at her own private joke.

"No, I don't want to take the chance they'll band together against us while we sleep. I'll try to make do with one, or maybe two, of them. Want me to grab you one?" She stood up, taking her empty dinner plate with her.

"Naw, I'll come along. I could use a cup of coffee, myself."

With a hand under her arm, he led her away from the warmth of the campfire.

"I'm dead." Claire flopped facedown on the sleeping bag in the tent, her arms falling lifelessly at her sides.

"Good, then you won't be able to resist me when I have my way with you." John rolled to his side and began nibbling her neck.

Claire giggled and turned to face him, "Funny, I never would have guessed you were a necrophiliac."

"I've often found the conversation is better that way."

Claire would have punched him if only she could have made her tired limbs respond.

John must have guessed her intent because he laughed

at her disgusted look, sat up, and began massaging her limp muscles.

"I thought with whitewater rafting the river was supposed to do all the work," she protested with a mouthful of sleeping bag.

John squeezed a particularly sore muscle and Claire groaned.

"Poor baby. And here I thought that your hour of yoga every day would have sufficiently prepared you for this," he mocked, then laughed when she sleepily muttered something that he declined to interpret.

John continued gently massaging her shoulder muscles, listening to the loud chirping of the crickets as twilight descended, feeling oddly content. Looking down at the small body beneath him, he marveled at his tired body's immediate response. He'd always been more attracted to brunettes and redheads, usually ones with mile-long legs and heavily endowed chests. But he had somehow found himself enchanted by this blond-haired, gray-eyed pixie with an addiction to her cell phone.

He had vowed that the next time he got involved with a woman, it wouldn't be with someone who valued her job over everything else, but his conversation with his mother this morning had made him see things from a different perspective. He'd never asked himself before what motivated the women in his life to care so much about their jobs. He'd always assumed it all boiled down to money, that being financially successful was the most important thing to them, but what if that reason just scratched the surface? What if there were far more important things that drove them? Like self-respect and the desire to feel needed?

John's earliest childhood memories were of time spent with his father. He'd told himself that he didn't have many memories of his mother because she'd been at work all the time, but he knew she hadn't started her cosmetics business until he was almost ten years old.

A memory swam to the surface of his mind, its edges blurry like an aged photograph.

His mother, her blond hair longer, softer, standing in the kitchen holding out a plate of cookies to a small boy in a tan uniform with a dark blue scarf knotted around his neck.

"Here, honey, I made these for you to take to Scouts. I saw on the sheet that it's your turn to bring treats."

"No, thanks, Mom. Dad said we could stop off at the grocery store and get store-bought cupcakes."

"But these are homemade. I made chocolate chip and oatmeal raisin."

"Store-bought's better." The boy shrugged, then hearing Dad's horn from the driveway, waved a nonchalant goodbye to his mother as he banged out the screen door.

Had it always been like that for his mother? He forced himself to look at the events of his life from a different angle.

He remembered begging his father to stay out camping or hiking or fishing for "just one more hour," coming home late on Sundays. His mother would usually be in bed by the time he and his dad trooped in, tired and dirty. Although she had professed to not be much of a cook, he always remembered something simmering on the stove for him and Dad when they'd dragged into the house late. They'd shed their wet, smelly clothes in the mudroom, expecting them to be magically returned clean and dry, as they always were, before their next adventure. They'd share a hasty meal, tossing dirty dishes in the sink without a thought, as though some midnight fairies would have them all washed up by morning.

John closed his eyes, rubbing a hand across his forehead. He and his father were all the family his mother had and they had shut her out. She had been there to cook, to keep the house clean, to make sure the laundry was done. He had never even wondered what she did to fill the time when she was alone, which was most of the time, he realized now.

It was no wonder she'd gone in search of something else to give purpose to her life, something she could do that would make her feel needed. And John had been jealous

because the few times he'd thought about including her in
his life, she'd been busy making something of herself.

And what about Delilah? he asked himself, trying to be
fair in his assessment. It was hard to do. She had left him
when he'd been at the lowest point in his life, left him
because he'd turned down a promotion at the FBI, couldn't
take one more day of death. She wanted to be married to
someone whose job was at least as prestigious as hers. She
loved telling people that John was with the FBI, enjoyed
the immediate respect that came with his job. He remembered broaching the subject of starting Outdoor Adventures,
remembered the contempt in her voice when she told him
she wasn't interested in being married to some glorified
forest ranger.

To Delilah, money and prestige had meant everything.
She had urged him to take on more and more cases in the
hope that he'd get promoted faster, but the emotional cost
was too high. After that last case, after seeing that little boy
dead, knowing there was nothing he could do to stop the
evil in the world, he had simply walked away. Delilah
hadn't understood.

Beside him, Claire shifted, reminding him where he was.
John untied Claire's hiking boots and pulled them off, then
nudged her to crawl into her sleeping bag. She made soft
little moaning sounds as she snuggled deeper into the plush
down. John slipped off his own boots, then sat looking
down at the silky strands of blond hair peeking out from
Claire's sleeping bag. She loved her work, as Delilah had,
but for different reasons. It wasn't the money or the prestige
that seemed to drive her, it was the feeling of being needed.

Making sure Claire was zipped tightly in her sleeping
bag, John slipped into the bag he'd dragged into the tent
for himself. He had been wrong about his mother, and he
was realizing that he had been wrong about Claire, as well.
He reached out a hand, touching a blond curl that lay outside the covers. Maybe all Claire needed was to know that
her employers and clients weren't the only ones who
wanted her around.

He pushed his sleeping bag closer to hers and gently laid an arm across her shoulders. "I need you, Claire," he said softly.

"Mmm." She rolled over in her sleep, curling into his chest with a drowsy sigh.

John held her tightly long after she'd fallen asleep, staring unseeing at the light green fabric of the tent as Claire nestled safely in his arms.

Robert Edwards gazed over the sleeping camp with narrowed eyes.

He had awakened before the first hint of dawn broke through the darkness and set off from the well-stocked vacation cabin he'd discovered last evening, following the river as the first weak rays of sun lightened the dark sky to find the rafters' camp. He had spent the entire evening yesterday making the final preparations for his plan.

If there was one thing Robert had learned in his life, it was the importance of proper planning. He would never have come as far as he had without making sure that he'd covered every angle, although he did admit he'd slipped up by not being prepared for Art Engleheart's illness. Art was only in his mid-forties and Robert hadn't known that a family history of heart disease left the man at a high risk for a heart attack. He'd figured he had a good ten years before having to worry about Art's replacement. He'd already started grooming someone for the job but, as he'd told the others, he couldn't suggest to Allied's management that he'd rather have a rookie on these accounts as opposed to one of Allied's best employees without arousing some suspicion. With Claire gone, however, he could get everything back on track, Robert thought as he waited for the chance to put his plan into action.

A familiar figure suddenly emerged groggily from one of the tents. Robert moved into plain view and waved at his son. Bryan stared dumbly toward him at first, then hastily made his way toward Robert's hiding place.

"Dad, what are you doing here?" Bryan whispered,

ducking behind a large bush. "I tried calling you this morning before we left the lodge, but your secretary said you
were home sick."

"I told her that to cover my tracks. I decided to come
here to make sure you did as I asked. Have you taken care
of Miss Brown?"

Bryan scuffled his feet across the carpet of decaying
leaves on the forest floor, refusing to meet his father's eyes.
"Not yet. Every time I had a chance, that damned John
McBride showed up. He's hovering around her like a dog
in heat."

Robert's eyes narrowed at the whining tone in his son's
voice. One thing he never could stand was someone who
made excuses for his failures.

"I even tried putting things in her food that might be
poisonous, but she kept picking them out."

"What do you mean, 'might be poisonous'?"

"Well, I couldn't get a straight answer from either of our
guides about what plants around here are edible, and it's
not like I'm carrying a set of encyclopedias around in my
pack. Besides, I was trying to avoid looking suspicious."

Sitting back on his haunches, Robert scanned the campsite for any signs of activity. "What did you plan to do
today?"

Bryan lowered his gaze to the leaf-strewn ground. "I
don't know," he mumbled. "More of the same, I guess."

Robert snorted, looking at his son with disgust. "Forget
it. I can see that I sent a boy to do a man's work. I'll take
over from here. You just stay out of my way, and keep
your mouth shut. Do you think you can manage that?"

"Of course, Dad. I'm not an idiot," Bryan protested.

Robert watched his son return to the camp, a mocking
curl to his lip. He'd always suspected his son was a wimp
who wouldn't be able to do what was necessary to succeed
when the chips were down, and now he had his proof.
When he got back to Seattle, he was going to start making
new plans for his own replacement since his son had proven
he didn't have the nerve for the job.

Robert unwrapped a grape-flavored sourball, tossing the wrapper at his feet as he popped the candy into his mouth. Then, resting his shoulder against a bushy pine tree, he waited patiently for his target to come into view.

Chapter 20

IT SOUNDED AS IF AN ENTIRE AVIARY WERE SINGING RIGHT outside her tent. Why did nature have to be so noisy? Claire grumpily pulled the sleeping bag up over her ears, then sighed, realizing it was no use trying to get back to sleep.

She stuck her head out of the warm cocoon of the sleeping bag.

And cold, she complained silently. Why does it always have to be so cold in the great outdoors?

Grimacing, she sat up and stretched her sore shoulder muscles, then smiled as she spied her hiking boots, which John had obviously taken off for her last night and stored upside down. Now, there was a good reason to get out of bed. She smiled, remembering the feel of his gentle hands on her aching muscles.

She looked over to the empty sleeping bag next to hers. Looks like Mr. Early Bird is already out catching worms, she thought, grateful that he hadn't woken her up when he left. Now, there was the kind of man to have. One who wouldn't insist that you get up to enjoy the sunrise just because he had to. Running her fingers through her messy morning hair, Claire found herself wondering what was going to happen after Sunday.

John must care a little bit for her. If he didn't, he wouldn't keep trying to reform her obsessive work habits, wouldn't care how she spent her time out of his bed. Maybe that wasn't enough to build a lifelong commitment on, but it was certainly more than anyone else had ever felt for her.

And how did she feel? Claire absently pulled on the pair of thick wool socks that John had left for her. She didn't want the relationship to end, couldn't imagine not seeing

John again after Sunday, but what was she going to do about it?

Claire gathered up her toothbrush and toothpaste and slipped on the pink sweatpants she'd brought in lieu of the fancy new clothes still tucked neatly in her suitcase back at the lodge. Was her job enough to keep her in Seattle? A week ago, she would have answered that question with a resounding yes, but was that because her job was *all* she had? Meg was really her only true friend, and her old college chum traveled most of the time since she'd officially retired rich at the age of thirty-two. Claire knew she had only herself to blame for the lack of other people in her life. How could she have a meaningful relationship with someone when all she did was work all the time?

A sudden memory popped into Claire's head. A loud table in a restaurant, filled with people. What had they been celebrating? Her birthday? She glanced at her watch as the seconds ticked by, thinking she'd been foolish to ride with someone else. She had things to get done back at the office, but a fresh round of drinks was on its way.

She'd turned to her ride, who had a brightly decorated hat on her head. "I need to get back to the office," she'd said.

"Come on, Claire. We all work long hours and this is our one day a month to have some fun," her co-worker had protested. Claire remembered insisting she had to leave, never mind the truth to the other woman's words.

It was the last time she'd been invited to go out with the others. And no wonder. Claire cringed at the memory. What was one two-hour lunch in the big scheme of things? Nothing, really, besides the chance for people who worked together year in and year out to get to know one another on a more personal basis.

How had she let herself fall into the trap of believing that work came before everything else, including people? Absently, she tossed on the red, white, and blue flannel shirt she'd become rather attached to these last few days, then left the tent to find the bathroom so she could brush her teeth and comb her unruly hair.

There was nothing wrong with liking a job. She'd always be the type of person to do a task to the best of her abilities. But what was wrong with liking *people*, too?

What about loving people? Claire stopped, standing as still as a marble statue in the middle of the chilly forest when the question popped unbidden into her head.

Yes, what about love? Hadn't it been nice to fall asleep in John's strong arms? Didn't it feel good to wake up, anticipating the moment when she'd see him again? What would her life be like ten years from now, if she chose to continue working like this? She could imagine it clearly, sitting alone at the dining room table in her townhouse, a laptop her only companion. Was the sacrifice going to be worth it then? She blinked back the sudden rush of tears in her eyes. She could feel the loneliness as if it were a tangible thing crawling over her skin.

No. No. That was not the life she wanted. She wanted the other vision, the one with the kids, and the dog, sitting by the fire, holding hands with the green-eyed man she loved.

"Good morning." John's arms reached around her waist.

Claire turned, startled, then wrapped her arms tightly around his waist, burrowing her nose into the opening of the shirt at his neck. "Good morning." She hid her blush at the thought that he had caught her in the act of virtually planning what to name their second child.

"Your nose is cold," John protested, rubbing his chin across the top of her head affectionately.

"Sorry," Claire mumbled, without moving.

"It's going to be a great day," he said, thankfully oblivious to her discomfort. "We may get a little rain, but we'll be wet out on the river anyway. Looks like the clouds should be gone by the time we pull out of the river this afternoon. Tomorrow should be a beautiful day."

Regaining her composure, Claire raised her eyebrows and met his cheery gaze.

He patted her backside and grinned down at her. "Not a morning person, huh?"

Claire snorted, leaving him in no doubt of her answer.

"That's all right. Why don't you go get some coffee and breakfast to wake yourself up? I've got to help Kyle with the equipment."

He patted her butt again, sending her off like a good little girl with a kiss on her forehead.

She took a few steps, then looked back to see John walking away. Her lips quirked up with a smile. No, there was nothing at all wrong with loving a person, she thought, making her way across the clearing.

She finished brushing her teeth and left the makeshift bathroom the lodge had provided for its guests, then went back to her tent to pack everything she wasn't taking on the raft into a backpack that she could throw into dry storage for safekeeping. Hauling the pack out of the tent, she walked into the woods behind the food tent in search of the dry-storage bin.

The trees in this forest must be hundreds of years old, Claire thought, marveling at the circumference of some of the larger ones. She'd driven down Highway 101 through the redwood forest of Northern California the first summer after she'd moved to the West Coast. The trees there were thousands of years old, and she'd almost cried when she'd seen that someone had cut a hole through one of the trees so people could drive through it. She figured they'd done it so the tourists could grasp the sheer immensity of the trees, but it seemed like such a desecration to her that she had dropped a check into the next "Save the Forest" collection box she saw. Then she realized that she obviously fit into the category of "liberal tree-huggers" that irritated her father so much, so she dropped in some more cash just out of spite.

Claire smiled at the remembered sense of freedom she'd felt stuffing her money into the collection box, then gasped as she was suddenly jerked off her feet.

She dropped her backpack, struggling to get her arms

free as a piece of silver duct tape was slapped across her mouth.

Stunned, she thought at first that she had been grabbed by a bear, but the arm attached to the hand clamped over her mouth was decidedly human. Besides, it was doubtful that wild animals had much access to the local hardware store.

Her second thought was that it was William Weber. He'd given her a wide berth after the last rafting trip, but Claire remembered the malevolent intent in his light brown eyes when he'd locked her in the cabin of the truck.

She kicked with all her might, landing a satisfying blow on her captor's left knee before he started dragging her into the woods. Claire drew a deep breath in through her nose, willing herself to stay calm and wait for a chance to escape. Running over her Guerrilla Yoga moves in her mind, she made herself go limp, making it harder for him to drag her. Time, she knew, was on her side. The camp was beginning to bustle; it wouldn't be long before both she and William were missed.

They were a good hundred yards away from camp when her captor dropped her in a heap next to a fast-moving stream. Claire winced as her sore shoulder took the brunt of her weight. With her arms tied behind her back, there was nothing to break her fall.

The strong tape across her mouth made it difficult to breathe and Claire fought to keep from hyperventilating. She struggled upright and tried to get her legs beneath her to run.

Her captor was shrugging into a light day pack, his back to her.

Claire pushed herself to her feet and began to run as fast as she could in the direction of the camp. She'd gone no more than ten paces when she was jerked off her feet. She fell backward, writhing in pain from arms that felt as if they'd been ripped out of their sockets. She couldn't stop the tears that came to her eyes.

"Not very smart, Miss Brown," her captor admonished as he held up the tether he'd attached to the rope binding her wrists.

Claire blinked back further tears and looked up. It was not William Weber's voice that had greeted her. Her eyes widened in astonishment. What in the world was Bryan's father doing here? And why had he kidnapped her?

He read the obvious question in her eyes. "Sorry. I don't have time to explain right now." He waved a vicious-looking knife under her nose. "Get up," he ordered.

Claire looked from the knife to the hollow expression in his light blue eyes as she struggled to her feet. Whatever was going on, it was clear to her that Robert Edwards was prepared to use the knife in his hands. It was equally clear to her that she was in no position to refuse. He ordered her forward and Claire groaned silently as her first step brought excruciating pain vibrating through her body. Shrugging forward, she heard the audible popping of her arms moving back into place as tears rolled down her face from the effort it had extracted from her.

Numbly, she placed one foot in front of the other.

She wanted to scream over her inability to take a deep breath, but forced herself to stay calm as Robert pushed her deeper into the forest. She stumbled over a tree root and fell to her knees, jarring her abused body again.

"Get up, we've got to keep moving," Robert said, not unkindly.

Claire tried to gesture at her mouth using her shoulder.

"No, I can't trust you not to scream. I'll take it off later, once we're farther away from camp. Go." He pointed to the left with the knife.

Claire felt her knees start to shake, more frightened than she had ever been in her life. She had no idea where Bryan's father was taking her, or why, but she had just seen the look of a madman and she knew that he did not intend for her to come out of this alive. She didn't know when or how it had happened, but this guy was obviously a few clicks left of true north himself.

She tried to take a deep breath, tried to look inside her-self for some sense of calm, but instead felt her teeth start chattering as the fear began to take root in her bones. A cold breeze pushed inside her unbuttoned flannel shirt, bringing a drop of rain with it. Claire shivered, trying to push her shirt together with her shoulders but the motion of her walking just pushed it back. She wished John were here, wanted his warmth, his strength, his arms wrapped around her keeping her safe. Blinking back another round of tears that threatened to spill down her face, Claire pic-tured his face, his dark green eyes looking into hers.

"I look for things that don't belong." Claire heard his voice as clearly as if he'd been standing right in front of her.

"A snapped branch too high up for some animal to have broken it, a piece of fabric, a strand of hair. Anything that seems out of place is a clue." John's words from the camp-fire last night came back to her, the things he'd told them he looked for when little Billy had gotten lost.

She stumbled clumsily, falling against an evergreen tree. A limb snapped, leaving half the branch dangling from a jagged cut. Righting herself, she planted the sole of her hiking boot firmly into the soft earth at the base of the tree.

Robert jerked her arms viciously. "Don't bother trying to leave a trail. By the time anyone notices you're gone, it will be too late."

A woman's screech brought John running into the campsite from the riverbed where he'd been busy sorting wet suits.

Peggy Weber stood in front of one of the tents, clutching her son's hand and screaming.

"What's wrong?" John asked.

Peggy stopped screaming, picked up little Billy, and moved out of the way, pointing.

John released his breath loudly as Cindy crawled out of the tent, her unbuttoned shirt clutched to her naked breasts. She was followed by William Weber, who was hastily try-ing to pull up a pair of navy blue running shorts.

"Cindy, what the hell is going on?" Bryan asked from behind John.

"Don't bother answering that, William. It's obvious what's going on. You'll have all the freedom you want to chase bimbos like that, starting right now. We're leaving," Peggy said, her voice icy calm now that she'd regained her composure.

For once, Billy refrained from crying. John was thankful, since he hadn't brought his wallet. He turned to find the entire camp watching an almost identical repeat of the scene they'd watched a week ago.

Except this time, I've escaped without a bloody nose, John thought wryly.

"Okay, everyone, let these folks work out their problems in private. There's coffee and breakfast set up in the clearing."

He herded the remaining guests away from the melee, searching the crowd for Claire's blond head.

"Has anybody seen Claire?" John asked as the group reached the breakfast table.

There was a general shaking of heads.

John made a quick run around the camp, sticking his head into their tent to make sure she hadn't gone back to sleep. More slowly now, he walked the perimeter of the camp, calling her name and looking for any sign of her. A set of tracks that could be hers led him behind the food tent, and he spotted her pack just ahead lying on its side.

"Claire, where are you?" he called.

His mother came up behind him and laid a calming hand on his forearm. "Perhaps she just stepped out of the clearing and got lost."

John took a deep breath. Surely she hadn't wandered off into the forest, not after his warning on their hike to the hot springs. The only reason she would have done so would be to hide the fact that she was working. Had she broken her promise to him again?

"Would you get my pack, Mom?" John asked, continuing to follow Claire's trail into the forest. He stopped at a place where she had paused, well within sight of the camp. John crouched over the print, inspecting the depression in the soft forest floor. It was deeper than the ones behind it, telling him she'd stopped here. He compared the size with his own. What size booties had Claire asked for? Six? The footprint in the dirt looked to be about right for a woman's size six.

He looked for the next set of prints, guessing the length of her stride and scanning the forest floor. He'd just discovered a larger set of prints when his mother returned with his backpack.

"Thanks, Mom," he said, then opened his pack. Claire's cell phone was right where he'd put it last night, apparently undisturbed.

The first hint of worry tickled the hairs at the nape of John's neck.

"Claire?" he yelled again. "Where are you?"

George Isler and his granddaughters came out of the camp and stood beside his mother. "What can we do?"

John was grateful for the older man's question. He spoke to the assembled group.

"Why don't you take a section of forest? But don't get too far from camp. Stay in line of sight with the person to your left at all times."

"What do we look for?" Mary Jane asked.

"Footprints. A path of broken brush." John shrugged, fighting a feeling of hopelessness. How could he communicate what signs to look for when sometimes it was just the feeling that something was out of place, not any real physical evidence, that kept him moving?

He closed his eyes, willing his mind to clear.

The searchers fanned out into the trees. John claimed the area where he'd found the first tracks, hoping that perhaps she'd simply taken an early morning stroll and was even now on her way back to camp. He'd be furious with her if that was the case, of course. He'd strangle her himself for ignoring his repeated warnings to stay out of the woods. How could she be so foolish as to go off into a forest without proper maps and a compass? Hadn't he told her how easy it was to get lost, even in a familiar wood, how all the trees started to look the same after awhile? Yes, he'd be angry with her for all of a second, then he'd kiss her to within an inch of her life—the rest of the guests be damned.

He looked back down at the second set of prints. They were larger than Claire's and appeared to be fairly fresh, the ridges hardly worn down. He followed them backward, behind some thick brush. He saw something out of place and knelt down on the ground to pick it up. It was a piece of cellophane, the kind used to wrap hard candies. John put the wrapper in his pocket, then followed the prints back out of the brush. He stood next to them, looking at Claire's smaller shoeprints in front of him. He imagined two people standing the way the footprints pointed. Why would the man have stood behind Claire like this? And why did Claire's prints suddenly disappear, replaced by two deep trenches heading deeper into the forest?

John knew the answer, but he didn't want to let the image form in his mind. It wasn't the first time he'd seen evidence of an abduction.

He closed his eyes, fighting the panic. He had to focus, had to be faster, smarter than ever before.

"Mr. McBride?" Lisa Isler waved to get his attention. "I think I've found something."

John rushed over to the girl and saw another footprint, clear as a picture, in the mud near a small stream. It was the same size as the one he'd just been studying. This print too looked fresh. The sides hadn't had time to collapse in on themselves or get eroded by the slight breeze that was blowing across the forest floor. John crouched down to look at the other evidence on the ground. A snakelike line, probably rope. Some handprints placed awkwardly close together.

Claire had not just wandered off into the forest by herself. John could tell from the evidence that someone—a man, judging by the boot prints—had taken her. He'd tied her wrists together before she'd fallen in the dirt, and then he'd forced her into the woods.

John couldn't tell, looking at the prints, why the man had taken Claire. And at this point, he didn't care. All he cared about was finding her, bringing her back safely. He was not going to let evil win this time.

"What do you think?" George Isler asked.

John looked up and met the other man's gaze. "I've got to go after her."

George nodded, his eyes serious. "I'll get help."

John watched as his mother came up beside the older man and put her hand in his. "We'll go."

"Hurry," was all John said before shouldering his back-pack and following the trail that led away from the camp.

Chapter 21

HER SHOULDER ACHED AND HER WRISTS BURNED WHERE they chafed against the rough rope Robert Edwards had bound her with, but Claire refused to let herself give up. She tried to keep her mind alert by looking for opportunities to escape and by devising ways to leave clues for John of the route they were taking. The ground they were traveling over now was hard and covered with a thick blanket of dried leaves and pine needles. She'd been watching to see if they left footprints in their wake, and was dismayed to see that they left behind no obvious marks on the forest floor. Whenever she thought Robert wasn't paying attention, she surreptitiously dragged her feet a bit to try to leave a trail in the debris.

When the hands tied behind her back brushed against the bottom of her flannel shirt, Claire had an idea. Trying not to attract Robert's attention, she worked at a tear in the fabric. Their footfalls on the dry brush cloaked the slight ripping sound as Claire managed to free a scrap of the cloth. She stopped and turned to Robert, gesturing with one aching shoulder at the duct tape still stuck over her mouth.

"No. We're still too close. Keep walking," he answered in response to her silent plea.

Hoping she had distracted him, Claire dropped the small scrap underfoot. She waited for him to jerk the rope as punishment, then sent up a silent prayer of thanks when he didn't.

Afraid to leave too many pieces of her shirt on the ground, Claire did her best to be patient and drop a clue at lengthy intervals. She had just dropped another scrap when Robert jerked her to a halt from behind. She clenched her teeth and choked back a groan from the strain on her shoulders.

Had he finally noticed her attempts to leave a clear trail for John to follow? Claire hurriedly glanced around for a possible means of escape but they were surrounded on all sides by dense forest. Even if she were able to get away from him, Robert would have an easy time following her, especially with her arms tied behind her back keeping her slightly off balance.

Claire blinked back tears of helpless frustration. She had to find some way to get away from him before they reached wherever they were going. She knew without a doubt that he intended to kill her, although she still had no idea why.

She felt his hands loosening the rope on her wrists, glad that shredding her shirt had forced herself to exercise her hands periodically so they hadn't become numb and useless.

"I'm going to take the lead now," Robert said, coming around to face her.

Claire eased her shoulders back and forth, trying to work out the kinks now that her arms were free.

"Give me your hands," Robert ordered, holding the rope out in front of him.

Claire made a split-second decision. She might not have much chance of getting away, but she'd have even less chance with her hands tied together again.

She made a move as if to hold her hands out, shifting her weight to the balls of her feet. Nathan would have been impressed at her perfectly executed combination of the Springing Deer and Striking Snake moves. In one fluid movement, she went from standing still to feet flying, landing a solid kick directly in the area of Robert's groin. She didn't stop to assess the extent of the damage, knowing that she'd won herself mere seconds of a head start as she sprang forward into the trees.

Crashing through the brush, she took off at a full run to her left, heading for what she hoped was the river. She had no idea how far away it might be, but at least it would provide her with something to navigate by.

Using one hand to ward off low-lying branches as she ran, she used the other to grasp at the tape covering her mouth. Without pausing, she yanked off the sticky silver tape, balancing the pain of her abused skin with the ability to finally take in an ample lungful of breath.

She heard Robert cursing behind her and urged her legs to move faster. She headed toward a crest ahead, hoping she wasn't going to find a cliff overlooking the river as in some Hollywood movie.

My James Bond tricks are just about used up by now, she thought, careening toward the crest of the hill.

John followed the trail of Claire and her kidnapper and silently praised her for the clues she'd left. The small pieces of fabric she'd dropped along the way shone like neon signs to his trained eye.

He came to a place where the debris on the ground lay in an unnatural pattern, disturbed by the skirmish that had taken place there. The footprints were harder to see here, there was no soft dirt to leave the perfect impressions like there was back near the campsite.

His eyes swept in an arc and John cursed. He didn't have time to slow down, had to reach Claire and her captor before it was too late. He wiped a bead of sweat from his brow and tried to push the cloudy fear from his mind. He crouched down, searching the broken pine needles for a clue.

There, to the left. A slight depression in the leaves, the curve at the top of the print too small to be the man's print. John looked to where he expected the next print to be and let out a breath when he found it. Soon, it became easier, broken limbs pointing the way Claire had taken.

He shouted her name, hoping to hear her reply but getting nothing in return.

As he followed the trail, John went over this stretch of the forest in his mind. The river lay just ahead. Claire must

have thought it was her safest means of escape, but couldn't
know she was approaching one of the most treacherous
stretches of the river and, without a raft or even a helmet
to protect her, she was in as much danger from the river as
she was from the man who had kidnapped her.

He came out of the forest at a dead run, just in time to
see Claire leap into the frigid water.

"Claire!" John yelled, all the fear and desperation he felt
packed into that one word.

She didn't turn around, didn't acknowledge that she'd
heard him.

With her head start, there was no way he could reach
her in time. John stopped abruptly, pictured the route the
river took, trying to think of the best place to intercept her.
Without a moment's hesitation he changed direction, charg-
ing into the forest as if chased by a pack of rabid wolves.

Robert cursed as a branch brushed against his injured groin.

He had obviously underestimated her. It was a mistake
he would not make again, he vowed as he watched Claire
disappear. He crested the hill at a full run and saw her
sliding down the rocky cliff ahead of him. It was a fairly
steep decline, unhindered by many trees or bushes. At the
bottom, the rocks leveled off, making way for the swiftly
moving river.

Robert started down after her, only to stop in his tracks
at the faint sound of someone calling Claire's name. Cautiously, he took a step backward into the cover of the trees
and looked down to see if she had heard it, as well.

She had not even paused in her progress toward the
river. He watched as she clambered over the last remaining
boulders.

Robert moved behind a large pine tree, positioning himself so he could see upstream where the shout had come
from and forcing himself to take deep, calming breaths. He
hadn't come this far only to have everything ruined by
some overeager Boy Scout. His mind raced. He berated
himself for not anticipating that someone might come after

her. He'd expected that the guides would call in the local
Search and Rescue, but figured he'd be finished with her
by the time any sort of rescue mission could be mounted.

Now, as he watched, a man emerged from the trees
about two hundred yards from where Robert stood.

"Claire!" the man yelled again, scanning the landscape.

Robert looked down to see if Claire had finally heard
someone calling her name. She obviously hadn't, because
she stood at the side of the river, hesitated for a split second, then threw herself into the fast-moving water.

The man disappeared back into the forest.

Robert had always prided himself on being a brilliant
strategic thinker. It was the one skill he possessed that had
enabled him to rise above other men both in his personal
and, more importantly, in his professional life. He had a
beautiful wife, a successful career, and an impressive home
in an elite neighborhood. He had been named Unity's pres-
ident of the year more times than he could remember. He
should have no problem figuring out how to handle this, he
told himself as he stood staring at the river.

Robert reached into his pack and drew out a pair of thin
cowhide gloves. He kept a careful eye on Claire's progress
as he pulled on the gloves and reached back into his pack
for the gun he'd bought just in case his original plan went
awry. Congratulating himself on being so well prepared, he
put the gun into an outside pocket of his pack where it
would be easily accessible and quietly began making his
way through the forest in pursuit of his prey.

She hadn't realized the water would be so cold.

Claire didn't even attempt to stop the chattering of her
teeth as she replayed the memory of John's description of
River Position as if her mind were a movie screen.

Struggling to point her toes downstream, she yelped as
her bottom hit against a barely submerged boulder. Her
body caught against the obstruction and the force of the
current pushed her, face first, into the river. She came up
sputtering and tried to get into position by planting her feet

on the river bottom, only to get pushed over by the current again.

Another rock loomed up ahead and she rolled over on her back, determined to use the power of the river to her advantage.

"I am one with the river," she chanted aloud, remembering John's joking comment about Zen whitewater rafters.

"I am—ouch!" She cursed as something hard struck her injured shoulder.

She reached out as the offending tree branch floated by. It wasn't a paddle, but it was relatively straight and much more buoyant than she was. Claire grabbed the branch and repeated John's instructions out loud.

"First, don't panic." She took a deep breath, then continued. "Feet downstream, check. Knees bent." She bent her knees. "Check. Bottoms up."

She stretched herself out to get her bottom half out of the water, feeling her head and shoulders go deeper into the river as a result. Her body instinctively fought the unnatural position, trying to bring her knees and shoulders closer together to get her head up out of the water. She felt herself slow down as the current caught her and started to drag at her. Claire again forced herself to stretch out, holding the tree branch across her chest and trying not to close her eyes as the next set of rapids appeared.

"I am one with the river. I am one with the river. I am—" She stopped her chant, closing her mouth as she slid over the first rock like silk sliding over bare skin.

Astonished that John's advice actually worked, Claire made every effort to fight her body's natural inclination to curl in on itself as she approached the next drop.

Afraid to move her head out of the water, Claire could only see snatches of the riverbank out of her peripheral vision. She didn't see Robert, but she knew he was following her. There had been something mad, yet determined, in his light blue eyes. Something that told her he wasn't going to give up this easily. She could only hope the river led her to safety, or that John would find her before Robert did.

Claire shook her head, clearing her eyes of water. She needed to focus on getting help, not waste time wondering about Robert's motives. She banished everything else to the back of her mind as she pushed a heavy log downstream with her makeshift oar.

She had been floating for about half an hour, Claire guessed, too content to lift her arm and look at her watch, which had probably stopped because she didn't think it was waterproof anyway. A strange lassitude stole into her bones. Must be the aftermath of the adrenaline rush she'd been on all day, Claire thought sleepily as she continued to float down the river. She felt her eyes start to close and woke herself with a giggle.

"You can't take a nap on the water," she said to herself with a smile as her eyes started to close again.

She had been cold in the beginning, but now she was beginning to feel warm, hot almost. She briefly considered getting rid of some of her clothes, but, besides not having the energy, she knew she had to stay in the River Position or risk getting banged up again.

Closing her eyes, Claire felt the soft caress of water against her cheeks as the current carried her gently downstream. She felt almost boneless as her body effortlessly slid over rocks and around obstacles. The steady roar of the river pushing against its banks seemed to get louder and louder as she lazily floated downstream.

John forced his eyes not to close as he peered over the edge of the cliff, watching as pebbles from the unstable outcropping he was perched on fell sixty feet into the river below.

He swallowed against the boulder lodged in his throat, then cursed fate for making this the best place to attempt a rescue. The river curved back here, making it the only place he could reach Claire before she hit the waterfall ahead.

Grabbing a nylon rope out of his backpack, he slung one end around a tree at the edge of the forest. The tree wasn't as strong as he would have liked, but he only had one rope and it looked as if he were going to need every foot as it was.

Knotting the end, he yanked backward with all his might, praying that it would hold. He tossed the length of rope over the cliff, put his pack back on, then lay down on the ground. Gripping the rope in both hands, he scooted backward toward the canyon, swallowing heavily when his feet touched nothing but air.

He closed his eyes, fighting back a shiver of fear.

"Just don't look down," he muttered as he pushed his body farther off terra-not-so-firma and into nothingness.

He wrapped a foot around the rope, using the leverage to ease the pressure on his hands as he forced himself to inch down the line.

His eyes flew open as a sudden shower of rocks pelted him from above. He tried not to think of the million and one things that could possibly go wrong here. Was Claire's captor at the top of the cliff right now, untying the rope? Was the rope, instead, rubbing against the sharp rocks like string against a knife? Pushing his thoughts of doom away, John slid another few feet down the thin line.

His downward momentum stopped abruptly as his foot hit a snag. John instinctively glanced down, then wished he hadn't as his stomach revolted.

"Damn it, damn it, damn it," he cursed again as he pulled himself up several feet.

Two things he had just seen, besides the alarming distance between himself and good ol' Mother Earth, were a tangle in his line that he'd have to get free before he could go any farther, and Claire floating quickly toward him, apparently blissfully unaware that she was heading straight toward a three-story drop.

John wrapped the rope around his right wrist for support, straining with his left hand to try to grab the tangled line he'd clenched between his feet. He grimaced as the nylon cut into his arm with the force of his entire weight. He stretched out his fingers to grab the knot and bring it up to where he could untangle it, grunting with frustration when it slipped through a sweat-slick hand.

He tried again, watching Claire's progress out of the corner of his eye. Another shower of pebbles hit him as his efforts to straighten out the rope caused him to start swinging like a pendulum.

"This is not good," John groaned as he swung closer to the cliff face. He grabbed hold of the knot just before his shoulder made contact with the cold, hard rock.

The fingers of his left hand frantically worked at the snarl as the rope swung him away from the cliff face. His right arm ached with the effort of holding him suspended and John cursed himself for not keeping up with the rigorous training he'd gone through when he'd been in the FBI.

The tangle came free just as John started swinging back toward the cliff. He wrapped the untangled rope around his foot to brace his weight, almost sighing with pleasure as the pressure against his right arm was relieved, and gripped the nylon cord with both hands again.

He swung his body around to take the brunt of the impact against the pack on his back.

"Oof," he grunted as he hit the face of the cliff. Grabbing at a spindly weed growing out of the rock to stop the swinging motion, John hurried to continue his downward slide. He was still about twenty feet above the river when he saw Claire come toward him from the mouth of the canyon.

"Claire, swim to the side," he yelled, gesturing wildly toward the opposite riverbank.

She didn't raise her head.

"Claire, damn it, listen to me!" he hollered, his voice echoing against the rocks. "There's a waterfall. Swim to the riverbank."

She didn't even twitch.

Maybe she'd hit her head on the way down. Had she been unconscious this whole time? Is that why she hadn't heard him calling her name? John looked upriver in desperation. Claire was lying very still, sliding down the river effortlessly, her eyes closed as if she were resting in a tub of warm bathwater.

John looked down. He was directly over the river. He had no idea how deep it was at this point, but he couldn't reach Claire fast enough by continuing his slide down the rope.

His fear of heights warred with his fear for Claire.

Claire won.

He let go of the rope.

His feet hit the river bottom and he let his knees go soft to absorb the fall. The cold water against skin that was burning with sweat seconds ago came as a shock as John used his legs to shove himself up out of the water. Something hard slammed into his chest as he popped out of the water.

It was Claire. Or, rather, the stick that was clenched between her pale white hands. He grabbed her arm with both hands, struggling to hold them against the strong current.

"Claire," he said loudly in her ear. "Are you hurt?"

She rolled her head toward him and smiled, surprising him when she opened her beautiful gray eyes sleepily.

"John, I was just having the most wonderful dream."

"Dream?" he yelled, shaking her arm.

Claire frowned, confused. "Why are you yelling at me?"

John tried to stay calm as he attempted to pull them toward the riverbank. She didn't appear to be injured, but she was exhibiting the warning signs of hypothermia. "Do you feel cold?"

"I don't know, do I?" Claire giggled sleepily.

"Claire?" John growled, shaking her.

"No, I'm warm." Claire's eyes slid closed again.

"Damn it. Claire, listen to me." He shook her arm. "You're getting hypothermia. You have to wake up."

"No, I'm warm," Claire repeated.

"I know you feel warm, but that's just one of the symp-

toms of hypothermia. You have to fight it. Come on, open
your eyes. You've got to help me."

"Umm." Claire shook her head.

John grabbed the stick she held tightly clenched across
her chest and yanked her into an upright position.

"Get moving," he ordered.

Claire struggled to get her legs under her. Her feet felt
as if they'd been made into concrete Popsicles. Her head
went under the water and she came up sputtering.

"Why'd you do that?" she asked John, glaring at him
crossly as her teeth started to chatter.

"I'm sorry, honey, but we have to get the blood circu-
lating again."

Claire nodded, the feeling of lassitude beginning to
evaporate as warm blood started to circulate again in her
veins now that she started to move.

John pushed her ahead of him, hoping the effort of fighting the river would be enough to stop the effects of the
cold. They had to get out of the water, and fast. Claire's
foot slipped on a rock and John grabbed her arm before
she could fall, then saw tears start to form in her eyes.

"I'm sorry I'm such a weakling," she sniffed.

If their situation weren't so dire, John would have
laughed at her pathos. As it was, he spared her a tender
smile as he continued urging her to move faster. "You're
hardly a weakling."

"Then why are you always having to come to my rescue? It's not fair, I'm a strong, capable woman not some
helpless, sniveling medieval damsel in distress."

John put an arm around her shoulder as they waded
through the river, quickly heading for the far side. "Tell
you what, when we get out of this, I'll let you rescue me
from something."

"Rescue you from what?"

"Technology. I hate computers. I make my employees
hand-write invoices and receipts."

"That's pathetic," Claire said.

Her teeth continued to chatter, but she seemed less

sleepy with every rushed, watery step. The going was a bit easier now that they'd almost reached the riverbank. The rocks at the bottom of the river were slippery, but they didn't have to fight the current with every step. John kept talking, hoping to keep her mind off the danger they were in. "Let's make a deal. I'll keep hauling you out of rivers, saving you from lecherous men, and generally making my body available to you for, uh, whatever type of rescue mission you want."

John stepped out of the water and pulled Claire behind him onto the rock-strewn riverbank.

"What do you get out of the deal?" she asked.

"You can rescue me from technology, help me overcome my fear of the twenty-first century. You can even automate the lodge and Outdoor Adventures." He shuddered, as if terrified by the idea.

John hurriedly picked his way across the smooth rocks on the bank of the river. Twenty more feet and they would be in the woods on the side of the river opposite from Claire's kidnapper.

Claire's rebuttal was cut off as a chip flew off a boulder right in front of them, effectively closing off their route to the forest. Their retreat hadn't been fast enough, and John's effort to distract Claire from her misery ended with the unmistakable retort of a gunshot.

"Get behind me," he ordered quietly.

"Robert Edwards was the one who kidnapped me. He's Bryan's father," she explained quickly.

"Mr. Edwards?" John yelled, scanning the landscape for the sniper.

He saw the top of a silvery blond head over a large rock on the opposite side of the river and guessed he'd found his man.

"Get behind that rock." John nudged Claire quietly backward, trying to get them into a more protected position so he could get his knife out of his ankle holster. He wished briefly he'd stowed his gun in the waterproof backpack he was carrying. He had planned to bring it as a precaution after his old friend's warning, but he had thought the danger was over when Derrick called the day before yesterday.

"Several of the guests are coming with help, Mr. Edwards," John lied, hoping he could convince the other man to give up.

Robert Edwards laughed. "Good try, but I think you're lying. Now why don't you and Miss Brown come over here so we can get on with this?"

"Why would we want to do that?" John asked conversationally.

"Because if you don't I'll simply shoot you right now and come after Miss Brown again momentarily."

"And if we give ourselves up?"

"There's a cabin about half a mile from here where you and Miss Brown can get warmed up. I even have some tea there. Really, all I want is to talk to Claire."

"He's lying, John. He's going to kill us both." Claire pushed the words out through chattering teeth.

John looked at Claire, at the paleness of her skin, her shivering shoulders, then back at the river. They could get back in and chance going over the falls, but Claire was cold and exhausted and, even if they survived the drop, their best chance of staying alive would be to stay in the river until they came upon help. Given the already chilled state of her body, John didn't think she'd make it that long.

He glanced toward the riverbank. They could try to make it to the forest, but there was no cover to protect them from the gun of the madman. He'd be able to pick them off easily if they tried to make a run for it. They were out of choices.

"Claire, we need to do what he says," John said quietly.

It looked as if she wanted to protest, but couldn't get any words past her chattering teeth. She nodded, holding out a hand to him as she stood up.

"I promise you, we'll get out of this, Claire." John enveloped her small cold hand in his large, warm one.

"Or die trying," Claire added, her teeth clattering to-

314   BEVERLY BRANDT

gether as she clung to his hand like the damsel in distress she had berated herself for being.

They waded back through the river, Robert's gun following them at each step. As soon as they were on the other side, Robert grabbed Claire and put the barrel of the gun against her temple.

"Empty out your pack. And don't try anything funny," he ordered, his empty blue eyes meeting John's.

"Give me that phone," Robert said, once John was finished laying each item in his pack out on the riverbank.

John handed him Claire's cell phone, watching the weapon aimed at her head for any sign of weakness. Robert pushed Claire out in front of him and gestured with the gun.

"Get moving."

"Let me give Claire my jacket first," John insisted. The bright yellow raingear would protect her wet clothing from the wind, and would help warm her with her own body heat.

Robert looked as if he were going to refuse, but shrugged after a moment's hesitation. "Fine, just hurry up."

John picked the bright yellow coat up off the ground, surreptitiously slipping a small flare gun that he'd managed to hide from Robert into one of the pockets before draping it over Claire's shoulders. "Here, this should help keep you warm."

"Thank you," she mumbled, sliding her hands in the pockets for warmth. Her eyes met his with sudden realization as her fingers encountered the weapon. John nodded, his gaze passing his strength to her as they trudged back into the silence of the forest.

Chapter 22

"HERE WE ARE," ROBERT EDWARDS SAID CHEERFULLY AS if they'd arrived at the cabin for a nice, friendly visit.

Claire looked at John, her eyes silently asking if she should try to use the flare gun now.

John gave an imperceptible shake of his head.

"Go on in," Robert ordered, shrugging carefully out of his backpack as he kept his gun pointed at Claire's chest. He let the pack slide to the ground outside the door and he urged them into the cabin.

Robert had tied their hands together, a smart move since it eliminated the chance that they might bolt in opposite directions, forcing Robert to decide which one to go after first. John opened the cabin door cautiously, preceding Claire inside so he could determine if Robert had set any traps.

The cabin was dusty but obviously well cared for, John noted as he scanned the interior. He was not surprised to find such a well-equipped house here, as many wealthy entertainers and business people had vacation homes in the area. Since money was no object to them, they spared no expense to provide themselves with all the modern amenities. The front door opened up into a great room with floor-to-ceiling windows along the opposite wall that provided a panoramic view of the canyon beyond. A set of French doors led to a balcony jutting out over the edge of the cliff the cabin was perched on. John swallowed hard, vowing that he'd kill Robert Edwards before stepping foot onto that balcony.

Claire pushed him farther into the cabin from behind as Robert prodded her with his gun.

"Please sit down. Take your coat off." Robert motioned

to a heavy pine picnic-style table in the kitchen with the silver barrel of his gun.

"I'm still cold. Do you mind if I leave it on?" Claire waited a tense second until Robert shrugged.

John slid across the bench seat with his back to the wall, facing the doorway. Claire was forced to sit on his left with her back to the balcony. She had stopped shivering during their walk to the cabin, but her clothes were still damp and he was afraid she'd start to get chilled again now that they were sitting still.

"Where's that tea you promised?" John asked quietly as Claire's teeth started to chatter.

Robert fished around in the pocket of his Dockers, never taking his eyes off them. He pulled out a pair of handcuffs and tossed them across the table.

Claire jumped nervously as the cuff landed in front of her with a heavy thud.

"Cuff him to the table," Robert commanded.

Claire looked at John.

"Do it or I shoot him now," Robert said.

John nodded imperceptibly. Claire picked up the handcuffs. John scooted closer to her on the bench, offering up his left hand to be cuffed to a piece of wood that attached the bench seat to the heavy table. He needed to keep his right hand free. If he could reach the knife in his boot, he'd only have one chance to hit Robert. He could throw fairly accurately with his left hand if he had to, but fairly accurate wasn't going to be enough in this situation.

"Why don't you let Claire make that tea now while you discuss whatever it is you needed to talk with her about?" John suggested, giving Robert his best I'm-just-a-harmless-country-boy look while silently vowing to disembowel the other man if he so much as disturbed a hair on Claire's head.

"All right," Robert agreed after a moment's hesitation.

Claire's hands fumbled with the knot as she hurried to untie their wrists. She'd figured John had some reason he wanted his right hand free and that he was using the tea as an excuse to get himself free and distract Robert at the same time.

"So what did you want to talk to me about?" Claire asked, rummaging through a cupboard. She remembered the saying that the kitchen was the most dangerous room in the house and quietly started opening drawers hoping to find something she could use against Robert.

"Nice try, Miss Brown, but I already took care of all the knives."

"I was just looking for the spoons," she answered innocently, holding one up as proof.

"Uh-huh. Put the mugs in the microwave for no more than thirty seconds. I won't have you tossing scalding water at me," he ordered.

Claire cursed silently as he foiled her plan.

She tapped her foot impatiently as the seconds ticked off. After thirty seconds, the water in the three mugs was no more than lukewarm. She brought the mugs to the table with the teabags and set John's in front of him apologetically. So far, the score was definitely in John's favor as far as rescuing went, she thought, shuffling her feet across the dusty wood floor as she sat down.

"Has anyone ever told you that you just might be too good at your job?" Robert watched her disinterestedly as he pulled something out of the pocket of his pants. Plastic crinkled as he unwrapped a piece of candy, tossing the wrapper on the floor of the cabin.

Claire pushed a strand of hair back over her ear and picked up her tepid tea. "Of course not."

"Well, then, let me be the first."

"What are you talking about?" John asked, shifting in his seat.

Claire noticed the movement and blinked as realization dawned. His knife, of course! He must keep it strapped to his ankle, like Indiana Jones. She hoped her face didn't give him away as she concentrated on wiping the triumphant expression from her eyes.

Robert abruptly stood up and John eased back in his seat.

"Claire figured out in less than one week something that nobody else in her company has," Robert continued, pacing the floor in front of them.

"What have I figured out?" Claire asked, genuinely puzzled. "All I know is that my boss was making fraudulent claims against some of your clients. I would have thought you'd be glad to stop the theft."

"Come, my dear, you're so close to the truth. Don't disappoint me. Do you really think my clients wouldn't notice this sort of thing? That they'd continue to make payments to deceased claimants?" Robert's words sounded slurred as he talked around the candy in his mouth.

Claire shook her head in frustration. "I don't know. The claims are pretty evenly spread throughout all the companies. I thought that perhaps nobody was paying attention and they'd just slipped through."

"Wrong." Robert shook his head as if he were disappointed with her conclusion.

A thought began to form in Claire's mind, one she voiced slowly. "But if a group of clients got together with an adjuster and decided to make some extra money for themselves, they could create bogus claimants, have the adjuster cut checks based on the dummy claims, and if the broker was in on the deal and agreed to look the other way, no one would ever find out."

Robert nodded, a gleeful light shining in his pale blue eyes. "And the broker who sets up and manages the scheme gets clients for life."

"By blackmailing them, I suppose?" John asked, disgust evident in his voice.

Robert glared at John. "I hardly have to blackmail anyone into accepting an extra half a million, tax-free, every year."

"What do you do when a new risk manager comes along?" Claire asked, trying to get Robert's attention away from John so he could get to his knife.

"I feel him out, get an idea of whether he would be amenable to the idea or not. It's usually very clear to me which ones are corruptible."

"And if they're not?"

Robert shrugged. "Then the company's claims costs improve and everyone's happy."

"How much does Bryan know about this?" Claire asked.

"He knows everything. He doesn't handle any of the accounts involved in our little scheme, but since I was grooming him to take over, he knew all about it."

"What do you mean, you 'were' grooming him?" John asked, still trying to buy time.

"After he botched killing Miss Brown, I realized he could never take my place."

Claire shook her head. So that's what Bryan's strange questions had been about. He was trying to poison her. She remembered John's remark about Bryan asking about hemlock trees. Didn't Bryan know that it was the hemlock plant that was poisonous, not the tree? Obviously he didn't, judging from the bark that had appeared in her dinner last night.

"How long have you been involved with this?" John asked, when Claire remained silent.

"Oh, quite a few years. It's been a very successful proposition for everyone concerned."

"And nobody's ever suspected a thing?" Claire asked incredulously, feeling sickened by the amount of money this man and his group had embezzled from their employers.

"Never," Robert answered, pride evident in his tone.

"Until I did."

"That's right, until you did." Irritation replaced the pride in his voice.

"Perhaps Claire would be interested in joining your group," John suggested.

Claire looked at him indignantly. "How could you think I'd even consider—" She broke off, belatedly realizing she'd ruined his ploy.

John looked as if he wanted to clap his free hand over her mouth. Claire wished he would have.

Robert gave a harsh laugh. "I counted on that being your answer." He grabbed her arm in a viselike grip and yanked her to her feet. "Come on outside, I'd like to show you the view."

"No!" John roared, slamming to his feet in an effort to reach her, only to be pulled up short by the handcuff attached to his left wrist.

Robert pulled her out of John's reach toward the French doors. Claire started to struggle.

"If you fight me, I'll put a bullet through him right now," Robert said softly.

Claire looked at the gun he had pointed right at John's head and didn't doubt his words.

"He's going to kill me anyway, Claire. Fight him," he snarled.

I am going to fight him, Claire thought, but if she could give John even the slightest edge, she had to try. Her eyes locked with his, green to gray, hero to heroine, and he must have read the promise in hers. She was going to rescue him, even if she had to sacrifice herself to do it.

"No." John shook his head. "Damn you, no."

Tears slipped down Claire's cheek. She had to tell him how she felt, just in case this didn't turn out the way she planned. He had to know what she'd so recently discovered, that her work meant nothing to her compared to her feelings for him.

"I love you," she said quietly.

"How touching," Robert said, shoving her outside and closing the door against John's frantic protests.

The soft wind blew a strand of hair across her face. Claire noticed that the clouds had burned off and the sky was now a beautiful light blue with only a few puffs of white cotton marring the perfection of the early autumn morning.

All in all, it was too lovely a day to die.

Chapter 23

STRANGELY, CLAIRE'S HEART SOARED. SO THIS WAS WHAT it felt like to be in love, she thought, mechanically following Robert's orders to move closer to the railing of the balcony. She had convinced herself twice before that she was in love, but now that she knew what the real thing felt like, she marveled at how shallow her previous relationships had been. This feeling was incredibly intense, like someone was squeezing her heart, but at the same time, it felt amazingly right that she should want to put John's well-being in front of her own.

She looked at Robert Edwards, and the knowledge that he was going to try to kill John once he thought he was done with her gave her a sudden rush of furious energy. She glanced over the balcony, stalling for time. As she put out a hand to steady herself from the dizzying drop, one of the boards came loose and plummeted down the ravine.

"You obviously want this to look like an accident," she said.

"Yes, I thought that would be for the best," Robert answered matter-of-factly.

"I can see how you're going to accomplish that with me, but you'll never get John out here," she said.

"I realize that. I can't risk taking off his handcuffs. He appears to be a very strong man so I think I'll shoot him first before uncuffing him from the table. Then I'll do my best to make it look like a suicide. The police will either think he pushed you off the balcony during a lovers' quarrel, then felt so remorseful that he killed himself, or they'll believe your death was accidental and your lover couldn't bear to live without you and took his own life. In either case, I doubt they'll suspect foul play. I'm sure the local authorities aren't quite the caliber we're used to in the city, so they'll probably not even dust the place for prints. Even if they do, I'm wearing gloves." He held up his hands to show her.

"I never realized what vivid imaginations you insurance brokers had," Claire said dryly.

Robert ignored her attempt at humor as he pulled another candy out of his pocket.

"Sourball?" he offered.

"No, thanks. I'd much rather die on an empty stomach," Claire answered.

"Suit yourself." Robert shrugged, popping a green sourball into his mouth. "Lean back against that rail," he ordered.

Claire glanced down, surveying the endless drop down the ravine. There was no way she'd survive a fall to the bottom of the canyon, but if she could manage to twist herself just right, she might be able to catch one of the balcony supports and pull herself up to safety.

It was her only hope.

She took a deep breath, knowing she had to try. Otherwise, Robert would simply shoot her and then she'd be no help to John at all.

Claire leaned against the rail, hearing it crack where Robert had sabotaged it. She braced her feet, mentally planning her fall, just like Nathan had taught in his yoga class.

"Feel your body's movements." She could almost hear his strident bark. "Control your fall, control yourself. Remember, it's your body and it will do what you tell it to do."

The railing splintered and Claire fought panic as her arms flailed against the nothingness below.

"Control it!" Nathan's almost-real voice barked.

She twisted, stretching out her arms.

Her hands touched wood.

She fought back a scream of pain as her aching shoulders took the full force of her drop and her body slammed against the cliff.

"Fight the pain. Fight the pain," she chanted silently as she struggled to gain a foothold among the rocks. The knowledge that Robert would see she hadn't fallen if he looked over the railing pushed her on.

Her toes latched on to a slight crack in the face of the cliff. Pushing upward with her tiptoes, Claire used all the strength remaining in her arms to pull herself astride one of the beams supporting the balcony. Panting from exertion, she hastily pulled the flare gun from the pocket of the bright yellow raincoat, then yanked the coat off and flung it down the hill with a prayer that it was heavy enough to get farther down the cliff than the next ten feet. If Robert looked over the balcony, he'd see the coat at the bottom of the ravine and be satisfied she was dead.

Claire scooted to the end of the beam and wrapped her arms around her knees as she heard Robert's footsteps on the boards above.

"Please let him think I'm dead," she whispered silently.

She felt sickened when she heard him whistling as he made his way back into the cabin.

As soon as she heard the doors closing, Claire scrambled across the ground under the balcony to the side of the cabin. As she ran, her eyes frantically searched for any kind of weapon that might be more powerful than the flare gun in her hands, but only found a few pieces of firewood. She could hear John's raised voice from inside as she ran, awkwardly holding the pistol out in front of her.

Rounding the corner of the cabin, she stopped at the sight of Robert's pack just outside the door. Until then, she'd forgotten that her new cell phone was inside Robert's pack. She didn't know how well it would work after being dunked in the river, but it was worth a try. She grabbed the phone out of the pack, then hesitated for a second. Should she make the emergency call first or try to rescue John?

From inside the cabin there was a loud crash, followed by a gunshot.

"No," Claire screamed as she burst in through the open doorway, the flare gun raised like a sword.

Robert turned toward her and she fired, the flare erupting with a loud hiss in the interior of the cabin.

Claire wasn't sure if it was a direct hit, but it was good enough. The flash ignited Robert's loose shirt and it exploded into flames. Obviously, he had never learned to stop, drop, and roll because, instead of following that advice, he ran outside onto the balcony, flapping his arms. This only fed more oxygen to the fire, which spread to his pants.

Ignoring Robert's flailing, Claire raced across the room to find John slumped on the floor next to the table.

"John, are you hurt?" she asked frantically, crouching down on the floor next to him.

He slowly opened his eyes and groaned. "My shoulder."

Claire felt herself go lightheaded at the sight of blood running down the arm that was still handcuffed to the table. She whipped off her tattered red, white, and blue plaid flannel shirt and held it up against the wound, then looked around for the cell phone she'd dropped by the door. "Hold this. I'll be right back," she said as she spotted it.

"Help Robert," John ground out, sweating with the attempt to keep the shirt pressed to his skin.

"He tried to kill you," Claire protested.

"I know, but you can't let him die like that."

Claire looked out the window, watching Robert continue to flap around in an attempt to put himself out. With a sigh, she stood up and grabbed the mugs off the table, then ran to the kitchen to fill them with tap water and raced outside. She tossed the water at him and some of the flames died out. Claire ran back to the kitchen, refilled the mugs, and doused Robert again. The remaining flames sizzled out, but Robert didn't stop flailing his arms and Claire noticed his face had turned a sickly shade of blue.

"I never knew fire would do that," she muttered.

It was only as Robert flung himself against the balcony railing that Claire realized it wasn't the fire that had turned his face that ghastly shade. He was choking on his sourball and was using the railing to administer the Heimlich maneuver to himself.

Claire stepped forward, intending to help, just as the damaged railing splintered under the force of Robert's thrusts. Before she could grab for him, he was gone. Claire heard Robert's scream as he plummeted to his death but, unlike him, she didn't stop to make sure he was gone. She had more important things to do.

Claire dropped the mugs on the balcony and ran back inside. She grabbed her cell phone off the floor where she'd dropped it and brought it back to where John lay, urging him to stay calm as she waited for the phone to power up. When it did, she dialed 911.

"What is the nature of your emergency?" the operator asked.

"My, uh . . ." Claire paused, looking into John's eyes. What was he? Her friend? Her lover? She hated this question.

"Your fiancé," John interrupted weakly.

Claire felt the smile stretching her face, wondered if he was blinded by the force of it.

"My fiancé has been shot. We need an ambulance right away."

"Yes, ma'am. Can you tell me where you are?"

Claire blinked. "Yes. Yes, I can. Just a minute." Turning the phone around, she surfed to the navigational aid feature of her new phone and told the operator their exact location. The operator gave her some rudimentary first-aid instructions and promised that help was on the way.

Claire ended the call, then sank down on the floor next to John. He scooted closer to the table, then carefully lifted his uninjured arm and put it over her shoulders. "You rescued me," he said, his voice strained.

Claire kept her hand pressed against his wound and rested her head against his chest. "Yes, and I never want to have to do it again."

John nuzzled his chin against the top of her head. "I thought I'd lost you, Claire. I saw you go over the edge of that balcony, and I thought I'd lost you." The arm around her shoulder tightened painfully.

"I was a little worried for a few seconds, myself." Claire hugged him back, trying to ease the anguish in his emerald-green eyes.

"I love you, Claire." He spoke the words softly, solemnly, like a vow.

She gazed up at the man she loved, and at that moment she realized what had been missing in her life. There was nothing wrong with liking her job and doing it well, but she deserved more out of life than that. She deserved someone who loved her with all his heart, someone who would look at her the way John McBride was looking at her now, someone who would miss her if she was gone from his life. That's what she wanted, not more money that she didn't have time to spend, or more work than she could possibly handle. She wanted someone to care about *her,* not about her productivity or her managerial skills, but *her,* Claire, the woman. She wanted John, just the way he was.

Claire smiled at him, offering up her lips to his. "I love you, too, John."

Their lips met, sealing the promise they'd made to one another.

The happiness is ringing in my ears, Claire thought, locked in John's embrace.

Her eyes popped open. It was not happiness that was ringing, it was her cell phone.

"Just a minute." She broke off the kiss, holding up a hand when John started to protest. "No, this is something I have to do."

Ignoring the disappointed look in John's eyes, she picked the cell phone up off the floor, eyeing the incoming number on the lighted display. It was her assistant, probably calling with some insurance emergency that only she could solve. She eased herself out from under John's grasp and stood up. The phone continued jangling in her hand as she walked through the French doors and out onto the balcony.

Reaching her arm back as far as it would go, Claire

hurled the phone over the edge of the cliff before turning back to her lover with a satisfied smile.

After all, she thought, who needs global satellite positioning when you've found your own true north?